THE CULTURE OF INDIA

UNDERSTANDING INDIA

THE CULTURE OF INDIA

EDITED BY KATHLEEN KUIPER, MANAGER, ARTS AND CULTURE

Britannica®
Educational Publishing

IN ASSOCIATION WITH

ROSEN
EDUCATIONAL SERVICES

Published in 2011 by Britannica Educational Publishing
(a trademark of Encyclopædia Britannica, Inc.)
in association with Rosen Educational Services, LLC
29 East 21st Street, New York, NY 10010.

Distributed exclusively by Rosen Educational Services.
For a listing of additional Britannica Educational Publishing titles, call toll free (800) 237-9932.

First Edition

Britannica Educational Publishing
Michael I. Levy: Executive Editor
J.E. Luebering: Senior Manager
Marilyn L. Barton: Senior Coordinator, Production Control
Steven Bosco: Director, Editorial Technologies
Lisa S. Braucher: Senior Producer and Data Editor
Yvette Charboneau: Senior Copy Editor
Kathy Nakamura: Manager, Media Acquisition
Kathleen Kuiper: Manager, Arts and Culture

Rosen Educational Services
Alexandra Hanson-Harding: Editor
Nelson Sá: Art Director
Cindy Reiman: Photography Manager
Matthew Cauli: Cover Design, Designer
Introduction by Smriti Jacobs

Library of Congress Cataloging-in-Publication Data

The culture of India / edited by Kathleen Kuiper.—1st ed.
   p. cm.—(Understanding India)
"In association with Britannica Educational Publishing, Rosen Educational Services."
Includes bibliographical references and index.
ISBN 978-1-61530-149-2 (library binding)
1. India—Civilization. I. Kuiper, Kathleen.
DS423.C875 2011
954—dc22

2010011743

Manufactured in the United States of America

On the cover: A young woman shows her henna-decorated hands as she prepares for her
wedding. © *www.istockphoto.com/Mihir Panchal*

On the back cover: The Temple at Khajuharo, India, is a UNESCO World Heritage Site.
© *www.istockphoto.com/Keith Molloy*

On pages 21, 53, 85, 122, 184, 240, 267, 296, 329, 331, 333, 335: Indian youth perform a
Punjabi traditional folk dance, the Giddha, during Republic Day celebrations at the Guru
Nanak Stadium in Amritsar on January 26, 2010. *NarinderNanu/AFP/Getty Images*

CONTENTS

50

56

61

88

109

114

CHAPTER 4: OTHER INDIGENOUS INDIAN RELIGIONS AND INDIAN PHILOSOPHY

CHAPTER 5: INDIAN VISUAL ARTS 184

173

174

199

208

221

233

245

263

280

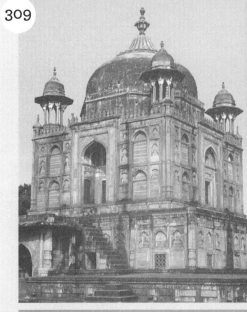

INTRODUCTION

In the Indian language of Hindi, the word *rasa* means flavour. A piece of art is considered to have different flavours, and savouring each distinct taste is considered part of the whole aesthetic experience. As readers page through this volume and learn about the peoples, languages, religions, arts, music, and architecture of India, they will begin to gain a sense of the multi-faceted *rasa* of India. They will sense it as they learn about India's vastly diverse peoples, from its modern city-dwellers to remote tribes that practice group marriage. They will learn about its richly spiced cuisine, its faiths, and its cultural traditions. As they read on, they will understand more about India's arts. From ancient sculptures to lovely Mughal miniature paintings, India has excelled in the visual arts. India has a rich tradition of dance, such as its gentle *manipuri* and fierce *kathikali* dance. They will they contemplate massive rock-cut temples, such as the Ellora caves. Packing more than 4,500 years of India's cultural history into a single book is a difficult venture. Even this extensive volume can be nothing more than an introduction to the flavour one of the world's most extraordinary and influential lands.

Readers will first be introduced to some of the many ethnic groups that make up India's population. The roots of some groups can be found in the sophisticated city states such as Harappa and Mohenjo-daro that thrived in the northern Indus River valley from 2500 BC, but the Dravidian people who founded them were later pushed south by the incoming Aryans of Central Asian origin. Waves of invasions by Persians, Scythians, Arabs, Mongols, Turks, and Afghans since that time have brought later contributions to the mix. Features of North Indians echo that later heritage, while ethnic groups such as the Nagas and Khasis in northeastern India resemble Tibetans and Southeast Asians. The population of South India is mainly of Dravidian origins.

Over the millennia, invasions, migration, marriage, and intermarriage have produced a vast population that exceeds a billion people.

India has a caste system that continues to be largely honoured today. The social stratification is made up of five levels broadly based on occupation. At the top of the hierarchy are the Brahmans, the priests; the Kshatriya, or the warrior class, are followed by the Vaishyas, mainly merchants. The Shudras—artisans and labourers—and the Scheduled castes (once known as the Untouchables, or Dalit) complete the system. Each of these divisions contains numerous subcastes.

The rock-cut Kailasa temple, part of the Ellora Caves in Maharashtra, India, was built in the 8th century AD. It is more than 100 feet (30 metres) high. **Abraham Nowitz/National Geographic/ Getty Images**

In line with its diverse ethnicities, India's languages include members of the Indo-European, Dravidian, Austroasiatic, and Sino-Tibetan families. Hindi, which is an Indo-Aryan language (a subdivision of Indo-European languages) and English, a Germanic language (also of the Indo European family) are the official languages of the nation. The states that make up the Hindi belt lie in the northern part of the country—although even in this region there are wide variations in dialect. The other official language, English, is a remnant of British rule. Its use makes India one of the largest English-speaking countries in the world. From the English-language press to film and television, English is a major lingua franca. It links the central government with non-Hindi speaking states.

In southern India, most states have their own languages. These include Telugu in Andhra Pradesh, Mayalayam in Kerala, and Tamil in Tamil Nadu. These Dravidian languages are quite distinct from Hindi. Though only 22 regional languages are listed in the constitution of India, there are hundreds of others. For example, those who live in the northeastern state of Assam converse in Assamese while those living on the western coast of Konkan speak Konkani. Many are fluent in more than one language, including their "mother tongue" and one or more of the common Indian languages. When it comes to writing these languages, Indic writing systems include Hindi's script, Devanagari, which stems from the classical language Sanskrit. Varieties of the Grantha alphabet are used to write a number of the Dravidian languages of South India.

India's people have shared respect for religion. This is the birthplace of two major world religions, Hinduism and Buddhism, in addition to smaller ones such as Sikhism and Jainism. Most Indians are Hindu, but minorities are present in nearly every state.

Hinduism evolved from the Vedic religion of early India. It is often described as a "way of life," since there is no central authority or organization. Hindus believe in one God, but with many manifestations, the primary three being Brahma the creator, Vishnu the preserver, and Shiva the destroyer. With hundreds of other minor deities, Hindus typically worship as they do in accordance with caste, subcaste, and other factors.

One of the core beliefs of Hinduism, the cycle of birth, death, and rebirth, is shared by Buddhism. The Buddha's enlightenment is seen as a triumph over this chain of reincarnation, brought about after several years of meditation. Though it originated in India, Buddhism is not a major religion of modern India. In fact, there are far more Muslims than Buddhists, a result of the proselytization of Muslim invaders from the 9th century AD on.

Jainism, which employs concepts from Hinduism and Buddhism, advocates a path to enlightenment through a disciplined life based upon the tenet of non-violence to all living creatures. The fundamental ethical virtue of Jainism is *ahimsa* ("noninjury"), the standard by which all actions are judged. The name Jainism comes from the Sanskrit verb meaning "to conquer." Jain monks and nuns believe they must fight against passions and bodily senses to gain omniscience and purity of soul.

Sikhism, which originated in the northern state of Punjab, combines elements of Hinduism and Islam and today is one of the largest minority religions. The Parsis, Zoroastrians from Persia, add to the mix, having migrated to western India when Islam spread through their homeland in present-day Iran.

Christianity, thought to have first been brought by St. Thomas, the only apostle to travel eastward, was later spread through colonizing efforts by Europeans such as the Portuguese and the British. Today, the largest population of Christians in India is Roman Catholic. There also are numerous tribal groups in India who live in remote areas and typically follow animistic religions.

Religion in India historically has been closely related to Indian philosophy, particularly with respect to Hinduism and Buddhism. The concepts of samsara—the cycle of life, death, and rebirth—and moksha, the release from this cycle, are central to Indian philosophy. Various forms of meditation, including Yoga, are considered methods by which to break this cycle. This thread of Vedic philosophy runs from ancient times until today.

Mahatma Gandhi was another prominent figure who put the Vedic doctrine of *ahimsa* into practice in the fight for India's independence from the British.

The art of India art dates back to limestone statuettes and bronze artifacts from the craft workshops of Mohenjo-daro and Harappa, two of the outstanding cities of the Indus Valley civilization.

In northern India, the Mauryan empire, which ruled from 321 to 185 BC, ushered in new styles in art, shown by examples such as highly polished stone pillars with beautifully modeled lions roaring from them. Between the first and third centuries AD, a distinctive style of relief carving developed in such places as Mathura, in which stories were told in rows of intricately detailed figures. Mathura was also noted for its sculptures of Buddha. The golden age of sculpture in North India was over by the 12th century, when Muslim rulers, who decried representational art, had taken over most of the region. Yet, despite the traditional Islamic prohibitions against painting pictures of people, the Islamic Mughal dynasty, which ruled from the mid-16th century, ushered in new styles of painting, such as tiny miniatures showing scenes from stories, portraits, and other features. South India, which mostly maintained itself as a Hindu stronghold, had its own artistic standards. Some of the most memorable artistic achievements of South Indian art are the elegant bronze statues of Shaiva and Vaishnava gods that were created during the early (9th-century) rule of the Chola dynasty. Chola bronzes have a technical sophistication and beauty that impress even today.

Indian music plays an integral role in Indian life. These old traditions span everything from the folk music of tribal groups to well-established classical Indian music systems. The instruments range from simple flutes to multi-string sitars. Musical forms include songs sung together in groups and long, instrumental and vocal expositions on exotic scales known as ragas. A raga, meaning "to colour," serves as a basis for composition and improvisation. So does the second element of Indian music, tala, a time measure.

The Hindustani classical music tradition, found mainly in North India, is based on the sitar and the tabla drums. Ragas are based on seasons, times of day, and various moods. The Karnatic tradition of South India features another lute-like instrument, the vina, in place of the sitar, and the double-ended *mridangam* drum instead of the tablas. The rhythms of the two regions differ, as do the musical scales.

In addition to its classical music, modern India is awash in the trendy music of Bollywood films. Bollywood is India's version of Hollywood, only it is much bigger in terms of film output and audience.

Folk dances such as the bhangra and the *dandiya raas* are exceedingly popular with the younger, more urban generation that is far removed from the village origins of these dances. Musicians are now creating bhangra songs that speak about contemporary concerns, such as AIDS and prejudice. Festivals in just about all the religious traditions will include some form of the many folk dances of India.

Classical dance meanwhile is still performed in India. Some of these dance-drama styles are the sensuous *bharata natyam* and *manipuri*, danced by women; the fierce *kathakali*, danced by men; and the *kathak*, danced by both. These classical forms are often used by dancers to enact stories from ancient Hindu text such as the *Mahabharata* and the *Ramayana*.

Texts such as these, with their narratives of mythological heroes, romances, and social and political events are also brought to life by actors in rural settings in folk theatre. These productions often use dance, exaggerated makeup, masks and music to dramatize tales, but different forms of folk theatre sport their own conventions. In the *ramlila*, for instance, characters playing the gods Krishna and Rama are always young boys, while some characters can remove their masks and remain on stage. In the *jatra*, only one character, the *vivek*, or "conscience," sings as he comments on the action.

India's architecture is also world famous. From the centres of the Indus valley civilization is evident an early element of urban planning—city streets on a grid pattern. And at Mohenjo-daro, for instance, visitors can see the remains of craft workshops, a granary, and the ruins of the massive Great Bath, which is 897 sq. feet (83 sq. metres) large.

The temples at Ellora and Ajanta, in the western state of Maharashtra, are huge monoliths painstakingly hewn from rock. These temples are rich in statues carved by monks paying homage to Buddhism, Hinduism, and Jainism. Religion has played an important role in many of India's most impressive architectural achievements, from towering Hindu temples, their roofs garnished with carvings of gods and goddesses, to magnificent Persian-influenced mosques built during the Mughal dynasty, such as the Jāmiʿ Masjid (Great Mosque) in the city of Fatehpur Sikri. The most famous Mughal building, however, is the Taj Mahal, a monument rich in inlaid marble built by Emperor Shah Jahan in the memory of his favourite wife, Mumtaz Mahal.

The British also contributed a number of fine buildings to India. One example is Mumbai's arresting Victoria Terminus railway station, now called the Chhatrapati Shivaji Terminus, which displays a spectacular Victorian Gothic Revival style.

Like the geography of the Indian subcontinent itself, which ranges from the Himalayan highlands of Ladakh in the extreme north to the tropical nature reserves of Kerala in the south, India's culture incorporates a wide range of styles and substance while projecting a commonality that is immediately and distinctly Indian. This volume will offer an insight into the many fascinating, rich, and colourful layers of Indian culture.

CHAPTER 1

THE PEOPLES OF INDIA AND THE CASTE SYSTEM

India is a diverse, multiethnic country that is home to thousands of small ethnic and tribal groups. This complexity developed from a lengthy and involved process of migration and intermarriage. The great urban culture of the vast Indus civilization, a society of the Indus River valley that is thought to have been Dravidian-speaking, thrived from roughly 2500 to 1700 BC. An early Indo-European civilization—dominated by peoples with linguistic affinities to peoples in Iran and Europe—came to occupy northwestern and then north-central India over the period from roughly 2000 to 1500 BC and subsequently spread southwestward and eastward at the expense of other indigenous groups. Despite the emergence of caste restrictions, this process was attended by intermarriage between groups that probably has continued to the present day, despite considerable opposition from peoples whose own distinctive civilizations had also evolved in early historical times. Among the documented invasions that added significantly to the Indian ethnic mix are those of Persians, Scythians, Arabs, Mongols, Turks, and Afghans. The last and politically most successful of the great invasions—namely, that from Europe—vastly altered Indian culture but had relatively little impact on India's ethnic composition.

Ghat (stepped bathing place) on the Yamuna River at Mathura, Uttar Pradesh, India. Globe

SELECTED GROUPS

Broadly speaking, the peoples of north-central and northwestern India tend to have ethnic affinities with European and Indo-European peoples from southern Europe, the Caucasus region, and Southwest and Central Asia. In northeastern India—West Bengal (to a lesser degree), the higher reaches of the western Himalayan region, and Ladakh (in Jammu and Kashmir state)—much of the population more closely resembles peoples to the north and east, notably Tibetans and Burmans. Many aboriginal ("tribal") peoples in the Chota Nagpur Plateau (northeastern peninsular India) have affinities to such groups as the Mon, who have long been established in mainland Southeast Asia. Much less numerous are southern groups who appear to be descended, at least in part, either from peoples of East African origin (some of whom settled in historical times on India's western coast) or from a population commonly designated as Negrito, now represented by numerous small and widely dispersed peoples from

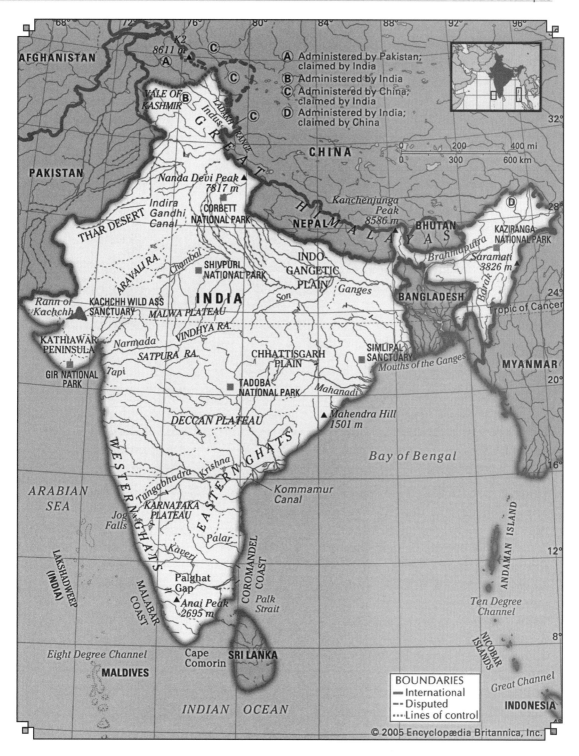

the Andaman Islands, the Philippines, New Guinea, and other areas.

Andamanese

The Andamanese, united by use of a common language, constitute the main aboriginal group of the Andaman Islands in the Bay of Bengal. Most have been absorbed into modern Indian life, but traditional culture survives among such groups as the Jarawa and Onge of the lesser islands. Late 20th-century estimates indicated approximately 50 speakers of Andamanese languages and perhaps 550 ethnic Andamanese.

Until the mid-19th century, the remoteness of these peoples and their strong territorial defenses helped them to avoid outside influences. Some of the Andamanese continue to live by hunting and collecting. The bow, once the only indigenous weapon, was used both for fishing and for hunting wild pigs; the Andamanese had no traps or fishhooks. Turtle, dugong, and fish are caught with nets and harpoons; the latter are used from single-outrigger canoes. Pottery is made, and iron, obtained from shipwrecks, has been used for arrowheads, knives, and adzes from at least the 18th century. It is shaped by breaking and grinding, a technique derived from the working of shell.

Badaga

The largest tribal group living in the Nilgiri Hills of Tamil Nadu state in southern India, the Badaga have increased very rapidly, from fewer than 20,000 in 1871 to about 140,000 in the late 20th century. Their language is closely akin to Kannada as spoken in Karnataka state to the north of the Nilgiris. The name Badaga means "northerner," and it is clear that the Badaga came into the Nilgiris from the north, perhaps impelled by economic or political pressures. The time of their migration has been dated sometime after the founding of the Lingayat Hindu sect in the 12th century and before 1602, when their settlement in the area was noted by Roman Catholic priests.

The Badaga were divided into six main endogamous groups that were ranked in ritual order. The two highest castes were priests and vegetarians; the lowest caste worked as servants for the other five. Traditional Badaga religion and economy also relied on goods and services supplied by the other Nilgiri peoples—Kota, Toda, and Kurumba.

The Badaga generally are agriculturists, but many are engaged in other professions. In addition to grain, Badaga farmers grow large crops of potatoes and vegetables. Many have altered their traditional practices. Improved agriculture, local and national policies, and high-caste Hindu tradition are the major concerns of the contemporary Badaga.

Bhil

The Bhil of western India are an ethnic group of nearly 2.5 million people. Many are tribal, and they have been known for rugged independence, sometimes associated with banditry.

They are distributed widely in upland areas from Ajmer in Rajasthan on the north to Thana in Maharashtra on the south, and eastward as far as Indore in Madhya Pradesh. Nearly all of them engage in agriculture, some of them using the slash-and-burn (*jhum*) method—in which secondary jungle is burnt and a crop is raised for one or two years in the ash—but most employing the plow. The highland Bhil generally live in scattered houses made of wattle and thatch.

The relationship between the Bhil and neighbouring peoples is not clear. The Bhil follow Rajasthani kinship usages in Rajasthan and Maharashtrian usages in Maharashtra, but with easier marriage and divorce procedures. Most Bhil worship local deities in varied pantheons only slightly touching the practices of higher Hinduism; a few aristocratic segments such as the Bhilala and some plains groups employ Brahman priests; others are converts to Islam. Their dialects are akin to Gujarati or to other Indo-Aryan languages rather than to the Munda or Dravidian tongues of most tribal peoples.

BHUTIA

The Bhutia (Bhotia, Bhote, Bhutanese) are a Himalayan people who are believed to have emigrated southward from Tibet in the 9th century or later. They constitute a majority of the population of Bhutan and form minorities in Nepal and India, particularly in the Indian state of Sikkim. They speak various languages of the Tibeto-Burman branch of the Sino-Tibetan language family.

The Bhutia are mountain dwellers, living in small villages and isolated homesteads separated by almost impassable terrain. They practice a terraced agriculture on the mountain slopes, their main crops being rice, corn (maize), and potatoes. Some of them are animal breeders, known for their cattle and yaks.

Their religion is Tibetan Buddhism, with an admixture of the pre-Buddhist shamanism known as Bon. They recognize the Dalai Lama as their spiritual leader. Their traditional society was feudal, with most of the population working as tenants of a landowning nobility, although there were few marked differences in ways of life between landowners and tenants. There were also slaves, most of them descended from captives taken in raids on Indian territory. In the 1960s the Bhutanese government formally abolished slavery and sought to break up the large estates; the nobility were also deprived of their hereditary titles.

The Bhutia trace their descent patrilineally. They are predominantly monogamous, but polygamy is still practiced in some areas.

BODO

The Bodo live in the northeastern Indian states of Assam and Meghalaya (as well as in Bangladesh) and speak Tibeto-Burman languages. They numbered about

1.5 million in the early 21st century. Dominant in Assam until about 1825, they are now the largest minority group in that state. They are concentrated in the northern areas of the Brahmaputra River valley. Most of them are settled farmers, though they formerly practiced shifting cultivation. The Bodo consist of a large number of tribes. Their western tribes include the Cutiya, Plains Kachari, Rabha, Garo, Mech, Koch, Dhimal, and Jaijong; the eastern tribes include the Dimasa (or Hill Kachari), Galong (or Gallong), Hojai, Lalung, Tippera, and Moran.

The Bodo tribes are not culturally uniform. The social system of some, such as the Garo, is matrilineal (descent traced through the maternal line), while other tribes are patrilineal. Several of the Bodo tribes were so influenced by Hindu social and religious concepts that in modern times they have regarded themselves as Hindu castes. Thus the Koch, for example, lay claim to the high Hindu status of Kshatriya (the warrior and ruling class); their claim is not generally admitted, however, and many of the subdivisions of the Koch rank very low in the caste hierarchy.

The Kachari tribe is divided into clans named after aspects of nature (e.g., heaven, earth, rivers, animals, and plants). Descent and succession to property are in the male line. They have a tribal religion, with an extensive pantheon of village and household gods. Marriage is usually arranged by the parents and involves the payment of a bride-price. Such institutions as the community

house for bachelors and many features of their religion link them with the Naga and other hill tribes of Assam, but the growing influence of Hindu ideas and customs works toward assimilation into the caste society of the Assam plains.

Among the Garo, the village headman is usually the husband of the heiress, the senior woman of the landowning lineage. He transmits his headman's office to his sister's son, who marries the headman's daughter (the next heiress). The lineages of the male headmen and the female heiresses are thus in perpetual alliance. Political title and land title are both transmitted matrilineally, one through one lineage, the other through the other. There are a dozen subtribes, with varying customs and dialects, but all are divided into matrilineal clans. Marriages involve members of different clans. Polygamy is practiced. A man must marry his wife's father's widow, who is in such cases the husband's father's sister, actual or classificatory. Such a wife takes precedence over her daughter, to whom the husband is already married. A man's sister's son, called his *nokrom,* stands therefore in intimate relationship to him, as the husband of one of his daughters and ultimately of his widow and the vehicle through which his family's interest in the property of his wife is secured for the next generation, for no male can inherit property.

BOHRAS

The name Bohra (Bohora) is applied in general to any Shī'ī Ismā'īlī Muslim of the

Musta'lī group living in western India. The name is a corruption of a Gujarati word, *vahaurau*, meaning "to trade." The Bohras include, in addition to this Shī'ī majority, often of the merchant class, a Sunnī minority who are usually peasant farmers. The Musta'lī group, which originated in Egypt and later moved its religious centre to Yemen, gained a foothold in India through missionaries of the 11th century. After 1539, by which time the Indian community had grown quite large, the seat of the group was moved from Yemen to Sidhpur, India. A split resulted in 1588 in the Bohra community between followers of Dā'ūd ibn Quṭb Shāh and Sulaymān, who both claimed leadership of the community. The followers of Dā'ūd and Sulaymān have since remained the two major groups within the Bohras, with no significant dogmatic differences, the *dā'ī*, or leader, of the Dā'ūdīs residing in Mumbai, the leader of the Sulaymānī in Yemen.

BUNDELA

The Bundelas are a Rajput clan for whom the region of Bundelkhand in north-central India is named. The Bundelas, whose origins are obscure, emerged in the 14th century. They won prominence when they resisted the Afghan emperor, Shēr Shah of Sūr, who was killed while besieging their fortress of Kalinjar in 1545. The Bundela Bir Singh of Orchha, in collusion with Akbar's son, Prince Salim (later Jahāngīr), ambushed and killed the Mughal emperor's confidant, Abu al-Faḍl 'Allāmī, in 1602.

The Bundela territories were important because through them ran the route from the Deccan to the Ganges-Yamuna Doab (river basin). But they were hilly, remote, and difficult to control. The Mughals suppressed many insurrections until the Bundelas called in the Marathas (1729). After many vicissitudes the tract passed under British control in the early 19th century. The fortress of Kalinjar was taken in 1812.

GOND

The Gond are aboriginal peoples of central India, numbering about 2 million. They live in the states of Madhya Pradesh, Maharashtra, Andhra Pradesh, Bihar, and Orissa. The majority speak various and, in part, mutually unintelligible dialects of Gondi, an unwritten language of the Dravidian family. Some Gond have lost their own language and speak Hindi, Marathi, or Telugu, whichever language is dominant in their area.

There is no cultural uniformity among the Gond. The most developed are the Raj Gond, who once had an elaborate feudal order. Local rajas, linked by ties of blood or marriage to a royal house, exercised authority over groups of villages. Aside from the fortified seats of the rajas, settlements were formerly of little permanence; cultivation, even though practiced with plows and oxen, involved frequent shifting of fields and clearing of new tracts of forest land. The Raj Gond continue to stand outside the Hindu caste system, neither acknowledging the superiority of Brahmans nor feeling bound by Hindu rules such as the ban on killing cows.

The highlands of Bastar in Madhya Pradesh are the home of three important Gond tribes: the Muria, the Bisonhorn Maria, and the Hill Maria. The last, who inhabit the rugged Abujhmar Hills, are the least developed. Their traditional type of agriculture is slash-and-burn (*jhum*) cultivation on hill slopes. Hoes and digging sticks are still used more often than plows. The villages are periodically moved, and the commonly owned land of each clan contains several village sites occupied in rotation over the years.

Bisonhorn Maria, so called after their dance headdresses, live in less hilly country and have more permanent fields that they cultivate with plows and bullocks.

The Muria are known for their youth dormitories, or *ghotul,* in the framework of which the unmarried of both sexes lead a highly organized social life; they receive training in civic duties and in sexual practices.

Indian women of the Muria Gond tribe in Chhattisgarh state collect drinking water. Noah Seelam/AFP/Getty Images

The religion of all Gonds centres in the cult of clan and village deities, together with ancestor worship.

HO

The Ho, also called Larka Kol, are a tribal people of the state of Bihar in India, concentrated in the area of Kolhan on the lower Chota Nagpur Plateau. They numbered about 1,150,000 in the late 20th century, mostly in Bihar and Orissa states of northeastern India. They speak a language of the Munda family (of Austroasiatic stock) and appear to have moved gradually into their territory from farther north. Their traditional social organization includes features common to those of other Munda-speaking tribes, including the institution of girls' and boys' dormitories, an elaborate system of village offices, and a territorial organization into quasi-military confederations. They trace their descent through the paternal line, and young people are expected to marry outside the paternal clan, but there is a prevalent custom of marrying one's cousin on the maternal side. Marriage by elopement and by abduction are also traditionally common. The Ho worship spirits, some of which they believe to cause disease. They approach them through divination and witchcraft.

The traditional economy of the Ho was hunting and a shifting agriculture. These pursuits have declined in favour of settled agriculture and livestock raising. Many of the men also work as labourers in mines and factories.

KADAR

A small tribe of southern India, the Kadar reside along the hilly border between Kochi in the state of Kerala and Coimbatore in the state of Tamil Nadu. They speak Tamil and Kannada, both Dravidian languages.

They live in the forests and do not practice agriculture, building shelters thatched with leaves and shifting location as their employment requires. They prefer to eat rice obtained in trade or as wages rather than to subsist on food of their own gathering. They have long served as specialized collectors of honey, wax, sago, cardamom, ginger, and umbrella sticks for trade with merchants from the plains. Many Kadar men work as labourers.

The Kadar population was estimated at approximately 2,000 individuals in the early 21st century. They worship jungle spirits and their own kindly creator couple as well as local forms of the Hindu deities. Marriage with cross-cousins (that is, the child of one's mother's brother or one's father's sister) is permitted.

KHARIA

The name Kharia refers to any of several groups of hill people living in the Chota Nagpur area of Orissa and Bihar states, northeastern India, and numbering more than 280,000 in the late 20th century. Most of the Kharia speak a South Munda language of the Munda family, itself a part of the Austroasiatic stock. They are of uncertain ethnic origin. The Kharia are usually subdivided into three groups: Hill Kharia, Dhelki, and Dudh. All are patrilineal, with the family as the basic unit, and are led by a tribal government consisting of a priest, a headman, and village leaders. The Hill Kharia speak an Indo-Iranian language and seem otherwise to be a totally separate group. The Dhelki and the Dudh, both of whom speak the Kharia language, recognize each other—but not the Hill Kharia—as Kharia.

The Dudh are the most numerous and progressive branch; they live along the Sankh and South Koel rivers. The Dhelki are concentrated near Gangpur. Both live in settled villages, and intervillage federations enforce the feeling of social solidarity. They traditionally build separate large dormitories for unmarried men and women, but this practice has been abandoned by Christian Kharia. The Kharia's traditional religion includes a form of sun worship, in which each family head makes five sacrifices to Bero, the sun god, to protect his generation.

The Hill Kharia live in small groups in remote areas of the Simlipal Range in Orissa state. They depend on shifting agriculture, growing rice and millet, but constantly face the problem of land scarcity. They also collect silk cocoons, honey, and beeswax for trade.

Khasi

The Khasi live in the Khasi and Jaintia hills of the state of Meghalaya in India. The Khasi have a distinctive culture. Both inheritance of property and succession to tribal office run through the female line, passing from the mother to the youngest daughter. Office and the management of property, however, are in the hands of men identified by these women and not in the hands of women themselves. This system has been modified by the conversion of many Khasi to Christianity, by the consequent conflict of ritual obligations under the tribal religion and the demands of the new religion, and by the right of the people to make wills in respect of self-acquired property.

The Khasi speak a Mon-Khmer language of the Austroasiatic stock. They are divided into several clans. Wet rice (paddy) provides the main subsistence; it is cultivated in the valley bottoms and in terrace gardens built on the hillsides. Many of the farmers still cultivate only by the slash-and-burn method, in which secondary jungle is burnt over and a crop raised for one or two years in the ash.

Under the system of administration set up in the district in the 1950s, the Khasi's elected councils enjoy a measure of political autonomy under the guidance of a deputy commissioner. In addition, seats in the state assembly and in the national parliament are reserved for representatives of the tribal people.

Khoja

The Khoja (Persian: Khvajeh) are a caste of Indian Muslims who were converted from Hinduism to Islam in the 14th century by the Persian *pīr* (religious leader, or teacher) Saḍr-ul-Dīn and adopted as members of the Nizārī Ismāʿīlī sect of the Shīʿites. Forced to feign either Hinduism, Sunni Islam, or Ithna ʿAshariyah in order to preserve themselves from persecution, some Khojas, in time, became followers of those faiths.

The term Khoja is not a religious designation but a purely caste distinction that was carried over from the Hindu background of the group. Thus, there are both Sunni and Shīʿite Khojas. Other Nizārī Ismāʿīlīs share the same beliefs, practices, and even language with the Khojas; however, one cannot enter the caste except by birth.

Khojas live primarily in India and East Africa. Every province with large numbers of them has an Ismāʿīlī council, the decisions of which are recognized as legal by the state. As Nizārī Ismāʿīlīs, Khojas are followers of the Aga Khan.

KHOND

The Khond (Kond, Kandh, Kondh) people, whose numbers are estimated to exceed 800,000, live in the hills and jungles of Orissa state, India. Most Khond speak Kui and its southern dialect, Kuwi, belonging to the Dravidian language family. Most are now rice cultivators, but there are still groups, such as the Kuttia Khond, who practice slash-and-burn agriculture.

The Khond have been in contact for many centuries with Oriya-speaking neighbours to the west, north, and east and with Telugu-speaking groups to the south. By degrees they have taken on the language and customs of their neighbours. In the Baudh Plains there are Khond who speak only Oriya; farther into the hills the Khond are bilingual; in the remoter jungles Kui alone is spoken. There is an analogous gradation in the practice of Hindu customs concerning caste and untouchability and in the knowledge of Hindu deities. The process of acculturation progressed rapidly in the late 20th century.

KOLI

The Koli constitute a large caste living in the central and western mountain area of India, and they numbered about 650,000 in the late 20th century. The largest group of Koli live in Maharashtra and Gujarat states. Although identified as cultivators and labourers, many Koli survive only by gathering firewood and hiring out as labourers, subsisting on berries and mangoes in summer when food is scarce. The coastal Koli fish, and a few literate Koli are employed in Mumbai schools or local government.

The Koli are organized into several clans and are largely Hinduized but retain some of their former animism. They believe sickness is caused by an angry spirit or deity and that a second marriage may awaken the spirit of the first spouse. Traditionally classified as a tribe, they were redesignated as a low

Hindu caste, containing the subcastes Agri and Ahir.

Korku

The tribal Korku people of central India are concentrated in the states of Maharashtra and Madhya Pradesh. At the end of the 20th century, they numbered about 560,000. However, poverty and restricted use of ancestral land due to government attempts to save the Bengal tiger have led to malnutrition and even starvation among the Korku. Most are settled agriculturalists, and many have substantial farms; others shifted as recently as the late 19th century from slash-and-burn jungle cultivation (*jhum*) to forestry and field labour. The Korku live in villages of thatched houses. They have hereditary headmen and trace their descent along paternal lines. They speak a language of the Munda family (Austroasiatic).

In religion the Korku are Hindus. Their ceremonies resemble those of the low castes in that they employ their own priests and mediums instead of Brahmans.

Kota

The Kota are a group of indigenous, Dravidian-speaking peoples of the Nilgiri Hills in the south of India. They lived in seven villages totalling about 2,300 inhabitants during the 1970s; these were interspersed among settlements of the other Nilgiri peoples, Badaga and Toda.

A village has two or three streets, each inhabited by the members of a single patrilineal clan. Most adult Kota also speak Tamil, another Dravidian tongue.

They were traditionally artisans and musicians. Each Kota family was associated with a number of Badaga and Toda families for whom they provided metal tools, wooden implements, and pots. They also furnished the music necessary for the ceremonies of their neighbours. From its associated families the Kota family received a share of grain from the Badaga harvest and some dairy products from the Toda. The Kota also cooperated with the jungle-dwelling Kurumbas, who provided forest products and magical protection. Because the Kota handled animal carcasses and had other menial occupations, their neighbours considered them to be of inferior caste.

Aboriginal Kota religion entails a family trinity of two brother deities and the goddess-wife of the elder. Each deity has a priest and a diviner in every village. The diviner becomes possessed on appropriate occasions and speaks with the voice of god.

After 1930 the traditional interdependence among the Nilgiri groups was abandoned, and only a few Kota families continue to supply tools and music. Kota livelihood depends mainly upon the cultivation of grain and potatoes.

Kuki

The Kuki are a Southeast Asian people living in the Mizo (formerly Lushai) Hills on the border between India and Myanmar (Burma) and numbering about 12,000 in the 1970s. They have been largely assimilated by the more populous Mizo and have adopted Mizo customs and language.

Traditionally the Kuki lived in small settlements in the jungles, each ruled by its own chief. The youngest son of the chief inherited his father's property, while the other sons were provided with wives from the village and sent out to found villages of their own. The Kuki live an isolated existence in the bamboo forests, which provide them with their building and handicraft materials. They grow rice, first burning off the jungle to clear the ground. They hunt wild animals and keep dogs, pigs, buffalo, goats, and poultry.

LEPCHA

The Lepcha (Rong) live in Sikkim state and the Darjeeling district of West Bengal in India, as well as in eastern Nepal and western Bhutan. They number about 36,000 in India. They are thought to be the earliest inhabitants of Sikkim, but they have adopted many elements of the culture of the Bhutia people, who entered the region from Tibet in the 14th century and afterward. The Bhutia are mainly pastoralists in the high mountains; the Lepcha usually live in the remotest valleys. While some intermarriage has occurred between the two groups, they tend to stay apart and to speak their own languages, which are dialects of Tibetan. Neither group has much to do with the Hindu Nepalese settlers, who entered

Sikkim since the 18th century and in the late 20th century comprised about two-thirds of the population.

The Lepcha are primarily monogamous, although a married man may invite a younger unmarried brother to live with him and share his fields and his wife. Occasionally, also, a man may have more than one wife. The Lepcha trace their descent through the paternal line and have large patrilineal clans.

They were converted to Tibetan Buddhism by the Bhutia, but still retain their earlier pantheon of spirits and their shamans, who cure illnesses, intercede with the gods, and preside over the rites accompanying birth, marriage, and death.

Traditionally hunters and gatherers, the Lepcha now also engage in farming and cattle breeding.

MAGAR

The Magar (Mangar) people of Nepal and Sikkim state, India, live mainly on the western and southern flanks of the Dhaulagiri mountain massif. They number about 390,000. The Magar speak a language of the Tibeto-Burman family. The northern Magar are Lamaist Buddhists in religion, while those farther south have come under strong Hindu influence. Most of them draw their subsistence from agriculture. Others are pastoralists, craftsmen, or day labourers. Along with the Gurung, Rai, and other Nepalese ethnic groups, they have won fame as the Gurkha soldiers of the British and Indian armies.

MARATHA

A major people of India, the Maratha (Mahratta, Mahratti) are famed in history as yeoman warriors and champions of Hinduism. Their homeland is the present state of Maharashtra, the Marathi-speaking region that extends from Mumbai to Goa along the west coast of India and inland about 100 miles (160 km) east of Nagpur.

The term Maratha is used in three overlapping senses: within the Marathi-speaking region it refers to the single dominant Maratha caste or to the group of Maratha and Kunbi (descendants of settlers who came from the north about the beginning of the 1st century AD) castes; outside Maharashtra, the term often loosely designates the entire regional population speaking the Marathi language, numbering some 80 million; and, used historically, the term denotes the regional kingdom founded by the Maratha leader Shivaji in the 17th century and expanded by his successors in the 18th century.

The Maratha group of castes is a largely rural class of peasant cultivators, landowners, and soldiers. Some Maratha and Kunbi have at times claimed Kshatriya (the warrior and ruling class) standing and supported their claims to this rank by reference to clan names and genealogies linking themselves with epic heroes, Rajput clans of the north, or historical dynasties of the early medieval period. The Maratha and Kunbi group of castes is divided into subregional groupings of coast, western hills, and Deccan Plains, among which there is little intermarriage. Within each subregion, clans of these castes are classed in social circles of decreasing rank. A maximal circle of 96 clans is said to include all true Maratha, but the lists of these 96 clans are highly varied and disputed.

MEITHEI

The dominant population of Manipur in northeastern India is Meithei, also called Manipuri. The area was once inhabited entirely by peoples resembling such hill tribes as the Naga and the Mizo. Intermarriage and the political dominance of the strongest tribes led to a gradual merging of ethnic groups and the formation finally of the Meithei, numbering about 1,200,000 in the late 20th century. They are divided into clans, the members of which do not intermarry.

Although they speak a Tibeto-Burman language, they differ culturally from the surrounding hill tribes by following Hindu customs. Before their conversion to Hinduism they ate meat, sacrificed cattle, and practiced headhunting, but now they abstain from meat (though they eat fish), do not drink alcohol, observe rigid rules against ritual pollution, and revere the cow. They claim high-caste status. The worship of Hindu gods, with especial devotion to Krishna, has not precluded the cult's worship of many pre-Hindu indigenous deities and spirits.

Rice cultivation on irrigated fields is the basis of their economy. They are keen

Boat on a canal south of Logtak Lake, near Imphal, Manipur, India. Most of Manipur's population is made up of Meithei people. Gerald Cubitt

horse breeders, and polo is a national game. Hockey, boat races, theatrical performances, and dancing (well known throughout India as the Manipuri style) are other pastimes.

MINA

The Mina (Meo, Mewati) are a tribe and caste inhabiting Rajasthan and Punjab states in northern India, as well as Punjab province, Pakistan. They speak Hindi and claim descent from the Rajputs. The Mina may have originated in Inner Asia, and tradition suggests that they migrated to India in the 7th century with the Rajputs, but no other link between the two has been substantiated. In the 11th century, the Meo branch of the Mina tribe converted from Hinduism to Islam, but they retained Hindu dress. Although the Mina and Meo are regarded as variants, some Meo claim that their ancestral home is Jaipur.

Originally a nomadic, warlike people practicing animal breeding and known for lawlessness, today most Mina and Meo are farmers with respected social positions. In the late 20th century the Mina in India numbered more than 1,100,000, and the Meo, concentrated in northeastern Punjab, Pakistan, numbered more than 300,000. Both are divided into 12 exogamous clans, led by a headman (*muqaddam*) and a council (*panch*) of tribe members. They trace descent patrilineally (through the male line) and divide themselves into three classes: landlords, farmers, and watchmen. Both the Mina and Meo permit widow divorce and remarriage, and the Meo allow

a man to exchange a sister or close female relative for his bride. Following Hindu tradition, the Mina cremate their dead while the Meo observe burial rites.

MIZO

The Mizo, also called Lushai (Lushei), are a Tibeto-Burman-speaking people who numbered about 540,000 in the late 20th century. They inhabit the mountainous tract on the India-Myanmar (Burma) border known as the Mizo (formerly Lushai) Hills, in the Indian state of Mizoram. Like the Kuki tribes, with which they have affinities, the Mizo traditionally practiced shifting slash-and-burn cultivation, moving their villages frequently. Their migratory habits facilitated rapid expansion in the 18th and 19th centuries at the expense of weaker Kuki clans.

Mizo villages traditionally were situated on the crests of hills or spurs and, until the pacification of the country under British rule, were fortified by stockades. Every village, though comprising members of several distinct clans, was an independent political unit ruled by a hereditary chief. The stratified Mizo society consisted originally of chiefs, commoners, serfs, and slaves (war captives). The British suppressed feuding and headhunting but administered the area through the indigenous chiefs.

MUNDA

The name Munda refers to any of several more or less distinct tribal groups inhabiting a broad belt in central and eastern India and speaking various Munda languages of the Austroasiatic stock. They numbered approximately 9 million in the early 21st century. In the Chota Nagpur Plateau in southern Bihar, adjacent parts of West Bengal and Madhya Pradesh, and the hill districts of Orissa, they form a numerically important part of the population.

Munda history and origins are matters of conjecture. The territory they now occupy was until recently difficult to reach and remote from the great centres of Indian civilization; it is hilly, forested, and relatively poor for agriculture. It is believed that the Munda were once more widely distributed but retreated to their present homelands with the advance and spread of other peoples. Nevertheless, they have not lived in complete isolation and share (with some tribal variation) many culture traits with other Indian peoples. Most Munda peoples are agriculturists. Along with their languages, the Munda have tended to preserve their own culture, although the government of India encourages their assimilation to the larger Indian society.

NAGA

Nagas constitute a group of tribes inhabiting the Naga Hills of Nagaland state in northeastern India. They include more than 20 tribes of mixed origin, varying cultures, and very different physical appearance. The numerous Naga languages (sometimes classified as dialects) belong to the Tibeto-Burman group of the Sino-Tibetan languages. Almost every village has its own dialect; to communicate with other Naga groups they typically use broken Assamese (Nagamese), English, or Hindi. The largest tribes are the Konyaks, Aos, Tangkhuls, Semas, and Angamis.

Most Nagas live in small villages strategically placed on hillsides and located near water. Shifting cultivation (*jhum*) is commonly practiced, although some tribes practice terracing. Rice and millet are staples. Manufactures and arts include weaving (on simple tension looms) and wood carving. Naga fishermen are noted for the use of intoxicants to kill or incapacitate fish.

Tribal organization has ranged from autocracy to democracy, and power may reside in a council of elders or tribal council. Descent is traced through the paternal line; clan and kindred are fundamental to social organization.

As a result of missionary efforts dating to the 19th-century British occupation of the area, a sizable majority of Nagas are Christians.

In response to nationalist political sentiment among the Nagas, the government of India created the state of Nagaland in 1961.

ORAON

The Oraon are an aboriginal people of the Chota Nagpur region in the state of Bihar, India. They call themselves Kurukh and speak a Dravidian language akin to Gondi and other tribal languages of central India. They once lived farther to the southwest on the Rohtas Plateau, but they were dislodged by other populations and migrated to Chota Nagpur, where they settled in the vicinity of Munda-speaking tribes.

Speakers of Oraon number about 1,900,000, but in urban areas, and particularly among Christians, many Oraon speak Hindi as their mother tongue. The tribe is divided into numerous clans associated with animal, plant, and mineral totems. Every village has a headman and a hereditary priest; a number of neighbouring villages constitute a confederation, the affairs of which are conducted by a representative council.

An important feature of the social life of a village is the bachelors' dormitory for unmarried males. The bachelors sleep together in the dormitory, which is usually on the outskirts of the village. There is a separate house for the females. The dormitory institution serves in the socializing and training of the young.

The traditional religion of the Oraon comprises the cult of a supreme god, Dharmes, the worship of ancestors, and the propitiation of numerous tutelary deities and spirits. Hinduism has influenced the ritual and certain beliefs. Many Oraon, including the majority of the educated, have become Christians.

Pahari

The Pahari people of India form a majority of the population of Himalayan India (in Himachal Pradesh and northern Uttar Pradesh), as well as three-fifths of the population of neighbouring Nepal.

They speak languages belonging to the Indo-Aryan branch of the Indo-European family and are also called Parbate, Khasa, or Chetri. The people are historically ancient, having been mentioned by the authors Pliny and Herodotus and figuring in India's epic poem, the *Mahabharata*. Their numbers were estimated to be about 20 million in the early 21st century.

The great majority of the Pahari are Hindus, but their caste structure is less orthodox and less complex than that of the plains to the south. Usually they are divided into the high "clean" or "twice-born" castes (Khasia, or Ka) and the low "unclean" or "polluting" castes (Dom). Most of the high-caste Pahari are farmers; the Dom work in a variety of occupations and may be goldsmiths, leather workers, tailors, musicians, drummers, and sweepers.

The Pahari have historically practiced a wide variety of marriage arrangements, including polyandry (several brothers sharing one or more wives), polygyny (several wives sharing a husband), group marriages (with an equal number of husbands and wives), and monogamy. Girls may be married before age 10, though they do not cohabit with their husbands until they are mature.

The Pahari are an agricultural people, cultivating terraces on the hillsides. Their chief crops are potatoes and rice. Other crops include wheat, barley, onions, tomatoes, tobacco, and various vegetables. Sheep, goats, and cattle are kept. The spinning of wool is done by everyone, while weaving is carried on by members of a lower caste.

SANSI

The Sansi are a nomadic criminal tribe originally located in the Rajputana area of northwestern India but expelled in the 13th century by Muslim invaders and now living in Rajasthan state as well as scattered throughout all of India. The Sansi claim Rajput descent, but, according to legend, their ancestors are the Beriya, another criminal caste. Relying on cattle thievery and petty crime for survival, the Sansi were named in the Criminal Tribes Acts of 1871, 1911, and 1924, which outlawed their nomadic lifestyle. Reform, initiated by the Indian government, has been difficult because they are a Scheduled Caste and sell or barter any land or cattle given to them.

Numbering some 60,000 in the early 21st century, the Sansi speak Hindi and divide themselves into two classes, the *khare* (people of pure Sansi ancestry) and the *malla* (people of mixed ancestry). Some are cultivators and labourers, although many are still nomadic. They trace their descent patrilineally and also serve as the traditional family genealogists of the Jat, a peasant caste. Their religion is simple Hinduism, but a few have converted to Islam.

SANTHAL

The tribal Santhal (Manjhi) people of eastern India, numbered about more than 5 million in the late 20th century. Their greatest concentration is in the states of Bihar, West Bengal, and Orissa. Smaller numbers live in Bangladesh and Nepal. Their language is Santhali, a dialect of Kherwari, a Munda language.

Many Santhal are employed in the coal mines near Asansol or the steel factories in Jamshedpur, while others work during part of the year as paid agricultural labourers. In the villages, where tribal life continues, the most important economic activity is the cultivation of rice. Each village is led by a hereditary headman assisted by a council of elders; he also has some religious and ceremonial functions. Groups of villages are linked together in a larger territorial unit termed a *pargana*, which also has a hereditary headman.

The Santhal have 12 clans, each divided into a number of subdivisions also based on descent, which is patrilineal (through the male line). Members of the same clan do not marry each other. Membership in the clan and subclan carries certain injunctions and prohibitions with regard to style of ornament, food, housing, and religious ritual. Marriage is generally monogamous; polygyny (having more than one wife at a time), though permitted, is rare. The traditional religion centres on the worship of spirits, and the ancestral spirits of the headmen are objects of an important cult.

SAVARA

The Savara (Saora, Sora, Saura) of eastern India are distributed mainly in the states of Orissa, Madhya Pradesh, Andhra Pradesh, and Bihar, with total numbers of about 310,000, most of whom are in Orissa.

Most Savara have become Hinduized and generally speak the Oriya language. Their traditional form of Munda dialect is preserved among those living in the hills, however. The Savara of the hill country are divided into subtribes mainly on the basis of occupation: the Jati Savara are cultivators; the Arsi, weavers of cloth; the Muli, workers in iron; the Kindal, basket makers; and the Kumbi, potters. The traditional social unit is the extended family, including both males and females descended from a common male ancestor.

TAMIL

The Tamil people, originally of southern India, make up the majority of the population of Tamil Nadu state and also inhabit parts of Kerala, Karnataka, and Andhra Pradesh states, all situated in the southernmost third of India. Their language, also called Tamil, is one of the principal languages of the Dravidian family. Altogether they numbered about 57 million in the late 20th century.

The Tamil area in India is a centre of traditional Hinduism. Tamil schools of personal religious devotion (bhakti) have long been important in Hinduism, being enshrined in a literature dating back to the 6th century AD. Buddhism and Jainism were widespread among the Tamil in the early Christian era, and these religions' literatures predate the early bhakti literature in the Tamil area. Although the present-day Tamil are mostly Hindus, there are Christians,

Muslims, and Jains among them. In the recent past, the Tamil area was also the home of the movement that calls for the desanskritization and debrahmanization of Tamil culture, language, and literature.

The Tamil have a long history of achievement; sea travel, city life, and commerce seem to have developed early among them. Tamil trade with the ancient Greeks and Romans is verified by literary, linguistic, and archaeological evidence. The Tamil have the oldest cultivated Dravidian language, and their rich literary tradition extends back to the early Christian era. The Chera, Chola, Pandya, and Pallava dynasties ruled over the Tamil area before the Vijayanagar empire extended its hegemony in the 14th century, and these earlier dynasties produced many great kingdoms. Under them the Tamil people built great temples, irrigation tanks, dams, and roads, and they played an important role in the transmission of Indian culture to Southeast Asia. The Chola, for example, were known for their naval power and brought the Malay kingdom of Sri Vijaya under their suzerainty in AD 1025. Though the Tamil area was integrated culturally with the rest of India for a long time, politically it was for most of the time a separate entity until the advent of British rule in India.

The Tamil in Sri Lanka today are of various groups and castes, though they are all Hindus. The so-called Ceylon Tamil, constituting approximately half of them, are concentrated in the northern part of the island. They are relatively well-educated, and many of them hold clerical

Interior of the Mahishasuramardini cave temple, Mahabalipuram, Tamil Nadu, India.
Frederick M. Asher

and professional positions. The so-called Indian Tamil of Sri Lanka were brought there by the British in the 19th and 20th centuries as workers on the tea estates, and they have been regarded as foreigners by the other ethnic groups. The Ceylon and Indian Tamil are organized under different caste systems and have little social intercourse with each other.

In the 1980s, growing tensions between the Ceylon Tamil and the Sinhalese Buddhist majority in Sri Lanka prompted Tamil militants to undertake a guerrilla war against the central government in hopes of creating a separate Tamil state for themselves in the north and northeast. The Tamil rebels' organization, the Liberation Tigers of Tamil Eelam (popularly, the "Tamil Tigers"), continued their insurgency until they were defeated by the Sri Lankan government in May 2009.

TODA

The Toda are a pastoral tribe of the Nilgiri Hills of southern India. Numbering only about 800 in the early 1960s, they had almost doubled in numbers by the mid-2000s because of improved health facilities. The Toda language is Dravidian but is the most aberrant of that linguistic stock.

Toda settlements contain from three to seven small thatched houses scattered over the pasture slopes. Built on a wooden framework, the typical house has an arched roof in the shape of a half barrel. The Toda traditionally trade dairy products, as well as cane and bamboo articles, with the other Nilgiri peoples, receiving Badaga grain and cloth and Kota tools and pottery in exchange. Kurumba people play music for Toda funerals and supply various forest products.

Toda religion centres on the all-important buffalo. Ritual must be performed for almost every dairy activity, from milking and giving the herds salt to churning butter and shifting pastures seasonally. There are ceremonies for the ordination of dairymen-priests, for rebuilding dairies, and for rethatching funerary temples. These rites and the complex funeral rituals are the major occasions of social intercourse, when intricate poetic songs alluding to the buffalo cult are composed and chanted.

Polyandry is fairly common; several men, usually brothers, may share one wife. When a Toda woman becomes pregnant one of her husbands ceremonially presents her with a toy bow and arrow, thus proclaiming himself the social father of her children.

Some Toda pasture land has come under recent cultivation by other peoples and much of it has been reforested. This threatens to undermine Toda culture by greatly diminishing the buffalo herds.

CASTE

A unique development of Hindu societies, castes are the ranked, hereditary social groups, often linked with occupation and marriage within their own group, that together constitute traditional societies in South Asia, particularly among Hindus in India.

Use of the term *caste* to characterize social organization in South Asia, particularly among the Hindus, dates to the middle of the 16th century. *Casta* (from Latin *castus,* "chaste") in the sense of purity of breed was employed by Portuguese observers to describe the division of Hindu society in western and southwestern India into socially ranked occupational categories. In an effort to maintain vertical social distance, these groups practiced mutual exclusion in matters relating to eating and, presumably, marrying. Subsequently, cast, or caste, became established in English and major European languages (notably Dutch and French) in the same specific sense. Caste is generally believed to be an ancient, abiding, and unique Indian institution upheld by a complex cultural ideology.

VARNAS

It is essential to distinguish between large-scale and small-scale views of caste society, which may respectively be said to represent theory and practice, or ideology and the existing social reality. On the large scale, contemporary students of Hindu society recall an ancient four-fold arrangement of socioeconomic categories called the *varnas*, which is traced back to an oral tradition preserved in the Rigveda (dating from perhaps 1000 BC). The Sanskrit word *varna* has many connotations including description, selection, classification, and colour. Of these, it is colour that appears to have been the intended meaning of the word as used by the authors of the Rigveda. The "Aryans" (*arya*, "noble," "distinguished") were the branch of Indo-European peoples that migrated about 1500 BC to northwestern India (the Indus Valley and the Punjab Plain), where they encountered the local, dark-skinned people they called the *daha* (enemies) or the *dasyus* (servants). It is also likely that the *daha* included earlier immigrants from Iran. The tendency of some 20th-century writers to reduce the ancient bipolar classification to racial differences on the basis of skin colour is misleading and rightly no longer in vogue.

The Indo-Europeans and the *dasyus* may have been antagonistic ethnic groups divided by physical features, culture, and language. Whatever their relations, it is likely that they gradually became integrated into an internally plural social order significantly influenced by the prior social organization of the Indo-Europeans. A threefold division of society into priests, warriors, and commoners was a part of the Indo-European heritage. In an early period, membership in a *varna* appears to

have been based mainly on personal skills rather than birth, status, or wealth. By the end of the Rigvedic period, however, the hereditary principle of social rank had taken root. Thus the Purusha (Universal Man) hymn of the Rigveda (probably a late addition to the text) describes the creation of humanity in the form of *varnas* from a self-sacrificial rite: Brahmans were the mouth of Purusha, from his arms were made the Rajanyas, from his two thighs, the Vaishyas, and the Sudras were born from his feet. The extent to which the ideology's hierarchical ordering of the four groups mirrored the social reality is unknown.

The highest ranked among the *varnas*, the Brahmans, were priests and the masters and teachers of sacred knowledge (*veda*). Next in rank but hardly socially inferior was the ruling class of Rajanya (kinsmen of the king), later renamed Kshatriya, those endowed with sovereignty and, as warriors, responsible for the protection of the dominion (*kshatra*). A complex, mutually reinforcing relationship of sacerdotal authority and temporal power was obviously shaped over a long period of time.

Clearly ranked below the two top categories were the Vaishyas (from *vish*, "those settled on soils"), comprising agriculturists and merchants. These three *varnas* together were deemed to be "twice-born" (*dvija*), as the male members were entitled to go through a rite of initiation during childhood. This second birth entitled them to participate in specified sacraments and gave them access to sacred knowledge. They were also entitled alongside their social superiors to demand and receive menial services from the Sudras, the fourth and lowest ranked *varna*. Certain degrading occupations, such as disposal of dead animals, excluded some Sudras from any physical contact with the "twice-born" *varnas*. As a Scheduled Caste, they were simply dubbed "the fifth" (*panchama*) category.

In the *varna* framework, the Brahmans have everything, directly or indirectly: "noble" identity, "twice-born" status, sacerdotal authority, and dominion over the Vaishyas and the Sudras, who accounted for the great majority of the people. This is not surprising, for the ancient Brahmans were the authors of the ideology. The four *varnas*, together with the notional division of the individual life cycle into four stages, or *ashramas* (*brahmacharya*, or the years of learning and extreme discipline; *garhasthya*, or householdership; *vanaprastha*, or retirement; and *sannyasa*, or renunciation of all worldly bonds) may at best be considered an archetypical blueprint for the good, moral life. Indeed, the Hindu way of life is traditionally called the *varnashrama dharma* (duties of the stages of life for one's *varna*). The *varna* order remains relevant to the understanding of the system of *jatis*, as it provides the ideological setting for the patterns of interaction that are continuously under negotiation.

JATIS

Although the term *caste* has been used loosely to stand for both *varna* and *jati*

(broadly, "form of existence fixed by birth"), it is *jati*—the small-scale perspective represented by local village societies—that most scholars have in mind when they write about the caste system of India. *Jatis* and relations among them have been accessible to observers from ancient times to the present. (Hereafter *jati* and *caste* will be used synonymously.)

Empirically, the caste system is one of regional or local *jatis*, each with a history of its own, whether this be Kashmir or Tamil Nadu, Bengal or Gujarat. History may differ, but the form of social organization does not. Everywhere castes have traditionally been endogamous; each *jati* was associated with one or more hereditary occupations, but certain occupations (for example, agriculture or nontraditional civil service) were caste-neutral; and there were *jati*-specific restrictions on what and with whom one could eat and drink. And, everywhere castes were ranked vertically, with the Brahmans at the top by virtue of their inherent condition of ritual purity, and the Sudras at the bottom. Those among the Sudras who disposed of impure substances (body emissions, dead animals, etc.) were the "untouchables." Between the top and bottom rungs there was considerable fluidity.

It is reasonable to assume that the caste system, contrary to the popular images of its changelessness, has always been characterized by the efforts of various *jatis* to raise themselves in the social order. Such efforts have been more successful in the case of low but ritually pure castes than in the case of those living below the line of pollution. As for "untouchability," this was declared unlawful in the Indian constitution framed after independence and adopted in 1949–50.

Two routes have been available to castes seeking upward mobility. The traditional route consists of the adoption of certain critical elements of the way of life of clean (upper) castes, such as the ritual of initiation into the status of a clean *jati*, wearing of the sacred thread (a loop of thread worn next to the skin over the left shoulder and across the right hip) symbolic of such status, vegetarianism, teetotalism, abstention from work that is considered polluting or demeaning, and prohibition of the remarriage of widows. The process is gradual and not always successful. The critical test of success lies in the willingness, first, of higher castes to accept cooked food from members of the upwardly mobile *jati* and, second, of equivalent-status castes to provide them services that are deemed demeaning.

Within the framework of traditional values, socially ambitious castes have also been known, when possible, to supplement the criterion of ritual purity by the secular criteria of numerical strength, economic well-being (notably in the form of land ownership), and the ability to mobilize physical force to emerge as the wielders of power in village affairs and in local politics. Such a *jati* is usually referred to as the "dominant caste." It is important to distinguish between status and dominance, although in historical practice they usually coincided. An important aspect of social change today is the dissociation of ritual status from secular economic and political power.

Although a great many spheres of life in modern India are little influenced by caste, most marriages are nevertheless arranged within the caste. This is in part because most people live in rural communities and because the arrangement of marriages is a family activity carried out through existing networks of kinship and caste.

CULTURAL MILIEU

The tempo of life in this large and diverse polyglot nation varies from region to region and from community to community. By the early 21st century the lifestyle of middle-class and affluent urban families differed little from that of urbanites in Europe, East Asia, or the Americas. For the most part, however, the flow of rural life continued much as it always had. Many small villages remained isolated from most forms of media and communications, and work was largely done by hand or by the use of animal power. Traditional forms of work and recreation only slowly have given way to habits and pastimes imported from the outside world. The pace of globalization was slow in much of rural India, and even in urban areas Western tastes in food, dress, and entertainment were adopted with discrimination. Indian fashions have remained the norm; Indians have continued to prefer traditional cuisine to Western fare; and, though Indian youths are as obsessed as those in the West with pop culture, Indians produce their own films and music (albeit, strongly influenced by Western styles), which have been extremely popular domestically and have been successfully marketed abroad.

Throughout India, custom and religious ritual are still widely observed and practiced. Among Hindus, religious and social custom follows the *samskara*, a series of personal sacraments and rites conducted at various stages throughout life. Observant members of other confessional communities follow their own rites and rituals. Among all groups, caste protocols have continued to play a role in enforcing norms and values, despite decades of state legislation to alleviate caste bias.

FAMILY AND KINSHIP

For almost all Indians the family is the most important social unit. There is a strong preference for extended families, consisting of two or more married couples (often of more than a single generation), who share finances and a common kitchen. Marriage is virtually universal, divorce rare, and virtually every marriage produces children. Almost all marriages are arranged by family elders on the basis of caste, degree of consanguinity, economic status, education (if any), and astrology. A bride traditionally moves to her husband's house. However, nonarranged "love marriages" are increasingly common in cities.

Within families, there is a clear order of social precedence and influence based on gender, age, and, in the case of a woman, the number of her male children. The senior male of the household—whether father, grandfather, or uncle—typically is the recognized family head, and his wife is the person who regulates the tasks assigned to female family members. Males enjoy higher status than females; boys are often pampered while girls are relatively neglected. This is reflected in significantly different rates of mortality and morbidity between the sexes, allegedly (though reliable statistics are lacking) in occasional female infanticide, and increasingly in the abortion of female fetuses following prenatal gender testing. This pattern of preference is largely connected to the institution of dowry, since the family's obligation to provide a suitable dowry to the bride's new family represents a major financial liability. Traditionally, women were expected to treat their husbands as if they were gods, and obedience of wives to husbands has remained a strong social norm. This expectation of devotion may follow a husband to the grave; within some caste groups, widows are not allowed to remarry even if they are bereaved at a young age.

Hindu marriage has traditionally been viewed as the "gift of a maiden" (*kanyadan*) from the bride's father to the household of the groom. This gift is also accompanied by a dowry, which generally consists of items suitable to start a young couple in married life. In some cases, however, dowries demanded by grooms and their families have become quite

The Chariot Festival of the Jagannatha temple, Puri, Orissa, India. © Dinodia/Dinodia Photo Library

extravagant, and some families appear to regard them as means of enrichment. There are instances, a few of which have been highly publicized, wherein young brides have been treated abusively—even tortured and murdered—in an effort to extract more wealth from the bride's father. The "dowry deaths" of such young women have contributed to a reaction against the dowry in some modern urban families.

A Muslim marriage is considered to be a contractual relationship—contracted by the bride's father or guardian—and, though there are often dowries, there is formal reciprocity, in which the groom promises a *mahr*, a commitment to provide his bride with wealth in her lifetime.

Beyond the family the most important unit is the caste. Within a village all members of a single caste recognize a fictive kinship relation and a sense of mutual obligation, but ideas of fictive kinship extend also to the village as a whole. Thus, for example, a woman who marries and goes to another village never ceases to be regarded as a daughter of her village. If she is badly treated in her husband's village, it may become a matter of collective concern for her natal village, not merely for those of her own caste.

FESTIVALS AND HOLIDAYS

Virtually all regions of India have their distinctive places of pilgrimage, local saints and folk heroes, religious festivals, and associated fairs. There are also innumerable festivals associated with individual villages or temples or with specific castes and cults. The most popular of the religious festivals celebrated over the greater part of India are Vasantpanchami (generally in February, the exact date determined by the Hindu lunar calendar), in honour of Sarasvati, the goddess of learning; Holi (February–March), a time when traditional hierarchical relationships are forgotten and celebrants throw coloured water and powder at one another; Dussehra (September–October), when the story of the *Ramayana* is reenacted; and Diwali, a time for lighting lamps and exchanging gifts. The major secular holidays are Independence Day (August 15) and Republic Day (January 26).

CUISINE

Although there is considerable regional variation in Indian cuisine, the day-to-day diet of most Indians lacks variety. Depending on income, two or three meals generally are consumed. The bulk of almost all meals is whatever the regional staple might be: rice throughout most of the east and south, flat wheat bread (chapati) in the north and northwest, and bread made from pearl millet (*bajra*) in Maharashtra. This is usually supplemented with the puree of a legume (called dal), a few vegetables, and, for those who can afford it, a small bowl of yogurt. Chilies and other spices add zest to this simple fare.

Spices are a distinctive feature of the cooking of India and Indonesia. In India, every good cook prepares a curry—a mixture of such fragrant powdered spices as cardamom, cinnamon, cloves, cumin, nutmeg, and turmeric. The spice blend is kept in a jar in the kitchen and is used to season all sorts of foods.

The Hindus of India have developed what is perhaps the world's greatest vegetarian cuisine. They use cereals, pulses (lentils, peas, and beans), and rice with great imagination to produce a widely varied but generally meatless cuisine.

Indian cooks prepare delicious chutneys, highly seasoned vegetables and fruits used as side dishes that must be fresh to be fully appreciated. They also make little delicacies such as *idlis*, cakes of rice and lentils that are cooked by steaming; *pakoras*, vegetables fried in chickpea batter; and *jalebis*, pretzel-like tidbits made by soaking a deep-fried batter of wheat and chickpea flour in a sweet syrup. *Raitas*, yogurt with fruits or vegetables, are another favourite. Other specialties include *biryani*, a family of complicated rice dishes cooked with meats or shrimp; *samosa*, a flaky, stuffed, deep-fried pastry; *korma*, lamb curry made with a thick sauce using crushed nuts and yogurt; *masala*, the dry or wet base for curry; and a great variety of breads and hot wafers, including *naan*, *pappadam*, *parathas*, and *chapatis*.

In southern India and especially in the historical region of Telingana, or Andhra, the food is seasoned with fresh chili peppers and can be fiery hot. Lamb is the most important meat served in northern India. It is prepared in hundreds of different ways as kabobs, curries, roasts, and in rice dishes. In pre-independence days the Mughal cuisine there ranked among the most lavish in the world. The Mughal cuisine developed during the Muslim empire of the great Mughal kingdom. It is based, mostly because of religious and geographic limitations, on lamb. The preparations are mostly roasted, barbecued dishes, also kabobs and the so-called dry curries, versus the stew-type cooking of the south.

Fish, fresh milk, and fruits and vegetables, however, are more widely consumed, subject to regional and seasonal availability. In general, tea is the preferred beverage in northern and eastern India, while coffee is more common in the south.

CLOTHING

Clothing for most Indians is also quite simple and typically untailored. Men

Indian men wearing dhotis, from a 19th-century painting. Courtesy of the Victoria and Albert Museum, London

(especially in rural areas) frequently wear little more than a broadcloth dhoti, worn as a loose skirtlike loincloth, or, in parts of the south and east, the tighter wraparound *lungi*. In both cases the body remains bare above the waist, except in cooler weather, when a shawl also may be worn, or in hot weather, when the head may be protected by a turban. The more-affluent and higher-caste men are likely to wear a tailored shirt, increasingly of Western style. Muslims, Sikhs, and urban dwellers generally are more inclined to wear tailored clothing, including various types of trousers, jackets, and vests.

Although throughout most of India women wear saris and short blouses, the way in which a sari is wrapped varies greatly from one region to another. In Punjab, as well as among older female students and many city dwellers, the characteristic dress is the *shalwar-kamiz*, a

Indian woman wearing a sari, detail of a gouache painting on mica from Tiruchchirappalli, India, c. 1850. Courtesy of the Victoria and Albert Museum, London

Detail of a patola sari from Gujarat, late 18th century; in the Prince of Wales Museum of Western India, Mumbai. Gujarat is famous for its skilled craftwork, including the making of silk patola fabric. P. Chandra

combination of pajama-like trousers and a long-tailed shirt (saris being reserved for special occasions). Billowing ankle-length skirts and blouses are the typical female dress of Rajasthan and parts of Gujarat. Most rural Indians, especially females, do not wear shoes and, when footwear is necessary, prefer sandals.

The modes of dress of tribal Indians are exceedingly varied and can be, as among certain Naga groups, quite ornate. Throughout India, however, Western dress is increasingly in vogue, especially among urban and educated males, and Western-style school uniforms are worn by both sexes in many schools, even in rural India.

SPORTS AND RECREATION

The history of sports in India dates to thousands of years ago, and numerous games, including chess, wrestling, and archery, are thought to have originated there. Contemporary Indian sport is a diverse mix, with traditional games, such as *kabaddi* and *kho-kho*, and those introduced by the British, especially cricket, football (soccer), and field hockey, enjoying great popularity.

Kabaddi, primarily an Indian game, is believed to be some 4,000 years old. Combining elements of wrestling and rugby, the team sport has been a regular part of the Asian Games since 1990. *Kho-kho*, a form of tag, ranks as one of the most popular traditional sports in India, and its first national championship was held in the early 1960s.

Indians are passionate about cricket, which probably appeared on the sub-continent in the early 18th century. The country competed in its first official test in 1932 and in 1983—led by captain Kapil Dev, one of the most successful cricketers in history—won the World Cup. Golf is also played throughout India. The Royal Calcutta Golf Club, established in Kolkata in 1829, is the oldest golf club in India and the first outside Great Britain.

India made its Olympic Games debut at the 1920 Games in Antwerp, though it did not form an Olympic association until 1927. The following year, in Amsterdam, India competed in field hockey for the first time. The national team's victory that year was the first of six consecutive gold medals in the event between 1928 and 1956; they won again in 1964 and 1980.

MEDIA AND PUBLISHING

Several thousand daily newspapers are published in India. Although English-language dailies and journals remain highly influential, the role of the vernacular press is increasing steadily in absolute and relative importance. Among the largest-circulating dailies are *The Times of India* and *Hindustan Times* (both in English), the *Hindustan* and the *Navbharat Times* (Hindi), and the *Anandabazar Patrika* (Bangla). Book publishing is a thriving industry. Academic titles account for a large portion of all works published, but there is also a considerable market for literature. On the whole, the press functions with little government censorship, and serious controls have been imposed only in matters of national security, in times of emergency, or when it is deemed necessary to avoid inflaming passions (e.g., after communal riots or comparable disturbances). The country's largest news agency, the Press Trust of India, was founded in 1947. The United News of India was founded in 1961.

Radio broadcasting began privately in 1927 but became a monopoly of the colonial government in 1930. In 1936 it was given its current name, All India Radio, and since 1957 it also has been known as Akashvani. The union government provides radio service throughout the country via hundreds of transmitters. Television was introduced experimentally by Akashvani in 1959, and regular broadcasting commenced in 1965. In 1976 it was made a separate service under the name Doordarshan, later changed to Doordarshan India ("Television India"). Television and educational programming are transmitted via the Indian National Satellite (INSAT) system. The country's first Hindi-language cable channel, Zee TV, was established in 1992, and this was followed by other cable and satellite services.

There is relatively dense telephone service in most urban areas, but many rural areas remain isolated. The same is true of cellular telephones, which are common in major cities. Internet cafés can be found in many affluent areas, and millions of Indian households are connected to the Internet via telephone and cable connections. There are numerous high-technology centres in the country, and India is connected to the outside world via international cables and across satellite networks.

CHAPTER 2

INDIAN LANGUAGES AND WRITING SYSTEMS

There are probably hundreds of major and minor languages and many hundreds of recognized dialects in India. There are also several isolate languages, such as Nahali, which is spoken in a small area of Madhya Pradesh state. The overwhelming majority of Indians speak Indo-Aryan or Dravidian languages.

The difference between language and dialect in India is often arbitrary, however, and official designations vary notably from one census to another. This is complicated by the fact that, owing to their long-standing contact with one another, India's languages have come to converge and to form an amalgamated linguistic area—a *Sprachbund*—comparable, for example, to that found in the Balkans. Languages within India have adopted words and grammatical forms from one another, and vernacular dialects within languages often diverge widely. Over much of India, and especially the Indo-Gangetic Plain, there are no clear boundaries between one vernacular and another (although ordinary villagers are sensitive to nuances of dialect that differentiate nearby localities). In the mountain fringes of the country, especially in the northeast, spoken dialects are often sufficiently different from one valley to the next to merit classifying each as a truly distinct language. There were at one time, for example, no fewer than 25 languages classified within the Naga group, not one of which was spoken by more than 60,000 people.

Lending order to this linguistic mix are a number of written, or literary, languages used on the subcontinent, each of which often differs markedly from the vernacular with which it is associated. Many people are bilingual or multilingual, knowing their local vernacular dialect ("mother tongue"), its associated written variant, and, perhaps, one or more other languages.

INDIAN LANGUAGES

The languages spoken in India are classified as belonging to the following families: Indo-European (the Indo-Aryan branch in particular), Dravidian, Austroasiatic (Munda in particular), and Sino-Tibetan (Tibeto-Burman in particular).

INDO-ARYAN (INDIC)

In the early 21st century, Indo-Aryan languages were spoken by more than 800 million people, primarily in India, Bangladesh, Nepal, Pakistan, and Sri Lanka. According to the 2001 census of India, Indo-Aryan languages accounted for more than 790,625,000 speakers, or more than 75 percent of the population. By 2003 the constitution of India included 22 officially recognized, or Scheduled, languages. However, this number does not distinguish among many speech communities that could legitimately be considered distinct languages. For example, the Hindi census category includes not only Hindi proper (about 422,050,000 speakers in 2001) but also such languages as Bhojpuri (about 33,100,000), Magahi (about 13,975,000), and Maithili (more than 12,175,000).

Other Indo-Aryan languages that have been officially recognized in the constitution are as follows (the approximate numbers of speakers for each are drawn from the census report of 2001): Asamiya (Assamese, about 13,175,000 speakers), Bangla (Bengali, 83,875,000), Gujarati (46,100,000), Kashmiri (5,525,000), Konkani (2,500,000), Marathi (71,950,000), Nepali (2,875,000), Oriya (33,025,000), Punjabi (29,100,000), Sindhi (2,550,000), and Urdu (51,550,000).

GENERAL CHARACTERISTICS

Linguists generally recognize three major divisions of Indo-Aryan languages: Old, Middle, and New (or Modern) Indo-Aryan. These divisions are primarily linguistic and are named in the order in which they initially appeared, with later divisions coexisting with rather than completely replacing earlier ones.

Old Indo-Aryan includes different dialects and linguistic states that are referred to in common as Sanskrit. The most archaic Old Indo-Aryan is found in Hindu sacred texts called the Vedas, which date to approximately 1500 BC. There is a clear-cut difference between Vedic and post-Vedic Sanskrit in that the former has certain formations that the latter has eliminated. The grammarian Panini (c. 5th–6th century BC) appropriately distinguishes between usage proper to the language of sacred texts— that is, Vedic usage—and what occurs in the spoken language of his time. Other distinctions are also made within the language, so scholars speak of Classical Sanskrit and Epic Sanskrit. Despite differences in genre, however, the Sanskrit found in such works generally agrees with the language Panini describes. So-called un-Paninian forms not only reflect the influence of vernaculars but also continue a freedom of usage already to be seen in aspects of the living spoken language Panini described.

Middle Indo-Aryan includes the dialects of inscriptions from the 3rd century BC to the 4th century AD as well as various literary languages. Apabhramsha dialects represent the latest stage of Middle Indo-Aryan development. Though all Middle Indo-Aryan languages are included under the name Prakrit, it is customary to speak of the Prakrits as excluding Apabhramsha.

Uncertainties regarding the course of Indo-Aryan migration make it difficult to determine the domain of Proto-Indo-Aryan, the ancestral language of all the known Indo-Aryan tongues, if indeed there was any such single region. All that can be said with certainty is that the Indo-Aryan speakers on the Indian subcontinent first occupied the area comprising most of present-day Punjab state (India), Punjab province (Pakistan), Haryana, and the Upper Doab (of the Ganges–Yamuna Doab) of Uttar Pradesh. The structure of Proto-Indo-Aryan must have been similar to that of early Vedic, albeit with dialect variations.

Some of the Indo-Aryan languages are used by relatively few speakers; others are used as the media of education and of official transactions. Hindi written in the Devanagari script is one of two official languages of the Republic of India (the other is English). It is widely used as a lingua franca throughout northern India, including Haryana and Madhya Pradesh, and in parts of the South. Asamiya, Bangla, Oriya, Punjabi, Gujarati, and Marathi are the state languages of Assam, West Bengal, Orissa, Punjab, Gujarat, and Maharashtra, respectively. There are other Modern Indo-Aryan languages with large numbers of speakers in India, though they lack official recognition; examples include various languages spoken in Rajasthan (e.g., Marwari, Mewari); several Pahari languages, spoken in Himachal Pradesh, Uttarakhand, and Sindhi, spoken by Sindhis in various parts of India. Each of the major state languages has several dialects in addition to the standard dialect adopted for official purposes, and Hindi has not only dialects but also several varieties according to the mother tongue of the area; e.g., Bombay Hindi and Calcutta Hindi.

Many New Indo-Aryan languages also have official status outside India. Urdu written in Perso-Arabic script is the official language of Pakistan, where it is spoken by most of the population

The Maharaja Sayajirao University of Baroda at Vadodara, Gujarat, India. Gujarati is the official language of Gujarat, used for educational and government purposes. Vidyavrata

as either a first or a second language. Structurally and historically, Hindi and Urdu are one, although they are now official languages of different countries, are written in different alphabets, and have been developing in divergent manners. The term *hindī* (also *hindvī*) is known from as early as the 13th century AD. The term *zabān-e-urdū* 'language of the imperial camp' came into use about the 17th century. In the south, Urdu was used by Muslim conquerors of the 14th century.

HINDI

Hindi is the preferred official language of India, although much national business is also done in English and the other languages recognized in the Indian constitution. In India, Hindi is spoken as a first language by nearly 425 million people and as a second language by some 120 million more. Significant Hindi speech communities are also found in South Africa, Mauritius, Bangladesh, Yemen, and Uganda.

Literary Hindi, written in the Devanagari script, has been strongly influenced by Sanskrit. Its standard form is based on the Khari Boli dialect, found to the north and east of Delhi. Braj Bhasha, which was an important literary medium from the 15th to the 19th century, is often treated as a dialect of Hindi, as are Awadhi, Bagheli, Bhojpuri, Bundeli, Chhattisgarhi, Garhwali, Haryanawi, Kanauji, Kumayuni, Magahi, and Marwari. However, these so-called dialects of Hindi are more accurately described as regional languages of the "Hindi zone" or "belt," an area that approximates the region of northern India, south through the state of Madhya Pradesh.

Within this zone, the degree to which regional languages resemble standard Hindi varies considerably. Maithili—the easternmost regional language of the Hindi belt—bears more historical resemblance to Bangla than to standard Hindi. Likewise, Rajasthani, the westernmost language of the belt, in some respects resembles Gujarati more than standard Hindi. Nevertheless, the majority of speakers of these regional languages consider themselves to be speaking a Hindi dialect. Among other reasons, they note that these languages were grouped with Hindi by the British in an attempt to classify languages in the early days of British rule. Furthermore, Hindi (rather than one of the regional languages) was chosen as the medium of instruction at the elementary-school level. In large part as a result of this colonial policy, members of the urban middle class and educated villagers throughout the zone claim to be speakers of Hindi because the use of these regional languages or dialects in public venues—that is, outside the circle of family and close friends—is perceived as a sign of inadequate education. In other words, speaking standard Hindi gives as much status to people in this region as speaking English gives in the south of India; both are treated as languages of upward social mobility. Thus, people in search of new jobs, marriages, and the like must use standard Hindi in everyday communication. In many cases, young people now have only a passive knowledge of the regional languages. Particularly since the 1950s, the prevalence of mass media (radio, television, and films) and growing literacy have led to an increase in the number of native speakers of standard Hindi.

Occasionally there are demands for the formation of separate states for the speakers of one or another regional language. Such demands are generally neutralized by counterdemands for the recognition of that regional language's many dialects. For instance, when the demand for the formation of a separate state of Maithili speakers was raised in Bihar in the 1960s and '70s, there was a counterdemand for the recognition of Angika in eastern Bihar and Bajjika in northwestern Bihar. The successful demands for forming the new states of Chhattisgarh (from territory once in Madhya Pradesh) and Uttaranchal (from territory in Uttar Pradesh) was more sociopolitical than linguistic.

Modern standard Hindi evolved from the interaction of early speakers of Khari Boli with Muslim invaders from Afghanistan, Iran, Turkey, Central Asia, and elsewhere. As the new immigrants settled and began to adjust to the Indian social environment, their languages— which were ultimately lost—enriched Khari Boli.

Most of the Persian words that were assimilated with Hindi concerned administration, such as *bahi* 'account book,' *faujdari* 'criminal (case),' *vazir* 'minister,' and *musahib* 'courtier.' Words such as *dalil* 'argument,' *faisla* 'judgment,' and *gavahi* 'witness' have been completely assimilated and are usually not recognized as loanwords. Persian names for items of dress and bedding (e.g., *pajama*, *chador*), cuisine (e.g., *korma, kabab*), cosmetics (e.g., *sabun* 'soap,' *hina* 'henna'), furniture (e.g., *kursi* 'chair,' *mez* 'table'), construction (e.g., *divar* 'wall,' *kursi* 'plinth'), a large number of adjectives and their nominal derivatives (e.g., *abad* 'inhabited' and *abadi* 'population'), and a wide range of other items and concepts are so much a part of the Hindi language that purists of the postindependence period have been unsuccessful in purging them.

While borrowing Persian and Arabic words, Hindi also borrowed phonemes, such as /f/ and /z/, though these were sometimes replaced by /ph/ and /j/. For instance, Hindi renders the word for 'force' as either *zor* or *jor* and the word for 'sight' as *nazar* or *najar*. In most cases

the sounds /g/ and /x/ were replaced by /k/ and /kh/, respectively. Contact with the English language has also enriched Hindi. Many English words, such as *button, pencil, petrol,* and *college* are fully assimilated in the Hindi lexicon.

Hindi has borrowed a number of prefixes and suffixes from Persian that, when combined with indigenous roots, have created new words. Similarly, the process of hybridization with English has produced a large number of derived nominals, such as *kaungresi* (*congress + i*), *Ameriki* (*America + i*), and *vaiscansalari* (*vice-chancellor + i*), in which the base word is English and the suffix is typically Hindi. Nouns that mix contributions from English and Persian, such as *table-kursi* 'tables and chairs' and *schoolimarat* 'school building,' are also found. In spoken Hindi, English-based complex verbs are used as well. For instance, one can say either *aram karna* or *rest karna* 'to rest,' *parhai karna* or *study karna* 'to study,' and *bahas karna* or *plead karna* 'to plead.'

In earlier Hindi the relative clause was placed either at the beginning or at the end of the main clause. For instance, one could render 'the boy who came here yesterday is my friend' in several ways: *wo larka mera dosht hai jo kal yaha aya tha,* literally 'that boy my friend is who yesterday came here'; *jo larka kal yaha aya tha, wo mera dosht hai,* literally 'which boy yesterday here came, he my friend is'; or *wo larka jo kal yaha aya tha, mera dosht hai,* literally 'that boy who yesterday here came, my friend is.' After colonization, Hindi syntax was influenced by English, though in a limited way. For instance, until the mid-19th century, Hindi had no form for indirect narration—one could formerly say *Ram ne kaha, mein nahi aaoonga* 'Ram said, "I won't come,"' and now one can also say *Ram ne kaha ki wo nahi ayega* 'Ram said that he won't come.'

From the mid-20th century, the use of Hindi on national television increased the use of a linguistic device called *code switching*, in which the speaker creates sentences by combining a Hindi phrase with another in English, as in *I told him that mai bimar hu* 'I told him that I am sick.' This device differs from *code mixing*, in which words of different origins are mixed: *usne sick leave ki application de hai* 'he has applied for sick leave.'

In 1931 linguist Sumit Kumar Chatterjee conducted a study in Calcutta (now Kolkata) detailing the use of a lingua franca that he called Bazaar Hindustani. It had minimal grammatical forms and a simplified basic vocabulary used by both Europeans and Indians who spoke such languages as Asamiya, Bangla, Oriya, Tamil, and Hindi. In the early 21st century, what came to be known simply as Hindustani—a colloquial spoken language that, depending on geographic location, draws extensively from Hindi and Sanskrit or from Urdu and Persian—continued to be the lingua franca of Kolkata and other cosmopolitan and industrial cities that had drawn people from all parts of India. As Hindi originated in just such a multilingual situation centuries ago, so may urbanism instigate the development of an even richer lexicon and even more flexible syntactic devices.

Pressure on standard Hindi is felt not only from non-Hindi speakers but also from the many Hindi speakers who have recently switched over from their dialects to standard Hindi without having entirely eliminated the influences of those regional languages. In such cases, sound systems often retain a regional touch; for instance, Biharis use /s/ in place of /sh/, and the hill peoples (the so-called Scheduled Tribes) of Uttar Pradesh use /sh/ for /s/. The syntax of such speakers may also have recognizable variants; for example, instead of the standard Hindi form *mujhey jana hai* 'I have to go,' Punjabis and Delhites say *maine jana hae*, Hindi speakers of Teangana say *maiku jana hai*, and people of western Madhya Pradesh and Maharashtra say *apanko jana hai*.

The Central Hindi Directorate, a government agency with the mission of standardizing and modernizing Hindi, is moving the language closer to Sanskrit. Non-Hindi speakers, however, are pulling the language in another direction by using increasing numbers of English words and phrases and by simplifying the complex rules of subject-verb agreement found in standard Hindi. Notably, both groups are motivated by the same goal—to widen the scope of Hindi by making it more comprehensible to non-Hindi speakers.

ASAMIYA (ASSAMESE)

The only indigenous Indo-Aryan language of the Assam valley, Asamiya has been affected in vocabulary, phonetics, and structure by its close association with Tibeto-Burman dialects in the region. Its grammar is noted for its highly inflected forms, and there are also different pronouns and noun plural markers for use in honorific and nonhonorific constructions. Asamiya is also closely related to Bangla; like Bangla and Oriya, Asamiya has no grammatical gender distinctions.

Asamiya literary tradition dates to the 13th century. Prose texts, notably *buranji*s (historical works), began to appear in the 16th century.

BANGLA (BENGALI)

Bangla is spoken in India primarily in the states of West Bengal, Assam, and Tripura.

There is general agreement that in the distant past Oriya, Asamiya, and Bangla formed a single branch, from which Oriya split off first and Asamiya later. This is one reason that the earliest specimens of Bangla language and literature, the *Charyapadas* (Buddhist mystic songs), are also claimed by speakers of Oriya and Asamiya as their own.

The Bangla linguists Suniti Kumar Chatterji and Sukumar Sen suggested that Bangla had its origin in the 10th century AD, deriving from Magahi Prakrit (a spoken language) through Magahi Apabhramsha (its written counterpart).

The Bengali scholar Muhammad Shahidullah and his followers offered a competing theory, suggesting that the language began in the 7th century AD and developed from spoken and written Gauda (also, respectively, a Prakrit and an Apabhramsha).

Although Bangla is an Indo-European language, it has been influenced by other language families prevalent in South Asia, notably the Dravidian, the Austroasiatic, and the Tibeto-Burman families, all of which contributed to Bangla vocabulary and provided the language with some structural forms. In the 1960s and '70s, Chatterji examined dictionaries from the early 20th century and attributed slightly more than half of the Bangla vocabulary to native words (i.e., naturally modified Sanskrit words, corrupted forms of Sanskrit words, and loanwords from non-Indo-European languages), about 45 percent to unmodified Sanskrit words, and the remainder to foreign words. Dominant in the last group was Persian, which was also the source of some grammatical forms. More recent studies suggest that the use of native and foreign words has been increasing, mainly because of the preference of Bangla speakers for the colloquial style.

There are two standard styles in Bangla: the Sadhubhasa (elegant or genteel speech) and the Chaltibhasa (current or colloquial speech). The former was largely shaped by the language of early Bangla poetical works. In the 19th century it became standardized as the literary language and also as the appropriate vehicle for business and personal exchanges. Although it was at times used for oration, Sadhubhasa was not the language of daily communication.

Chaltibhasa is based on the cultivated form of the dialects of Kolkata (Calcutta) and its neighbouring small towns on the Bhagirathi River. It has come into literary use since the early 20th century, and by the early 21st century it had become the dominant literary language as well as the standard colloquial form of speech among the educated. The pronouns and verb forms of the Sadhubhasa are contracted in Chaltibhasa. There is also a marked difference in vocabulary.

Although distinctions in the use of Bangla are associated with social class, educational level, and religion, the greatest differences are regional. The four main dialects roughly approximate the ancient political divisions of the Bangla-speaking world, known as Radha (West Bengal proper); Pundra, or Varendra (the northern parts of West Bengal and Bangladesh); Kamrupa (northeastern Bangladesh); and Bangla (the dialects of the rest of Bangladesh. In addition,

Indian women in Kolkata celebrate Vasantotsav, the Bengali festival of spring on February 28, 2010. Deshakalyan Chowdhury/AFP/Getty Images

two cities, Sylhet and Chittagong, have developed dialects with lexical and phonological characteristics that are mostly unintelligible to other speakers of Bangla.

The Bangla script is derived from Brahmi, one of the two ancient Indian scripts, and particularly from the eastern variety of Brahmi. Bangla script followed a different line of development from that of Devanagari and Oriyan scripts, but the characters of Bangla and Asamiya scripts generally coincided. By the 12th century AD the Bangla alphabet was nearly complete, although natural changes continued to take place until the 16th century. Some conscious alterations were also made in the 19th century.

Bangla is written from left to right. There are no capital letters. The script is characterized by many conjuncts, upstrokes, downstrokes, and other features that hang from a horizontal line. The punctuation marks, save one, are all taken from 19th-century English.

Bangla spelling was more or less standardized through a set of reforms that were initiated by the University of Calcutta in 1936. However, the standardization process continued throughout the 20th and into the early 21st century. For instance, the Bangla Academy in Dhaka prefers a set of alternatives offered by the 1936 reforms, while the Bangla Academy in West Bengal has proposed new reforms. Visva-Bharati, the university founded by the Bengali poet and Nobelist Rabindranath Tagore, has also effected several spelling variations. Finally, some newspapers and publishers have their own house styles. Not surprisingly, these independent efforts to standardize Bangla orthography have helped to create a degree of confusion.

DOGRI

Dogri is spoken in the Indian state of Jammu and Kashmir. The earliest written reference to it (using the paleonym [ancient name] Duggar) is found in the *Nuh sipihr* ("The Nine Heavens"), written by the poet Amīr Khosrow in AD 1317.

Dogri is descended from Classical Sanskrit, the language of the *Vedas* (1500–1200 BC). The development of Dogri from the Vedic period to its present form has been traced through changes in phonology. For example, the word *son* is rendered as *putra* in Old Indo-Aryan (perhaps 1200–250 BC), *putta* in Middle Indo-Aryan (approximately 400 BC–AD 1100), and *putter* in Dogri (since perhaps AD 1100). Documented phonological changes include nasalization, metathesis (the transposition of phonemes within a word), and shifts in voice and aspiration. Dogri uses length, nasalization, juncture, stress, and three tones (level, falling, and rising) to differentiate between its 10 vowel phonemes and 28 consonant phonemes.

Dogri vocabulary (but not grammatical structure) has been influenced by other languages, notably Persian and English. Within the language, variety is for the most part geographically based.

Dogri was once written in Dogra or Dogra Akkhar, the official script of Jammu and Kashmir state during the reign of Ranbir Singh (1857–85). However, Dogra was for the most part replaced by Devanagari script during the 20th century.

GUJARATI

Most of the 46 million people who speak Gujarati reside in the Indian state of Gujarat, though there are significant diaspora communities around the world, especially in the United Kingdom and the United States.

The development of the language can traced to approximately the 12th century AD. Gujarati inflection is fairly complex, marking three genders (masculine, feminine, and neuter), two numbers (singular and plural), and three cases (nominative, oblique, and agentive-locative) for nouns. It is usually written with a cursive form of Devanagari script.

Differences in religion, caste, ethnicity, profession, and education overlap with regional distinctions to create a complex system of language varieties in which sharp dialect boundaries cannot be drawn. Linguists have discerned two general pairs of dialect groups, however. The first is based on differing phonology: some groups use a "tight" phonation, spoken with a raised larynx; others use a "murmured" phonation, spoken with the intermittent lowering of the larynx. The second dialect pair is based on ethnicity, as there are recognizable distinctions between speakers who are Parsi and those who are Bohra.

KASHMIRI

Kashmiri is spoken in the Vale of Kashmir and the surrounding hills. By origin it is a Dardic language, but it has become predominantly Indo-Aryan in character. Reflecting the history of the area, the Kashmiri vocabulary is mixed, containing Dardic, Sanskrit, Punjabi, and Persian elements. Religious differences are evident in vocabulary and choice of alphabet. Muslims employ Persian and Arabic words freely; they also use the Persian form of the alphabet to write Kashmiri, although the Persian alphabet is not truly suited to the task, because it lacks symbols for the many Kashmiri vowel sounds. Kashmiri Hindus favour words derived from Sanskrit and write Kashmiri in the Sarada alphabet, a script of Indian origin. In printed books, the Devanagari character is used. There is a small amount of Kashmiri literature. The only important spoken dialects are Kishtwari, Poguli, and Rambani.

KONKANI

Konkani, the language of some 2.5 million people, is spoken on the central west coast of India, where it is the official language of Goa state. It is also associated particularly with the city of Mangalore (Mangaluru) in southwestern Karnataka and is spoken especially along the west coast of Maharashtra state. Because of the language's proximity to Marathi, it bears some resemblance to that language, but it precedes Marathi in date of origination. The first known Konkani inscription dates to 1187.

MAITHILI

With Magadhi (Magahi) and Bhojpuri, Maithili is one of the major languages of Bihar state. Maithili is the language of old Mithila (the area of ancient Videha, now Tirhut), which is dominated by orthodoxy and the Maithil Brahman way of life. Maithili is the only Bihari language with a script of its own, called Tirhuta, and a strong literary history; one of the earliest and most celebrated writers in Maithili was Vidyapati (Bidpai; 15th century), noted for his lyrics of love and devotion.

MARATHI

Marathi is spoken in western and central India. Its range extends from north of Mumbai down the western coast past Goa and eastward across the Deccan; in 1966 it became the official language of the state of Maharashtra. The standard form of speech is that of the city of Pune (Poona).

Descended from the Maharashtri Prakrit, Marathi has a significant literature. Books are printed in Devanagari script, which is also used for handwriting, although for handwriting there is also an alternate cursive form of Devanagari called Modi. Eastern Hindi is the Indo-Aryan language most closely related to Marathi. Like Hindi, Marathi has lost most of its inflectional system to indicate case, using instead postpositions (like prepositions, only following the word) with an oblique "case" to serve the function originally filled by inflection.

NEPALI

Nepali (also called Gurkha, Gorkhali, Gurkhali, or Khaskura) is spoken by more than 17 million people, more than 2.8 million of whom live in parts of India bordering on Nepal.

Patterns of phonological change suggest that Nepali is related to the languages of northwestern India, and particularly to Sindhi, Lahnda, and Punjabi. Comparative reconstructions of vocabulary have supported this appraisal, relating Nepali to proto-Dardic, Pahari, Sindhi, Lahnda, and Punjabi.

Investigations of archaeology and history indicate that modern Nepali is a descendant of the language spoken by the ancient Khasha people. The word Khasha appears in Sanskrit legal, historical, and literary texts such as the *Manu-smriti* (1st century BC), Kalhana's *Rajatarangini* (AD 1148), and the *Puranas* (AD 350–1500). The Khashas ruled over a vast territory comprising what are now western Nepal, parts of Garhwal and Kumaon (India), and parts of southwestern Tibet. Ashoka Challa (AD 1255–78) called himself *khasha-rajadhiraja* ("emperor of the Khashas") in a copperplate inscription found in Bodh Gaya. His descendants used old

Nepali to inscribe numerous copperplates during the 14th century.

After the Muslim conquest, the Rajputs of Chittaurgarh, the Brahmans of Kannauj, and many others fled to the foothills of the Himalayas for shelter. The pressure of the migrants and the rising ambition of the local powers caused the Khasha kingdom to fissure into smaller principalities. Some Khasha moved to the eastern parts of present-day Nepal, where their language became a common method of communication for the region's linguistically diverse ethnic groups.

Eventually Prithvi Narayan Shah (1723?–75) unified the smaller principalities. During and after unification, the Nepalese were identified as Gurkhas or Ghurkhalis, while their language was referred to by the singular forms of those names. With the growth of linguistic nationalism, the name Nepali became increasingly popular among the Nepalese living in Nepal and India.

Nepali includes three regional dialect groups: the western, the central, and the eastern. There is also a distinct dialect used by the members of the royal family and the upper classes. This dialect has a special lexicon and a four-level honorific system, and it is increasingly being adopted by the educated middle class and the newly wealthy.

Nepali has a rich heritage of oral literature as well as a body of written literature that has been developed during last two and half centuries. The vocabulary and style of written Nepali are influenced by Sanskrit and recorded with the Devanagari script.

As a medium of law and administration, the register of legal Nepali has been developed and enriched with Persian and Arabic words. Technical terms for the various administrative branches of government have been devised and borrowed from Sanskrit and English as needed. Modern spoken Nepali has borrowed vocabulary from Hindi, Sanskrit, and English.

Oriya

Oriya is the main official language of the Indian state of Orissa. The language has several dialects; Mughalbandi (Coastal Oriya) is the standard dialect and the language of education.

Oldest of the eastern group of the Indo-Aryan family, Oriya is derived from Ardhamagadhi Prakrit. Oriya arguably dates back to the 10th century AD, though it was almost indistinguishable from Bangla until the 11th century. The first poetic classic was composed in the 15th century, and literary prose began to take shape in the 18th century.

Oriya has been heavily influenced by the Dravidian languages as well as Arabic, Persian, and English. Its lexicon has been enriched by borrowings from these languages as well as from Tamil, Telugu, Marathi, Turkish, French, Portuguese, and Sanskrit. Words borrowed from Sanskrit occur in two forms: *tatsama* (close to the original form) and *tadbhava* (remote from the original form).

Oriya allows compounding, but unlike Sanskrit it does not allow elision (the slurring or omission of a final unstressed vowel). The use of compounds is more a feature of written than of spoken Oriya. Oriya has 6 pure vowels, 9 diphthongs, 28 consonants (3 of them retroflex—i.e., produced with the tip of the tongue curled back toward the hard palate), 4 semivowels, and no consonant-ending words.

Oriya grammar distinguishes between singular and plural number; first, second, and third person; and masculine and feminine gender. It is an inflectionally rich language. Nominals carry number and case inflections, while adjectives carry inflections indicating degree and, for the *tatsama* adjectives, gender.

In Oriya inscriptions from between the 12th and the 14th century, word order is relatively free, and verb–object sequence (with the subject before or after) is not infrequent. Other historical changes include the loss of some plural markers and some postpositions. The indirect speech, relative clauses, and passive constructions found in English have emerged in Oriya, although these are considered nonstandard forms. New discursive forms such as the essay and news reporting and analysis have also come to Oriya from English. Scholarly speech and writing still remain fairly Sanskritized, however.

PUNJABI

The Punjabi (Panjabi) language is spoken by more than 100 million people in Punjab, a territory that was divided between India and Pakistan during partition; the former territory now comprises both Punjab state in India and Punjab province in Pakistan. Smaller speech communities exist in Canada, Malaysia, South Africa, the United Arab Emirates, the United Kingdom, the United States, and elsewhere.

There are two major varieties of Punjabi. The western variety is known as Lahnda, while the eastern variety is known as Gurmukhi. Punjabi is generally written with either Perso-Arabic script or the Gurmukhi alphabet, which was devised by the Sikh Guru Angad (ruled 1539–52) for scriptural use; it is now employed for general purposes as well. Occasionally, Punjabi is written with Devanagari script.

The Punjabi language evolved from Shauraseni Apabhramsha. Traces of earlier Prakrits, especially Pali, and of proto-Indo-Aryan and pre-Indo-Aryan languages also appear in Punjabi phonology and morphology.

The most distinctive feature of modern Punjabi is its use of tones to differentiate words that are otherwise identical. The language uses three contour tones (tones that change over the course of a word). These are realized over two successive syllables and are expressed phonetically as high rising-falling, mid rising-falling, and very low rising.

Punjabi does not have the voiced aspirates of other Indo-Aryan languages. Generally, the consonant /h/ corresponds to high tone. Through analogic development, tones have also evolved in places and positions where one does not expect aspirates or /h/. Another significant feature of Punjabi is a large number of words—especially ancient place-names, and nouns and adjectives evolved from them—that have retroflex sounds. The majority of such words are from the western pre-Indo-European civilizations.

The earliest Punjabi literature has been traced to the Natha era (9th to 14th century AD), when Punjab was the main centre of socioreligious movements. The language of these compositions is morphologically closer to Shauraseni Apabhramsha, but the vocabulary and rhythm reflect colloquial speech forms.

SANSKRIT

The word *Sanskrit* comes from a Sanskrit word (*saṃskṛta*) meaning "adorned, cultivated, purified." It is an Old Indo-Aryan language in which the most ancient documents are the Vedas, composed in what is called Vedic Sanskrit. Although Vedic documents represent the dialects then found in the northern midlands of the Indian subcontinent and areas immediately east thereof, the very earliest texts—including the Rigveda ("The Veda Composed in Verses"), which scholars generally ascribe to approximately 1500 BC—stem from the northwestern part of the subcontinent, the area of the ancient seven rivers (*sapta sindhavaḥ*).

What is generally called Classical Sanskrit—but is actually a language close to late Vedic as then used in the northwest of the subcontinent—was elegantly described in one of the finest grammars ever produced, the *Astadhyayi* ("Eight Chapters") composed by Panini (c. 6th–5th century BC). The *Astadhyayi* in turn was the object of a rich commentatorial literature, documents of which are known from the time of Katyayana (4th–3rd century BC) onward. In the same Paninian tradition there was a long history of work on semantics and the philosophy of language, the pinnacle of which is represented by the *Vakyapadiya* ("Treatise on Sentence and Words") of Bhartrhari (late 6th–7th century AD).

Over its long history, Sanskrit has been written both in Devanagari script and in various regional scripts, such as Sharada from the north (Kashmir), Bangla in the east, Gujarati in the west, and various southern scripts, including the Grantha alphabet, which was especially devised for Sanskrit texts. Sanskrit texts continue to be published in regional scripts, although in fairly recent times Devanagari has become more generally used.

There is a large corpus of literature in Sanskrit covering a wide range of subjects. The earliest compositions are the Vedic texts. There are also major works of drama and poetry, although the exact dates of many of these works and their creators have not been definitively established. Important authors and works include Bhasa (for example, his *Svapnavasvavadatta* ["Vasavadatta in a Dream"]), who is assigned widely varying dates but definitely worked prior to Kalidasa, who mentions him; Kalidasa, dated anywhere from the 1st century BC to the 4th century AD, whose works include *Shakuntala* (more fully, *Abhijnanashakuntala*; "Shakuntala Recalled Through Recognition" or "The Recognition of Shakuntala"), *Vikramorvashiya* ("Urvashi Won Through Valour"), *Kumarasambhava* ("The Birth of Kumara"), and *Raghuvamsha* ("The Lineage of Raghu"); Shudraka and his *Mrcchakatika* ("Little Clay Cart"), possibly dating to the 3rd century AD; Bharavi and his *Kiratarjuniya* ("Arjuna and the Mountain Man"), from approximately the 7th century; Magha, whose *Shishupalavadha* ("The Slaying of Shishupala") dates to the late 7th century; and from about the early 8th century Bhavabhuti, who wrote *Mahaviracarita* ("Deeds of the Great Hero"), *Malatimadhava* ("Malati and Madhava"), and *Uttararamacarita* ("The Last Deed of Rama"). The two epics *Ramayana* ("Life of Rama") and *Mahabharata* ("Great Tale of the Bharatas") were also composed in Sanskrit, and the former is esteemed as the first poetic work (*adikavya*) of India.

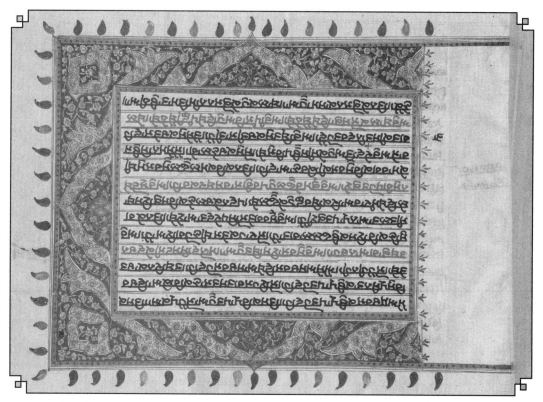

This illuminated Sikh manuscript shows Devanagari script. Réunion des Musées Nationaux/ Art Resource, NY

The *Panchatantra* ("Treatise in Five Chapters") and *Hitopadesha* ("Beneficial Instruction") are major representatives of didactic literature. Sanskrit was also used as the medium for composing treatises of various philosophical schools, as well as works on logic, astronomy, and mathematics.

Sanskrit is not restricted to Hindu compositions. It has also been used by Jaina and Buddhist scholars, the latter primarily Mahayana Buddhists. Further, Sanskrit is recognized in the constitution of India as both a classical language and an official language and continues to be used in scholarly, literary, and technical media, as well as in periodicals, radio, television, and film.

In its grammatical structure, Sanskrit is similar to other early Indo-European languages such as Greek and Latin. It is an inflected language. For instance, the Sanskrit nominal system—including nouns, pronouns, and adjectives—has three genders (masculine, feminine, and neuter), three numbers (singular, dual, and plural), and seven syntactic cases (nominative, accusative, instrumental, dative, ablative, genitive, and locative), in addition to a vocative.

SINDHI

The Sindhi language is spoken by some 2.5 million people in India and tens of millions more in Pakistan. Smaller speech communities exist in the United Kingdom, the United States, Oman, the Philippines, and Singapore.

The origin of the Sindhi language can be traced to an Old Indo-Aryan dialect, or primary Prakrit, that was spoken in the region of Sindh at the time of compilation of the *Vedas* (1500–1200 BC) or perhaps some centuries before that. Glimpses of that dialect can be seen to some extent in the literary language of the hymns of the *Rigveda*.

Like other languages of this family, Sindhi has passed through Old Indo-Aryan (Sanskrit) and Middle Indo-Aryan (Pali, secondary Prakrits, and Apabhramsha) stages of growth, and it entered the New Indo-Aryan stage around the 10th century AD.

The language has several salient linguistic features. The most important phonological features are the four voiced implosive phonemes, or sounds produced by suddenly drawing air into the mouth (/b/, /d/, /g/, and /j/). In terms of morphology, Sindhi is known for the use of passive and impersonal verb stems, as with *likh-ij-e* 'may be written.' It also uses suffixal pronouns with nouns, postpositions, and verbs, as with *pina-si* 'his/her father' (literally 'father [of] his/hers'), *khe-si* 'to him/her,' and *likhya-in-si* 'he wrote him/her.'

Sindhi has preserved many archaic words and grammatical forms from Sanskrit and the Prakrits. Examples include Sindhi *jhuru* 'old' from Vedic Sanskrit *juryah*, *jui* 'place' from Vedic Sanskrit *yuti*, and *vuttho* 'rained' from Prakrit *vuttha*. Sindhi has also inherited an abundance of vowel-ending words, most ending in *-u* and *-o*, from the Prakrits.

Historically, the Sindh region suffered frequent invasions. It was conquered by the forces of Islam in AD 712 and remained under Muslim rule until the British conquest in 1843. Hence, the Sindhi language borrowed many Arabic and Persian words. In spite of this, the basic vocabulary and grammatical structure of Sindhi has remained mostly unchanged.

Sindhi has been one of the major literary languages of the Indo-Pakistan subcontinent, though its literary prominence is being surpassed in some areas by Urdu. Sindhi is written mainly in two scripts. The first is a modified and enlarged form of the Arabic alphabet that was standardized by the British government in 1852 and consists of 52 characters; it is known as the Arabic-Sindhi script. The second is the Devanagari-Sindhi script, comprising Devanagari and an additional four letters used to express the special implosive sounds of Sindhi. Use of the Devanagari-Sindhi script has helped to preserve and promote the literary and cultural heritage of the region and its language.

In addition, Sindhi can be written with an indigenous script (also called Sindhi) that derives from proto-Devanagari, Brahmi, and Indus valley scripts. A small number of traders use it for commercial correspondence, and it is the script of choice for the religious texts of Isma'ili Khoja Muslims. Sindhi can be written with the Gurmukhi alphabet and Gujarati characters as well.

The folk literature of Sindhi is as old as the language itself. It has been collected and compiled from oral tradition and published in more than 40 volumes by the Sindhi Adabi Board, a government institution that was established in 1955 for the promotion of the language. Written Sindhi literature is first attested in the 8th century AD, when references to an independent, Sindhi version of the *Mahabharata* appear. However, the earliest well-attested written records in Sindhi belong to the 15th century AD.

Medieval Sindhi devotional literature (1500–1843) comprises Sufi poetry and Advaita Vedanta poetry. Sindhi literature has flourished during the modern period (since 1843), although the language and literary style of contemporary Sindhi writings in Pakistan and India had noticeably diverged by the late 20th century; authors from the former country were borrowing extensively from Persian and Arabic vocabulary, while those from the latter were highly influenced by Hindi.

Urdu

Urdu is spoken by more than 50 million people in India and by millions more in Pakistan. Significant speech communities exist in the United Arab Emirates, the United Kingdom, and the United States as well. Notably, Urdu and Hindi are mutually intelligible.

Urdu developed in the 12th century AD from the regional Apabhramsha of northwestern India, serving as a linguistic *modus vivendi* after the Muslim conquest. Its first major poet was Amīr

Khosrow (1253–1325), who composed *dohas* (couplets), folksongs, and riddles in the newly formed speech, then called Hindvi. This mixed speech was variously called Hindvi, Zaban-e-Hind, Hindi, Zaban-e-Delhi, Rekhta, Gujari, Dakkhani, Zaban-e-Urdu-e-Mualla, Zaban-e-Urdu, or just Urdu, literally 'the language of the camp.' Major Urdu writers continued to refer to it as Hindi or Hindvi until the beginning of the 19th century, although there is evidence that it was called Hindustani in the late 17th century (Hindustani now refers to a simplified speech form that is India's largest lingua franca).

Urdu is closely related to Hindi, a language that originated and developed in the Indian subcontinent. They share the same Indic base and are so similar in phonology and grammar that they appear to be one language. In terms of lexicon, however, they have borrowed extensively from different sources—Urdu from Arabic and Persian, Hindi from Sanskrit—so they are usually treated as independent languages. Their distinction is most marked in terms of writing systems: Urdu uses a modified form of Perso-Arabic script, while Hindi uses Devanagari.

Phonologically, the Urdu sounds are the same as those of Hindi except for slight variations in short vowel allophones. Urdu also retains a complete set of aspirated stops (sounds pronounced with a sudden release with an audible breath), a characteristic of Indo-Aryan, as well as retroflex stops. Urdu does not retain the complete range of Perso-Arabic consonants, despite its heavy borrowing from that tradition. The largest number of sounds retained is among the spirants, a group of sounds uttered with a friction of breath against some part of the oral passage, in this case /f/, /z/, /zh/, /x/, and /g/. One sound in the stops category, the glottal /q/, has also been retained from Perso-Arabic.

From the grammatical point of view, there is not much difference between Hindi and Urdu. One distinction is that Urdu uses more Perso-Arabic prefixes and suffixes than Hindi; examples include the prefixes *dar-* 'in,' *ba-/baa-* 'with,' *be-/bila-/la-* 'without,' and *bad-* 'ill, miss' and the suffixes *-dar* 'holder,' *-saz* 'maker' (as in *zinsaz* 'harness maker'), *-khor* 'eater' (as in *muftkhor* 'free eater'), and *-posh* 'cover' (as in *mez posh* 'table cover').

DRAVIDIAN

The Dravidian language family consists of some 70 languages spoken primarily in South Asia. They are spoken by more than 215 million people in India, Pakistan, and Sri Lanka. Dravidian languages are spoken by about one-fourth of all Indians, overwhelmingly in southern India. Dravidian speakers among tribal peoples (e.g., Gonds) in central India, in eastern Bihar, and in the Brahui-speaking region of the distant Pakistani province of Balochistan suggest a much wider distribution in ancient times.

The Dravidian languages are divided into South, South-Central, Central, and North groups; these groups are further organized into 24 subgroups. The four major literary languages—Telugu, Tamil, Malayalam, and Kannada—are recognized by the constitution of India. They are also the official languages of the states of Andhra Pradesh, Tamil Nadu, Kerala, and Karnataka (formerly Mysore), respectively.

THE HISTORY OF THE DRAVIDIAN LANGUAGES

There is considerable literature on the theory that India is a linguistic area where different language families have developed convergent structures through extensive regional and societal bilingualism. It is now well established that the Indo-Aryan and Dravidian language families developed convergent structures in sound system (phonology) and grammar owing to contact going back to the 2nd millennium BC. The earliest varieties of Indo-Aryan are forms of Sanskrit. More than a dozen Dravidian loanwords can be detected in the Sanskrit text of the Rigveda (1500 BC), including *ulūkhala-* 'mortar,' *kuṇḍa* 'pit,' *khála-* 'threshing floor,' *kāṇá-* 'one-eyed,' and *mayūra* 'peacock.' The introduction of retroflex consonants (those produced by the tongue tip raised against the middle of the hard palate) has also been credited to contact between speakers of Sanskrit and those of the Dravidian languages.

The presence of Dravidian loanwords in the Rigveda implies that speakers of Dravidian and Indo-Aryan languages were, by the time of its composition, fused into one speech community in the great Indo-Gangetic Plain, while independent communities of Dravidian speakers had moved to the periphery of the Indo-Aryan area (Brahui in the northwest, Kurukh-Malto in the east, and Gondi-Kui in the east and central India). Notably, the most ancient forms of the Dravidian languages are found in southern India, which was not exposed to Sanskrit until the 5th century BC. This suggests that the south was populated by the speakers of the Dravidian languages even before the entry of Indo-Europeans into India.

The word *drāviḍa/drāmiḍa* and its adjectival forms occur in Classical Sanskrit literature from the 3rd century BC as the name of a country and its people. *Drāviḍa* as the name of a language occurs in Kumarila-Bhatta's *Tantravartika* ("Exposition on the Sacred Sciences") of approximately the 7th century AD. In these and almost all similar cases, there is reason to believe that the name referred to the Tamil country, Tamil people, and Tamil language. Robert Caldwell, the Scottish missionary and bishop who wrote the first comparative grammar of the Dravidian languages (1856), argued that the term sometimes referred ambiguously to South Indian people and their languages; he adopted it as a generic name for the whole family since Tamil (*tamiẓ*) was already the established name of a specific language.

DRAVIDIAN STUDIES

In 1816, Englishman Francis Whyte Ellis of the Indian Civil Service (at the time a division of the East India Company) introduced the notion of a Dravidian family. His *Dissertation of the Telugu Language* was initially published as "Note to the Introduction" of British linguist A.D. Campbell's *A Grammar of the Teloogoo Language*. Ellis's monograph provided lexical and grammatical evidence to support the hypothesis that Tamil, Telugu, Kannada, Malayalam, Tulu, Kodagu, and Malto were members of "the family of languages which may be appropriately called the dialects of Southern India."

The next major publication on the Dravidian languages was Robert Caldwell's *A Comparative Grammar of the Dravidian or South Indian Family of Languages* (1856). A missionary who left his native Scotland for a lifetime of work in India, he demonstrated that the Dravidian languages were not genetically related to Sanskrit, thus disproving a view that had been held by Indian scholars for more than two millennia. Caldwell identified 12 Dravidian languages; to the 7 already noted by Ellis, he added Toda and Kota of South Dravidian, Gondi and Kui-Kuvi of South-Central Dravidian, and Kurukh of North Dravidian. He also discussed Brahui.

The 20th century was marked by considerable research and publication on the Dravidian language family and its members, particularly in three realms of study. The first was the collection of cognates (related words) and the discovery of sound correspondences (related sounds) among the different languages; these led to the reconstruction of the hypothetical parent language called Proto-Dravidian. The second area of investigation focused on the study of the various inscriptions, literary texts, and regional dialects of the four literary languages, which allowed scholars to identify the historical evolution of those languages. A third area of interest involved the discovery and linguistic description of new languages within the family.

Several new languages were added to the Dravidian family in the 20th century, including Kota, Kolami, Parji, Pengo, Ollari, Konda/Kubi, Kondekor Gadaba, Irula, and Toda. Progress was also made in describing nonliterary languages, notably Brahui, Kurukh, Malto, Kui, Kuvi, Gondi (various dialects), Kodagu, and Tulu.

The most significant and monumental work of the 20th century was *A Dravidian Etymological Dictionary* ([DED] 1961; revised 1984) by British linguist Thomas Burrow and Canadian linguist Murray B. Emeneau. Much that has been accomplished in comparative phonology and reconstruction is indebted to this work. The early 21st century saw a continuation of studies in comparative morphology, though much work on the comparative syntax of the family remains to be done.

KANNADA

Kannada, also called Kanarese or Kannana, is the official language of the state of Karnataka in southern India. It is also spoken in the states that border Karnataka. Early 21st-century census data indicated that some 38 million individuals spoke Kannada as their first language; another 9 to 10 million were thought to speak it as a secondary language. In 2008 the government of India granted Kannada classical-language status.

Kannada is the second oldest of the four major Dravidian languages with a literary tradition. The oldest Kannada inscription was discovered at the small community of Halmidi and dates to about AD 450. The Kannada script evolved from southern varieties of the Ashokan Brahmi script. The Kannada script is closely related to the Telugu script; both emerged from an Old Kannarese (Karnataka) script. Three historical stages are recognized: Old Kannada (450–1200), Middle Kannada (1200–1700), and Modern Kannada (1700–present).

The word order is subject–object–verb, as in the other Dravidian languages. Verbs are marked for person, number, and gender. The case-marking pattern is nominative-accusative, with experiencer subjects taking the dative inflection. Most inflection is rendered through affixation, especially of suffixes. The language uses typical Dravidian retroflex consonants (sounds pronounced with the tip of the tongue curled back against the roof of the mouth), such as /ḍ/, /ṇ/, and /ṭ/, as well as a series of voiced and voiceless aspirates borrowed from the Indo-Aryan language family.

Three regional varieties of Kannada are identifiable. The southern variety is associated with the cities of Mysore and Bangalore, the northern with Hubli-Dharwad, and the coastal with Mangalore. The prestige varieties are based on the Mysore-Bangalore variety. Social varieties are currently characterized by education and class or caste, resulting in at least three distinct social dialects: Brahman, non-Brahman, and Scheduled Caste (Dalit; formerly untouchable). A diglossia or dichotomy also exists between formal literary varieties and spoken varieties.

Kannada literature began with the *Kavirajamarga* of Nripatunga (9th century AD) and was followed by Pampa's *Bharata* (AD 941). The earliest extant grammar is by Nagavarma and dates to the early 12th century; the grammar of Keshiraja (AD 1260) is still respected. Kannada literature was influenced by the Lingayat (Virasaiva) and the Haridasa movements. In the 16th century the Haridasa movement of vernacular devotional song reached its zenith with Purandaradasa and Kanakadasa, the former considered the father of Karnatak music, the classical music of southern India.

MALAYALAM

Malayalam is spoken mainly in India, where it is the official language of the state of Kerala and the union territory of Lakshadweep. It is also spoken by bilingual communities in contiguous parts of Karnataka and Tamil Nadu. In the early 21st century, Malayalam was spoken by more than 35 million people.

Malayalam has three important regional dialects and a number of smaller ones. There is some difference in dialect along social, particularly caste, lines. As a result of these factors, the Malayalam language has developed diglossia, a distinction between the formal, literary language and colloquial forms of speech.

Malayalam evolved either from a western dialect of Tamil or from the branch of Proto-Dravidian from which modern Tamil also evolved. The earliest record of the language is an inscription dated to approximately AD 830. An early and extensive influx of Sanskrit words influenced the Malayalam script. Known as Koleluttu ("Rod Script"), it is derived from the Grantha script, which in turn is derived from Brahmi. Koleluttu has letters to represent the entire corpus of sounds from both Dravidian and Sanskrit.

Like the Dravidian languages generally, Malayalam has a series of retroflex consonants (/ḍ/, /ṇ/, and /ṭ/) made by curling the tip of the tongue back to the roof of the mouth. It uses subject–object–verb word order and has a nominative-accusative case-marking pattern. Its pronominal system has "natural" gender, a form that marks the gender of humans masculine or feminine while designating all nonhuman nouns as neuter.

The earliest extant literary work in Malayalam is *Ramacharitam*, an epic poem written in the late 12th or early 13th century. In the subsequent centuries, besides a popular *pattu* ("song") literature, there flourished a literature of mainly erotic poetry composed in the *manipravalam* ("ruby coral") style, an admixture of Malayalam and Sanskrit.

TAMIL

Tamil is the official language of the Indian state of Tamil Nadu and the union territory of Puducherry (Pondicherry). It is also an official language in Sri Lanka and Singapore and has significant numbers of speakers in Malaysia, Mauritius, Fiji, and South Africa. In the early 21st century more than 66 million people were Tamil speakers.

The earliest Tamil writing is attested in inscriptions and potsherds from the 5th century BC. Three periods have been distinguished through analyses of grammatical and lexical changes: Old Tamil (from about 450 BC to AD 700), Middle Tamil (700–1600), and Modern Tamil (from 1600). The Tamil writing system evolved from the Brahmi script. The shape of the letters changed enormously over time, eventually stabilizing when printing was introduced in the 16th century AD. The major addition to the alphabet was the incorporation of Grantha letters to write unassimilated Sanskrit words, although a few letters with irregular shapes were standardized during the modern period. A script known as Vatteluttu ("Round Script") is also in common use.

Spoken Tamil has changed substantially over time, including changes in the phonological structure of words. This has created diglossia—a system in which there are distinct differences between colloquial forms of a language and those that are used in formal and written contexts. The major regional variation is between the form spoken in India and that spoken in Jaffna (Sri Lanka), capital of a former Tamil city-state, and its surrounds. Within Tamil Nadu there are phonological differences between the northern, western, and southern speech. Regional varieties of the language intersect with varieties that are based on social class or caste.

Like the other Dravidian languages, Tamil is characterized by a series of retroflex consonants (/ḍ/, /ṇ/, and /ṭ/) made by curling the tip of the tongue back to the roof of the mouth. Structurally, Tamil is a verb-final language that allows flexibility regarding the order of the subject and the object in a sentence.

TELUGU

The largest member of the Dravidian language family, Telugu is primarily spoken in southeastern India. It is the official language of the state of Andhra Pradesh. In the early 21st century Telugu had more than 75 million speakers.

The first written materials in the language date from AD 575. The Telugu script is derived from that of the 6th-century Chalukya dynasty and is related to that of the Kannada language. Telugu literature begins in the 11th century with a version of the Hindu epic *Mahabharata* by the writer Nannaya.

There are four distinct regional dialects in Telugu, as well as three social dialects that have developed around education, class, and caste. The formal, literary language is distinct from the spoken dialects—a situation known as diglossia.

Like the other Dravidian languages, Telugu has a series of retroflex consonants (/ḍ/, /ṇ/, and /ṭ/) pronounced with the tip of the tongue curled back against the roof of the mouth. Grammatical categories such as case, number, person, and tense are denoted with suffixes. Reduplication, the repetition of words or syllables to create new or emphatic meanings, is common (e.g., *pakapaka* 'suddenly bursting out laughing,' *garagara* 'clean, neat, nice').

OTHER LANGUAGES AND LINGUA FRANCAS

Manipuri and Bodo, both Sino-Tibetan languages and official languages of India, and other Sino-Tibetan languages are spoken by small numbers of people in northeastern India. So, too, Santhali, a Munda (Austroasiatic) language, has official status.

When a language is used as a means of communication between populations speaking vernaculars that are not mutually intelligible, it is known as a lingua franca. The two major lingua francas in India are Hindustani and English.

MUNDA

Some 9 million people (the Munda) in northern and central India speak Munda languages. Some scholars divide these into two subfamilies: the North Munda (spoken in the Chota Nagpur Plateau of Bihar, Bengal, and Orissa) including Korku, Santhali, Mundari, Bhumij, and Ho; and the South Munda (spoken in central Orissa and along the border between Andhra Pradesh and Orissa). The latter family is further split into Central Munda, including Kharia and Juang, and Koraput Munda, including Gutob, Remo, Sora (Savara), Juray, and Gorum. The classification of these languages is controversial.

North Munda (of which Santhali is the chief language) is the more important of the two groups; its languages are spoken by about nine-tenths of Munda speakers. After Santhali, the Mundari and Ho languages rank next in number of speakers, followed by Korku and Sora. The remaining Munda languages are spoken by small, isolated groups of people and are little known.

Characteristics of the Munda languages include three numbers (singular, dual, and plural), two gender classes (animate and inanimate) for nouns, and the use of either suffixes or auxiliaries for indicating the tenses of verb forms. In Munda sound systems, consonant sequences are infrequent, except in the middle of a word. Except in Korku, where syllables show a distinction between high and low tone, accent is predictable in the Munda languages.

Santhali is spoken primarily in the east-central Indian states of West Bengal, Jharkhand, and Orissa. At the turn of the 21st century there were approximately 4.8 million speakers of Santhali in India. Of these, more than 2 million Santhals lived

These flags, carried by proponents of the Telugu Dasam political party in Andhra Pradesh, show Grantha script. Noah Seelam/AFP/Getty Images

in Jharkhand, nearly 2 million in West Bengal, several hundred thousand in Orissa, and about 100,000 in Assam.

TIBETO-BURMAN

At the end of the 20th century, India had some 5.5 million speakers of Tibeto-Burman (TB) languages. The great Sino-Tibetan (ST) language family, comprising Chinese on the one hand and

Tibeto-Burman on the other, is comparable in time-depth and internal diversity to the Indo-European language family and is equally important in the context of world civilization.

After the existence of the Tibeto-Burman family was posited in the mid-19th century, British scholars, missionaries, and colonial administrators in India and Burma (now Myanmar) began to study some of the dozens of little-known "tribal" languages of the region that seemed to be genetically related to the two major literary languages, Tibetan and Burmese. This early work was collected by Sir George Abraham Grierson in the *Linguistic Survey of India* (1903–28), three sections of which (vol. 3, parts 1, 2, and 3) are devoted to word lists and brief texts from TB languages.

Further progress in TB studies had to wait until the late 1930s, when Robert Shafer headed a project called Sino-Tibetan Linguistics at the University of California, Berkeley. This project assembled all the lexical material then available on TB languages, enabling Shafer to venture a detailed subgrouping of the family at different taxonomic levels, called (from higher to lower) *divisions, sections, branches, units, languages,* and *dialects.* This work was finally published in a two-volume, five-part opus called *Introduction to Sino-Tibetan* (vol. 1, 1966–67; vol. 2, 1974).

Basing his own work on the same body of material, Paul K. Benedict produced an unpublished manuscript titled "Sino-Tibetan: A Conspectus": (henceforth referred to as the *Conspectus*) in the early 1940s. In that work he adopted a more modest approach to supergrouping and subgrouping, stressing that many TB languages had so far resisted precise classification. Benedict's structural insight enabled him to formulate sound correspondences (regular phonological similarities between languages) with greater precision and thereby to identify exceptional phonological developments. A revised and heavily annotated version of the *Conspectus* was published in 1972, ushering in the modern era of Sino-Tibetan historical/comparative linguistics.

In part because the Tibeto-Burman family extends over such an enormous geographic range, it is characterized by great typological diversity. Influences from Chinese on the one hand and Indo-Aryan languages on the other have contributed significantly to the diversity of the TB family. It is convenient to refer to the Chinese and Indian spheres of cultural influence as the Sinosphere and the Indosphere. Some languages and cultures are firmly in one or the other: the TB languages of Nepal and much of the Kamarupan branch of TB are Indospheric, as are the Munda and Khasi branches of Austroasiatic.

Any given language of TB is likely to be known by several names, including its autonym (what its speakers call it), one or more exonyms (what other groups call it), paleonyms (old names, some of which are now thought to be pejorative), and neonyms (new names) that have often replaced the old. To take a relatively simple case, the Lotha Naga of India are a Scheduled (officially recognized) Tribe of fewer than 100,000 people, yet the people and their language are called by at least three exonyms—Chizima, Choimi, and Miklai, by the neighbouring Angami, Sema, and Assamese peoples, respectively. The paleonyms Lolo, Lushai, Abor, Dafla, and Mikir have for the most part been replaced by Yi, Mizo, Adi, Nyishi, and Karbi, respectively.

Manipuri

Also called Meithei (Manipuri: Meiteilon), Manipuri is spoken predominantly in Manipur, a northeastern state of India. Smaller speech communities exist in the Indian states of Assam, Mizoram, and Tripura, and it is also spoken in Bangladesh and Myanmar. There are approximately 1.9 million speakers of Manipuri, which is used as a lingua franca among the 29 different ethnic groups of Manipur. In 1992 it became the first TB language to receive recognition as an official, or "Scheduled," language of India.

Manipuri has its own script, locally known as Meitei Mayek. Manipur state and its surroundings are the locus from which the Tibeto-Burman family spread and diversified, making the genetic assignment of the region's languages very difficult. During the 19th and 20th centuries, different linguists conjectured that Manipuri belonged to one of several TB subdivisions. In the early 21st century, the consensus view placed Manipuri

in its own subdivision of the so-called Kamarupan group—a geographic (or areal) rather than a genetic designation but one that must suffice until more definitive information becomes available.

Bodo

The Bodo language, which has several dialects, belongs to the Tibeto-Burman branch of Sino-Tibetan languages. It is spoken in the northeastern Indian states of Assam and Meghalaya and in Bangladesh. It is related to Dimasa, Tripura, and Lalunga languages, and it is written in Latin, Devanagari, and Bengali scripts.

INDIAN ENGLISH

English, which is an official language of India, is its most widely used lingua franca. The great size of India's population makes it one of the largest English-speaking communities in the world, although English is claimed as the mother tongue by only a small number of Indians and is spoken fluently by less than 5 percent of the population. English serves as the language linking the central government with the states, especially with those in which Hindi is not widely understood. English is also the principal language of commerce, the language of instruction in almost all of the country's prestigious universities and private schools, and the language of scientific research. The English-language press remains highly influential; scholarly publication is predominantly in English (almost exclusively so in science); and many Indians are devotees of literature in English (much of it written by Indians), as well as of English-language film, radio, television, popular music, and theatre.

In 1950, when India became a federal republic within the Commonwealth of Nations, Hindi was declared the first national language. English, it was stated, would "continue to be used for all official purposes until 1965." In 1967, however, by the terms of the English Language Amendment Bill, English was proclaimed "an alternative official or associate language with Hindi until such time as all non-Hindi states had agreed to its being dropped."

English was thereby acknowledged to be indispensable. It is the only practicable means of day-to-day communication between the central government at New Delhi and states with non-Hindi speaking populations, especially with the Deccan, or "South," where millions speak Dravidian languages.

HINDUSTANI

Hindustani began to develop during the 13th century AD in and around the Indian cities of Delhi and Meerut in response to the increasing linguistic diversity that resulted from Muslim hegemony. In the 19th century its use was widely promoted by the British, who initiated an effort at standardization. Hindustani is widely recognized as India's most common lingua franca, but its status as a vernacular renders it difficult to measure precisely its number of speakers.

Hindustani was initially used to facilitate interaction between the speakers of Khari Boli (a regional dialect that developed out of Shauraseni Apabhramsha and is now considered a variety of Hindi) and the speakers of Persian, Turkish, and Arabic who migrated to North India after the establishment of Muslim hegemony in the early 13th century AD.

Hindustani's popularity increased as a result of its use by poets such as Amīr Khosrow (1253–1325), Kabir (1440–1518), Dadu (1544–1603), and Rahim (1556–1627), the court poet of Akbar. Its use by Sufi saints such as Baba Farid (flourished late 12th century) and various poets of the Natha tradition (which combined practices from Buddhism, Shaivism, and Hatha Yoga in an effort to reach immortality) also increased its popularity.

Though Khari Boli supplied its basic vocabulary and grammar, Hindustani also borrowed freely from Persian. Among the Persian words that became common are many concerning administration (e.g., *adalat* 'court,' *daftar* 'office,' *vakil* 'pleader,' *sipahi* 'soldier,' *shahar* 'city,' *kasba* 'small town,' *zila* 'district'), dress (e.g., *kamiz* 'shirt,' *shal* 'shawl'), cosmetics (e.g., *itra* 'perfume,' *sabun* 'soap'), furniture (e.g., *kursi* 'chair,' *mez* 'table,' *takht* 'dais'), and professions (e.g., *bajaj* 'draper,' *chaprasi* 'peon,' *dukandar* 'shopkeeper,' *haqim* 'physician,' *dalal* 'broker,' *halvai* 'confectioner').

Hindustani also borrowed Persian prefixes to create new words. Persian affixes became so assimilated that they were used with original Khari Boli words as well. The process of hybridization also led to the formation of words in which the first element of the compound was from Khari Boli and the second from Persian, such as *rajmahal* 'palace' (*raja* 'noble, prince' + *mahal* 'house, place') and *rang-mahal* 'fashion house' (*rangi* 'colouring, dyeing' + *mahal* 'house, place').

As Muslim rule expanded, Hindustani speakers traveled to distant parts of India as administrators, soldiers, merchants, and artisans. As it reached new areas, Hindustani further hybridized with local languages. In the Deccan, for instance, Hindustani blended with Telugu and came to be called Dakhani. In Dakhani, aspirated consonants were replaced with their unaspirated counterparts; for instance, *dekh* 'see' became *dek*, *ghula* 'dissolved' became *gula*, *kuch* 'some' became *kuc*, and *samajh* 'understand' became *samaj*.

When the British colonized India, they chose to instruct their officers in Hindustani. Colonization intensified existing conflicts between the Hindu population and the Muslim population even as it motivated efforts toward linguistic standardization. During the process of creating a literary, standard form of Hindustani, Hindus introduced increasing numbers of Sanskrit words, and Muslims introduced increasing numbers of Persian and Arabic words.

Mahatma Gandhi realized that the standardization process was dangerously divisive. He emphasized the importance of keeping Hindustani as colloquial as possible and of avoiding the addition of unfamiliar Sanskrit, Persian, and Arabic words. He also pleaded for the use of both Devanagari and Persian Arabic script for writing Hindustani. However, the religious difference proved intractable, and with partition Hindustani was split into two distinct (if closely related) official languages, Hindi in India and Urdu in Pakistan. Despite this division, many basic terms, such as the names of the parts of the human body and of relatives, pronouns, numerals, postpositions, and verbs, are the same in both Sanskritized Hindi and Persianized Urdu.

In a study of Calcutta (now Kolkata), the Indian linguist Sumit Kumar Chatterjee in 1931 detailed the use of a lingua franca that he named Bazaar Hindustani. He noted that the language was greatly simplified, with minimal grammatical forms, vocabulary, idioms, and expressions, and that it was used by Indians and Europeans who spoke language as diverse as Asamiya, Bangla, Oriya, and Tamil.

In the 21st century, this simplified version of Hindustani continues to be used as a lingua franca not only in Kolkata but in all of the cities of India, especially in non-Hindi-speaking areas. More than 100 million individuals, including more than 50 million people in India, speak Urdu; many of these individuals may actually use Hindustani for ordinary communication. Approximately 550 million people speak Hindi, and sizable portions of this group, especially those who live in cities, are known to use Hindustani rather than Sanskritized Hindi in ordinary speech. Thus, while Hindustani may not survive as a literary language, it continues to thrive as a vernacular.

INDIC WRITING SYSTEMS

Two scripts are attested in ancient India: the syllabic Kharosthi and semialphabetic Brahmi scripts of ancient India. No systems of writing subsequently developed from the Kharosthi script. Brahmi, however, is thought to be the forerunner of all of the scripts used for writing the languages of India, Tibet, Southeast Asia, and Indonesia (exceptions include those areas in which native writing systems have been replaced by the Latin or Arabic alphabet or by Chinese).

KHAROSTHI

The earliest extant inscription in Kharosthi dates from 251 BC, and the latest from the 4th–5th century AD. The system probably derived from the Aramaic alphabet while northwestern India was under Persian rule in the 5th century BC. Aramaic, however, is a Semitic alphabet of 22 consonantal letters, while Kharosthi is syllabic and has 252 separate signs for consonant and vowel combinations. A cursive script written from right to left, Kharosthi was used for commercial and calligraphic purposes. It was influenced

somewhat by Brahmi, which eventually superseded it.

BRAHMI

Of Aramaic derivation or inspiration, the Brahmi script can be traced to the 8th or 7th century BC, when it may have been introduced to Indian merchants by people of Semitic origin. Brahmi is semi-alphabetic, each consonant having either an inherent a sound pronounced after it or a diacritic mark to show another vowel; initial vowels have separate characters. In most cases Brahmi and its derivatives are written from left to right, but a coin of the 4th century BC, discovered in Madhya Pradesh, is inscribed with Brahmi characters running from right to left. Among the many descendants of Brahmi are Devanagari (used for Sanskrit, Hindi, and other Indian languages), the Bangla and Gujarati scripts, and those of the Dravidian languages.

GUPTA SCRIPTS

The Gupta scripts are a group of alphabetic writing systems (sometimes modified to represent syllables instead of single sounds). They derived from a northern Indian alphabet of the 4th–6th century AD. The ruling Gupta state at that time gave the script its name. It was developed out of Brahmi and was spread with the Gupta empire over large areas of conquered territory, with the result that the Gupta alphabet was the ancestor (for the most part via Devanagari) of most later Indian scripts.

The original Gupta alphabet had 37 letters, including 5 vowels, and was written from left to right. Four main subtypes of Gupta script developed from the original alphabet: eastern, western, southern, and Central Asian. The Central Asian Gupta can be further divided into Central Asian Slanting Gupta and its Agnean and Kuchean variants and Central Asian Cursive Gupta, or Khotanese. A western branch of eastern Gupta gave rise to the Siddhamatrka script (*c.* AD 500), which, in turn, evolved into the Devanagari alphabet (*c.* AD 700), the most widespread of the modern Indian scripts.

GRANTHA ALPHABET

The earliest inscriptions in Grantha, dating from the 5th–6th century AD, are on copper plates from the kingdom of the Pallavas (near modern Chennai [Madras]). The form of the alphabet used in these inscriptions, classified as Early Grantha, is seen primarily on copper plates and stone monuments. Middle Grantha, the form of the script used from the mid-7th to the end of the 8th century, is also known from inscriptions on copper and stone. The script used from the 9th to the 14th century is called Transitional Grantha; from approximately 1300 on, the modern script has been in use. Currently two varieties are used: Brahmanic, or "square," and Jain, or

"round." The Tulu-Malayalam script is a variety of Grantha dating from the 8th or 9th century AD. The modern Tamil script may also be derived from Grantha, but this is not certain.

Originally used for writing Sanskrit only, Grantha in its later varieties is also used to write a number of the Dravidian languages indigenous to southern India. The script has 35 letters, five of them vowels, and is written from left to right.

DEVANAGARI

The Devanagari script is used to write the Sanskrit, Prakrit, Hindi, Marathi, and Nepali languages, developed from the North Indian monumental script known as Gupta and ultimately from the Brahmi alphabet, from which all modern Indian writing systems are derived. In use from the 7th century AD and occurring in its mature form from the 11th century onward, Devanagari is characterized by long, horizontal strokes at the tops of the letters, usually joined in modern usage to form a continuous horizontal line through the script when written.

The word *Devanagari* is from the Sanskrit words *deva*, meaning "god," and *nāgarī (lipi)*, meaning "[script] of the city." The script is also called Nagari.

The Devanagari writing system is a combination of syllabary and alphabet. One of its more notable characteristics is the convention that a consonantal symbol lacking diacritics is read as the consonant followed by the letter *a*—that is, the *a* is implied rather than written as a separate character.

Another notable characteristic is that the most common traditional listing of Devanagari symbols follows a phonetic order in which the vowels are recited before the consonants; in contrast, most alphabets follow an order that mixes vowels and consonants together (e.g., *A, B, C*). Furthermore, Devanagari arranges the vowels and consonants in an order that starts with sounds pronounced at the back of the oral cavity and proceeds to sounds produced at the front of the mouth.

The Devanagari consonants are divided into classes of stops (sounds that are pronounced by stopping and then releasing the airflow, such as *k, c, ṭ, t, p*), semivowels (*y, r, l, v*), and spirants (*ś, ṣ, s, h*; *h* comes last because it has no unique place of articulation).

The name of each vowel is designated by its sound plus the suffix *-kāra*; thus, *akāra* is the name for *a* and *ākāra* for *ā*. A consonant is usually referred to by its sound plus the default vowel *a* and the suffix *-kāra*: *kakāra* is the name for *k*, *khakāra* for *kh*, *gakāra* for *g*, *ghakāra* for *gh*, *ṇakāra* for *ṇ*, *yakāra* for *y*, *śakāra* for *ś*, *hakāra* for *h*, and so on. The names of a few letters are irregular, notably *repha* (for *r*), *anusvāra* (for *ṃ*), and those of *ḫk*, *ḫp*, and *ḫ*, as noted earlier.

CHAPTER 3

HINDUISM

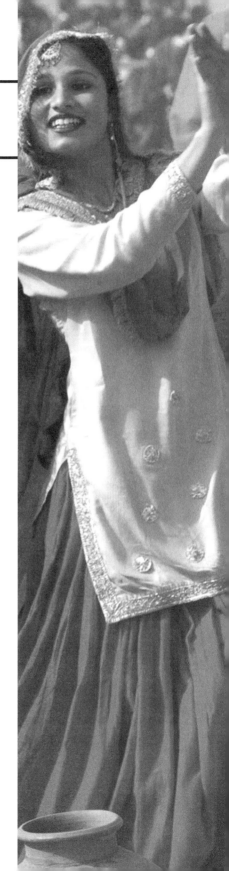

Hinduism is a major world religion originating on the Indian subcontinent and comprising several and varied systems of philosophy, belief, and ritual. Although the name Hinduism is relatively new, having been coined by British writers in the first decades of the 19th century, it refers to a rich cumulative tradition of texts and practices, some of which date to the 2nd millennium BC or possibly earlier. If the Indus valley civilization (3rd–2nd millennium BC) was the earliest source of these traditions, as some scholars hold, then Hinduism is the oldest living religion on Earth. Its many sacred texts in Sanskrit and vernacular languages served as a vehicle for spreading the religion to other parts of the world, though ritual and the visual and performing arts also played a significant role in its transmission. In the early 21st century Hinduism had nearly one billion adherents worldwide and was the religion of about 80 percent of India's population. Despite its global presence, however, it is best understood through its many distinctive regional manifestations.

THE TERM *HINDUISM*

The term *Hinduism* became familiar as a designator of religious ideas and practices distinctive to India with the publication of books such as *Hinduism* (1877) by Sir Monier Monier-Williams, the notable Oxford scholar and author of an influential Sanskrit diction-ary. Initially it was an outsiders' term, building on centuries-old usages of the word *Hindu*. Early travelers to the Indus valley, beginning with the Greeks and Persians, spoke of its inhabitants as "Hindu" (Greek: '*indoi*), and, in the 16th century, residents of India them-selves began very slowly to employ the term to distinguish themselves from the Turks. Gradually the distinction became primarily religious rather than ethnic, geographic, or cultural.

Since the late 19th century, Hindus have reacted to the term *Hinduism* in several ways. Some have rejected it in favour of indigenous formulations. Those preferring *Veda* or *Vedic religion* want to embrace an ancient textual core and the tradition of Brahman learning that preserved and interpreted it. Those pre-ferring *sanatana dharma* ("eternal law") emphasize a broader tradition of belief and practice (such as worship through images, dietary codes, and the venera-tion of the cow) that is not necessarily mediated by Brahmans (members of the highest social class who are usually priests). Still others, perhaps the majority, have simply accepted the term *Hinduism* or its analogues, especially *hindu dharma* (Hindu moral and religious law), in vari-ous Indic languages.

Since the early 20th century, text-books on Hinduism have been written by Hindus themselves, often under the rubric of *sanatana dharma*. These efforts at self-explanation have been intended to set Hinduism on a par with other religious traditions and to teach it systematically to Hindu youths. They add a new layer to an elaborate tradition of explaining practice and doctrine that dates to the 1st millen-nium BC. The roots of this tradition can be traced back much farther—textually, to the schools of commentary and debate preserved in epic and Vedic writings from the 2nd millennium BC; and visu-ally, through artistic representations of yakshas (luminous spirits associated with specific locales and natural phenomena) and nagas (cobralike divinities), which were worshipped from about 400 BC. The roots of the tradition are also sometimes traced back to the female terra-cotta figu-rines found ubiquitously in excavations of sites associated with the Indus valley civilization (3rd–2nd millennium BC) and sometimes interpreted as goddesses. In recognition of this ancient tradition of self-explanation, present-day Hindus often assert that theirs is the world's old-est religion.

GENERAL NATURE OF HINDUISM

More strikingly than any other major religious community, Hindus accept—and indeed celebrate—the organic, multileveled, and sometimes internally inconsistent nature of their tradition. This expansiveness is made possible by the widely shared Hindu view that truth or reality cannot be encapsulated in any creedal formulation, a perspective expressed in the Hindu prayer "May good thoughts come to us from all sides." Thus, Hinduism maintains that truth must be sought in multiple sources, not dogmatically proclaimed.

Anyone's view of the truth—even that of a *guru* regarded as possessing superior authority—is fundamentally conditioned by the specifics of time, age, gender, state of consciousness, social and geographic location, and stage of attainment. These multiple perspectives enhance a broad view of religious truth rather than diminish it; hence, there is a strong tendency for contemporary Hindus to affirm that tolerance is the foremost religious virtue. On the other hand, even cosmopolitan Hindus living in a global environment recognize and value the fact that their religion has developed in the specific context of the Indian subcontinent. Such a tension between universalist and particularist impulses has long animated the Hindu tradition. When Hindus speak of their religious identity as *sanatana dharma*, a formulation made popular late in the 19th century, they emphasize its continuous, seemingly eternal (*sanatana*) existence and the fact that it describes a web of customs, obligations, traditions, and ideals (*dharma*) that far exceeds the Western tendency to think of religion primarily as a system of beliefs. A common way in which English-speaking Hindus often distance themselves from that frame of mind is to insist that Hinduism is not a religion but a way of life.

THE FIVE TENSILE STRANDS

Across the sweep of Indian religious history, at least five elements have given shape to the Hindu religious tradition: doctrine, practice, society, story, and devotion. These five elements, to adopt a typical Hindu metaphor, are understood as relating to one another as strands in an elaborate braid. Moreover, each strand develops out of a history of conversation, elaboration, and challenge. Hence, in looking for what makes the tradition cohere, it is sometimes better to locate central points of tension than to expect clear agreements on Hindu thought and practice.

DOCTRINE

The first of the five strands of Hinduism is doctrine, as expressed in a vast textual tradition anchored to the Veda ("Knowledge"), the oldest core of Hindu religious utterance, and organized through the centuries primarily by members of the learned Brahman class. Here several characteristic tensions appear. One concerns the status of the One in relation to the Many—issues of belief in several deities, monotheism, and monism. Another tension concerns the disparity between the world-preserving ideal of *dharma* and that of *moksha* (release from an inherently flawed world). A third tension exists between individual destiny, as shaped by *karma* (the influence of one's actions on one's present and future lives), and the individual's deep bonds to family, society, and the divinities associated with these concepts.

Practice

The second strand in the fabric of Hinduism is practice. Many Hindus, in fact, would place this first. Despite India's enormous diversity, a common grammar of ritual behaviour connects various places, strata, and periods of Hindu life. While it is true that various elements of Vedic ritual survive in modern practice and thereby serve a unifying function, much more influential commonalities appear in the worship of icons or images (*pratima*, *murti*, or *arca*). Broadly, this is called *puja* ("honouring [the deity]"), or *archana* if performed in a temple by a priest. It echoes conventions of hospitality that might be performed for an honoured guest, especially the giving and sharing of food. Such food is called *prasada* (Hindi, *prasad*: "grace"), reflecting the recognition that when human beings make offerings to deities, the initiative is not really theirs. They are actually responding to the generosity that bore them into a world fecund with

A Hindu worship service in Pune (Poona), India, following an ancient ritual. C.M. Natu

life and possibility. The divine personality installed as a home or temple image receives *prasada*, tasting it (Hindus differ as to whether this is a real or symbolic act, gross or subtle) and offering the remains to worshipers. Consuming these leftovers, worshipers accept their status as beings inferior to and dependent upon the divine. An element of tension arises because the logic of *puja* and *prasada* seems to accord all humans an equal status with respect to God, yet exclusionary rules have often been sanctified rather than challenged by *prasada*-based ritual. Specifically, lower-caste people and those perceived as outsiders or carriers of pollution have historically been forbidden to enter certain Hindu temples, a practice that continues even today.

SOCIETY

The third strand that has served to organize Hindu life is society. Early visitors to India from Greece and China and, later, others such as the Persian scholar and scientist al-Bīrūnī, who traveled to India in the early 11th century, were struck by the highly stratified (if locally variant) social structure that has come to be called familiarly the caste system. While it is true that there is a vast disparity between the ancient vision of society as divided into four ideal classes (*varna*s) and the contemporary reality of thousands of endogamous birth-groups (*jati*s, literally "births"), few would deny that Indian society is notably plural and hierarchical. This fact has much to do

with an understanding of truth or reality as being similarly plural and multilayered—though it is not clear whether the influence has proceeded chiefly from religious doctrine to society or vice versa. Seeking its own answer to this conundrum, a well-known Vedic hymn (Rigveda 10.90) describes how, at the beginning of time, a primordial person underwent a process of sacrifice that produced a four-part cosmos and its human counterpart, a four-part social order comprising Brahmans (priests), Kshatriyas (nobles), Vaishyas (commoners), and Sudras (servants).

The social domain, like the realms of religious practice and doctrine, is marked by a characteristic tension. There is the view that each person or group approaches truth in a way that is necessarily distinct, reflecting its own perspective. Only by allowing each to speak and act in such terms can a society constitute itself as a proper representation of truth or reality. Yet this context-sensitive habit of thought can too easily be used to legitimate social systems based on privilege and prejudice. If it is believed that no standards apply universally, one group can too easily justify its dominance over another. Historically, therefore, certain Hindus, while espousing tolerance at the level of doctrine, have maintained caste distinction in the social realm. Responding to such oppression, especially when justified by allegedly Hindu norms, lower-caste groups have sometimes insisted, "We are not Hindus!" Yet their own communities may enact similar inequities, and their religious practices and beliefs often continue to tie them to the greater Hindu fold.

STORY

Another dimension drawing Hindus into a single community of discourse is narrative. For at least two millennia, people in almost all corners of India—and now well beyond—have responded to stories of divine play and of interactions between gods and humans. These stories concern major figures in the Hindu pantheon: Krishna and his lover Radha, Rama and his wife Sita and brother Lakshmana, Shiva and his consort Parvati (or, in a different birth, Sati), and the Great Goddess Durga, or Devi as a slayer of the buffalo demon Mahisasura. Often such narratives illustrate the interpenetration of the divine and human spheres, with deities such as Krishna and Rama entering entirely into the human drama. Many tales focus in different degrees on genealogies of human experience, forms of love, and the struggle between order and chaos or between duty and play. In generating, performing, and listening to these stories, Hindus have often experienced themselves as members of a single imagined family.

Yet, simultaneously, these narratives serve to articulate tensions. Thus, the *Ramayana*, traditionally a testament of Rama's righteous victories, is sometimes told by women performers as the story of Sita's travails at Rama's hands. South Indian performances may emphasize the

Ravana, the 10-headed demon king, detail from a Guler painting of the Ramayana, *c. 1720.* Courtesy of the Cleveland Museum of Art, Ohio, gift of George P. Bickford

virtues of Rama's enemy Ravana as equal to or even surpassing those of Rama himself. And in North India lower-caste musicians present religious epics such as *Alha* or *Dhola* in terms that reflect their own experience of the world rather than the upper-caste milieu of the great Sanskrit religious epic the *Mahabharata*, which these epics nonetheless echo. To the broadly known pan-Hindu, male-centred narrative traditions, these variants provide both resonance and challenge.

DEVOTION

There is a fifth strand that contributes to the unity of Hindu experience through time: *bhakti* ("sharing" or "devotion"), a broad tradition of a loving God that is especially associated with the lives and words of vernacular poet-saints throughout India. Devotional poems attributed to these inspired figures, who represent both genders and all social classes, have elaborated a store of images and moods to which access can be had in a score of languages; *bhakti* verse first appeared in Tamil in South India and moved northward into other regions with different languages. Individual poems are sometimes strikingly similar from one language or century to another, without there being any trace of mediation through the pan-Indian, distinctly upper-caste language Sanskrit. Often, individual motifs in the lives of *bhakti* poet-saints also bear strong family resemblances. With its central affirmation that religious enthusiasm is more fundamental than rigidities of practice or doctrine, *bhakti* provides a common challenge to other aspects of Hindu life. At the same time, it contributes to a common Hindu heritage—even a common heritage of protest. Yet certain expressions of *bhakti* are far more confrontational than others in their criticism of caste, image worship, and the performance of vows, pilgrimages, and acts of self-mortification.

CENTRAL CONCEPTIONS

In the following sections, various aspects of this complex whole will be addressed, relying primarily on a historical perspective of the development of the Hindu tradition. This approach has its costs, for it may seem to give priority to aspects of the tradition that appear in its earliest extant texts. These texts owe their preservation mainly to the labours of upper-caste men, especially Brahmans, and often reveal far too little about the perspectives of others. They should be read, therefore, both with and against the grain, with due attention paid to silences and absent rebuttals on behalf of women, regional communities, and people of low status—all of whom nowadays call themselves Hindus or identify with groups that can sensibly be placed within the broad Hindu span.

VEDA, BRAHMANS, AND ISSUES OF RELIGIOUS AUTHORITY

For members of the upper castes, a principal characteristic of Hinduism has traditionally been a recognition of the Veda, the most ancient body of Indian religious literature, as an absolute authority revealing fundamental and unassailable truth. The Veda is also regarded as the basis of all the later *shastra* texts, which stressed the religious merits of the Brahmans—including, for example, the medical corpus known as the *Ayur Veda*. Parts of the Veda are quoted in essential Hindu rituals (such as the wedding ceremony), and it is the source of many enduring patterns of Hindu thought, yet its contents are practically unknown to most Hindus. Still, most Hindus venerate it from a distance, and groups who reject its authority outright (such as Buddhists and Jains) are regarded by Hindus as deviating from their common tradition.

Another characteristic of much Hindu thought is its special regard for Brahmans as a priestly class possessing spiritual supremacy by birth. As special manifestations of religious power and as bearers and teachers of the Veda, Brahmans have often been thought to represent an ideal of ritual purity and social prestige. Yet this has also been challenged, either by competing claims to religious authority—especially from kings and other rulers—or by the view that Brahmanhood is a status attained by depth of learning, not birth. Evidence of both these challenges can be found in Vedic literature itself, especially the Upanishads (speculative religious texts that provide commentary on the Vedas), and *bhakti* literature is full of vignettes in which the small-mindedness of Brahmans is contrasted with true depth of religious experience, as exemplified by poet-saints such as Kabir and Ravidas.

DOCTRINE OF *ATMAN-BRAHMAN*

Most Hindus believe in *brahman*, an uncreated, eternal, infinite, transcendent, and all-embracing principle. *Brahman* contains in itself both being and non-being, and it is the sole reality—the ultimate cause, foundation, source, and goal of all existence. As the All, *brahman* either causes the universe and all beings to emanate from itself, transforms itself into the universe, or assumes the appearance of the universe. *Brahman* is in all things and is the self (*atman*) of all living beings. *Brahman* is the creator, preserver, or transformer and reabsorber of everything. Hindus differ, however, as to whether this ultimate reality is best conceived as lacking attributes and qualities—the impersonal *brahman*—or as a personal God, especially Vishnu, Shiva, or Shakti (these being the preferences of adherents called Vaishnavas, Shaivas, and Shaktas, respectively). Belief in the importance of the search for a One that is the All has been a characteristic feature of India's spiritual life for more than 3,000 years.

KARMA, *SAMSARA*, AND *MOKSHA*

Hindus generally accept the doctrine of transmigration and rebirth and the complementary belief in *karma*. The whole process of rebirth, called *samsara*, is cyclic, with no clear beginning or end, and encompasses lives of perpetual, serial attachments. Actions generated by desire and appetite bind one's spirit (*jiva*) to an endless series of births and deaths. Desire motivates any social interaction (particularly when involving sex or food), resulting in the mutual exchange of good and bad *karma*. In one prevalent view, the very meaning of salvation is emancipation (*moksha*) from this morass, an escape from the impermanence that is an inherent feature of mundane existence. In this view the only goal is the one permanent and eternal principle: the One, God, *brahman*, which is totally opposite to phenomenal existence. People who have not fully realized that their being is identical with *brahman* are thus seen as deluded. Fortunately, the very structure of human experience teaches the ultimate identity between *brahman* and *atman*. One may learn this lesson by different means: by realizing one's essential sameness with all living beings, by responding in love to a personal expression of the divine, or by coming to appreciate that the competing attentions and moods of one's waking consciousness are grounded in a transcendental unity—one has a taste of this unity in the daily experience of deep, dreamless sleep.

DHARMA AND THE THREE PATHS

Hindus disagree about the best way (*marga*) to attain such release. The *Bhagavadgita* ("Song of the Lord"; *c.* AD 100), an extremely influential Hindu text, presents three paths to salvation: the *karma-marga* ("path of duties"), the disinterested discharge of ritual and social obligations; the *jnana-marga* ("path of knowledge"), the use of meditative concentration preceded by long and systematic ethical and contemplative training (Yoga) to gain a supraintellectual insight into one's identity with *brahman*; and the *bhakti-marga* ("path of devotion"), love for a personal God. These ways are regarded as suited to various types of people, but they are interactive and potentially available to all.

Although the pursuit of *moksha* is institutionalized in Hindu life through ascetic practice and the ideal of withdrawing from the world at the conclusion of one's life, many Hindus ignore such practices. The *Bhagavadgita* states that because action is inescapable, the three paths are better thought of as simultaneously achieving the goals of world maintenance (*dharma*) and world release (*moksha*). Through the suspension of desire and ambition and through a taste for the fruits (*phala*) of one's actions, one is enabled to float free of life while engaging it fully. This matches the actual goals of most Hindus, which include executing properly one's social and ritual duties; supporting one's caste, family, and profession; and working to achieve a broader stability in the cosmos, nature, and society. The designation of Hinduism as *sanatana dharma* emphasizes this goal of maintaining personal and universal equilibrium, while at the same time calling attention to the important role played by the performance of traditional religious practices in achieving that goal. Because no one person can occupy all the social, occupational, and age-defined roles that are requisite to maintaining the health of the life-organism as a whole, universal maxims (e.g., ahimsa, the desire not to harm) are qualified by the more-particular *dharmas* that are appropriate to each of the four major *varnas*: Brahmans (priests), Kshatriyas (warriors and kings), Vaishyas (the common people), and Sudras (servants). These four categories are superseded by the more practically applicable *dharmas* appropriate to each of the thousands of particular castes (*jatis*). And these, in turn, are crosscut by the obligations appropriate to one's gender and stage of life (*ashrama*). In principle then, Hindu ethics is exquisitely context-sensitive, and Hindus expect and celebrate a wide variety of individual behaviours.

ASHRAMAS: THE FOUR STAGES OF LIFE

European and American scholars have often overemphasized the so-called "life-negating" aspects of Hinduism—the rigorous disciplines of Yoga, for example. The polarity of asceticism and sensuality, which assumes the form of a conflict between the aspiration for liberation and the heartfelt desire to have descendants and continue earthly life, manifests itself in Hindu social life as the tension between the different goals and stages of life. For many centuries the relative value of an active life and the performance of meritorious works (*pravritti*), as opposed to the renunciation of all worldly interests and activity (*nivriti*), has been a much-debated issue. While philosophical works such as the Upanishads emphasized renunciation, the *dharma* texts argued that the householder who maintains his sacred fire, begets children, and performs his ritual duties well also earns religious merit. Nearly 2,000 years ago these *dharma* texts elaborated the social doctrine of the four *ashramas* ("abodes"). This concept was an attempt to harmonize the conflicting tendencies of Hinduism into one system. It held that a male member of any of the three higher classes should first become a chaste student (*brahmacharin*); then become a married householder (*grihastha*), discharging his debts to his ancestors by begetting sons and to the gods by sacrificing; then retire (as a *vanaprastha*), with or without his wife, to the forest to devote himself to spiritual contemplation; and finally, but not mandatorily, become a homeless wandering ascetic (*sannyasin*). The situation of the forest dweller was always a delicate compromise that remained problematic on the mythological level and was often omitted or rejected in practical life.

Although the householder was often extolled—some authorities, regarding studentship a mere preparation for this *ashrama*, went so far as to brand all other stages inferior—there were always people who became wandering ascetics immediately after studentship. Theorists were inclined to reconcile the divergent views and practices by allowing the ascetic way of life to those who were entirely free from worldly desire (owing to the effects of restrained conduct in former lives), even if they had not gone through the traditional prior stages.

The texts describing such life stages were written by men for men; they paid scant attention to stages appropriate for women. The *Manu-smriti* (200 BC–AD 300; *Laws of Manu*), for example, was content to regard marriage as the female equivalent of initiation into the life of a student, thereby effectively denying the student stage of life to girls. Furthermore, in the householder stage, a woman's purpose was summarized under the heading of service to her husband. What we know of actual practice, however, challenges the idea that these patriarchal norms were ever perfectly enacted or that women entirely accepted the values they presupposed. While some women became ascetics, many more focused their religious lives on realizing a state of blessedness that was understood to be at once this-worldly and expressive of a larger cosmic well-being. Women have often directed the cultivation of the auspicious life-giving force (*shakti*) they possess to the benefit of their husbands and families, but, as an ideal, this force has independent status.

PRACTICAL HINDUISM

Practical Hinduism is both a quest to achieve well-being and a set of strategies for locating sources of affliction and removing or appeasing them. Characterized in this way, it has much in common with the popular beliefs and practices of many other religions. For example, Roman Catholicism as practiced in many parts of Europe or Mahayana Buddhism in Korea and Taiwan involve, as does Hinduism, petitions and offerings to enshrined divine powers in order to engage their help with all manner of problems and desires. Thus, religions which could hardly differ more vastly in their understanding of the nature of divinity, reality, and causality may nonetheless converge at the level of popular piety.

The presumption that assigns "practical" Hinduism to peasants, labourers, or tribal peoples—while assuming that the high-born, wealthy, and educated would be concerned with spiritual enlightenment and Hinduism's ultimate aim of liberation (*moksha*)—is false. Hindu farmers care about their souls at least as much as do Hindu business or professional men and women (if less single-mindedly than world renouncers, who come from all ranks of life). Farmers' uncertain livelihoods, however, may influence them to dedicate more time and energy to rituals designed to obtain prosperity or to remove troubles, to bring rain to parched fields or to prevent damaging hail, to advance their children's education and careers, or to protect their families from ill health. Although rural Hindus may have little time for meditative practices, they are fully aware of ultimate truths transcending the everyday. By the same token, the pious urban elite, if more likely to pursue spiritual disciplines, frequently sponsor worship in temples or homes to ensure worldly success. At all levels of the social hierarchy, Hinduism lives through artistic performances: dance and dance-drama, representational arts, poetry, music, and song serve not only to please deities but to transmit the religion's meaningful narratives and vital truths.

Both adherents of the faith and those who study it describe Hinduism as a way of life. Thus, they implicitly contrast Hinduism to religions that appear to be primarily located in spaces and times set apart from the everyday—such as "church on Sunday." Although Hindus have magnificent sacred architecture and a vital tradition of calendrical festivals, the "way of life" description means that religious attitudes and acts permeate ordinary places, times, and activities. For example, bathing, dressing, cooking, eating, disposing of leftovers, and washing the dishes may all be subject to ritual prescriptions in Hindu households. Motivations for such ritualized actions are ascribed to considerations of purity—an interest that is often linked to maintaining status in a hierarchical social system.

When Hindus interact with deities, considerations of purity may or may not be important. In some Vaishnava traditions, for example, one must remain in a relatively pure state in order to be fit to worship. A Brahman priest of a Krishna temple in the Vallabha sect might refuse food and water from the hands of non-Brahmans, not to show he is better than they are but because his work in the temple demands that he maintain such boundaries. Should he inadvertently lower his own ritual purity, he might displease or offend the deity with whom he is in regular contact, which could threaten human well-being in general.

Vaishnava traditions, however, include an alternative perspective that is conveyed in a well-known tale about Rama. This tale, frequently portrayed in poetry and art, tells of an outcaste tribal woman named Shabari who meets Rama in the forest. Her simple-hearted love for him is so great that she offers him wild berries, which are all she has. She bites

each one first to test its sweetness before giving it to her lord, and in so doing she contaminates the berries with saliva, a major source of pollution. Although the berries are highly unacceptable according to the standards of ritual purity, Rama accepts them and eats them blissfully. The message is that the polluted offerings of a lowborn person given to God with a heart full of love are far more pleasing than any ritually pure gift from a less-devout being. Purity of heart, therefore, is more important than bodily purity.

The capacity to see both sides of most matters—cognitive flexibility rather than dogmatic fixity—is one of the most important characteristics of practical Hinduism, which lacks dogma altogether. In this regard, persistent continuities with Hinduism's ancient roots in Vedic traditions can be discerned. The elaborate sacrificial rituals of Vedic religion have often been described as being focused on obtaining the goods of life—neatly summarized as prosperity, health, and progeny—from divine powers through exacting ritual behaviours. However, in the Upanishads, the last of the Vedic texts, voices emerge that care for neither the rituals nor their promised fruits but are concerned above all with learning the nature of ultimate reality and how the human soul may recognize that indescribable essence in itself. One quest never supplants the other. In Hinduism today there remains a vital creative tension between, on the one hand, faith in the efficacy of ritual and desire for its worldly fruits and, on the other, disregard for all external practices and material results. Farmers consistently deride the notion that sins are washed away in the waters of sacred rivers, yet they spend small fortunes to travel to and bathe in them.

DEVOTION

Devotion (*bhakti*) effectively spans and reconciles the seemingly disparate aims of obtaining aid in solving worldly problems and locating one's soul in relation to divinity. It is the prime religious attitude in much of Hindu life. The term *bhakti* is derived from a root that literally means "having a share"; devotion unites without totally merging the identities of worshipers and deities. While some traditions of *bhakti* radically speak out against ritual, devotion in ordinary life is usually embedded in worship, vows, and pilgrimages—three major elements within practical Hinduism.

Theistic devotion presents itself as an easy path, obliterating the need for expensive sacrificial rituals, difficult ascetic practices, and scriptural knowledge. All of these are understood as restricted to high-caste males, and in practice specifically to the rich, the spiritually gifted, or the learned. But *bhakti* is for all human beings, regardless of their rank, gender, or talent. Any person's chosen deity may help him obtain life's rewards or avoid its disasters. At the same time, such a chosen deity may be the subject of pure, unmotivated devotional love, recollected in a few moments of morning meditation, in prayers uttered before a shrine, or in the lighting of incense.

DEITIES

As one Hindu author Sitansu Chakravarti helpfully explains in *Hinduism: A Way of Life* (1991),

> *Hinduism is a monotheistic religion which believes that God manifests Himself or Herself in several forms. One is supposed to worship the form that is most appealing to the individual without being disrespectful to other forms of worship.*

Although the specific details of ritual action and the names and appearances of deities vary vastly across the subcontinent, commonalities in ritual structure and attitude override the great diversity of ritual practices and associated mythic tales. Whether offering soaked raw chickpeas to Shiva's agent Bhairuji in Rajasthan or a buffalo to Draupadi in Tamil Nadu or water to Krishna's devoted basil plant in Bengal, Hindus approach deities through similarly structured actions. These are just as pan-Hindu as the eternal Vedas or the three important deities—Shiva, Vishnu, and the Devi, whose forms and names vary widely but are nonetheless recognizable to Hindus throughout the world.

Ethnographies of rural Hindu practices reveal a wide variety of human relationships with multiple divine beings. These relationships are based not only on family and community affiliations but also on individual life experiences, so that individuals and families often develop idiosyncratic religiosities while remaining well within the range of normative patterns. A household of Gujars (a community associated with herding, dairy production, and agriculture) in a Rajasthani village presents one representative example. This family is particularly devoted to two deities from whom they believe they have received special blessings: Dev Narayan, a regional hero considered to be an avatar or incarnation of Vishnu, and Sundar Mata ("Beautiful Mother"), a local goddess, or village mother.

Dev Narayan is worshipped at multiple sites throughout Rajasthan. However, each of his shrines—in Puvali, in Banjari, and so forth—has its own identity. This particular family lives a short walk from Puvali's Dev Narayan, but they believe that the more remote Banjari's Dev Narayan—located near their ancestral home—has blessed two generations with long-awaited sons. They go weekly for *darshan* (divine vision of a deity's image) to Puvali's Dev Narayan, as it is convenient. But when the time comes to hold a major feast of thanksgiving to the deity who granted their prayers, they go to a great deal of extra trouble and added expense to hold this feast at the more remote place of Banjari. If questioned, the adults in this family would state conclusively that there is no difference between the two places and moreover that God

is ultimately singular and to be found nowhere on the face of the earth but rather in one's own body and heart. An everyday Hinduism embedded in materiality motivates the distinction between Banjari and Puvali, while a Hinduism that dissolves differences and seeks transcendent unity denies it. Most persons live their lives holding and moving between both these orientations.

Sundar Mata has only one place, on the edge of the Gujar family's home village. She has helped them with various problems over the years. In times of trouble, devotees sometimes make inner vows to Sundar Mata (or any deity), no matter where they are. But to fulfill that vow, thankful persons must present themselves and their offerings in her particular place. Sundar Mata's shrine, like most Hindu places of worship, accumulates gifts dedicated by grateful worshipers. For example, the largest iron trident at Sundar Mata's shrine was offered by a migrant labourer who lost his suitcase on the train back from Delhi. He vowed to give his village goddess a huge trident if he got the bag back, which he miraculously did.

Although a local deity, Sundar Mata is related to pan-Hindu goddesses such as Lakshmi, Parvati, or Durga. They are all thought to be manifestations of a single goddess; name and form are ultimately not significant. Yet again it should be noted that human worshipers attach themselves to certain images and localities, and, for those devoted to Sundar Mata, not any goddess will do.

Durga killing the buffalo demon Mahisasura, Rajasthani miniature of the Mewar school, mid-17th century, in a private collection. Pramod Chandra

This family that honours Dev Narayan and Sundar Mata also worships lineage deities at home. Ritual attention to the spirits of deceased uncles and infants ensures their household's well-being, and each domestic group takes similar care of loved ones who have died. Several members of the Gujar family portrayed here have taken a once-in-a-lifetime pilgrimage as far as Haridwar in Uttar Pradesh, Gaya in south-central Bihar, and Puri in eastern Orissa. Mementos of these journeys—such as framed images of the sacred Ganges River's descent to earth or the central icons from the temple of Puri in Orissa—are placed in their home shrine. Home shrines in general accumulate sacred objects and images eclectically. Images are treasured and are believed to manifest miraculous powers, but images are also understood to be lifeless and dispensable—another reflection of the Hindu genius for seeing both sides.

WORSHIP

Worship, or *puja*, is the central action of practical Hinduism. Scholars describe

Hindu worship as a preeminently transactional event; through worship, humans approach deities by respectful interactions with their powers. At every level, from elaborate temple rituals to simple home practice, worship consists of offerings made and blessings received; reverence is rendered and grace pours down. The purpose of many rituals is to promote auspiciousness (*kalyana, mangala, shri*)—a pervasive Hindu concept indicating all kinds of good fortune or well-being.

Ritual manuals in vernacular languages offer explicit instructions on exactly what should be offered and declare what benefits may be obtained through specific acts of worship. Benefits may be as general as health and prosperity or as specific as the removal of a particular illness. They also conventionally include rewards after death—thus uniting this-worldly and other-worldly blessings. Devotional songs and statements, however, persistently deny all mechanical views of divine exchanges, insisting that humans have nothing to give, that everything belongs to God, and that no truly religious action should ever be performed instrumentally. Thus, the key tension between external ritual and internal realization that originated in Vedic times and was perpetuated in devotional teachings is sustained in popular present-day ritual action.

One key element in all worship is *prasad*, translated simply as "blessing" or "grace" and sometimes more literally as "blessed leftovers." This term refers to the returned portion of a worshiper's or pilgrim's offering, which is understood as having value added by the intangible process of a deity's consumption. *Prasad* to be used for offerings is hawked by vendors on the road to a temple, but this food does not truly become graced until it has been given as an offering and received back. Many foodstuffs are used as *prasad*; bananas or other raw fruits and coconuts are particularly common, as are various candies and milk products. Fresh flowers are often included on an offering tray and may also be returned as *prasad*. Other substances commonly distributed at temples include the water in which icons have been ritually bathed, called *charanamrit* ("foot nectar"), and the ash from burnt offerings. What all these have in common is contact with the deity's power in the process of worship and service.

Another important element of temple worship is seeing the deity: *darshan*. Here again, a two-way but fundamentally unequal flow takes place. An image is always enlivened and given eyes; the worshiper's delighted gaze at the deity engages the deity's awareness of the worshiper, and a channel of grace is formed. Sound and scent also alert deities to humans in their presence. Ringing bells, blowing conch shells, singing or playing instrumental music, burning incense, and pouring clarified butter onto smoldering coals are among the activities intended to alert the deity of the devotee's presence. Worshipers commonly prostrate themselves, symbolically offering respect and their own bodies. A circumambulation of the deity's altar is another physical mode of engagement with divine power. Hindu worship is accurately described as involving all the senses.

Worship is by no means confined to temples. It may be performed at a home altar, a wayside shrine, or anywhere a devotee decides to mark off a sacred space. Actions at home may be far less elaborate than those at temples, more routinized as part of daily household life, and are performed without priestly expertise. South Indian housewives traditionally turn their thresholds into auspicious altars for the goddess each morning as they draw ritual designs, which are almost instantly trampled back into dust.

Conceptually distinct from worship yet often conflated with it is *seva*, or service. This refers to regular, respectful attentions to the needs of enshrined deities, or icons (*murti*). Service in many temples is twice daily or more often. At shrines it may involve bathing an icon, changing its ornaments, ringing bells, and waving lights before it (*arati*). In temples the person who does *seva* is normally a ritual expert, regularly present. Although *seva* is never done with an aim in mind, it is understood to keep the gods beneficently inclined, and flawed *seva* may cause trouble. Performing *seva* is good for the soul of the server.

DIVINATION, SPIRIT POSSESSION, AND HEALING

Simple practices of divination are common to practical Hinduism. Everyone wants to know: Will my wish be fulfilled? Will my prayer be granted? The answers to such yes-no questions may be revealed by any of a number of practices. Plucking grains between thumb and finger from a pile and counting them to see if they add up to an auspicious number, pressing flowers to the wall and waiting for them to fall, and pouring clarified butter on coals and seeing if a flame rises up are common practices in more than one region of India.

A more elaborate mode of communicating with divine power is spirit possession, in which a human being, male or female, is thought to act as a vehicle for a deity's mind and voice. This practice is also found in every geographic region where Hinduism flourishes. Although more common to rural areas, it is not absent from urban religion. A possessed priest or priestess is able to provide answers more complex than "yes" or "no." A medium possessed by a deity may identify certain spirits of the dead who are troubling someone with symptoms of physical and mental illness. Usually these spirits are understood to cause trouble because they are not satisfied with the attention they are getting. The medium will prescribe ritual actions designed to transform the spirit from a source of affliction to a benevolent or neutral power or to send the spirit away. Purely malevolent beings, including jealous "witches" or nameless wandering ghosts, are cajoled, bullied, or even frightened into departure.

Practical Hinduism is greatly concerned with maintaining mental and physical health. Although a possessed priest occasionally forbids resort to doctors and their remedies, in the majority of cases healing rituals operate in conjunction with medicines, injections, and operations. Familial problems are often untangled with the help of a possessed priest in consultations sometimes likened by observers to group therapy.

WOMEN'S RELIGIOUS PRACTICES

Women's rituals comprise an important part of practical Hinduism. Some male-authored Hindu scriptures limit women's religious roles, consider women more subject than men to bodily impurities, and subordinate them to their fathers and husbands. Priests in temples and other public spaces are predominantly—though not exclusively—male. Most domestic Hindu rituals, however, lie in the hands and hearts of women. Women perform their own *seva* and *puja* at permanent or temporary domestic shrines, are the chief ritual experts at many calendrical festivals, and are responsible for many ritual aspects of weddings and other life-cycle celebrations. Women more frequently than men undertake personal vows (*vrata*)—individually or collectively—to ensure the well-being of their families.

The elements of a *vrata* usually include a partial fast, simple worship in a domestic space temporarily purified for this purpose, and often the retelling of one or more stories honouring the deities and exemplifying the rewards or

describing the origins of the ritual. The event may conclude with the consumption of special food to break the fast. Vows are often associated with calendrical cycles, whether solar, lunar, or both. For example, each day of the week is identified with a particular deity: Monday with Shiva, Tuesday with Hanuman, Wednesday with Ganesha, and so forth. If a woman undertakes a Monday *vrata*, she will fast and worship Shiva and tell his story every Monday. Or, a person may do an eleventh *vrata*, a vow for the eleventh day of the lunar calendar, which would come twice a month in the waxing and waning halves of the moon. Some vows are undertaken for the occasional potent convergence of both calendrical systems, such as *somavati amavasa*, a Monday dark moon.

Women's ritually performed stories feature heroines who may be devotees of the deity being honoured, daughters of female devotees, or persons ignorant of that particular deity who then learn about its power and blessings in the course of severe tribulations. Notably, the heroines of women's devotional stories exemplify moral virtues, ritual knowledge, devotional fervour, and transformative agency. The power accumulated by women through their ritual actions should never be used exclusively for their own well-being. Selflessness is a very important virtue that is exemplified by self-denial in fasting. Nonetheless, because women's well-being is connected to familial well-being, women see their rituals as productive of better circumstances for themselves and their loved ones. For women, practical Hinduism is a space where they express their competence, self-respect, and power and see themselves as protectors of husbands, brothers, and sons. Even while critiquing the ways in which some Hindu traditions disadvantage women, Indian feminists have located important resources for women in goddess worship, in *vrata* narratives, and in the sense of gender solidarity and self-worth that women's rituals produce.

PILGRIMAGE

Pilgrimage in Hinduism, as in other religions, is the practice of journeying to sites where religious powers, knowledge, or experience are deemed especially accessible. Hindu pilgrimage is rooted in ancient scriptures. According to textual scholars, the earliest reference to Hindu

Pilgrims bathing in the Ganges River at Haridwar, India. Paul Popper Ltd.

pilgrimage is in the Rigveda (c. 1500 BC), in which the "wanderer" is praised. Numerous later texts, including the epic *Mahabharata* (c. 300 BC–AD 300) and several of the mythological Puranas (c. AD 300–750), elaborate on the capacities of particular sacred sites to grant boons, such as health, wealth, progeny, and deliverance after death. Texts enjoin Hindu pilgrims to perform rites on behalf of ancestors and recently deceased kin. Sanskrit sources as well as devotional literature in regional vernacular languages praise certain places and their miraculous capacities.

Pilgrimage has been increasingly popular since the 20th century, facilitated by ever-improving transportation. Movement over actual distance is critical to pilgrimage, for what is important is not just visiting a sacred space but leaving home. Most pilgrimage centres hold periodic religious fairs called *melas* to mark auspicious astrological moments or important anniversaries. In 2001, for example, the Kumbh Mela in Allahabad was attended during a six-week period by tens of millions of pilgrims.

Because of shared elements in rituals, a pilgrim from western Rajasthan does not feel alienated in the eastern pilgrimage town of Puri, even though the spoken language, the landscape and climate, the deities' names and appearances, and the food offerings are markedly different from those the pilgrim knows at home. Moreover, pilgrimage works to propagate practices among diverse regions because stories and tales of effective and attractive ritual acts circulate along with pilgrims.

Pilgrimage sites are often located in spots of great natural beauty thought to be pleasing to deities as well as humans. Environmental activists draw on the mythology of the sacred landscapes to inspire Hindu populations to adopt sustainable environmental practices. The Sanskrit and Hindi word for pilgrimage centre is *tirtha*, literally a river ford or crossing place. The concept of a ford is associated with pilgrimage centres not simply because many are on riverbanks but because they are metaphorically places for transition, either to the other side of particular worldly troubles or beyond the endless cycle of birth and death.

RITUALS, SOCIAL PRACTICES, AND INSTITUTIONS

A number of rituals, social practices, and institutions are associated with Hinduism. These vary considerably according to beliefs and doctrines.

TEMPLE WORSHIP

Image worship in sectarian Hinduism takes place both in small household shrines and in the temple. Many Hindu authorities claim that regular temple worship to one of the deities of the devotional cults procures the same results for the worshiper as did the performance

Shiva temple, Bhumara. Frederick M. Asher

of one of the great Vedic sacrifices, and one who provides the patronage for the construction of a temple is called a "sacrificer" (*yajamana*).

Building a temple, which belongs to whoever paid for it or to the community that occupies it, is believed to be a meritorious deed recommended to anyone desirous of heavenly reward. The choice of a site, which should be serene and lovely, is determined by astrology and divination as well as by its proximity to human dwellings. The size and artistic value of temples range widely, from small village shrines with simple statuettes to great temple-cities whose boundary walls, pierced by monumental gates (*gopura*), enclose various buildings, courtyards, pools for ceremonial bathing, and sometimes even schools, hospitals, and monasteries.

Temple services, which may be held by any qualified member of the community, are neither collective nor carried out at fixed times. Those present experience, as spectators, the fortifying and beneficial influence radiating from the sacred acts. Sometimes worshipers assemble to meditate, to take part in chanting, or to listen to an exposition of doctrine. The *puja* (worship) performed in public "for the well-being of the world" is, though sometimes more elaborate, largely identical with that executed for personal interest. There are, however, many regional differences and even significant variations within the same community.

SHAIVA RITES

Ascetic tendencies were much in evidence among the Pashupatas, the oldest Shaiva tradition in northern India. Their Yoga, consisting of a constant meditative contact with God in solitude, required that they frequent places for cremating bodies. One group that emerged out of the Pashupata sect carried human skulls (hence the name Kapalikas, from *kapala*, "skull"). The Kapalikas used the skulls as bowls for liquor into which they projected and worshipped Shiva as Kapalika, the "Skull Bearer," or Bhairava, the "Frightful One," and then drank to become intoxicated. Their belief was that an ostentatious indifference to anything worldly was the best method of severing the ties of *samsara*.

The view and way of life peculiar to the Virashaivas, or Lingayats (Lingam-Bearers), in southwestern India is characterized by a deviation from common Hindu traditions and institutions such as sacrificial rites, temple worship, pilgrimages, child marriages, and inequality of the sexes. Initiation (*diksa*) is, on the other hand, an obligation laid on every member of the community. The spiritual power of the *guru* is bestowed upon the newborn and converts, who receive the eightfold shield (which protects devotees from ignorance of the supremacy of God and guides them to final beatitude) and the lingam. The miniature lingam, the centre and basis of all their religious practices and observances, which they always bear on their body, is held to be God himself concretely represented. Worship is due it twice or three times a day. When a Lingayat "is absorbed into the lingam" (i.e., dies), his body is not cremated, as is customary in Hinduism, but is interred, like ascetics of other groups. Lingayats who have reached a certain level of holiness are believed to die in the state of emancipation.

Shaivism, though inclined in doctrinal matters to inclusiveness, inculcates some fundamental lines of conduct: one should worship one's spiritual preceptor (*guru*) as God himself, follow his path, consider him to be present in oneself, and dissociate oneself from all opinions and practices that are incompatible with the Shaiva creed. Yet some of Shiva's devotees also worship other gods, and the "Shaivization" of various ancient traditions is sometimes rather superficial.

Like many other Indian religions, the Shaiva-siddhanta has developed an elaborate system of ethical philosophy, primarily with a view to preparing the way for those who aspire to liberation. Because *dharma* leads to happiness, there is no distinction between sacred and secular duties. All deeds are performed as services to God and with the conviction that all life is sacred and God-centred. A devout way of living and a nonemotional mysticism are thus much recommended. Kashmir Shaivism developed the practice of a simple method of salvation: by the recognition (*pratyabhijna*)—direct, spontaneous, technique-free, but full of *bhakti*—of one's identity with God.

VAISHNAVA RITES

The faithful Shrivaishnava Brahman arranges his day around five pursuits: purificatory rites, collecting the requisites for worship, acts of worship, study and contemplation of the meaning of the sacred books, and meditative concentration on the Lord's image. Lifelong obligations include the performance of sacrifices and other rites, restraint of the senses, fasting and soberness, worship, recitation of the scriptures, and visits to sacred places. Ramanuja, the great theologian and philosopher of the 12th century, recommended, in addition to these practices, concentration on God, a virtuous way of living, and insensibility to luck and misfortune.

According to Madhva (*c.* 1199–*c.* 1278), faithful observance of all regulations of daily conduct—including bathing, breath control, etc.—will contribute to eventual success in the quest for liberation. Devout Vaishnavas emphasize God's omnipotence and the far-reaching effects of his grace. They attach much value to the repetition of his name or of sacred formulas (*japa*) and to the praise

Ramanuja, bronze sculpture, 12th century; from a Vishnu temple in Thanjavur (Tanjore) district, India. Courtesy of the Institut Français d'Indologie, Pondicherry

and commemoration of his deeds as a means of self-realization and of unification with his essence. Special stress is laid on *ahimsa* ("noninjury"), the practice of not killing or not causing injury to living creatures.

SACRED TIMES AND FESTIVALS

Hindu festivals are combinations of religious ceremonies, semi-ritual spectacles, worship, prayer, lustrations, processions, music, dances, magical acts—participants throw fertilizing water or, during the

Holi festival, coloured powder at each other—eating, drinking, lovemaking, licentiousness, feeding the poor, and other activities of a religious or traditional character. The original purpose of these activities was to purify, avert malicious influences, renew society, bridge over critical moments, and stimulate or resuscitate the vital powers of nature (hence the term *utsava*, meaning both the generation of power and a festival). Because Hindu festivals relate to the cyclical life of nature, they are supposed to prevent it from stagnating. These cyclic festivals—which may last for many days—continue to be celebrated throughout India.

Such festivals refresh the mood of the participants, further the consciousness of their own power, and help to compensate for their sensations of fear and inferiority concerning the forces of nature. Such mixtures of worship and pleasure require the participation of the entire community and create harmony among its members, even if not all contemporary participants are aware of the festival's original character. There are also innumerable festivities in honour of specific gods, celebrated by individual temples, villages, and religious communities.

An important festival, formerly celebrating Kama, the god of sexual desire, survives in the Holi, a saturnalia connected with the spring equinox and in western India with the wheat harvest. Although commemorated throughout India, the rituals associated with Holi vary regionally. Among the Marathas, a people who live along the west coast of India from Mumbai to Goa, the descendants of heroes who died on the battlefield perform a dance, sword in hand, in honour of their ancestors until they believe themselves possessed by the spirits of the heroes. In Bengal swings are made for Krishna; in other regions a bonfire is also essential. The tradition that accounts for the festival of Holi describes how young Prahlada, in spite of his demonic father's opposition, worshipped Vishnu and was carried into the fire by the female demon Holika, the embodiment of evil, who was believed to be immune to the ravages of fire. Through Vishnu's intervention, Prahlada emerged unharmed, while Holika was burned to ashes. The bonfires are intended to commemorate this event or rather to reiterate the triumph of virtue and religion over evil and sacrilege. This explains why objects representing the sickness and impurities of the past year—the new year begins immediately after Holi—are thrown into the bonfire, and it is considered inauspicious not to look at it. Moreover, people pay or forgive debts, reconcile quarrels, and try to rid themselves of the evils, conflicts, and impurities they have accumulated during the preceding months, translating the central conception of the festival into a justification for dealing anew with continuing situations in their lives.

Hindus celebrate a number of other important festivals, including Diwali, in which all classes of society participate, though it is believed to have been given

DIWALI

One of the major religious festivals in Hinduism, Diwali (Divali) lasts for five days from the 13th day of the dark half of the lunar month Ashvina to the second day of the light half of Karttika. (The corresponding dates in the Gregorian calendar usually fall in late October and November.) The name is derived from the Sanskrit term dipavali meaning "row of lights," which are lit on the new-moon night to bid the presence of Lakshmi, the goddess of wealth. In Bengal, however, the goddess Kali is worshiped, and in north India the festival also celebrates the return of Rama, Sita, Lakshmana, and Hanuman to the city of Ayodhya, where Rama's rule of righteousness would commence.

During the festival, small earthenware lamps filled with oil are lighted and placed in rows along the parapets of temples and houses and set adrift on rivers and streams. The fourth day—the main Diwali festival day and the beginning of the lunar month of Karttika—marks the beginning of the new year according to the Vikrama calendar. Merchants perform religious ceremonies and open new account books. It is generally a time for visiting, exchanging gifts, cleaning and decorating houses, feasting, setting off fireworks displays, and wearing new clothes.

Krishna and Radha, detail of a Kishangarh painting, mid-18th century; in a private collection. *P. Chandra*

Gambling is encouraged during this season as a way of ensuring good luck for the coming year and in remembrance of the games of dice played by the Lord Shiva and Parvati on Mount Kailasa or similar contests between Radha and Krishna. Ritually, in honour of Lakshmi, the female player always wins.

Diwali is also an important festival in Jainism. For the Jain community, many of whose members belong to the merchant class, the day commemorates the passing into nirvana of Mahavira, the most recent of the Jain Tirthankaras. The lighting of the lamps is explained as a material substitute for the light of holy knowledge that was extinguished with Mahavira's passing. Since the 18th century Diwali has been celebrated in Sikhism as the time Guru Hargobind returned to Amritsar from a supposed captivity in Gwalior—apparently an echo of Rama's return to Ayodhya. Residents of Amritsar are said to have lighted lamps throughout the city to celebrate the occasion.

by Vishnu to the Vaishyas (traders, et al.). It takes place in October and features worship and ceremonial lights in honour of Lakshmi, the goddess of wealth and good fortune; fireworks to chase away the spirits of the deceased; and gambling, an old ritual custom intended to secure luck for the coming year. The nine-day Durga festival, or Navaratri, is, especially in Bengal, splendid homage to Shakti; in South India it is a celebration of Rama's victory over Ravana.

CULTURAL EXPRESSIONS: VISUAL ARTS, THEATRE, AND DANCE

The structure of Indian temples, the outward form of images, and indeed the very character of Indian art are largely determined by the religion and unique worldview of India, which penetrated the other provinces of culture and welded them into a homogeneous whole. Moreover, the art that emerged is highly symbolic. The much-developed ritual-religious symbolism presupposes the existence of a spiritual reality that may make its presence and influence felt in the material world and can also be approached through its representative symbols.

The production of objects of symbolic value is therefore more than a technique. The artisan can begin work only after entering into a state of supranormal consciousness and must model a cult image after the ideal prototype. After undergoing a process of spiritual transformation, the artisan is believed to transform the material used to create the image into a receptacle of divine power. Like the artisan, the worshiper (sadhaka, "the one who wishes to attain the goal"), must grasp the esoteric meaning of a statue, picture, or pot and identify his or her self with the power residing in it. The usual offering, a handful of flowers, is the means to convey the worshiper's "life-breath" into the image.

TYPES OF SYMBOLS

If they know how to handle the symbols, the worshipers have at their disposal an instrument for utilizing the possibilities lying in the depths of their own subconscious as well as a key to the mysteries of the forces dominating the world.

Yantra and Mandala

The general term for an "instrument [for controlling]" is yantra, which is especially applied to ritual diagrams but can also be applied to cult images, pictures, and other such aids to worship. Any yantra represents some aspect of the divine and enables devotees to worship it immediately within their hearts while identifying themselves with it. Except in its greater complexity, a mandala does not differ from a yantra, and both are drawn during a highly complex ritual in a purified and ritually consecrated place. The meaning and the use of both are similar, and they may be permanent or provisional.

A *mandala*, delineating a consecrated place and protecting it against disintegrating forces represented in demoniac cycles, is the geometric projection of the universe, spatially and temporally reduced to its essential plan. It represents in a schematic form the whole drama of disintegration and reintegration, and the adept can use it to identify with the forces governing these. As in temple ritual, a vase is employed to receive the divine power so that it can be projected into the drawing and then into the person of the adept. Thus, the *mandala* becomes a support for meditation, an instrument to provoke visions of the unseen.

A good example of a *mandala* is the *shrichakra*, the "Wheel of Shri" (i.e., of God's *shakti*), which is composed of four isosceles triangles with the apices upward, symbolizing Shiva, and five isosceles triangles with the apices downward, symbolizing Shakti. The nine triangles are of various sizes and intersect with one another. In the middle is the power point (*bindu*), visualizing the highest, the invisible, elusive centre from which the entire figure and the cosmos expand. The triangles are enclosed by two rows of (8 and 16) petals, representing the lotus of creation and reproductive vital force. The broken lines of the outer frame denote the figure to be a sanctuary with four openings to the regions of the universe. A "spiritual" foundation is provided by a *yantra*, called the *mandala* of the Purusha (spirit) of the site, that is also drawn on the site on which a temple is built. This rite is a reenactment of a variant of the myth of Purusha, an immortal primeval being who obstructed both worlds until he was subdued by the gods; the parts of his body became the spirits of the site.

Lingam and Yoni

One of the most common objects of worship, whether in temples or in the household cult, is the lingam. Often much stylized and representing the cosmic pillar, it emanates its all-producing energy to the four quarters of the universe. As the symbol of male creative energy it is frequently combined with its female counterpart (yoni), the latter forming the base from which the lingam rises. Although the lingam originally may have had no relation to Shiva, it has from ancient times been regarded as symbolizing Shiva's creative energy and is widely worshipped as his fundamental form.

Visual Theology in Icons

The beauty of cult objects is believed to contribute to their power as sacred instruments, and their ornamentation is held to facilitate the process of inviting the divine power into them. Statues of gods are not intended to imitate ideal human forms but to express the supernatural. A divine figure is a "likeness" (*pratima*), a temporary benevolent or terrifying expression of some aspect of a god's nature. Iconographic handbooks

Vishnu on the serpent Shesha, Badami, India. Frederick M. Asher

"fear-not" gesture (*abhaya-mudra*), bestows protection. Every iconographic detail has its own symbolic value, helping devotees to direct their energy to a deeper understanding of the various aspects of the divine and to proceed from external to internal worship. For many Indians, a consecrated image is a container of concentrated divine energy, and Hindu theists maintain that it is an instrument for ennobling the worshiper who realizes God's presence in it.

THE ARTS

Like literature and the performing arts, the visual arts contributed to the perpetuation of myths. Images sustain the presence of the god: when Devi is shown seated on her lion, advancing against the buffalo demon, she represents the affirmative forces of the universe and the triumph of divine power over wickedness. Male and female figures in uninterrupted embrace, as in Shaiva iconography, signify the union of opposites and the eternal process of generation.

Religious Principles in Sculpture and Painting

In Hindu sculpture the tendency is toward hieratic poses of a god in a particular conventional stance (*murti*; image), which, once fixed, perpetuates itself. An icon is a frozen incident of a myth. For example, one *murti* of Shiva is the "destruction of the elephant," in which

attach great importance to the ideology behind images and reveal, for example, that Vishnu's eight arms stand for the four cardinal and intermediate points of the compass and that his four faces, illustrating the concept of God's fourfoldness, typify his strength, knowledge, lordship, and potency. The emblems express the qualities of their bearers—e.g., a deadly weapon symbolizes destructive force, many-headedness omniscience. Much use is made of gestures (*mudras*); for example, the raised right hand, in the

Agni with characteristic symbol of the ram, wood carving; in the Guimet Museum, Paris. Giraudon/Art Resource, New York

Shiva appears dancing before and below a bloody elephant skin that he holds up before the image of his horrified consort; the stance is the summary of his triumph over the elephant demon. A god may also appear in a characteristic pose while holding in his multitudinous hands his various emblems, on each of which hangs a story. Lovers sculpted on temples are auspicious symbols on a par with foliage, water jars, and other representatives of fertility. Carvings, such as those that appear on temple chariots, tend to be more narrative; even more so are the miniature paintings of the Middle Ages. A favourite theme in the latter is the myth of the cowherd god Krishna and his love of the female cowherders (*gopis*).

Religious Organization of Sacred Architecture

Temples must be erected on sites that are *shubha*—i.e., suitable, beautiful, auspicious, and near water—because it is thought that the gods will not come to other places. However, temples are not necessarily designed to be congenial to their surroundings, because a manifestation of the sacred is an irruption, a break in phenomenal continuity. Temples are understood to be visible representations of a cosmic pillar, and their sites are said to be navels of the world and are believed to ensure communication with the gods. Their outward appearance must raise the expectation of meeting with God. Their erection is a reconstruction

and reintegration of Purusha-Prajapati, enabling him to continue his creative activity, and the finished monuments are symbols of the universe that is the unfolded One. The owner of the temple (i.e., the individual or community that paid for its construction)—also called the sacrificer—participates in the process of reintegration and experiences his spiritual rebirth in the small cella, aptly called the "womb room" (*garbhagriha*), by meditating on the God's presence, symbolized or actualized in his consecrated image. The cella is in the centre of the temple above the navel—i.e., the foundation stone—and it may contain a jar filled with the creative power (*shakti*) that is identified with the goddess Earth (who bears and protects the monument), three lotus flowers, and three tortoises (of stone, silver, and gold) that represent earth, atmosphere, and heaven. The tortoise is a manifestation of Vishnu bearing the cosmic pillar; the lotus is the symbol of the expansion of generative possibilities. The vertical axis or tube, coinciding with the cosmic pillar, connects all parts of the building and is continued in the finial on the top; it corresponds to the mystical vertical vein in the body of the worshiper through which his soul rises to unite itself with the Highest.

The designing of Hindu temples, like that of religious images, was codified in the Shilpa-shastras (craft textbooks), and every aspect of the design was believed to offer the symbolic representation of some feature of the cosmos. The idea of microcosmic symbolism is strong in Hinduism and comes from Vedic times; the Brahmanas are replete with similar cosmic interpretations of the many features of the sacrifice. The Vedic idea of the correspondence (*bandhu*) between microcosm and macrocosm was applied to the medieval temple, which was laid out geometrically to mirror the structure of the universe, with its four geometric quarters and a celestial roof. The temple also represents the mountain at the navel of the world and often somewhat resembles a mountain. On the periphery were carved the most worldly and diverse images, including battles, hunts, circuses, animals, birds, and gods.

The erotic scenes carved at Khajuraho in Madhya Pradesh and Konarak in Orissa express a general exuberance that may be an offering of thanksgiving to the gods who created all. However, that same swarming luxuriance of life may also reflect the concern that one must set aside worldly temptations before entering the sacred space of the temple, for the carvings decorate only the outside of the temple; at the centre, the sanctum sanctorum, there is little if any ornamentation, except for a stark symbol of the god or

Detail of a wall of the Lakshmana temple at Khajuraho, Madhya Pradesh, India, c. 941. P. Chandra goddess. Thus, these carvings simultaneously express a celebration of *samsara* and a movement toward *moksha*.

Theatre and Dance

Theatrical performances are events that can be used to secure blessings and happiness; the element of recreation is indissolubly blended with edification and spiritual elevation. The structure and character of classical Indian drama reveal its origin and function: it developed from a magico-religious ceremony, which survives as a ritual introduction, and begins and closes with benedictions. Drama is produced for festive occasions with a view to spiritual and religious success (*siddhi*), which must also be prompted by appropriate behaviour from the spectators; there must be a happy ending; the themes are borrowed from epic and legendary history; the development and unraveling of the plot are retarded; and the envy of malign influences is averted by the almost obligatory buffoon (*vidusaka*, "the spoiler"). There are also, in addition to films, which often use the same religious and mythic themes, *yatra*s, a combination of stage play and various festivities that have contributed much to the spread of the Puranic view of life.

Dancing is not only an aesthetic pursuit but also a divine service. The dance executed by Shiva as king of dancers (Nataraja), the visible symbol of the rhythm of the universe, represents God's five activities: he unfolds the universe out of the drum held in one of his right hands; he preserves it by uplifting his other right hand in *abhaya-mudra*; he reabsorbs it with his upper left hand, which bears a tongue of flame; his transcendental essence is hidden behind the garb of apparitions, and grace is bestowed and release made visible by the foot that is held aloft and to which the hands are made to point; and the other foot, planted on the ground, gives an abode to the tired souls struggling in *samsara*. Another dance pose adopted by Shiva is the doomsday *tandava*, executed in his destructive Bhairava manifestation, usually with 10 arms and accompanied by Devi and demons. The related myth is that Shiva conquered a mighty elephant demon whom he forced to dance until he fell dead; then, wrapped in the blood-dripping skin of his victim, the god executed a horrendous dance of victory.

There are halls for sacred dances annexed to some temples because of this association with the divine. The rhythmic movement has a compelling force, generating and concentrating power or releasing superfluous energy. It induces the experience of the divine and transforms the dancer into whatever he or she impersonates. Thus, many tribal dances consist of symbolic enactments of events (harvest, battles) in the hope that they will be accomplished successfully. Musicians and dancers accompany processions to expel the demons of cholera or cattle plague. Even today, religious themes and the various relations between humans and God are danced and made visual by the codified symbolic meanings of gestures and movements.

HINDUISM AND THE WORLD BEYOND

Because religion forms a crucial aspect of identity for most Indians, much of India's history can be understood through the interplay among its diverse religious groups. Hindus are in the majority in every Indian state except Jammu and Kashmir (where Muslims form roughly two-thirds of the population); Punjab (roughly three-fifths Sikh); Meghalaya, Mizoram, and Nagaland (mainly Christian); and Arunachal Pradesh (predominantly animist). Hindus also form the majority in every union territory except Lakshadweep (more than nine-tenths Muslim). Almost everywhere, however, significant local minorities are present. Only in the states of Orissa and Himachal Pradesh do Hindus constitute virtually the entire population.

In 1947, with the partition of the subcontinent and loss of Pakistan's largely Muslim population, India became even more predominantly Hindu. The concomitant emigration of perhaps 10 million Muslims to Pakistan and the immigration of nearly as many Hindus and Sikhs from Pakistan further emphasized this change. Hindus now make up about three-fourths of India's population. Muslims, however, are still the largest single minority faith (more than one-ninth of the total

population), with large concentrations in many areas of the country, including Jammu and Kashmir, western Uttar Pradesh, West Bengal, Kerala, and many cities. India's Muslim population is greater than that found in any country of the Middle East and is only exceeded by that of Indonesia and, slightly, by that of Pakistan or Bangladesh.

HINDUISM AND ISLAM

Hindu relations with Islam and Christianity are in some ways quite different from the ties and tensions that bind together religions of Indian origin. Hindus live with a legacy of domination by Muslim and Christian rulers that stretches back many centuries—in North India, to the Delhi Sultanate established at the beginning of the 13th century. It is hardly the case that Muslim rule was generally loathsome to Hindus. Direct and indirect patronage from the Mughal emperors Akbar and Jahāngīr (1569–1627), whose chief generals were Hindu Rajputs, laid the basis for the great burst of Krishnaite temple and institution building that transformed the Braj region beginning in the 16th century. Moreover, close proximity and daily interaction throughout the centuries has led to efforts to accommodate the existence of the two religions. One manifestation of such syncretism occurred among mystically inclined groups who believed that one God, or the "universal principle," was the same regardless of whether it was called Allah or *brahman*. Various syntheses between the two religions that emphasize nonsectarianism have arisen in northern India.

Yet there were periods when the political ambitions of Islamic rulers took strength from iconoclastic aspects of Muslim teaching and led to the devastation of many major Hindu temple complexes, from Mathura and Varanasi in the north to Chidambaram and Madurai in the far south; other temples were converted to mosques. Episodically, since the 14th century, this history has provided rhetorical fuel for Hindu warriors eager to assert themselves against Muslim rivals. The bloody partition of the South Asian subcontinent into India and Pakistan in 1947 added a new dimension. Mobilizing Hindu sensibilities about the sacredness of the land as a whole, extremists have sometimes depicted the creation of Pakistan as a rape of the body of India, in the process demonizing Muslims who remain within India's political boundaries.

These strands converged at the end of the 20th century in a campaign to destroy the mosque built in 1528 by a lieutenant of the Mughal emperor Babur in Ayodhya, a city that has traditionally been identified as the place where Rama was born and ruled. In 1992 Hindu militants from all over India, who had been organized by the Vishwa Hindu Parishad (VHP; "World Hindu Council"), the Rashtriya Swayamsevak Sangh (RSS; "National Volunteer Alliance"), and the

Rama and Lakshmana attended by Hanuman in the forest, detail of relief inspired by the Ramayana, *from Nacna Kuthara, Madhya Pradesh, 5th century AD. P. Chandra*

Bharatiya Janata Party (BJP; "Indian People's Party"), destroyed the mosque in an effort to "liberate" Rama and establish a huge "Rama's Birthplace Temple" on the spot. In the aftermath, several thousand people—mostly Muslims—were killed in riots that spread across North India.

HINDUISM AND CHRISTIANITY

Relations between Hinduism and Christianity have also been shaped by unequal balances of political power and cultural influence. Although communities of Christians have lived in South

India since the middle of the 1st millennium, the great expansion of Indian Christianity followed the efforts of missionaries working under the protection of British colonial rule. Their denigration of selected features of Hindu practice—most notably image worship, suttee, and child marriage (the first two were also criticized by Muslims)—was shared by certain Hindus. Beginning in the 19th century and continuing into the 21st, a movement that might be called neo-Vedanta has emphasized the monism of certain Upanishads, decried "popular" Hindu "degenerations" such as the worship of idols, acted as an agent of social reform, and championed dialogue between other religious communities.

Many Hindus are ready to accept the ethical teachings of the Gospels, particularly the Sermon on the Mount (whose influence on Gandhi is well known), but reject the theological superstructure. They regard Christian conceptions about love and its social consequences as a kind of *bhakti* and tend to venerate Jesus as a saint, yet many resent the organization, the reliance on authorities, and the exclusiveness of Christianity, considering these as obstacles to harmonious cooperation. They subscribe to Gandhi's opinion that missionaries should confine their activities to humanitarian service and look askance at conversion, finding also in Hinduism what might be attractive in Christianity. Such sentiments took an unusually extreme form at the end of the 20th

century, when Hindu activists attacked Dalit Christians and their churches in various parts of India, especially Orissa and Gujarat. A far more typical sentiment is expressed in the eagerness of Hindus of all social stations, especially the middle class, to send their children to high-quality (often English-language) schools established and maintained by Christian organizations. No great fear exists that the religious element in the curriculum will cause Hindu children to abandon their parents' faith.

DIASPORIC HINDUISM

Since the appearance of Swami Vivekananda at the World's Parliament of Religions in Chicago in 1893 and the subsequent establishment of the Vedanta Society in various American and British cities, Hinduism has had a growing missionary profile outside the Indian subcontinent. Conversion as understood by Christians or Muslims is usually not the aim. As seen in the Vedanta Society, Hindu perspectives are held to be sufficiently capacious that they do not require new adherents to abandon traditions of worship with which they are familiar, merely to see them as part of a greater whole. The Vedic formula "Truth is one, but scholars speak of it in many ways" ("Akam sat vipra bahudhe vadanti") is much quoted. Many transnational Hindu communities—including Radha Soami Satsang Beas, Transcendental Meditation, the self-realization fellowship

Siddha Yoga, the Sathya Sai Baba Satsang, and the International Society for Krishna Consciousness (ISKCON, popularly called Hare Krishna)—have focused on specific *gurus*, particularly in their stages of most rapid growth. They frequently emphasize techniques of spiritual discipline more than doctrine. Of these groups, only ISKCON has a deeply exclusivist cast—which makes it, in fact, generally more doctrinaire than the Gaudiya Vaishnava lineages out of which its founding *guru*, A.C. Bhaktivedanta, emerged.

At least as important as these *guru*-centred communities in the increasingly international texture of Hindu life are communities of Hindus who have emigrated from South Asia to other parts of the world. Their character differs markedly according to region, class, and the time at which emigration occurred. Tamils in Malaysia celebrate a festival to the god Murukan (Thaipusam) that accommodates body-piercing vows long outlawed in India itself. Formerly indentured labourers who settled on the Caribbean island of Trinidad in the mid-19th century have consolidated doctrine and practice from various locales in Gangetic India, with the result that Rama and Shita have a heightened profile. Many migrants from rural western India, especially Gujarat, became urbanized in East Africa in the late 19th century and resettled in Britain. Like those Gujaratis who came directly to the United States from India since the liberalization of U.S. immigration laws in 1965, once abroad they are more apt to embrace the reformist *guru*-centred Swaminarayan faith than they would be in their native Gujarat, though this is by no means universal.

Professional-class emigrants from South India have spearheaded the construction of a series of impressive Shrivaishnava-style temples throughout the United States, sometimes receiving financial and technical assistance from the great Vaishnava temple institutions at Tirupati. The placement of some of these temples, such as the Penn Hills temple near Pittsburgh, Pa., reveals the desire to evoke Tirupati's natural environment on American soil. Similarly, Telugu-speaking priests from the Tirupati region have been imported to serve at temples such as the historically important Ganesha temple, constructed from a preexisting church in Queens, New York, in 1975–77. Yet the population worshipping at these temples is far more mixed than that in India. This produces on the one hand sectarian and regional eclecticism and on the other hand a vigorous attempt to establish doctrinal common ground. As Hindu scholar Vasudha Narayanan observed, educational materials produced at such temples typically hold that Hinduism is not a religion but a way of life, that it insists in principle on religious tolerance, that its Godhead is functionally trinitarian (the male *trimurti* of Brahma, Vishnu, and Shiva is meant, although temple worship is often very active at goddesses' shrines), and that Hindu rituals have inner meanings consonant with scientific principles and are conducive to good health.

Pacific and ecumenical as this sounds, members of such temples are also important contributors to the VHP, whose efforts since 1964 to find common ground among disparate Hindu groups have sometimes also contributed to displays of Hindu nationalism such as were seen at Ayodhya in 1992. As the 21st century opened, there was a vivid struggle between "left" and "right" within the Hindu fold, with diasporic groups playing a more important role than ever before. Because of their wealth and education, because globalizing processes lend them

prestige and enable them to communicate constantly with Hindus living in South Asia, and because their experience as minorities tends to set them apart from their families in India itself, their contribution to the evolution of Hinduism has been a very interesting one.

"Hinduism" was originally an outsider's word, and it designates a multitude of realities defined by period, time, sect, class, and caste. Yet the veins and bones that hold this complex organism together are not just chimeras of external perception. Hindus themselves—particularly diasporic Hindus—affirm them, continuing and even accelerating a process of self-definition that has been going on for millennia.

CHAPTER 4

OTHER INDIGENOUS INDIAN RELIGIONS AND INDIAN PHILOSOPHY

Hinduism, Buddhism, and Jainism originated in the same milieu: the circles of world renouncers of the 6th century BC. All share certain non-Vedic practices (such as renunciation itself and various Yogic meditational techniques) and doctrines (such as the belief in rebirth and the goal of liberation from perpetual transmigration), but Buddhists and Jains do not accept the authority of the Vedic tradition and therefore are regarded as less than orthodox by Hindus. From the 6th to the 11th century there was strong and sometimes bloody competition for royal patronage between the three communities—with Brahmans representing Hindu values—as well as between Vaishnavas and Shaivas. In general, the Brahman groups prevailed. In a typically absorptive gesture, Hindus in time recognized the Buddha as an incarnation of Vishnu, usually the ninth; it was often held, however, that Vishnu assumed this form to mislead and destroy the enemies of the Veda. Hence, the Buddha avatar is rarely worshipped by Hindus, though it is often highly respected by them. At an institutional level, certain Buddhist shrines, such as the one marking the Buddha's enlightenment at Bodh Gaya, have remained partly under the supervision of Hindu ascetics and are visited by Hindu pilgrims.

Buddhists living near the Chinese (Tibetan) border generally follow Tibetan Buddhism, sometimes designated as Vajrayana (Sanskrit: "Vehicle of the Thunderbolt"), while those living near the border with Myanmar adhere to the Theravada (Pali: "Way of the Elders"). Neo-Buddhists in Maharashtra do not have a clear sectarian affiliation.

Hinduism has much in common with Jainism, which until the 20th century remained an Indian religion, especially in social institutions and ritual life; for this reason, many Hindus still consider it a Hindu sect. The points of difference—e.g., a stricter practice of *ahimsa* ("noninjury") and the absence of sacrifices for the deceased in Jainism—do not give offense to orthodox Hindus. Moreover, many Jain laypeople worship images as Hindus do, though with a different rationale. There are even places outside India where Hindus and Jains have joined to build a single temple, sharing the worship space.

RELIGIONS

Other important religious minorities in India include Christians, most heavily concentrated in the northeast, Mumbai, and the far south; and Sikhs, mostly in Punjab and some adjacent areas. Buddhists live mostly in Maharashtra, Sikkim, Arunachal Pradesh, and Jammu and Kashmir; and Jains are most prominent in Maharashtra, Gujarat, and Rajasthan. Those practicing the Bahā'ī

faith, formerly too few to be treated by the census, have dramatically increased in number as a result of active proselytization. There are also some Zoroastrians (the Parsis), largely concentrated in Mumbai and in coastal Gujarat, who wield influence out of all proportion to their small numbers because of their prominence during the colonial period. Several tiny but sociologically interesting communities of Jews are located along the western coast. India's tribal peoples live mostly in the northeast; they practice various forms of animism, which is perhaps the country's oldest religious tradition.

SIKHISM

The practitioners of Sikhism are known as Sikhs. They call their faith Gurmat (Punjabi: "the Way of the Guru"). According to Sikh tradition, Sikhism was established by Guru Nanak (1469–1539) and subsequently led by a succession of nine other Gurus. All 10 human Gurus, Sikhs believe, were inhabited by a single spirit. Upon the death of the 10th, Guru Gobind Singh (1666–1708), the spirit of the eternal Guru transferred itself to the sacred scripture of Sikhism, *Guru Granth Sahib* ("The Granth as the Guru"), also known as the *Adi Granth* ("First Volume"), which thereafter was regarded as the sole Guru. In the early 21st century there were nearly 25 million Sikhs worldwide, the great majority of them living in the Indian state of Punjab.

History and Doctrine

Sikh in Punjabi means "learner," and those who joined the Sikh community, or Panth ("Path"), were people who sought spiritual guidance. In its earliest stage Sikhism was clearly a movement within the Hindu tradition; Nanak was raised a Hindu and eventually belonged to the Sant tradition of northern India, a movement associated with the great poet and mystic Kabir (1440–1518). The Sants, most of whom were poor, dispossessed, and illiterate, composed hymns of great beauty expressing their experience of the divine, which they saw in all things. Their tradition drew heavily on the Vaishnava bhakti (the devotional movement within the Hindu tradition that worships the god Vishnu), though there were important differences between the two. Like the followers of bhakti, the Sants believed that devotion to God is essential to liberation from the cycle of rebirth in which all human beings are trapped; unlike the followers of bhakti, however, the Sants maintained that God is *nirgun* ("without form") and not *sagun* ("with form"). For the Sants, God can be neither incarnated nor represented in concrete terms.

Certain lesser influences also operated on the Sant movement. Chief among them was the Nath tradition, which comprised a cluster of sects, all claiming descent from the semilegendary teacher Gorakhnath and all promoting Hatha Yoga as the means of spiritual liberation. Although the Sants rejected the physical aspects of Hatha Yoga in favour of meditation techniques, they accepted the Naths' concept of spiritual ascent to ultimate bliss. Some scholars have argued that the Sants were influenced by Islam through their contact with the Mughal rulers of India from the early 16th century, but there is in fact little indication of this, though Sufism (Islamic mysticism) may have had a marginal effect.

The 10 Gurus

The following discussion of the lives of the 10 Gurus relies on the traditional Sikh account, most elements of which are derived from hagiographic legend and lore and cannot be verified historically.

Guru Nanak

A member of the Khatri (trading) caste and far from illiterate, Nanak was not a typical Sant, yet he experienced the same spirit of God in everything outside him and everything within him as did others in the movement he founded. He was born in the Punjab, which has been the home of the Sikh faith ever since.

Nanak composed many hymns, which were collected in the *Adi Granth* by Guru Arjan, the fifth Sikh Guru, in 1604. Nanak's authorship of these works is beyond doubt, and it is also certain that he visited pilgrimage sites throughout India. Beyond this very little is known. The story of his life has been the imagined product of the legendary *janam-sakhis* ("life stories"), which were composed between 50 and 80 years after the Guru's death in 1539, though only a tiny fraction of the material found in them can be affirmed as factual.

The first *janam-sakhis* were attributed to the lifelong companion of Nanak, Bhai Bala (1466–1544), who composed an account of the Guru's life that was filled with miracles and wonder stories. By the end of the 19th century, the Bala version had begun to create serious unease among Sikh scholars, who were greatly relieved when a more rational version, since known as the *Puratan* ("Ancient") tradition, was discovered in London, where it had arrived as a gift for the library of the East India Company. Although it too contained fantastic elements, it had far fewer miracle stories than the Bala version, and it presented a more plausible account of the course of Guru Nanak's journeys. When supplemented by references from a discourse by the poet Bhai Gurdas (1551–1637), the *Puratan* seems to provide a satisfactory description of the life of Guru Nanak.

According to this version, Nanak made five trips, one in each of the four directions of the cardinal points of the compass, followed by one within the Punjab. He traveled first to the east and then to the south, reaching Sri Lanka. He then journeyed to the north, deep in the Himalayas, where he debated with Nath masters known as Siddhs, who were believed to have attained immortality through the practice of Yoga. His trip to the west took him to Baghdad, Mecca, and Medina. He then settled in Kartarpur, a village on the right bank of the Ravi River in the Punjab. After visiting southern Punjab, he died in Kartarpur, having appointed a loyal disciple as his successor.

The hagiographic character of the *Puratan* tradition is well illustrated by the story of Nanak's visit to Mecca. Having entered the city, Nanak lay down with his feet pointing at the mihrab (the niche in a mosque indicating the direction of the Ka'bah). An outraged *qāẓī* (judge) found him there and demanded an explanation. In reply Nanak asked him to drag his feet away from the mihrab. This the *qāẓī* did, only to discover that, wherever he placed Nanak's feet, there the mihrab moved. The lesson of the story is that God is everywhere, not in any particular direction.

Another popular *Puratan* story concerns Nanak's visit to the "Land Ruled by Women" in eastern India. Mardana, Nanak's faithful minstrel and travel companion, went ahead to beg for food but was turned into a sheep by one of the women. When Nanak arrived, he caused a pot to adhere to the woman's head and restored Mardana to his original form after instructing him to say "Vahi Guru" ("Praise to the Guru"). The women then tried all manner of fearsome magic on the pair, without success. After the queen of the Land Ruled by Women, Nur Shah, failed in her attempt to seduce Nanak, the women finally submitted.

Nanak was certainly no admirer of the Naths, who apparently competed with him for converts. (The *janam-sakhi* anecdotes give considerable prominence to debates between Nanak and the Siddhs, in which Nanak invariably gets the better of his opponents.) By contrast, he accepted the message of the Sants, giving it expression in hymns of the most compelling beauty. He taught that all people are subject to the transmigration of souls and that the sole and sufficient means of liberation from the cycle of rebirth is meditation on the divine *nam* (Persian: "name"). According to Nanak, the *nam* encompasses the whole of creation—everything outside the believer and everything within him. Having heard the divine word (*shabad*) through a grace bestowed by God, or Akal Purakh (one of Nanak's names for God), and having chosen to accept the word, the believer undertakes *nam simaran*, or meditation on the name. Through this discipline, he gradually begins to perceive manifold signs of the *nam*, and the means of liberation are progressively revealed. Ascending to ever-higher levels of mystical experience, the believer is blessed with a mounting sense of peace and joy. Eventually the *sach khand* ("abode of truth") is reached, and the believer passes into a condition of perfect and absolute union with Akal Purakh.

Sikhs believe that the "voice" with which the word is uttered within the believer's being is that of the spirit of the eternal Guru. Because Nanak performed the discipline of *nam simaran*, the eternal Guru took flesh and dwelt within him. Upon Nanak's death the eternal Guru was embodied, in turn, in each of Nanak's successors until, with the death of Guru Gobind Singh, it was enshrined in the holy scripture of the Sikhs, the *Guru Granth Sahib*.

The fourth Guru, Ram Das, introduced two significant changes: he introduced the appointment of *masands* (vicars), charged with the care of defined congregations (*sangats*), and he founded the important centre of Amritsar. The chief contribution of Arjan, the fifth Guru, was the compilation of the Sikhs' sacred scripture, using the *Goindval Pothis*, which had been prepared at the instructions of Guru Amar Das. All of the Gurus continued the teaching of Nanak concerning liberation through meditation on the divine name. The first five Gurus were, therefore, one as far as the central belief was concerned.

Under the sixth Guru, however, the doctrine of *miri/piri* emerged. Like his predecessors, the Guru still engaged in *piri*, spiritual leadership, but to it he now added *miri*, the rule of a worldly leader. The Panth was thus no longer an exclusively religious community but was also a military one that was commonly involved in open warfare. All Sikhs were expected to accept the new dual authority of the Gurus.

The final contribution of the Gurus came with Gobind Singh. As before, there was no weakening of the doctrine affirming meditation on the divine name. Guru Gobind Singh, however, believed that the forces of good and evil fell out of balance on occasion, and at times the latter increased enormously. Akal Purakh then intervened in human history to correct the balance, choosing as his agents particular individuals who fought the forces of evil that had acquired excessive power. Gobind Singh believed that the Mughals, through Emperor Aurangzeb, had tipped the scale too far toward evil and that he had been divinely appointed to restore the balance between good and evil. He also believed that drawing the sword was justified to rein in evil.

Guru Angad

In 1539 Nanak died, having first appointed Guru Angad (1504–52) as his successor. Originally known as Lahina, Angad had been a worshipper of the Hindu goddess Durga. While leading a party to the holy site of Javalamukhi (a temple in a town of the same name in Himachal Pradesh state, India), he passed by Kartarpur and was instantly won over by the beauty of Nanak's hymns. Thereafter the future Guru was completely loyal to his new master, and his behaviour persuaded Nanak that he would be a more suitable successor than either of the Guru's two sons. A thoroughly obedient disciple, Angad made no innovations in Nanak's teachings, and the period of his leadership was uneventful.

Guru Amar Das

When Angad died, the title of Guru was passed to Amar Das (1479–1574), who was distinguished by his total loyalty to the second Guru. According to tradition, Amar Das was a Vaishnava who had

spent his life looking for a Guru. While on a trip to the Ganges River, he decided to become a Sikh when he overheard the daughter of Angad singing a hymn by Nanak. Amar Das, who was 73 years old when he became Guru, assumed responsibility for the Panth at a time when it was settling down after the first flush of its early years. Many Sikhs had been born into the Panth, and the enthusiasm and excitement that characterized the religion under Nanak had dissipated. Believing that rituals were necessary to confirm the Sikhs in their faith, Amar Das ordered the digging of a sacred well (*baoli*), which he designated as a pilgrimage site; created three festival days (Baisakhi, Maghi, and Diwali); and compiled a scripture of sacred hymns, the so-called *Goindval Pothis*. In addition, because the Sikhs had spread throughout the Punjab, he established *manjis* (dioceses) to help spread the faith and better organize its adherents. Despite these changes, there was no weakening of the obligation to meditate on the *nam*.

Guru Ram Das

Guru Ram Das (1534–81), the fourth Guru, was the son-in-law of Guru Amar Das. He is perhaps best known as the founder of the town of Amritsar ("Pool of Nectar"), which became the capital of the Sikh religion and the location of the Harimandir (later known as the Golden Temple), the chief house of worship in Sikhism. He also replaced the *manjis* with *masands* (vicars), who were charged with the care of defined *sangats* (congregations) and who at least once a year presented the Guru with reports on and gifts from the Sikh community. Particularly skilled in hymn singing, Guru Ram Das stressed the importance of this practice, which remains an important part of Sikh worship. A member of the Khatri caste and the Sodhi family, Ram Das appointed his son Arjan as his successor, and all subsequent Gurus were his direct descendants.

Guru Arjan

Prithi Chand, the oldest brother of Guru Arjan (1563–1606), took a distinctly hostile view of his brother's appointment and in retaliation attempted to poison Hargobind, Arjan's only son. Prithi Chand and his followers also circulated hymns that they alleged were written by the earlier Gurus. This prompted Arjan to compile an authentic version of the hymns, which he did using Bhai Gurdas as his scribe and the *Goindval Pothis* as a guide. The resulting *Adi Granth*, in a supplemented version, became the *Guru Granth Sahib*. It remains the essential scripture of the faith, and Sikhs always show it profound respect and turn to it whenever they need guidance, comfort, or peace.

During Arjan's lifetime the Panth steadily won converts, particularly among members of the Jat agrarian caste. The Mughal governor of the Punjab was concerned about the growth of the religion, and Emperor Jahāngīr was influenced by rumours concerning Arjan's alleged support for Jahāngīr's rebellious son Khusro. Guru Arjan was arrested and tortured to death by the Mughals. Before he died, however, he urged his son—Hargobind, the sixth Guru—always to carry arms.

Guru Hargobind: A New Direction for the Panth

The appointment of the sixth Guru, Guru Hargobind (1595–1644), marks a transition from a strictly religious Panth to one that was both religious and temporal. Arjan's command to his son was later termed *miri/piri* ("temporal authority"/"spiritual authority"). Hargobind was still the Guru, and as such he continued the pattern established by his five predecessors. He was, in other words, a *pir*, or spiritual leader, but he was also a *mir*, or chieftain of his people, responsible for protecting them against tyranny with force of arms. The new status of the Guru and the Panth was confirmed by the actions of Hargobind and came to be reflected in the architecture of Amritsar. Opposite the Harimandir, the symbol of *piri*, there is a building known as Akal Takht, the symbol of *miri*. Thus, when Hargobind stood between the Harimandir and the Akal Takht and buckled on two swords, the message was clear: he possessed both spiritual and temporal authority.

Hargobind fought intermittently with Mughal forces in the Punjab. Following four such skirmishes, he withdrew from Amritsar and occupied Kiratpur in the foothills of the Shiwalik Hills. This was a much more suitable position because it was outside the territory directly controlled by the Mughal administration. There he remained until his death in 1644.

Before he died, the question of who should succeed him emerged. Although it was certain that the successor should be a descendant of his, it was far from clear which of his children or grandchildren should take his place. Hargobind had three wives who bore him six children. The eldest son, Gurditta, who was evidently his favourite for the position, had predeceased him, and none of the remaining five seemed suitable for the position. The older son of Gurditta, Dhir Mal, was rejected because, from his seat in Jalandhar district, he had formed an alliance with Emperor Shāh Jahān. This meant that the younger son of Gurditta, Har Rai, would become the seventh Guru. But Dhir Mal continued to make trouble for the orthodox Panth and attracted many Sikhs as his followers. He also claimed to possess the sacred scripture prepared by Guru Arjan and used it to buttress his claims to be the only legitimate Guru.

Guru Har Rai

The period of Guru Har Rai (1630–61) was a relatively peaceful one. He withdrew from Kiratpur and moved farther back into the Shiwalik Hills, settling with a small retinue at Sirmur. From there he occasionally emerged onto the plains of the Punjab to visit and preach to the Sikhs. In this regard he was well served by several *masands*, who brought him

news about the Sikhs and offerings of money to pay the expenses of the Panth.

The period of peace did not last, however. Guru Har Rai faced the same problems with the Mughals as Guru Arjan had. Aurangzeb, the successful contender for the Mughal throne, defeated his elder brother Dara Shikoh and established himself in Delhi. He then sent a message to Har Rai requiring him to deliver his son Ram Rai as a hostage for Har Rai's reputed support of Dara Shikoh. Aurangzeb evidently wished to educate the future Guru in Mughal ways and to convert him into a supporter of the Mughal throne. In an episode that illustrated the success of this quest, Aurangzeb once asked Ram Rai to explain an apparently demeaning line in the *Adi Granth*, which claimed that earthenware pots were *mitti musalaman ki*, or formed from deceased Muslim bodies. Ram Rai replied that the words had been miscopied. The original text should have been *mitti beiman ki*, the dust that is formed from the bodies of faithless people. When this answer was reported to Har Rai, he declared his intention never to see Ram Rai again. Because he had committed the serious crime of altering the words of Guru Nanak, Ram Rai could never be the Guru, and the position passed instead to his younger brother, Hari Krishen, who inherited the title when he was only five years old.

Guru Hari Krishen

Aurangzeb summoned Guru Hari Krishen (1656–64) to Delhi from the Shiwalik Hills.

While in Delhi, Hari Krishen contracted smallpox, which proved fatal. Before he died, he uttered the words "Baba Bakale," which indicated to his followers the identity of his successor, the *baba* ("old man") who is in the village of Bakala. Hari Krishen meant to identify Tegh Bahadur, who dwelt in Bakala and was the son of Guru Hargobind by his second wife and the half brother of Guru Hari Krishen's grandfather.

Guru Tegh Bahadur

As soon as these words became known, many hopeful persons rushed to Bakala to claim the title. Sikh tradition records that Makhan Shah, a trader, had been caught by a violent storm at sea and in his distress vowed to give the Sikh Guru 501 gold mohurs (coins) if he should be spared. After the storm abated, the survivor traveled to the Punjab, and, learning that the Guru resided in Bakala, he proceeded there. He discovered that several people claimed the title following the death of Guru Hari Krishen. He decided to test them all, laying before each claimant two gold mohurs. Finally he reached Tegh Bahadur, who asked him for the remainder of what he had promised. Rushing up to the rooftop, Makhan Shah proclaimed that he had indeed found the true Guru.

The period of Guru Tegh Bahadur (1621–75) is important for two reasons. The first is that several hymns that Tegh Bahadur wrote were added by Guru Gobind Singh to the collection originally made by Guru Arjan; the canon was then closed, and the *Adi Granth* has remained inviolable ever since. The second concerns the manner of Tegh Bahadur's death. Sikh tradition maintains that he was arrested by Mughal authorities for having aided Kashmiri Brahmans against Mughal attempts to convert them to Islam. Offered the choice of conversion or death, he chose the latter and was immediately beheaded.

A Sikh who witnessed the execution spirited away Tegh Bahadur's headless body and lodged it in his house outside Delhi. To cremate the body without raising suspicion, he burned the whole house. Meanwhile, three outcaste Sikhs secured the head of the Guru and carried it in secret up to Anandpur, a service which earned them and all their successors the right to be called Ranghreta Sikhs, an honoured group of outcaste followers of the Guru. Arriving in Anandpur, they produced the severed head amidst cries of great lamentation.

Guru Gobind Singh and the Founding of the Khalsa

Following the death of Tegh Bahadur, Guru Gobind Singh (1666–1708), the most important of all the Gurus with the exception of Guru Nanak, assumed leadership of the Sikhs. Gobind Rai, whose name was altered to Gobind Singh possibly at the time of the creation of the Khalsa, was born in Patna, the only child of Guru Tegh Bahadur. At the age of five he was brought to Anandpur and educated in

Sanskrit and Persian and in the arts of poetry and warfare. His father's execution in Delhi by Aurangzeb must have made a deep impression on the child. For several years after his succession as Guru, he continued his education in the Shiwalik Hills. He grew to manhood as the ruler of a small Shiwalik state, participating in various wars against other Shiwalik chieftains and demonstrating a particular delight in the sport of hunting.

According to Sikh tradition, on Baisakhi Day (the Indian New Year) late in the 17th century (the exact year is uncertain, though it was probably 1699), a fair was held at Anandpur, and all Sikhs were ordered to attend. The Guru remained concealed until the celebrations were at their height, when he suddenly appeared from a tent carrying a drawn sword and demanding the head of one of his loyal followers. At once the crowd became silent, wondering what had happened. The Guru repeated the command, and eventually Daya Singh volunteered and was taken behind a screen to be dispatched. Gobind Singh then reappeared, his sword dripping blood, and demanded a second victim. He too was escorted behind the screen, and again the sound of the sword could be heard. In this manner five loyal Sikhs agreed to die for their master. When he had apparently dispatched the fifth, the screen was removed, and all five were seen to be very much alive. At their feet lay five slaughtered goats. The five volunteers became the Panj Piare, the "Cherished Five," who had proved that their loyalty was beyond question.

Guru Gobind Singh explained that he desired the Panj Piare to be the beginning of a new order, the Khalsa ("the Pure," from the Persian *khalisah*, also meaning "pure"). The *masands* (many of whom had become quarrelsome or corrupt) would be eliminated, and all Sikhs, through their initiation into the Khalsa, would owe allegiance directly to the Guru. Gobind Singh then commenced the *amrit sanskar* ("nectar ceremony"), the service of initiation for the Panj Piare. When the rite was concluded, the Guru himself was initiated by the Panj Piare. The order was then opened to anyone wishing to join, and Sikh tradition reports that enormous crowds responded.

It should be noted that, contrary to the belief of many Sikhs, some central features of the present-day Khalsa did not exist in Gobind Singh's time. For example, although the Guru required that those initiated into the Khalsa carry arms and never cut their hair (so that at least the men would never be able to deny their identity as Khalsa Sikhs), the wearing of the "Five Ks"—*kes* or *kesh* (uncut hair), *kangha* (comb), *kachha* (short trousers), *kara* (steel bracelet), and *kirpan* (ceremonial sword)—did not become an obligation of all Sikhs until the establishment of the Singh Sabha, a religious and educational reform movement of the late 19th and the early 20th century. The Sikh wedding ceremony, in which the bride and groom walk around the *Guru Granth Sahib*, is also a modern development, having replaced the essentially Hindu rite, in which the bride and groom walk around

a sacred fire, by the Anand Marriage Act of 1909. The names Singh ("Lion") for Sikh males and Kaur ("Princess") for Sikh females, formerly adopted upon initiation into the Khalsa, are now bestowed to all Sikhs in a birth and naming ceremony. All of these changes have been incorporated into the *Rahit*, the Sikh code of belief and conduct, which reached nearly its final form in the early 20th century.

Guru Gobind Singh believed that the forces of good and evil in the world sometimes fall out of balance. When the forces of evil become too great, Akal Purakh intervenes in human history to correct the balance, using particular human individuals as his agents. In Gobind Singh's time the forces of evil, represented by the Mughals under Aurangzeb, had gained the ascendance, and it was Gobind Singh's task, he believed, to right the balance. In the service of this mission, the Sikhs were justified in drawing the sword. He expressed this conviction in *Zafarnama* ("Epistle of Victory"), a letter that he addressed late in life to Aurangzeb.

Soon after the creation of the Khalsa, the Guru was attacked by other Shiwalik chieftains in league with the Mughal governor of the town of Sirhind. In 1704 he was compelled to withdraw from Anandpur, losing two of his four sons in the battle that followed. The two remaining sons were taken prisoner and delivered to the governor of Sirhind, who cruelly executed them by bricking them up alive. The fate of these two children has remained an agonizing tale for Sikhs ever since.

From Anandpur Gobind Singh escaped to southern Punjab, where he inflicted a defeat on his pursuers at Muktsar. He then moved on to Damdama, remaining there until 1706 and, according to tradition, occupying himself with the final revision of the *Adi Granth*. When Aurangzeb died in 1707, Gobind Singh agreed to accompany Aurangzeb's successor, Bahādur Shāh, to southern India. Arriving at Nanded on the banks of the Godavari River in 1708, he was assassinated by agents of the governor of Sirhind.

Guru Gobind Singh is without doubt the beau ideal of the Sikhs. Illustrations of him and of Guru Nanak are commonly found in Sikh homes. He is regarded as the supreme exemplar of all that a Sikh of the Khalsa (a Gursikh) should be. His bravery is admired, his nobility esteemed, his goodness profoundly revered. The duty of every Khalsa member, therefore, is to follow his path and to perform works that would be worthy of him.

THE 18TH AND 19TH CENTURIES

The most significant figure in Sikh history of the 18th century is Lacchman Dev, who was probably born in Punch in

Kashmir and had become a Vaishnava ascetic known as Madho Das. He journeyed to the south and was in the vicinity of Nanded at the time of Guru Gobind Singh's arrival. The two met shortly before the Guru's death, and Madho Das was instantly converted to the Sikh faith and renamed Banda ("the Slave"). The Guru also conferred on him the title of Bahadur ("the Brave"); he has been known as Banda Bahadur ever since.

According to tradition, Banda Bahadur was commissioned by Gobind Singh to mount a campaign in the Punjab against the governor of Sirhind. A *hukamnama*, or letter of command, from the Guru was entrusted to him certifying that he was the Guru's servant and encouraging all Sikhs to join him. Arriving in the Punjab with a group of 25 Sikhs, Banda issued a call to join him, and, partly because the peasants were struggling against the excessive land tax of the Mughals, he had considerable success. The fact that he had been commissioned by the 10th Guru also counted for much. The process evidently took some time, and it was not until late 1709 that Banda and his army of peasants were able to mount an attack, sacking the towns of Samana and Sadhaura.

Banda then turned his attention to the town of Sirhind and its governor, who had bricked up the two younger sons of Guru Gobind Singh. For this and many other crimes, the Sikhs believed that he merited death. Banda's army, fighting with great determination, attacked and overwhelmed Sirhind, and the governor was put to the sword. Thereafter much of the Punjab was plunged into turmoil, though Banda's army clearly was the dominant force in the early years of the rebellion. Many of the peasants had rallied to Banda, and the Mughals were exceedingly hard-pressed to maintain control. Finally, after six years of fighting, Banda was cornered in the village of Gurdas Nangal, where he chose to construct a defense by flooding a surrounding canal. This proved to be a mistake, since the Mughals only had to wait until hunger drove Banda's army to surrender. Banda was put in chains and carried to Delhi in a cage, and in June 1716 he was tortured and barbarously executed.

Although Banda is greatly admired by Sikhs for his bravery and his loyalty to the 10th Guru, he has never commanded the complete approval of the Panth. This is presumably because he introduced changes to the Khalsa, including a new greeting, "Fateh darshan" ("Facing victory!"), in place of the traditional "Fateh Vahi Guruji" ("Victory to the Guru!"). He also required his followers to be vegetarians and to wear red garments instead of the traditional blue. Those who accepted these changes were called Bandai Sikhs, while those opposed to them—led by Mata Sundari, one of Guru Gobind Singh's widows—called themselves the Tat Khalsa (the "True" Khalsa or "Pure" Khalsa), which should not be confused with the Tat Khalsa segment of the Singh Sabha, discussed below.

After the execution of Banda, the Sikhs endured several decades of persecution by the Mughals, though there were occasional periods of peace. Only the Sikhs of the Khalsa—whose identity could be easily recognized by their uncut hair and flowing beards—were persecuted; other Sikhs were seldom affected. This period, nonetheless, is remembered by Sikhs as one of great suffering, accompanied by acts of great bravery by many Khalsa Sikhs in their struggle against the Mughal authorities in Lahore.

Beginning in 1747, the ruler of Afghanistan, Aḥmad Shāh Durrānī, led a series of nine invasions of the Punjab that eventually brought Mughal power in the region to an end. In rural areas, the Sikhs took advantage of the weakening of Mughal control to form several groups later known as *misls* or *misals*. Beginning as warrior bands, the emergent *misls* and their *sardars* (chieftains) gradually established their authority over quite extensive areas.

As Mughal power declined, the *misls* eventually faced the Afghan army of Aḥmad Shāh, with whom an important Sikh tradition is associated. After the Afghans occupied the Harimandir in 1757, Dip Singh, a member of the Shahid *misl*, pledged to free the shrine or die in the attempt. His small army was met by a much larger one several kilometres from Amritsar, and in the ensuing battle Dip Singh's head was cut off. According to one version of events, the body of Dip Singh, holding the head in one hand, continued fighting, eventually dropping dead in the precincts of the Harimandir. Another account reports that the body

fought its way to the outskirts of Amritsar and then hurled the head toward the Harimandir, the head landing very close to the shrine; the place where the head is believed to have landed is marked by a hexagonal stone.

By the end of Aḥmad Shāh's invasions in 1769, the Punjab was largely in the hands of 12 *misls*, and, with the external threat removed, the *misls* turned to fighting between themselves. Eventually, one *misldar* (commander), Ranjit Singh, the leader of the Sukerchakia *misl* (named after the town of Sukkarchak in what is now northeastern Punjab province, Pakistan), which included territories north and west of Lahore, won almost complete control of the Punjab. The lone exception was the Phulkian *misl* (so called after its founder, Phul, the disciple of Guru Har Rai) on the southeastern border of the Punjab, which survived because the English East India Company had reached the Sutlej River and Ranjit Singh recognized that he was not yet ready to fight the British army. For their part, the British recognized that Ranjit Singh was in the process of establishing a strong kingdom, and, for as long as it survived, they were content to have it as a buffer state between their territories and their ultimate objective, Afghanistan.

Sikhs remember Ranjit Singh with respect and affection as their greatest leader after the Gurus. He succeeded as Sukerchakia *misldar* when his father died in 1792. By 1799 he had entered Lahore, and in 1801 he proclaimed himself maharaja of the Punjab. He sheathed the two upper stories of the Harimandir in gold leaf, thereby converting it into what became known as the Golden Temple. Within the kingdom that replaced the *misl* system, Sikhs of the Khalsa received special consideration, but places were also found for Hindus and Muslims. The army was Ranjit Singh's particular interest. His objective was to create an entirely new army on a Western model, and for this purpose he employed numerous Europeans, only the British being excepted. When his new army was ready to do battle, the city of Multan, the Vale of Kashmir, and the citadel of Peshawar were all added to the kingdom of the Punjab.

Notwithstanding his many accomplishments, Ranjit Singh failed to provide a firm financial footing for his government, nor was he interested in training a successor. When he died in 1839, he was succeeded by his eldest son, Kharak Singh, though effective authority was exercised by Kharak Singh's son Nau Nihal Singh. Kharak Singh died in 1840 as a result of excessive opium consumption, and Nau Nihal Singh was killed by a falling arch on the day of his father's funeral. The Punjab quickly descended into chaos, and, following two wars with the British, the state was annexed in 1849 to become a part of British India. After annexation, the British favoured the Sikhs for recruitment as soldiers, and many Sikhs made the British army their career.

For their loyalty to the British administration during the unsuccessful Indian Mutiny of 1857–58, the Sikhs were rewarded with grants of land and other privileges. Peace and prosperity within the Punjab made possible the founding of the first Singh Sabha, a religious and educational reform movement, in Amritsar in 1873. Its purpose was to demonstrate that Sikhs were not involved in the Indian Mutiny and to respond to signs of decay within the Panth, such as haircutting and tobacco smoking. Because the men who gathered in Amritsar were, for the most part, large landowners and persons of high status, the positions they adopted were generally conservative. In response a more radical branch of the Singh Sabha was established in Lahore in 1879. The Amritsar group came to be known as the Sanatan ("Traditional") Sikhs, whereas the radical Lahore branch was known as the Tat Khalsa.

The differences between the two groups were considerable. The Sanatan Sikhs regarded themselves as part of the wider Hindu community (then the dominant view within the Panth), and they tolerated such things as idols in the Golden Temple. The Tat Khalsa, on the other hand, insisted that Sikhism was a distinct and independent faith. The pamphlet *Ham Hindu Nahin* (1898; "We Are Not Hindus"), by the Tat Khalsa writer Kahn Singh Nabha, provided an effective slogan for the movement. Other radical adherents, influenced by Western standards of scholarship, set out to revise and rationalize the *rahit-namas* (the manuals containing the *Rahit*), removing parts that were erroneous, inconsistent, or antiquated. Many prohibitions were eliminated, though tobacco and halal meat (flesh of an animal killed according to Muslim ritual) continued to be enjoined. Their work eventually resulted in a clear statement of the Five Ks, which has since been adopted by all orthodox Sikhs. Marriage was also reformed according to Tat Khalsa views.

The controversy between the Sanatan Sikhs and the Tat Khalsa Sikhs continued for some time, as other factions within the Singh Sabha lent their support to one group or the other. Most factions, however, supported the radical group, and, by the beginning of the 20th century, the dominance of the Tat Khalsa movement had become apparent. Eventually its victory was total, and, during the early decades of the 20th century, it converted the Panth to its distinctive way of thinking, so much so that the accepted contemporary understanding of the Sikh faith is the Tat Khalsa interpretation.

THE 20TH CENTURY TO THE EARLY 21ST CENTURY

During the early 1920s the Akali movement, a semimilitary corps of volunteers raised to oppose the British government, disputed with the British over control of the larger *gurdwaras* (Punjabi: "doorways to the Guru"), the Sikh houses of worship, in the Punjab. This conflict led eventually to the adoption by the Legislative Council of the Punjab of the Sikh Gurdwaras Act of 1925, whereby the principal *gurdwaras* were entrusted to Sikh control. The *gurdwaras* have been governed ever since

by the Shiromani Gurdwara Prabandhak Committee, an elected body that is regarded by many Sikhs as the supreme authority within the Panth.

The Punjabi *Suba*

During India's struggle for independence, the Sikhs were on both sides of the conflict, many continuing to serve in the British military and others opposing the colonial government. The partition between India and Pakistan in 1947 produced deep dissatisfaction among the Sikhs, who saw the Punjab divided between the two new states. Almost all Sikhs in the western Punjab migrated to the portion retained by India. Having settled there, however, they soon felt that the government of the Indian National Congress lacked sympathy for them, a situation that was put right by the creation in 1966 of the Punjabi *suba*, or the Punjabi state, within the union of India. Because the boundaries of the Punjab were redrawn to embrace those whose first language was Punjabi, the Sikhs constituted a majority in the new state.

For four decades following partition, the Sikhs enjoyed growing prosperity, including greater educational opportunities. Tat Khalsa Sikhs had long emphasized female education at the primary and secondary levels; now stress was laid upon tertiary education for both sexes. Punjabi University in Patiala was opened in 1962 with strong Sikh support, followed by Guru Nanak University (now Guru Nanak Dev University) in Amritsar in 1969, founded to honour the quincentenary of the birth of Guru Nanak. (Another reason for the establishment of Guru Nanak University was that Punjabi University tended to favour the trading castes; Guru Nanak University, by contrast, favoured the Jats.)

The growth of the Punjab was interrupted in the mid-1980s by conflict between the central government and Sikh fundamentalists, who were demanding a separate Sikh nation-state. In an effort to reign in the principal Sikh political party, the Shiromani Akali Dal ("Leading Akali Party"), the government unwisely enlisted the support of a young Sikh fundamentalist, Jarnail Singh Bhindranwale. In 1984 Bhindranwale and his armed followers occupied the Akal Takht in the Golden Temple complex in Amritsar. In response, Indian Prime Minister Indira Gandhi ordered a military assault on the complex, which proved much more difficult than had been anticipated and led to severe damage to some of the temple buildings. Later in the year, Gandhi was assassinated by two of her Sikh bodyguards in retaliation for the assault. This in turn prompted a pogrom against the Sikhs, particularly in the Delhi area, and led to guerrilla warfare against the central government in the Punjab that lasted until 1992. At the start of the 21st century, the demands of the fundamentalists still had not been met, but at least the Punjab was quiet. Meanwhile, the appointment of Manmohan Singh, a Sikh, as prime minister in 2004 was the source of great pride in the Sikh community.

The Sikh Diaspora

Until well into the modern era, most migrant Sikhs were traders who settled in India outside the Punjab or in neighbouring lands to the west. In the late 19th century, the posting of Sikh soldiers in the British army to stations in Malaya and Hong Kong prompted Sikh emigration to those territories, which eventually became jumping-off points for further migration to Australia, New Zealand, and Fiji, especially for those seeking temporary employment as unskilled labourers. Others Sikhs discovered opportunities along the west coast of North America, the first emigrants evidently arriving in 1903. Semiskilled artisans were also transported from the Punjab to British East Africa to help in the building of railways. After World War II, Sikhs emigrated from both India and Pakistan, most going to the United Kingdom but many also headed for North America. Some of the Sikhs who had settled in eastern Africa were expelled by Ugandan dictator Idi Amin in 1972; most of them moved to the United Kingdom. In the early 21st century the Sikh population in that country was more than 300,000, and there are communities of 180,000 to 200,000 members each in the United States and Canada.

SIKH PRACTICE

A Sikh *gurdwara* includes both the house of worship proper and its associated *langar*, or communal refectory. The *Adi*

Granth must be present at the *gurdwara*, and all attending must enter with heads covered and feet bare.

THE WORSHIP SERVICE

Sikhs show their reverence by bowing their foreheads to the floor before the sacred scripture. Worship consists largely of singing hymns from the scripture, and every service concludes with Ardas, a set prayer that is divided into three parts. The first part consists of a declaration of the virtues of all the Gurus, and the last part is a brief salutation to the divine name; neither part can be changed. The middle part of the Ardas is a list, in a generally agreed form, of the trials and the triumphs of the Khalsa, which are recited in clusters by a prayer leader. The congregation responds to each cluster with a fervent "Vahiguru," which originally meant "Praise to the Guru" but is now accepted as the most common word for God. The conclusion of the service is followed by the distribution of *karah prasad*, a sacramental food that consists of equal parts of coarsely refined wheat flour, clarified butter, and raw sugar.

THE REJECTION OF CASTE

The *Adi Granth* contains a forthright condemnation of caste, and consequently there is no toleration of caste in its presence (normally in a *gurdwara*). The Gurus denounced caste as holding no importance whatsoever for access to liberation. In the *langar*, therefore, everyone must sit in a straight line, neither ahead to lay claim to higher status nor behind to denote inferiority. Indeed, the distinctive Sikh *langar* originated as a protest against the caste system. Another signal of the Sikhs' rejection of caste is the distribution of the *karah prasad*, which is prepared or donated by people of all castes.

In two areas of Sikh society, however, caste is still observed. Sikhs are normally expected to marry within their caste: Jat marries Jat, Khatri marries Khatri, and Dalit marries Dalit. In addition, Sikhs of some castes tend to establish *gurdwaras* intended for their caste only. Members of the Ramgarhia caste, for example, identify their *gurdwaras* in this way (particularly those established in the United Kingdom), as do members of the Dalit caste.

More than 60 percent of Sikhs belong to the Jat caste, which is a rural caste. The Khatri and Arora castes, both mercantile castes, form a very small minority, though they are influential within the Sikh community. Other castes represented among the Sikhs, in addition to the distinctive Sikh caste of Ramgarhias (artisans), are the Ahluwalias (formerly Kalals [brewers] who have raised their status considerably) and the two Dalit castes, known in Sikh terminology as the Mazhabis (the Chuhras) and the Ramdasias (the Chamars).

RITES AND FESTIVALS

Sikh Rahit Marayada, the manual that specifies the duties of Sikhs, names four rituals that qualify as rites of passage. The first is a birth and naming ceremony, held in a *gurdwara* when the mother is able to rise and bathe after giving birth. A hymn is selected at random from the *Guru Granth Sahib*, and a name beginning with the first letter of the hymn is chosen. Singh is added to the names of males and Kaur to females. A second rite is the *anand karaj* ("blissful union"), or marriage ceremony, which clearly distinguishes Sikhs from Hindus. The bride and groom are required to proceed four times around the *Guru Granth Sahib* to the singing of Guru Ram Das's *Suhi Chhant 2,* which differs from the Hindu custom of circling a sacred fire. The third rite—regarded as the most important—is the *amrit sanskar,* the ceremony for initiation into the Khalsa. The fourth rite is the funeral ceremony. In all cases the distinction between Sikhs and Hindus is emphasized.

The initiation rite, as set down in *Sikh Rahit Marayada,* is conducted by six initiated Sikhs, five of whom conduct the actual rite while the sixth sits in attendance on the *Guru Granth Sahib,* which must be present on such occasions. The ritual involves pouring water into a large iron bowl and adding soluble sweets. This represents the *amrit* ("nectar"), which is stirred with a double-edged sword by one of the five Sikhs. After the recitation of certain works of the Gurus, which is followed by Ardas, the candidates for initiation drink five handfuls of *amrit* offered to them. Each time, the Sikh giving it to them cries, "Vahi Guruji ka Khalsa, Vahi Guruji ki fateh" ("Praise to the Guru's Khalsa! Praise to the Guru's victory!"). *Amrit* is sprinkled over the initiates' hair and eyes five times, and they drink the remainder of the *amrit* from the same bowl. They repeat five times the *Mul Mantra* (the superscription at the beginning of the *Guru Granth Sahib*), after which the *Rahit* is expounded to them by one of the five Sikhs. They are required to wear the Five Ks and to avoid four particular sins: cutting one's hair, eating halal meat, having sexual intercourse with anyone other than one's spouse, and using tobacco. The Sikh who commits any of these cardinal sins must publicly confess and be reinitiated. Anyone who violates the *Rahit* and does not confess is branded a *patit* (apostate). If a candidate has not received a name from the *Guru Granth Sahib,* one is conferred. Finally, *karah prasad* is distributed, all taking it from the same dish.

Sikhism observes eight major festivals, as well as several others of lesser importance. Four of the main festivals are *gurpurabs,* or events commemorating important incidents in the lives of the Gurus, such as the birthdays of Nanak and Gobind Singh and the martyrdoms of Arjan and Tegh Bahadur. The remaining four are the installation of the *Guru Granth Sahib,* the New Year festival of Baisakhi, Diwali, and Hola Mahalla. Festivals are marked by processions in the streets and visits to *gurdwaras,* particularly to those associated with one of the Gurus or with some historical event. Speeches are commonly made to crowds of worshipers. Diwali, the Festival of Light, is observed by both Hindus and Sikhs; the Sikh celebration centres on the Golden Temple, which is illuminated for the occasion. For Sikhs, Diwali commemorates the release of Guru Hargobind from imprisonment by the Mughal emperor Jahāngīr in Gwalior. Hola Mahalla, which is held the day after the Hindu festival of Holi, was established by Gobind Singh as an alternative to the Hindu holiday. It was originally observed with displays of martial skills and mock battles and is now celebrated with military parades.

Sects and Other Groups

In addition to the orthodox, there are several Sikh sects. Four of these are particularly important. Sikhs can be grouped not only by their sect but also by their style of dress and by the strictness with which they observe the *Rahit*. Contrary to common belief, not all Sikhs wear uncut hair and turbans—two groups do, and two do not. Of these four groups, three have names to distinguish them; the fourth, though unnamed, is numerous and includes many Sikhs of the diaspora.

Sects

Of the four significant sects, the Nirankaris and the Nam-Dharis, or Kuka Sikhs, emerged in northwestern Punjab during the latter part of Ranjit Singh's reign. The Nirankaris were members of trading castes and followers of Baba Dayal, who had preached a return to the doctrine of *nam simaran*. With the advent of the Tat Khalsa this goal was largely achieved, and today the Nirankaris differ from orthodox Sikhs only in their recognition of a continuing line of Gurus. The Nam-Dharis also recognize a continuing line, believing that Guru Gobind Singh did not die in Nander but lived in secret until he passed the title to Balak Singh. Under the second Nam-Dhari Guru, Ram Singh, the movement's centre moved to Bhaini Sahib, where trouble with British authorities led to Ram Singh's imprisonment in Rangoon, Burma (Yangon, Myanmar). Almost all Nam-Dharis are from the carpenter caste, and most adult male Nam-Dharis are easily recognized by their white homespun turbans, which they tie horizontally across the forehead.

The third sect, the Akhand Kirtani Jatha, emerged during the early 20th century. The members of this group are distinguished by their divergent interpretation of one of the Five Ks. Instead of accepting the *kes*, or uncut hair, they maintain that the command really stands for *keski*, which means a small turban that is normally worn under the main turban. In this group, men and women must wear this variety of turban. The group is strict in its beliefs, attaching great importance to *kirtan*, or the singing of hymns, and frequently devoting the whole night to the exercise. Leadership of the sect is now largely in the hands of the trading castes, though it originally comprised followers of Randhir Singh, who was a Jat.

Another group that requires women to wear turbans is the Sikh Dharma of the Western Hemisphere, founded in the United States in 1971 by Harbhajan Singh, who was always known as Yogi Bhajan. It is commonly known as the 3HO movement (Healthy Happy Holy Organization), though this is, strictly speaking, the name only of its educational branch. Most of its followers are white Americans who lay considerable emphasis on the discipline of meditation and who practice what they call kundalini Yoga. The Sikh Dharma's relations with the orthodox Khalsa are distinctly mixed, with many other Sikhs questioning both its teachings and its economic activities. The group's observance of the *Rahit* is, however, generally acknowledged to be of a very high order.

OTHER GROUPS

As mentioned above, style of dress and strictness of observance are other ways of distinguishing among Sikhs. The Kes-Dhari, for example, is composed of Sikhs who wear the *kes*, uncut hair, required as one of the Five Ks, and includes all those whom the popular view regards as Sikhs. Not all Kes-Dharis wear all of the Five Ks, but they will at least wear the wrist ring (the *kara*), and the men will have beards and wear the Sikh turban. In some cases, beards may be surreptitiously trimmed, and, instead of wearing a standard *kirpan* (ceremonial sword), members may carry a tiny replica measuring barely one centimetre in length, which is fastened to the comb (*kangha*) that holds the hair in place under the turban. All males bear the name Singh and all females the

name Kaur, and all accept the *Rahit* to a greater or lesser degree. Many are punctilious in their acceptance of it, obeying all the regulations laid down in *Sikh Rahit Marayada*. Others are rather less observant, though they are usually careful not to violate the *Rahit* while they are in the public gaze.

The Kes-Dhari Sikhs constitute a very substantial part of the Panth, especially in the Punjab, though their exact numbers there and in the rest of the world are impossible to determine. Although the vast majority of Kes-Dharis have not been initiated into the Khalsa, in practice they are regarded (and regard themselves) as Khalsa Sikhs.

A second group comprises those who have undertaken initiation. Because this involves *amrit* ("nectar"), these Sikhs are known as Amrit-Dhari Sikhs. They are also, of course, Kes-Dharis. Thus, all Amrit-Dharis are Kes-Dharis, though not all Kes-Dharis are Amrit-Dharis. Here too any estimate of numbers must rely on guesswork, but it is likely that Amrit-Dharis account for 15 to 18 percent of all Sikhs.

The Sahaj-Dharis are one of two groups of Sikhs that do not wear uncut hair. They also reject other injunctions of the *Rahit*, and they do not adopt typical Sikh personal names. Tat Khalsa scholars once believed that *sahaj-dhari* meant "slow-adopter" and was used to designate Sikhs who were on the path to full Khalsa membership. It is more probable, however, that the term is derived from Guru Nanak's use of the word *sahaj*, meaning the ineffable bliss of the soul's liberation.

Sahaj-Dhari Sikhism is based partly on caste, attracting many members of relatively high castes who do not observe the *Rahit* for fear of losing their high-caste status. Thus, the group includes many members of the trading castes but very few Jats, the agrarian caste that constitutes more than 60 percent of the Panth. It is impossible to determine the exact number of Sahaj-Dharis, partly because many families of the trading castes have only the eldest son initiated and leave the remainder of the family free to call themselves Sikh or Hindu.

The fourth category of Sikhs consists of those who have a traditional Kes-Dhari background but who cut their hair and wear distinctive turbans only when they attend a service in their *gurdwaras*. Although they do not always use their formal Khalsa names, they do use Singh or Kaur. This variety of Sikh is particularly common in countries outside India. There is still no widely accepted term for them, though they are frequently called Mona Sikhs, *mona* meaning "shaven." This term, however, is unsuitable because it does not clearly distinguish this group of Sikhs from the Sahaj-Dharis and because it has pejorative overtones.

CONCLUSION

The Sikhs understand their religion as the product of five pivotal events. The first was the teaching of Guru Nanak: his message of liberation through meditation on the divine name. The second was the arming of the Sikhs by Guru Hargobind. The third was Guru Gobind Singh's founding of the Khalsa, its distinctive code to be observed by all who were initiated. At his death came the fourth event, the passing of the mystical Guru from its 10 human bearers to the *Guru Granth Sahib*. The final event took place early in the 20th century, when Sikhism underwent a profound reformation at the hands of the Tat Khalsa. Sikhs are universally proud of the distinct faith thus created.

JAINISM

Jainism teaches a path to spiritual purity and enlightenment through a disciplined mode of life founded upon the tradition of *ahimsa*, nonviolence to all living creatures. Beginning in the 7th–5th century BC, Jainism evolved into a cultural system that has made significant contributions to Indian philosophy and logic, art and architecture, mathematics, astronomy and astrology, and literature. Along with Hinduism and Buddhism, it is one of the three most ancient Indian religious traditions still in existence.

While often employing concepts shared with Hinduism and Buddhism, the result of a common cultural and linguistic background, the Jain tradition must be regarded as an independent phenomenon. It is an integral part of South Asian religious belief and practice, but it is not a Hindu sect or Buddhist heresy, as earlier scholars believed.

The name *Jainism* derives from the Sanskrit verb *ji*, "to conquer." It refers to the ascetic battle that it is believed Jain renunciants (monks and nuns) must fight against the passions and bodily senses to gain omniscience and purity of soul or enlightenment. The most illustrious of those few individuals who have achieved enlightenment are called *Jina* (literally, "Conqueror"), and the tradition's monastic and lay adherents are called *Jain* ("Follower of the Conquerors"), or *Jaina*. This term came to replace a more ancient designation, *Nirgrantha* ("Bondless"), originally applied to renunciants only.

Jainism has been confined largely to India, although the recent migration of Indians to other, predominantly English-speaking countries has spread its practice to many Commonwealth nations and to the United States. Precise statistics are not available, but it is estimated that there are roughly four million Jains in India and 100,000 elsewhere.

History

Jainism originated in the 7th–5th century BC in the Ganges basin of eastern India. This area was then the scene of intense religious speculation and activity. Buddhism also appeared in this region, as did other belief systems that renounced the world and opposed the ritualistic Brahmanic schools whose prestige derived from their claim of purity and their ability to perform the traditional rituals and sacrifices and to interpret their meaning. These new religious perspectives promoted asceticism, the abandonment of ritual, domestic and social action, and the attainment of

gnosis (illumination) in an attempt to win, through one's own efforts, freedom from repeated rebirth.

Early History (7th Century BC–c. 5th Century AD)

The first Jain figure for whom there is reasonable historical evidence is Parshvanatha (or Parshva), a renunciant teacher who may have lived in the 7th century BC and founded a community based upon the abandonment of worldly concerns. Jain tradition regards him as the 23rd Tirthankara (literally, "Ford-maker," i.e., one who leads the way across the stream of rebirths to salvation) of the current age (*kalpa*). The 24th and last Tirthankara of this age was Vardhamana, who is known by the epithet Mahavira ("Great Hero") and is believed to have been the last teacher of "right" knowledge, faith, and practice. Although traditionally dated to 599–527 BC, Mahavira must be regarded as a close contemporary of the Buddha (traditionally believed to have lived in 563–483 BC but who probably flourished about a century later). The legendary accounts of Mahavira's life preserved by the Jain scriptures provides the basis for his biography and enable some conclusions to be formulated about the nature of the early community he founded.

Mahavira, like the Buddha, was the son of a chieftain of the Kshatriya (warrior) class. At age 30 he renounced his princely status to take up the ascetic life. Although he was accompanied for a time by the eventual founder of the Ajivika sect, Goshala Maskariputra, Mahavira spent the next 12½ years following a path of solitary and intense asceticism. He then converted 11 disciples (called *ganadharas*), all of whom were originally Brahmans. Two of these disciples, Indrabhuti Gautama and Sudharman, both of whom survived Mahavira, are regarded as the founders of the historical Jain monastic community, and a third, Jambu, is believed to be the last person of the current age to gain enlightenment. Mahavira is believed to have died at Pavapuri, near modern Patna.

The community appears to have grown quickly. According to Jain tradition, it numbered 14,000 monks and 36,000 nuns at the time of Mahavira's death. From the beginning the community was subject to schisms over technicalities of doctrine, however, these were easily resolved. The only schism to have a lasting effect concerned a dispute over proper monastic practice, with the Shvetambara ("White-robed") sect arguing that monks and nuns should wear white robes and the Digambaras ("Sky-clad," i.e., naked) claiming that a true monk (but not a nun) should be naked. This controversy gave rise to a further dispute as to whether or not a soul can attain liberation from a female body (a possibility the Digambaras deny).

This sectarian division, still existent today, probably took time to assume formal shape. Its exact origins remain unclear, in part because the stories describing the origins of the schism were designed to justify each sect's authority and denigrate the other. These accounts were written centuries after the fact and are valueless as genuine historical testimony. The consolidation of the Shvetambara-Digambara division was probably the result of a series of councils held to codify and preserve the Jain scriptures, which had existed as oral tradition long after Mahavira's death. Of the councils recorded in Jain history, the last one, held at Valabhi in Saurashtra (in modern Gujarat) in either AD 453 or 456, without Digambara participation, codified the Shvetambara canon that is still in use. The Digambara monastic community denounced the codification, and the schism between the two communities became irrevocable.

During this period, Jainism spread westward to Ujjain, where it apparently enjoyed royal patronage. Later, in the 1st century BC, according to tradition, a monk named Kalakacarya apparently overthrew King Gardabhilla of Ujjain and orchestrated his replacement with the Shahi kings (who were probably of Scythian or Persian origin). During the reign of the Gupta dynasty (AD 320–c. 600), a time of Hindu self-assertion, the bulk of the Jain community migrated to central and western India, becoming stronger there than it had been in its original home in the Ganges basin.

EARLY MEDIEVAL DEVELOPMENTS (500–1100)

There is archaeological evidence of the presence of Jain monks in southern

India from before the Common era, and the Digambara sect has had a significant presence in what is now the state of Karnataka for almost 2,000 years. The early medieval period was the time of Digambara Jainism's greatest flowering. Enjoying success in modern-day Karnataka and in neighbouring Tamil Nadu state, the Digambaras gained the patronage of prominent monarchs of three major dynasties in the early medieval period—the Gangas in Karnataka (3rd–11th century); the Rashtrakutas, whose kingdom was just north of the Ganga realm (8th–12th century); and the Hoysalas in Karnataka (11th–14th century). Digambara monks are reputed to have engineered the succession of the Ganga and the Hoysala dynasties, thus stabilizing uncertain political situations and guaranteeing Jain political protection and support.

The Digambaras' involvement in politics allowed Jainism to prosper in Karnataka and the Deccan. Many political and aristocratic figures had Jain monks as spiritual teachers and advisers. Epigraphical evidence reveals an elaborate patronage system through which kings, queens, state ministers, and military generals endowed the Jain community with tax revenues and with direct grants for the construction and upkeep of temples. Most famously, in the 10th century the Ganga general Chamundaraya oversaw the creation of a colossal statue of Bahubali (locally called Gommateshvara; son of Rishabhanatha, the first Tirthankara) at Shravana Belgola.

During this period Digambara writers produced numerous philosophical treatises, commentaries, and poems, which were written in Prakrit, Kannada, and Sanskrit. A number of kings provided patronage for this literary activity, and some wrote various works of literature themselves. The monk Jinasena, for example, wrote Sanskrit philosophical treatises and poetry with the support of the Rashtrakuta king Amoghavarsha I. An author in Kannada and Sanskrit, Amoghavarsha apparently renounced his throne and became a disciple of Jinasena in the early 9th century.

The Shvetambaras in the north were less prominently embroiled in dynastic politics than their southern counterparts, though there is evidence of such activity in Gujarat and Rajasthan. They supported the accession of kings such as Vanaraja in the 8th century and Kumarapala, whose accession was masterminded by Hemacandra, the great Shvetambara scholar and minister of state, in the 12th century. The Shvetambaras were no less productive than their Digambara contemporaries in the amount and variety of literature they produced during this period.

While Mahavira had rejected the claims of the caste system that privileged Brahman authority on the basis of innate purity, a formalized caste system nonetheless gradually appeared among the Digambara laity in the south. This hierarchy was depicted and sanctioned by Jinasena in his *Adipurana*, a legendary biography of the Tirthankara

Rishabhanatha and his two sons Bahubali and Bharata. The hierarchy differed from the Hindu system in that the Kshatriyas were assigned a place of prominence over the Brahmans and in its connection of purity, at least theoretically, with a moral rather than a ritual source. In addition, Jinasena did not see the caste system as an inherent part of the universe, as did Hindu theologians and lawgivers.

LATE MEDIEVAL–EARLY MODERN DEVELOPMENTS (1100–1800)

In the period of their greatest influence (6th–late 12th century), Jain monks of both sects, perhaps influenced by intense lay patronage, turned from living as wandering ascetics to permanent residence in temples or monasteries. A legacy of this transformation is the contemporary Digambara practice of the *bhattaraka*, through which a cleric takes monastic initiation but, rather than assuming a life of naked ascetic wandering, becomes an orange-robed administrator and guardian of holy places and temples. Some medieval Jain writers saw this compromise with ancient scriptural requirements as both a cause of and evidence for the religion's inexorable decline. However, Jainism's marginalization in India can best be ascribed to sociopolitical factors.

The Shvetambara Jain community's eclipse was greatly accelerated by the successful invasion of western and northern India by Muslim forces in the 12th century. Although it faced persecution and the destruction of important shrines, the Jain community perhaps suffered most from the sudden shift of political control from indigenous to foreign hands and the loss of direct access to sources of power. While some Jain laymen and monks served Muslim rulers as political advisers or teachers—including Hiravijaya, who taught the Moghul emperor Akbar—the Shvetambara community was gradually compelled to redefine itself and today thrives as a mercantile group.

At roughly the same time, various Shvetambara monastic subsects (*gaccha*) appeared, forming on the basis of both regional and teacher associations. Some of the most important of these subsects still exist, such as the Kharatara Gaccha (founded 11th century) and the Tapa Gaccha (founded 13th century). The *gacchas* included lay followers, often differed markedly from one another over issues of lineage, ritual, and the sacred calendar, and claimed to represent the true Jainism. According to tradition, their leading teachers sought to reform lax monastic practice and participated in the conversion of Hindu Rajput clans in western India that subsequently became Shvetambara Jain caste groups.

Although most *gacchas* accepted the practice of image worship, the Lumpaka, or Lonka Gaccha, did not. Founded by the mid-15th-century layman Lonka Shah, the Lonka Gaccha denied the scriptural warranty of image worship and in the 17th century emerged as the non-image-worshiping Sthanakavasi sect. At the end of the 18th century, the Sthanakavasi underwent a schism when Acarya Bhikshu founded the Terapanthi ("Following the 13 Tenets") sect, which claims to have avoided heresy and laxity throughout its history by investing authority in a single teacher.

In the south, Digambara Jainism, for all its prominence in aristocratic circles, was attacked by Hindu devotional movements that arose in Tamil Nadu as early as the 6th century. One of the most vigorous of these Hindu movements was that of the Lingayats, or Virashaivas, which appeared in full force in the 12th century in northern Karnataka, a stronghold of Digambara Jainism. The Lingayats gained royal support, and many Jains themselves converted to the Lingayat religion in the ensuing centuries. With the advent of the Vijayanagar empire in the 14th century, the Digambara Jains lost much of their royal support and survived only in peripheral areas of the southwest and in pockets of the north.

As with the Shvetambaras, the Digambara laity were among the most strident critics of their community's deteriorating situation. The most significant Digambara reform movement occurred in the early 17th century, led by the layman and poet Banarsidas. This movement stressed the mystical elements of the Jain path and attacked what it saw as the emptiness of Digambara temple ritual and the profligacy of the community's clerical leaders.

LATER JAIN HISTORY

By the middle of the 19th century, image-worshiping Shvetambara monks had virtually disappeared, and control of temples and ritual passed into the hands of quasi-monastic clerics known as *yati*. Monastic life, however, experienced a revival under the auspices of charismatic monks such as Atmaramji (1837–96), and the number of Shvetambara image-worshiping renunciants grew to approximately 1,500 monks and 4,500 nuns in the 20th century. The Tapa Gaccha is the largest subsect; the non-image-worshiping Shvetambara sects (the Sthanakavasis and Terapanthis) are smaller in number. The Digambara monastic community also experienced a revival of its ideals in the early 20th century with the ascendence of the great monk Acarya Shantisagar, from whom virtually all the 120 or so contemporary Digambara monks claim lineal descent.

In modern times the Shvetambara and Digambara communities in India have devoted much energy to preserving temples and publishing their religious texts. The Jains also have been involved in general welfare work, such as drought relief in Gujarat in the 1980s, support for Jain widows and the poor, and, as part of their philosophy of nonviolence and vegetarianism, maintaining shelters to save old animals from slaughter.

During the 20th century, Jainism evolved into a worldwide faith. As a result of age-old trading links, many Jains from western India settled in eastern African countries, most notably Kenya and Uganda. Political unrest in the 1960s compelled many of them to relocate to the United Kingdom, where the first Jain temple outside India was consecrated in Leicester, and then increasingly to the United States and Canada, where they successfully assumed their traditional mercantile and professional occupations. A desire to preserve their religious identity has led expatriate Jains to form trans-sectarian organizations such as the Jain Samaj, founded in Europe in 1970, and the Federation of Jain Associations in North America, founded in 1981. English-language publications such as *Jain Digest* and *Jain Spirit* have presented Jain ideals, such as nonviolence, vegetarianism, and, most recently, environmentalism, to members of the Jain diaspora and the wider world.

IMPORTANT FIGURES OF JAIN LEGEND

The Jains developed their own legendary history, the *Deeds of the 63 Illustrious Men*, which Western scholars call the *Universal History*. The most important figures in this history are the 24 Tirthankaras, perfected human beings who appear from time to time to preach and embody the faith. Other important figures in the history are from the Hindu tradition, most notably Krishna—regarded by the Jains as a cousin of the 22nd Tirthankara, Arishtanemi—and the hero Rama, who is treated as a pious, nonviolent Jain. By incorporating yet redefining such important Hindu figures, the Jains were able to both remain part of and separate from the surrounding Hindu world.

DOCTRINES OF JAINISM

Even though Jain doctrine holds that no one can achieve liberation in this corrupt time, the Jain religious goal is the complete perfection and purification of the soul. This, they believe, occurs only when the soul is in a state of eternal liberation from corporeal bodies. Liberation of the soul is impeded by the accumulation of *karman*s, bits of material, generated by a person's actions, that attach themselves to the soul and consequently bind it to physical bodies through many births. This has the effect of thwarting the full self-realization and freedom of the soul. As a result, Jain renunciants do not seek immediate enlightenment; instead, through disciplined and meritorious practice of nonviolence, they pursue a human rebirth that will bring them nearer to that state. To understand how the Jains address this problem, it is first necessary to consider the Jain conception of reality.

TIME AND THE UNIVERSE

Time, according to the Jains, is eternal and formless. It is understood as a wheel with 12 spokes (*ara*), the equivalent of ages, six of which form an ascending arc and six a descending one. In the ascending arc (*utsarpini*), humans progress in knowledge, age, stature, and happiness, while in the descending arc (*avasarpini*) they deteriorate. The two cycles joined together make one rotation of the wheel of time, which is called a *kalpa*. These *kalpas* repeat themselves without beginning or end.

The Jain world is eternal and uncreated. Its constituent elements, the five basics of reality (*astikayas*), are soul, matter, space, the principles of motion, and the arrest of motion; for the Digambaras there is a sixth substance, time. These elements are eternal and indestructible, but their conditions change constantly, manifesting three characteristics: arising, stability, and falling away. On this basis, Jainism claims to provide a more realistic analysis of the world and its complexities than Hinduism or Buddhism.

Jains divide the inhabited universe into five parts. The lower world (*adholoka*) is subdivided into seven tiers of hells, each one darker and more painful than the one above it. The middle world (*madhyaloka*) comprises a vast number of concentric continents separated by seas. At the centre is the continent of Jambudvipa. Human beings occupy Jambudvipa, the second continent contiguous to it, and half of the third. The focus of Jain activity, however, is Jambudvipa, the only continent on which it is possible for the soul to achieve liberation. The celestial world (*urdhvaloka*) consists of two categories of heaven: one for the souls of those who may or may not have entered the Jain path and another for those who are far along on the path, close to their emancipation. At the apex of the occupied universe is the *siddhashila*, the crescent-shaped abode of liberated souls (*siddhas*). Finally, there are some areas inhabited solely by *ekendriyas*, single-sense organisms that permeate the occupied universe.

JIVA AND AJIVA

Jain reality comprises two components, *jiva* ("soul," or "living substance") and *ajiva* ("nonsoul," or "inanimate substance"). *Ajiva* is further divided into two categories: nonsentient material entities and nonsentient nonmaterial entities.

The essential characteristics of *jiva* are consciousness (*cetana*), bliss (*sukha*), and energy (*virya*). In its pure state, *jiva* possesses these qualities limitlessly. The souls, infinite in number, are divisible in their embodied state into two main classes, immobile and mobile, according to the number of sense organs possessed by the body they inhabit. The first group consists of souls inhabiting immeasurably small particles of earth, water, fire, and air, along with the vegetable kingdom, which possess only the sense of touch. The second group comprises souls that inhabit bodies that have between two and five sense organs. Moreover, the universe is populated with an infinite number of minute beings, *nigodas*, some of which are slowly evolving while the rest have no chance of emerging from their hapless state.

Formless and genderless, *jiva* cannot be directly perceived by the senses. Like the universe, it is without a point of ultimate origin or end. While not all-pervasive, it can, by contraction or expansion, occupy various amounts of space. Like the light of a lamp in a small or a large room, *jiva* can fill both the smaller and the larger bodies it occupies. The soul assumes the exact dimensions of the body it occupies, but it is not identical with that body. On death it assumes the shape of the last physical body that housed it.

Matter (*pudgala*) has the characteristics of touch, taste, smell, and colour; however, its essential characteristic is lack of consciousness. The smallest unit of matter is the atom (*paramanu*). Heat, light, and shade are all forms of fine matter.

The nonsentient nonmaterial substances are space, time, and the principles of motion and its arrest. They are always pure and are not subject to defilement. The principles of motion and its arrest permeate the universe; they do not exist independently but rather form a necessary precondition for any object's movement or coming to rest.

KARMAN

The fundamental tenet of Jain doctrine is that all phenomena are linked in a universal chain of cause and effect. Every event has a definite cause. By nature each soul is pure, possessing infinite knowledge, bliss, and power; however, these faculties are restricted throughout time by the soul's contact with matter. This matter, which produces the chain of cause and effect, of birth and death, is *karman* (anglicized as *karma*), an atomic substance and not a process, as it is in Hinduism and Buddhism. To be free from the shackles of *karman*, a person must

stop the influx of new *karmans* and eliminate the acquired ones.

Karmic particles are acquired as the result of intentional "passionate" action, though the very earliest Jain teachings on this subject claimed that any action, even if unintentional, attracted *karman*. Acquired *karmans* can be annihilated through a process called *nirjara* ("wearing away"), which includes fasting, restricting diet, controlling taste, retreating to lonely places, along with mortifications of the body, atonement and expiation for sins, modesty, service, study, meditation, and renunciation of the ego. *Nirjara* is, thus, the calculated cessation of passionate action.

Because of *karman* a soul is imprisoned in a succession of bodies and passes through various stages of spiritual development before becoming free from all karmic bondage. These stages of development (*gunasthanas*) involve progressive manifestations of the innate faculties of knowledge and power and are accompanied by decreasing sinfulness and increasing purity.

THEORIES OF KNOWLEDGE AS APPLIED TO LIBERATION

In Jain thought, four stages of perception—observation, will to recognize, determination, and impression—lead to subjective cognition (*matijnana*), the first of five kinds of knowledge (*jnana*). The second kind, *shrutajnana*, derives from the scriptures and general information. Both are mediated cognition, based on external conditions perceived by the senses. In addition there are three kinds of immediate knowledge—*avadhi* (supersensory perception), *manahparyaya* (reading the thoughts of others), and *kevala* (omniscience). *Kevala* is necessarily accompanied by freedom from karmic obstruction and by direct experience of the soul's pure form unblemished by attachment to matter. Omniscience, the foremost attribute of a liberated *jiva*, is the emblem of its purity; thus, a liberated soul, such as a Tirthankara, is called a *kevalin* ("possessor of omniscience"). However, not all *kevalins* are Tirthankaras: becoming a Tirthankara requires the development of a particular type of karmic destiny.

For the Jains all knowledge short of omniscience is flawed. Because reality is characterized by arising, change, and decay, as opposed to simple permanence (for the Hindus) and impermanence (for the Buddhists), the Jains developed an epistemological system based on seven perspectives (*naya*). This system, *anekanta-vada*, "the many-pointed doctrine," takes into account the provisional nature of mundane knowledge. To gain some approximation to reality, a judgment must ideally be framed in accord with all seven perspectives.

According to Jainism, Yoga, the ascetic physical and meditative discipline of the monk, is the means to attain omniscience and thus *moksha*, or liberation. Yoga is the cultivation of true knowledge of reality, faith in the teachings of the Tirthankaras, and pure conduct; it is thus intimately connected to the Three Jewels (*ratnatraya*) of right knowledge, right faith, and right practice (respectively, *samyagjnana*, *samyagdarshana*, and *samyakcaritra*).

JAIN ETHICS

The Three Jewels constitute the basis of the Jain doctrinal and ethical stance. Right knowledge, faith, and practice must be cultivated together because none of them can be achieved in the absence of the others. Right faith leads to calmness or tranquillity, detachment, kindness, and the renunciation of pride of birth, beauty of form, wealth, scholarship, prowess, and fame. Right faith leads to perfection only when followed by right practice. Yet, there can be no virtuous conduct without right knowledge, the clear distinction between the self and the nonself. Knowledge without faith and conduct is futile. Without purification of mind, all austerities are mere bodily torture. Right practice is thus spontaneous, not a forced mechanical quality. Attainment of right practice is a gradual process, and a layperson can observe only partial self-control; a renunciant, however, is able to observe more comprehensive rules of conduct.

Two separate courses of conduct are laid down for the ascetics and the laity. In both cases the code of morals is based on the doctrine of *ahimsa*, or nonviolence. Because thought gives rise to action, violence in thought merely precedes violent behaviour.

Violence in thought, then, is the greater and subtler form of violence because it arises from ideas of attachment and aversion, grounded in passionate states, which result from negligence or lack of care in behaviour. Jainism enjoins avoidance of all forms of injury—whether committed by body, mind, or speech—and subscribes emphatically to the teaching that "nonviolence is the highest form of religious practice." For Jains, this principle, which manifests itself most obviously in the form of vegetarianism, is the single most important component of their tradition's message. Notable in this connection is the friendship between the Jain layman Raychandrabhai Mehta and Mohandas (later Mahatma) Gandhi, who considered his interactions with Mehta to have been important in formulating his own ideas on the use of nonviolence as a political tactic.

RITUAL PRACTICES AND RELIGIOUS INSTITUTIONS

Along with Buddhism, Jainism is the only surviving religion to have begun as a purely monastic religion. The rules for the laity are derived from monastic rules.

MONKS, NUNS, AND THEIR PRACTICES

Shvetambara monks are allowed to retain a few possessions such as a robe, an alms bowl, a whisk broom, and a *mukhavastrika* (a piece of cloth held over the mouth to protect against the ingestion of small insects), which are presented by a senior monk at the time of initiation. For the non-image-worshiping Sthanakavasis and the Terapanthis, the *mukhavastrika* must be worn at all times. After initiation a monk must adhere to the "great vows" (*mahavratas*) to avoid injuring any life-form, lying, stealing, having sexual intercourse, or accepting personal possessions. To help him keep his vows, a monk's life is carefully regulated in all details by specific ordinances and by the oversight of his superiors. For example, to help him observe the vow of nonviolence, a monk may not take his simple, vegetarian meals after dark, because to do so would increase the possibility of harming insects that might be attracted to the food. In addition, drinking water must first be boiled to ensure that there are no life-forms in it. Monks are expected to suffer with equanimity hardships imposed by the weather, geographic terrain, travel, or physical abuse; however, exceptions are allowed in emergencies, since a monk who survives a calamity can purify himself by confession and by practicing even more rigorous austerities.

Digambara monks take the same "great vows" as do the Shvetambara, but in acknowledgement of a much more intense interpretation of the vow of nonpossession, full-fledged Digambara monks remain naked, while lower-grade Digambara monks wear a loincloth and keep with them one piece of cloth not more than 1.5 yards (1.4 metres) long. Digambara monks use a peacock-feather duster to sweep the ground where they walk to avoid injuring any life-forms and drink water from a gourd. They beg for their only meal of the day using the cupped palms of their hand as an alms bowl. They regard their interpretation of the Jain monastic vocation as more in accord with the ancient model than that followed by the Shvetambaras.

All Jain renunciants must exercise the three *guptis* (care in thought, speech, and action) and the five *samitis* (types of vigilance over conduct). Essential to regular monastic ritual are the six "obligatory actions" (*avashyaka*), practiced daily and at important times of the ritual calendar: equanimity (*samayika*, a form of contemplative activity, which, in theory operates throughout the monk's entire career); praise of the Tirthankaras; obeisance to the Tirthankaras, teachers, and scriptures; confession; resolution to avoid sinful activities; and "abandonment of the body" (standing or sitting in a meditative posture).

The type of austerities in which a monk engages, the length of time he practices them, and their severity are carefully regulated by his preceptor, who

Two Indian Jain monks walk barefoot in Mumbai, India. Jain monks spread word of the Jain religion and preach the principle of ahimsa, or non-violence. *Sebastian D'Souza/AFP/ Getty Images*

takes into account the monk's spiritual development, his capacity to withstand the austerities, and his ability to understand how they help further his spiritual progress. The theoretical culmination of a monk's ascetic rigours is the act of *sallekhana*, in which he lies on one side on a bed of thorny grass and ceases to move or eat. This act of ritual starvation is the monk's ultimate act of nonattendance, by which he lets go of the body for the sake of his soul. Jain ideology views this as the ultimate act of self-control and triumph over the passions, rather than simply as suicide. While widely followed in ancient and medieval times, *sallekhana* is much less common today.

Both the Shvetambaras and Digambaras allow the initiation of nuns, and among the Shvetambaras, nuns outnumber monks by a ratio of approximately 3 to 1. Nevertheless, the status of Jain nuns is less prestigious than that of monks, to whom they are obliged by convention and textual stipulation to defer, despite the fact that these nuns are often women of great learning and spiritual attainment. In Digambara Jainism, nuns, who wear robes, accept the necessity of being reborn as men before they can advance significantly on the ascetic path.

RELIGIOUS ACTIVITY OF THE LAITY

While Jain literature from earliest times emphasizes the place of the monk and his concerns, it is clear that almost from the religion's outset the majority of Jains have been laypersons who support the community of renunciants. The medieval period was a time of particularly intense reflection by both Shvetambara and Digambara monks on the role of the laity. Many treatises discussing the layman's religious behaviour and vows were produced between the 5th and 17th century. According to these writings, lay behaviour should mirror the ascetic "great vows." Jain doctrine, however, holds that while the ascetic path can lead to the destruction (*nirjara*) of *karman*, the lay path allows only for the warding off (*samvara*) of new *karman* and thus does not radically alter an individual's karmic status.

The layman (Jainism's focus is invariably upon the male) is enjoined to observe eight basic rules of behaviour, which vary but usually include the avoidance of night eating, as well as a diet that excludes meat, wine, honey, and types of fruits and roots deemed to harbour life-forms. There are also 12 vows to be taken: five *anuvrata*s ("little vows"), three *gunavrata*s, and four *shikshavrata*s. The *anuvrata*s are vows to abstain from violence, falsehood, and stealing; to be content with one's own wife; and to limit one's possessions. The other vows are supplementary and meant to strengthen and protect the *anuvrata*s. They involve avoidance of unnecessary travel, of harmful activities, and of the pursuit of pleasure; fasting and control of diet; offering gifts and service to monks, the poor, and fellow believers; and voluntary death if the observance of the major vows proves impossible.

Lay people are further enjoined to perform the six "obligatory actions" at regular intervals, especially the *samayika*, a meditative and renunciatory ritual of limited duration. This ritual is intended to strengthen the resolve to pursue the spiritual discipline of Jain *dharma* (moral virtue) and is thought to bring the lay votary close to the demands required of an ascetic. It may be performed at home, in a temple, in a fasting hall, or before a monk.

Dating from early in the history of Jainism are 11 stages of a layman's spiritual progress, or *pratima* ("statue").

Medieval writers conceived *pratima* as a ladder leading to higher stages of spiritual development. The last two stages lead logically to renunciation of the world and assumption of the ascetic life.

It was natural for monastic legislators to portray the careers of idealized lay people as a preparatory stage to the rigours of ascetic life, but for Jain lay life to have meaning it need not necessarily culminate in initiation as a monk. With its careful rules about food, its regular ceremonies and cultural traditions, Jainism

Jain worshipers offer prayers at Hutheesing Jain Temple in Ahmedabad, Gujarat, in 2009, during the first day of the holiday of Holy Parushan Parva. Sam Panthaky/AFP/Getty Images

provides the laity a rounded social world. Typically, Jain lay life is characterized by strict vegetarianism, disciplined business or professional activity, and responsible conduct of family affairs with a view to establishing a sound social reputation. Lay Jains believe that pious activity—including fasting and almsgiving, and especially the practice of nonviolence—enables an individual not only to advance a little further along the path to final liberation but to improve his current material situation. As a result, there is a stark contrast between the great prosperity of the Jain lay community and the austere self-denial of the monks and nuns it supports.

Until very recently Jainism had not developed any distinctive life-cycle rituals for events such as birth and marriage, although in the 9th century the Digambara monk Jinasena attempted to legislate in this area. In general, practice has tended to conform to prevailing local custom, provided this does not infringe on basic Jain principles.

IMAGE WORSHIP

Temple worship is mentioned in early texts that describe gods paying homage to images and relics of Tirthankaras in heavenly eternal shrines. While Mahavira himself appears to have made no statement regarding image worship, it quickly became a vital part of the Jain tradition. Numerous images of Tirthankaras in the sitting and standing postures dating from the early Common era have been uncovered in excavations of a Jain stupa, or funerary monument, at Mathura in Uttar Pradesh. The earliest images of Tirthankaras are all nude and distinguished by carved inscriptions of their names on the pedestals. By the 5th century, symbols specific to each Tirthankara (e.g., a lion for Mahavira) began to appear. The practice of associating one of the 24 shasanadevatas ("doctrine goddesses") with images of individual Tirthankaras began in the 9th century. Some of these goddesses, such as Ambika ("Little Mother"), who is associated with the Tirthankara Arishtanemi, continue to have great importance for the Jain devotee. The images are generally located near the entrance to Jain temples and can be propitiated for aid in worldly matters.

Closely associated with the obligatory rites of the laity, worship (puja) can be made to all liberated souls, to monks, and to the scriptures. The focus for most image-worshiping Jains (murtipujaka) is the icon of the Tirthankara located in the central shrine room of the temple or, alternatively, in a domestic shrine. Temples also house subsidiary Tirthankara images. Although Tirthankaras remain unaffected by offerings and worship and cannot, as individuals who are liberated from rebirth, respond in any way, such devotional actions serve as a form of meditative discipline. Daily worship includes hymns of praise and prayers, the recitation of sacred formulas and the names of the Tirthankaras, and idol worship—bathing the image and making offerings to it of flowers, fruit, and rice. Shvetambaras also decorate images with clothing and ornaments. A long-standing debate within both Jain communities concerns the relative value of external acts of worship and internalized acts of mental discipline and meditation. Monks and nuns of all sects are prohibited from displays of physical worship.

Festivals

Important days in the Jain calendar are called *parvan*, and on these days religious observances, such as structured periods of fasting and festivals, take place. The principal Jain festivals can generally be connected with the five major events in the life of each Tirthankara: descent into his mother's womb, birth, renunciation, attainment of omniscience, and final emancipation.

The Jain calendar includes many festivals. Among them is the Shvetambara fasting ceremony, *oli*, which is celebrated for nine days twice a year (in March–April and September–October) and which corresponds to the mythical celestial worship of the images of the Tirthankaras. The most significant time of the Jain ritual year, however, is the four-month period, generally running from late July to early November, when monks and nuns abandon the wandering life and live in the midst of lay communities. For Shvetambaras, the single most important festival, Paryushana, occurs in the month of Bhadrapada (August–September). *Paryushana* ("Abiding") designates, on

the one hand, pacification by forgiving and service with wholehearted effort and devotion and, on the other, staying at one place for the monsoon season. The festival is characterized by fasting, preaching, and scriptural recitation. On its last day, Samvatsari ("Annual"), alms are distributed to the poor, and a Jina image is ceremonially paraded through the streets. A communal confession is performed by the laity, and letters are sent asking for forgiveness and the removal of all ill feelings about conscious or unconscious misdeeds during the past year. The equivalent Digambara festival is called Dashalakshanaparvan ("Observance Day of the 10 Religious Qualities") and centres on the public display of an important text, the *Tattvartha-sutra*.

On the full-moon day of the month of Karttika (October–November), at the same time that Hindus celebrate Diwali (the festival of lights), Jains commemorate the nirvana (final liberation) of Mahavira by lighting lamps. Another important Shvetambara ceremony, Jnanapancami (literally "Knowledge Fifth," where "Fifth" signifies a date), occurs five days later and is celebrated with temple worship and with reverence of the scriptures. The equivalent Digambara festival takes place in May–June. Mahavira Jayanti, the birthday of Mahavira, is celebrated by both sects in early April with public processions.

The most famous of all Jain festivals, Mastakabhisheka ("Head Anointment"), is performed every 12 years at the Digambara sacred complex at Shravana

Belgola ("White Lake of the Ascetics") in Karnataka state. In this ceremony, the 57-foot- (17-metre-) high statue of Bahubali is anointed from above with a variety of substances (water, milk, flowers, etc.) in the presence of an audience that can approach one million.

Pilgrimage

Pilgrimage, viewed as a particularly meritorious activity, is popular among renunciants and laity alike. Places of pilgrimage were created during the medieval period at sites marking the principal events in the lives of Tirthankaras, some of which were destroyed during the Muslim invasions, which started in the eighth century. Parasnath Hill and Rajgir in Bihar state and Shatrunjaya and Girnar hills on the Kathiawar Peninsula are among such important ancient pilgrimage sites. Other shrines that have become pilgrimage destinations are Shravana Belgola in Karnataka state, Mounts Abu and Kesariaji in Rajasthan state, and Antariksha Parshvanatha in Akola district of Maharashtra. For those unable to go on pilgrimage to the most famous sites, it is possible to worship their depictions in local temples. Small regional networks of shrines are also regarded as simulacra of the great pilgrimage sites.

JAINISM AND OTHER RELIGIONS

Jainism, Hinduism, and Buddhism share many key concepts derived from the Sanskrit language and dialects that have enabled them to hone their religious debates. For example, all three traditions share a notion of *karman* as the actions of individuals that determine their future births; yet each has attached unique connotations to the concept. This is also true with terms such as *dharma* (often translated "duty," "righteousness," or "religious path"), *yoga* ("ascetic discipline"), and *yajna* ("sacrifice," or "worship"). This Sanskritic discourse has shaped the religious and philosophical speculations, as well as the polemics, of each of these traditions.

The same circumstance occurs in the ritual and literature of each religion. In the ritual sphere, for example, the *abhiseka*, or head-anointing ritual, has had great significance in all three religions. The best-known example of this ritual is the one performed every 12 to 14 years on the statue of Bahubali at the Jain pilgrimage site at Shravana Belgola. The structure of this ritual is similar in each religious context, but it has a unique meaning in each tradition. In the literary sphere, each tradition developed an extensive corpus of canonical and commentarial literature, and each has developed a body of narrative literature. For example, so great was the influence of the story of Rama in the classical Hindu *Ramayana* that the Buddhists and Jains felt obliged to retell the story in their own terms. Jain literature includes 16 different versions of this story in Sanskrit and Prakrit.

Muslim influence on Jainism can be seen in a number of areas. It has been suggested that the concept of *ashatanas*—activities that are unsuitable or indecent in a temple—reveals a notion of the sanctity of the temple that recalls Muslim *barakah* ("holiness") more than any traditional Jain attitude. The most obvious Islamic influence is in the repudiation of image worship by the Shvetambara Lonkasaha sect.

Jain influence at the Mughal court of Akbar is a bright chapter in Jain history. Akbar honoured Hiravijaya Suri, then the leader of the Shvetambara Tapa Gaccha. His disciples and other monks gained the respect of the Mughal emperors Jahangir and Shah Jahan and even the Muslim chauvinist Aurangzeb. Moreover, Akbar prohibited animal slaughter near important Jain sites during the Paryushana festival. Jahangir also issued decrees for the protection of Shatrunjaya, and Aurangzeb recognized Jain proprietary rights over Mount Shatrunjaya. Mughal painting, influential in different schools of Indian painting, also influenced Jain miniature painting. In this way these ancient religions demonstrated respect for other traditions, which is one of the great strengths of Indian civilization.

BUDDHISM

Buddhism arose in northeastern India sometime between the late 6th century and the early 4th century BC, a period of great social change and intense religious activity. There is disagreement among scholars about the dates of the Buddha's birth and death. Many modern scholars believe that the historical Buddha lived from about 563 to about 483 BC. Many others believe that he lived about 100 years later (from about 448 to 368 BC). At this time in India, there was much discontent with Brahmanic (Hindu high-caste) sacrifice and ritual. In northwestern India there were ascetics who tried to create a more personal and spiritual religious experience than that found in the Vedas (Hindu sacred scriptures). In the literature that grew out of this movement, the Upanishads, a new emphasis on renunciation and transcendental knowledge can be found. Northeastern India, which was less influenced by those who had developed the main tenets and practices of the Vedic Hindu faith, became the breeding ground of many new sects. Society in this area was troubled by the breakdown of tribal unity and the expansion of several petty kingdoms. Religiously, this was a time of doubt, turmoil, and experimentation.

A proto-Samkhya group (i.e., one based on the Samkhya school of Hinduism founded by Kapila) was already well established in the area. New sects abounded, including various skeptics (e.g., Sanjaya Belatthiputta), atomists (e.g., Pakudha Kaccayana), materialists (e.g., Ajita Kesakambali), and antinomians (i.e., those against rules or laws—e.g., Purana Kassapa). The most important sects to arise at the time of the Buddha, however, were the Ajivikas (Ajivakas), who emphasized the rule of fate (*niyati*), and the Jains, who stressed the need to free the soul from matter. Although the Jains, like the Buddhists, have often been regarded as atheists, their beliefs are actually more complicated. Unlike early Buddhists, both the Ajivikas and the Jains believed in the permanence of the elements that constitute the universe, as well as in the existence of the soul.

Despite the bewildering variety of religious communities, many shared the same vocabulary—*nirvana* (transcendent freedom), *atman* ("self" or "soul"), *yoga* ("union"), *karma* ("causality"), *Tathagata* ("one who has come" or "one who has thus gone"), *buddha* ("enlightened one"), *samsara* ("eternal recurrence" or "becoming"), and *dhamma* ("rule" or "law")—and most

involved the practice of Yoga. According to tradition, the Buddha himself was a yogi—that is, a miracle-working ascetic.

Buddhism, like many of the sects that developed in northeastern India at the time, was constituted by the presence of a charismatic teacher, by the teachings this leader promulgated, and by a community of adherents that was often made up of renunciant members and lay supporters. In the case of Buddhism, this pattern is reflected in the Triratna—i.e., the "Three Jewels" of Buddha (the teacher), *dharma* (the teaching), and *sangha* (the community).

In the centuries following the founder's death, Buddhism developed in two

BUDDHA

(fl. c. 6th–4th century BC, Lumbini, near Kapilavastu, Shakya republic, Kosala kingdom [now in Nepal]—d. Kusinara, Malla republic, Magadha kingdom [now Kasia, India])

Born Siddhartha Gautama, Buddha became the spiritual leader and founder of Buddhism. The term buddha *(Sanskrit: "awakened one") is a title rather than a name, and Buddhists believe that there are an infinite number of past and future buddhas. The historical Buddha, referred to as the Buddha Gautama or simply as the Buddha, was born a prince of the Shakyas, on the India-Nepal border. He is said to have lived a sheltered life of luxury that was interrupted when he left the palace and encountered an old man, a sick man, and a corpse. Renouncing his princely life, he spent six years seeking out teachers and trying various ascetic practices, including fasting, to gain enlightenment. Unsatisfied with the results, he meditated beneath the bodhi tree, where, after temptations by Mara, he realized the Four Noble Truths and achieved enlightenment. At Sarnath he preached his first sermon to his companions, outlining the Eightfold Path, which offered a middle way between self-indulgence and self-mortification and led to the liberation of nirvana. The five ascetics who heard this sermon became not only his first disciples but also arhats who would enter nirvana upon death. His mission fulfilled, the Buddha died after eating a meal that may accidentally have contained spoiled pork and escaped the cycle of rebirth; his body was cremated, and stupas were built over his relics.*

directions represented by two different groups. One was called the Hinayana (Sanskrit: "Lesser Vehicle"), a term given to it by its Buddhist opponents. This more conservative group, which included what is now called the Theravada (Pali: "Way of the Elders") community, compiled versions of the Buddha's teachings that had been preserved in collections called the *Sutta Pitaka* and the *Vinaya Pitaka* and retained them as normative. The other major group, which calls itself the Mahayana (Sanskrit: "Greater Vehicle"), recognized the authority of other teachings that, from the group's point of view, made salvation available to a greater number of people. These supposedly more advanced teachings were expressed in sutras that the Buddha purportedly made available only to his more advanced disciples.

As Buddhism spread, it encountered new currents of thought and religion. In some Mahayana communities, for example, the strict law of karma (the belief that virtuous actions create pleasure in the future and nonvirtuous actions create pain) was modified to accommodate new emphases on the efficacy of ritual actions and devotional practices. During the second half of the 1st millennium AD, a third major Buddhist movement, Vajrayana (Sanskrit: "Diamond Vehicle"), or Esoteric Buddhism, developed in India. This movement was influenced by gnostic and magical currents pervasive at that time, and its aim was to obtain spiritual liberation and purity more speedily.

Despite these vicissitudes, Buddhism did not abandon its basic principles. Instead, they were reinterpreted, rethought, and reformulated in a process that led to the creation of a great body of literature. This literature includes the Pali *Tipitaka* ("Three Baskets")—the *Sutta Pitaka* ("Basket of Discourse"), which contains the Buddha's sermons; the *Vinaya Pitaka* ("Basket of Discipline"), which contains the rule governing the monastic order; and the *Abhidhamma Pitaka* ("Basket of Special [Further] Doctrine"), which contains doctrinal systematizations and summaries. These Pali texts have served as the basis for a long and very rich tradition of commentaries that were written and preserved by adherents of the Theravada community. The Mahayana and Vajrayana/Esoteric traditions have accepted as Buddhavacana ("the word of the Buddha") many other sutras and tantras, along with extensive treatises and commentaries based on these texts. Consequently, from the first sermon of the Buddha at Sarnath to the most recent derivations, there is an indisputable continuity—a development or metamorphosis around a central nucleus—by virtue of which Buddhism is differentiated from other religions.

THE BUDDHA'S MESSAGE

The teaching attributed to the Buddha was transmitted orally by his disciples, prefaced by the phrase "evam me sutam" ("thus have I heard"); therefore, it is difficult to say whether or to what extent

This 2nd-century BC stone statue of Buddha begging for alms is located in the Ajanta caves in Maharashtra, India. Dinodia Photos/Hulton Archive/Getty Images

his discourses have been preserved as they were spoken. They usually allude to the place and time they were preached and to the audience to which they were addressed. Buddhist councils in the first centuries after the Buddha's death attempted to specify which teachings attributed to the Buddha could be considered authentic.

SUFFERING, IMPERMANENCE, AND NO-SELF

The Buddha based his entire teaching on the fact of human suffering and the ultimately dissatisfying character of human life. Existence is painful. The conditions that make an individual are precisely those that also give rise to dissatisfaction and suffering. Individuality implies limitation; limitation gives rise to desire; and, inevitably, desire causes suffering, since what is desired is transitory.

Living amid the impermanence of everything and being themselves impermanent, human beings search for the way of deliverance, for that which shines beyond the transitoriness of human existence—in short, for enlightenment. The Buddha's doctrine offered a way to avoid despair. By following the "path" taught by the Buddha, the individual can dispel the "ignorance" that perpetuates this suffering.

According to the Buddha of the early texts, reality, whether of external things or the psychophysical totality of human individuals, consists of a succession and concatenation of microelements called dhammas (these "components" of reality are not to be confused with dhamma meaning "law" or "teaching"). The Buddha departed from traditional Indian thought in not asserting an essential or ultimate reality in things. Moreover, he rejected the existence of the soul as a metaphysical substance, though he recognized the existence of the self as the subject of action in a practical and moral sense. Life is a stream of becoming, a series of manifestations and extinctions. The concept of the individual ego is a popular delusion; the objects with which people identify themselves—fortune, social position, family, body, and even mind—are not their true selves. There is nothing permanent, and, if only the permanent deserved to be called the self, or atman, then nothing is self.

To make clear the concept of no-self (anatman), Buddhists set forth the theory of the five aggregates or constituents (khandhas) of human existence: (1) corporeality or physical forms (rupa), (2) feelings or sensations (vedana), (3) ideations (sanna), (4) mental formations or dispositions (sankhara), and (5) consciousness (vinnana). Human existence is only a composite of the five aggregates, none of which is the self or soul. A person is in a process of continuous change, and there is no fixed underlying entity.

KARMA

The belief in rebirth, or samsara, as a potentially endless series of worldly existences in which every being is caught up was already associated with the doctrine of karma (Sanskrit: *karman*; literally "act" or "deed") in pre-Buddhist India, and it was accepted by virtually all Buddhist traditions. According to the doctrine, good conduct brings a pleasant and happy result and creates a tendency toward similar good acts, while bad conduct brings an evil result and creates a tendency toward similar evil acts. Some karmic acts bear fruit in the same life in which they are committed, others in the immediately succeeding one, and others in future lives that are more remote. This furnishes the basic context for the moral life.

The acceptance by Buddhists of the teachings of karma and rebirth and the concept of the no-self gives rise to a difficult problem: how can rebirth take place without a permanent subject to be reborn? Indian non-Buddhist philosophers attacked this point in Buddhist thought, and many modern scholars have also considered it to be an insoluble problem. The relation between existences in rebirth has been explained by the analogy of fire, which maintains itself unchanged in appearance and yet is different in every moment—what may be called the continuity of an ever-changing identity.

THE FOUR NOBLE TRUTHS

Awareness of these fundamental realities led the Buddha to formulate the Four Noble Truths: the truth of misery (*dukkha*), the truth that misery originates within us from the craving for pleasure and for being or nonbeing (*samudaya*), the truth that this craving can be eliminated (*nirodhu*), and the truth that this elimination is the result of following a methodical way or path (*magga*).

THE LAW OF DEPENDENT ORIGINATION

The Buddha, according to the early texts, also discovered the law of dependent origination (*paticca-samuppada*), whereby one condition arises out of another, which in turn arises out of prior conditions. Every mode of being presupposes another immediately preceding mode from which the subsequent mode derives, in a chain of causes. According to the classical rendering, the 12 links in the chain are: ignorance (*avijja*), karmic predispositions (*sankharas*), consciousness (*vinnana*), form and body (*nama-rupa*), the five sense organs and the mind (*salayatana*), contact (*phassa*), feeling-response (*vedana*), craving (*tanha*), grasping for an object (*upadana*), action toward life (*bhava*), birth (*jati*), and old age and death (*jaramarana*). According to this law, the misery that is bound with sensate existence is accounted for by a methodical chain of causation. Despite a diversity of interpretations, the law of dependent origination of the various aspects of becoming remains fundamentally the same in all schools of Buddhism.

THE EIGHTFOLD PATH

The law of dependent origination, however, raises the question of how one may escape the continually renewed cycle of birth, suffering, and death. It is not enough to know that misery pervades all existence and to know the way in which life evolves; there must also be a means to overcome this process. The means to this end is found in the Eightfold Path, which is constituted by right views, right aspirations, right speech, right conduct, right livelihood, right effort, right mindfulness, and right meditational attainment.

NIRVANA

The aim of Buddhist practice is to be rid of the delusion of ego and thus free oneself from the fetters of this mundane world. One who is successful in doing so is said to have overcome the round of rebirths and to have achieved enlightenment. This is the final goal in most Buddhist traditions, though in some cases (particularly though not exclusively in some Pure Land schools in China and Japan) the attainment of an ultimate paradise or a heavenly abode is not clearly distinguished from the attainment of release.

The living process is again likened to a fire. Its remedy is the extinction of the fire of illusion, passions, and cravings. The Buddha, the Enlightened One, is one who is no longer kindled or inflamed. Many poetic terms are used to describe the state of the enlightened human being— the harbour of refuge, the cool cave, the place of bliss, the farther shore. The term that has become famous in the West is *nirvana*, translated as passing away or dying out—that is, the dying out in the heart of the fierce fires of lust, anger, and delusion. But nirvana is not extinction, and indeed the craving for annihilation or nonexistence was expressly repudiated by the Buddha. Buddhists search for salvation, not just nonbeing. Although nirvana is often presented negatively as "release from suffering," it is more accurate to describe it in a more positive fashion: as an ultimate goal to be sought and cherished.

In some early texts the Buddha left unanswered certain questions regarding the destiny of persons who have reached this ultimate goal. He even refused to speculate as to whether fully purified saints, after death, continued to exist or ceased to exist. Such questions, he maintained, were not relevant to the practice of the path and could not in any event be answered from within the confines of ordinary human existence. Indeed, he asserted that any discussion of the nature of nirvana would only distort or misrepresent it. But he also asserted with even more insistence that nirvana can be experienced—and experienced in the present existence—by those who, knowing the Buddhist truth, practice the Buddhist path.

EXPANSION OF BUDDHISM

The Buddha was a charismatic leader who founded a distinctive religious community based on his unique teachings. Some of the members of that community were, like the Buddha himself, wandering ascetics. Others were laypersons who venerated the Buddha, followed certain aspects of his teachings, and provided the wandering ascetics with the material support that they required.

In the centuries following the Buddha's death, the story of his life was remembered and embellished, his teachings were preserved and developed, and the community that he had established became a significant religious force. Many of the wandering ascetics who followed the Buddha settled in permanent monastic establishments and developed monastic rules. At the same time, the Buddhist laity came to include important members of the economic and political elite.

During its first century of existence, Buddhism spread from its place of origin in Magadha and Kosala throughout much of northern India, including the areas of Mathura and Ujjayani in the west. According to Buddhist tradition, invitations to the Council of Vesali (Sanskrit: Vaishali), held just over a century after the Buddha's death, were sent to monks living throughout northern and central India. By the middle of the 3rd century BC, Buddhism had gained the favour of a Mauryan king, Ashoka, who had established an empire that extended from the Himalayas in the north to almost as far as Sri Lanka in the south.

To the rulers of the republics and kingdoms arising in northeastern India, the patronage of newly emerging sects such as Buddhism was one way of counterbalancing the political power exercised by Brahmans (high-caste Hindus). The first Mauryan emperor, Chandragupta (c. 321–c. 297 BC), patronized Jainism and, according to some traditions, finally became a Jain monk. His grandson, Ashoka, who ruled over the greater part of the subcontinent from about 268 to 232 BC, traditionally played an important role in Buddhist history because of his support of Buddhism during his lifetime. He exerted even more influence posthumously, through stories that depicted him as a *chakravartin* ("a great wheel-rolling monarch"). He is portrayed as a paragon of Buddhist kingship who accomplished many fabulous feats of piety and devotion. It is therefore very difficult to distinguish the Ashoka of history from the Ashoka of Buddhist legend and myth.

The first actual Buddhist "texts" that are still extant are inscriptions (including a number of well-known Ashokan pillars) that Ashoka had written and displayed in various places throughout his vast kingdom. According to these inscriptions, Ashoka attempted to establish in his realm a "true *dhamma*" based on the virtues of self-control, impartiality, cheerfulness, truthfulness, and goodness. Although he promoted Buddhism, he did not found a state church, and he was known for his respect for other religious traditions. He sought to maintain unity in the Buddhist monastic community, however, and he promoted an ethic that focused on the layman's obligations in this world. His aim, as articulated in his edicts, was to create a religious and social milieu that would enable all "children of the king" to live happily in this life and to attain heaven in the next. Thus, he set up medical assistance for human beings and beasts, maintained reservoirs and canals, and promoted trade. He established a system of *dhamma* officers (*dhamma-mahamattas*) in order to help govern the empire. And he sent diplomatic emissaries to areas beyond his direct political control.

Ashoka's empire began to crumble soon after his death, and the Mauryan dynasty was finally overthrown in the early decades of the 2nd century BC. There is some evidence to suggest that Buddhism in India suffered persecution during the Shunga-Kanva period (185–28 BC). Despite occasional setbacks, however, Buddhists persevered; and before the emergence of the Gupta dynasty, which created the next great pan-Indian empire in the 4th century AD, Buddhism had become a leading if not dominant religious tradition in India.

During the approximately five centuries between the fall of the Mauryan dynasty and the rise of the Gupta dynasty, major developments occurred in all aspects of Buddhist belief and practice. Well before the beginning of the Common Era, stories about the Buddha's many previous lives, accounts of important events in his life as Gautama, stories of his "extended life" in his relics, and other aspects of his sacred biography were elaborated on. In the centuries that followed, groups of these stories were collected and compiled in various styles and combinations.

Beginning in the 3rd century BC, and possibly earlier, magnificent Buddhist

The south gateway (torana) *and the Great Stupa (Stupa 1), Sanchi, Madhya Pradesh, India.* Milt and Joan Mann/ CameraMann International

monuments such as the great stupas at Bharhut and Sanchi were built. During the early centuries of the 1st millennium AD, similar monuments were established virtually throughout the subcontinent. Numerous monasteries emerged too, some in close association with the great monuments and pilgrimage sites. Considerable evidence, including inscriptional evidence, points to extensive support from local rulers, including the women of the various royal courts.

During this period Buddhist monastic centres proliferated, and there developed diverse schools of interpretation concerning matters of doctrine and monastic discipline. Within the Hinayana tradition there emerged many different schools, most of which preserved a variant of the *Tipitaka* (which had taken the form of written scriptures by the early centuries of the Common Era), held distinctive doctrinal positions, and practiced unique forms of monastic discipline. The traditional number of schools is 18, but the situation was very complicated, and exact identifications are hard to make.

About the beginning of the Common Era, distinctively Mahayana tendencies began to take shape. It should be emphasized, however, that many Hinayana and Mahayana adherents continued to live together in the same monastic institutions. In the 2nd or 3rd century, the Madhyamika school, which has remained one of the major schools of Mahayana philosophy, was established, and many other expressions of Mahayana belief, practice, and communal life appeared. By the beginning of the Gupta era, the Mahayana had become the most dynamic and creative Buddhist tradition in India.

At this time Buddhism also expanded beyond the Indian subcontinent. It is most likely that Ashoka sent a diplomatic mission to Sri Lanka and that Buddhism was established there during his reign. By the beginning of the Common Era, Buddhism, which had become very strong in northwestern India, had followed the great trade routes into Central Asia and China. According to later tradition, this expansion was greatly facilitated by Kanishka, a great Kushana king of the 1st or 2nd century AD, who ruled over an area that included portions of northern India and Central Asia.

BUDDHISM UNDER THE GUPTAS AND PALAS

By the time of the Gupta dynasty (c. AD 320–c. 600), Buddhism in India was being influenced by the revival of Brahmanic religion and the rising tide of bhakti (a devotional movement that emphasized the intense love of a devotee for a personal god). During this period, for example, some Hindus practiced devotion to the Buddha, whom they regarded as an avatar (incarnation) of the Hindu deity Vishnu, and some Buddhists venerated Hindu deities who were an integral part of the wider religious context in which they lived.

Throughout the Gupta and Pala periods, Hinayana Buddhists remained a major segment of the Indian Buddhist community. Their continued cultivation of various aspects of Buddhist teaching led to the emergence of the Yogacara school, the second great tradition of Mahayana philosophy. A third major Buddhist tradition, the Vajrayana or Esoteric tradition, developed out of the Mahayana school and became a powerful and dynamic religious force. The new form of text associated with this tradition, the tantras, appeared during the Gupta period, and there are indications that distinctively Tantric rituals began to be employed at this time as well. It was during the Pala period (8th–12th centuries), however, that the Vajrayana/Esoteric tradition emerged as the most dynamic component of Indian Buddhist life.

Also during the Gupta period, there emerged a new Buddhist institution, the Mahavihara ("Great Monastery"), which often functioned as a university. This institution enjoyed great success during the reign of the Pala kings. The most famous of these Mahaviharas, located at Nalanda, became a major centre for the study of Buddhist texts and the refinement of Buddhist thought, particularly Mahayana and Vajrayana thought. The monks at Nalanda also developed a curriculum that went far beyond traditional Buddhism and included much Indian scientific and cultural knowledge. In subsequent years other important Mahaviharas were established, each with its own distinctive emphases and characteristics. These great Buddhist monastic research and educational institutions exerted a profound religious and cultural influence not only in India but throughout many other parts of Asia as well.

Although Buddhist institutions seemed to be faring well under the Guptas, Chinese pilgrims visiting India between AD 400 and 700 discerned a decline in the Buddhist community and the beginning of the absorption of Indian Buddhism by Hinduism. Among these pilgrims was Faxian, who left China in 399, crossed the Gobi Desert, visited various holy places in India, and returned to China with numerous Buddhist scriptures and statues. The most famous of the Chinese travelers, however, was the 7th-century monk Xuanzang. When he arrived in northwestern India, he found "millions of monasteries" reduced to ruins by the Huns, a nomadic Central Asian people. In the northeast Xuanzang visited various holy places and studied Yogacara philosophy at Nalanda. After visiting Assam and southern India, he returned to China, carrying with him copies of more than 600 sutras.

After the destruction of numerous Buddhist monasteries in the 6th century AD by the Huns, Buddhism revived, especially in the northeast, where it flourished for many more centuries under the kings of the Pala dynasty. The kings protected the Mahaviharas, built new centres at Odantapuri, near Nalanda, and established a system of supervision for all such institutions. Under the Palas the Vajrayana/Esoteric form of Buddhism became a major intellectual and religious force. Its adherents introduced important innovations into Buddhist doctrine and symbolism. They also advocated the practice of new Tantric forms of ritual practice that were designed both to generate magical power and to facilitate more rapid progress along the path to enlightenment. During the reigns of the later Pala kings, contacts with China decreased as Indian Buddhists turned their attention toward Tibet and Southeast Asia.

The Demise of Buddhism in India

With the collapse of the Pala dynasty in the 12th century, Indian Buddhism suffered yet another setback, from which it did not recover. Although small pockets of influence remained, the Buddhist presence in India became negligible.

Scholars do not know all the factors that contributed to Buddhism's demise in its homeland. Some have maintained that it was so tolerant of other faiths that it was simply reabsorbed by a revitalized Hindu tradition. This did occur, though Indian Mahayanists were occasionally hostile toward bhakti and toward Hinduism in general. Another factor, however, was probably much more important. Indian Buddhism, having become primarily a monastic movement, seems to have lost touch with its lay supporters. Many monasteries had become very wealthy, so much so that they were able to employ indentured slaves and paid labourers to care for the monks and to tend the lands they owned. Thus, after the Muslim invaders sacked the Indian monasteries in the 12th and 13th centuries, the Buddhist laity showed little interest in a resurgence.

CONTEMPORARY REVIVAL

In the 19th century Buddhism was virtually extinct in India. In far eastern Bengal

Prayer flags and pilgrim under the Bo tree at Bodh Gaya, Bihar, India. Milt and Joan Mann/ CameraMann International

and Assam, a few Buddhists preserved a tradition that dated back to pre-Muslim times, and some of them experienced a Theravada-oriented reform that was initiated by a Burmese monk who visited the area in the mid-19th century. By the end of that century, a very small number of Indian intellectuals had become interested in Buddhism through Western scholarship or through the activities of the Theosophical Society, one of whose leaders was the American Henry Olcott. The Sinhalese reformer Anagarika Dharmapala also exerted some influence, particularly through his work as one of the founders of the Mahabodhi Society, which focused its initial efforts on restoring Buddhist control of the pilgrimage site at Bodh Gaya, the presumed site of the Buddha's enlightenment.

Beginning in the early 20th century, a few Indian intellectuals became increasingly interested in Buddhism as a more rational and egalitarian alternative to Hinduism. Although this interest remained limited to a very tiny segment of the intellectual elite, a small Buddhist movement with a broader constituency developed in South India. Even as late as 1950, however, an official government census identified fewer than 200,000 Buddhists in the country, most of them residing in east Bengal and Assam.

Since 1950 the number of Buddhists in India has increased dramatically. One very small factor in this increase was the flood of Buddhist refugees from Tibet following the Chinese invasion of that country in 1959. The centre of the Tibetan refugee community, both in India and around the world, was established in Dharmsala, but many Tibetan refugees settled in other areas of the subcontinent as well. Another very small factor was the incorporation of Sikkim—a region with a predominantly Buddhist population now in the northeastern part of India—into the Republic of India in 1975.

The most important cause of the contemporary revival of Buddhism in India was the mass conversion, in 1956, of hundreds of thousands of Hindus living primarily in Maharashtra state who had previously been members of the so-called Scheduled castes (Dalits; formerly called untouchables). This conversion was initiated by Bhimrao Ramji Ambedkar, a leader of the Scheduled castes who was also a major figure in the Indian independence movement, a critic of the caste policies of Mahatma Gandhi, a framer of India's constitution, and a member of India's first independent government. As early as 1935 Ambedkar decided to lead his people away from Hinduism in favour of a religion that did not recognize caste distinctions. After a delay of more than 20 years, he determined that Buddhism was the appropriate choice. He also decided that 1956—the year in which Theravada Buddhists were celebrating the 2,500th year of the death of the Buddha—was the appropriate time. A dramatic conversion ceremony, held in Nagpur, was attended by hundreds of thousands of people. Since 1956 more than three million persons (a very conservative estimate) have joined the new Buddhist community.

Young Indian Buddhist monks play at the main entrance of the Tawang Monastery in Arunachal Pradesh state in India. Diptendu Dutta/AFP/Getty Images

The Buddhism of Ambedkar's community is based on the teachings found in the ancient Pali texts and has much in common with the Theravada Buddhist communities of Sri Lanka and Southeast Asia. There are important differences that distinguish the new group, however. They include the community's reliance on Ambedkar's own interpretations, which are presented in his book *The Buddha and His Dhamma*; the community's emphasis on a mythology concerning the Buddhist and aristocratic character of the Mahar (the largest of the Scheduled castes); and its recognition of Ambedkar himself as a saviour figure who is often considered to be a bodhisattva (future buddha). Another distinguishing characteristic of the Mahar Buddhists is the absence of a strong monastic community, which has allowed laypersons to assume the primary leadership roles. During the last several decades, the group has produced its own corpus of Buddhist songs and many vernacular books and pamphlets that deal with various aspects of Buddhist doctrine, practice, and community life.

INDIAN PHILOSOPHY

The systems of thought and reflection that were developed by the civilizations of the Indian subcontinent include both orthodox (*astika*) systems, namely, the Nyaya, Vaishesika, Samkhya, Yoga, Purva-mimamsa, and Vedanta schools of philosophy, and unorthodox (*nastika*) systems, such as Buddhism and Jainism. Indian thought has been concerned with various philosophical problems, significant among them the nature of the world (cosmology), the nature of reality (metaphysics), logic, the nature of knowledge (epistemology), ethics, and religion.

SIGNIFICANCE OF INDIAN PHILOSOPHIES IN THE HISTORY OF PHILOSOPHY

In relation to Western philosophical thought, Indian philosophy offers both surprising points of affinity and illuminating differences. The differences highlight

The Hindu deity Krishna, an avatar of Vishnu, mounted on a horse pulling Arjuna, hero of the epic poem Mahabharata; *17th-century illustration.* Photos.com/Jupiterimages

certain fundamentally new questions that the Indian philosophers asked. The similarities reveal that, even when philosophers in India and the West were grappling with the same problems and sometimes even suggesting similar theories, Indian thinkers were advancing novel formulations and argumentations. Problems that the Indian philosophers raised for consideration, but that their Western counterparts never did, include such matters as the origin (*utpatti*) and apprehension (*jnapti*) of truth (*pramanya*). Problems that the Indian philosophers for the most part ignored but that helped shape Western philosophy include the question of whether knowledge arises from experience or from reason and distinctions such as that between analytic and synthetic judgments or between contingent and necessary truths. Indian thought, therefore, provides the historian of Western philosophy with a point of view that may supplement that gained from Western thought. A study of Indian thought, then, reveals certain inadequacies of Western philosophical thought and makes clear that some concepts and distinctions may not be as inevitable as they may otherwise seem. In a similar manner, knowledge of Western thought gained by Indian philosophers has also been advantageous to them.

Vedic hymns, Hindu scriptures dating from the 2nd millennium BC, are the oldest extant record from India of the process by which the human mind makes its gods and of the deep psychological processes of mythmaking leading to profound cosmological concepts. The *Upanishads* (Hindu philosophical treatises) contain one of the first conceptions of a universal, all-pervading, spiritual reality leading to a radical monism (absolute nondualism, or the essential unity of matter and spirit). The *Upanishads* also contain early speculations by Indian philosophers about nature, life, mind, and the human body, not to speak of ethics and social philosophy. The classical, or orthodox, systems (*darshanas*) debate, sometimes with penetrating insight and often with a degree of repetition that can become tiresome to some, such matters as the status of the finite individual; the distinction as well as the relation between the body, mind, and the self; the nature of knowledge and the types of valid knowledge; the nature and origin of truth; the types of entities that may be said to exist; the relation of realism to idealism; the problem of whether universals or relations are basic; and the very important problem of *moksha,* or salvation—its nature and the paths leading up to it.

GENERAL CHARACTERISTICS OF INDIAN PHILOSOPHY

The various Indian philosophies contain such a diversity of views, theories, and systems that it is almost impossible to single out characteristics that are common to all of them. Acceptance of the authority of the Vedas characterizes all the orthodox (*astika*) systems, but not the unorthodox (*nastika*) systems, such as Carvaka (radical materialism),

Buddhism, and Jainism. Moreover, even when philosophers professed allegiance to the Vedas, their allegiance did little to fetter the freedom of their speculative ventures. On the contrary, the acceptance of the authority of the Vedas was a convenient way for a philosopher's views to become acceptable to the orthodox, even if a thinker introduced a wholly new idea. Thus, the Vedas could be cited to corroborate a wide diversity of views; they were used by the Vaishesika thinkers (i.e., those who believe in ultimate particulars, both individual souls and atoms) as much as by the Advaita (monist) philosophers.

COMMON CONCERNS

In most Indian philosophical systems, the acceptance of the ideal of *moksha*, like allegiance to the authority of the scriptures, was only remotely connected with the systematic doctrines that were being propounded. Many epistemological, logical, and even metaphysical doctrines were debated and decided on purely rational grounds that did not directly bear upon the ideal of *moksha*. Only the Vedanta ("end of the Vedas") philosophy and the Samkhya (a system that accepts a real matter and a plurality of the individual souls) philosophy may be said to have a close relationship to the ideal of *moksha*. The logical systems—Nyaya, Vaishesika, and Purvamimamsa—are only very remotely related. Also, both the philosophies and other scientific treatises, including even the *Kama-sutra* ("Aphorisms on Love") and

the *Arthashastra* ("Treatise on Material Gain"), recognized the same ideal and professed their efficacy for achieving it.

When Indian philosophers speak of intuitive knowledge, they are concerned with making room for it and demonstrating its possibility, with the help of logic—and there, as far as they are concerned, the task of philosophy ends. Indian philosophers do not seek to justify religious faith; philosophic wisdom itself is accorded the dignity of religious truth. Theory is not subordinated to practice, but theory itself, as theory, is regarded as being supremely worthy and efficacious.

Three basic concepts form the cornerstone of Indian philosophical thought: the self, or soul (*atman*), works (*karma*, or *karman*), and salvation (*moksha*). Leaving the Carvakas aside, all Indian philosophies concern themselves with these three concepts and their interrelations, though this is not to say that they accept the objective validity of these concepts in precisely the same manner. Of these, the concept of *karma*, signifying moral efficacy of human actions, seems to be the most typically Indian. The concept of *atman*, not altogether absent in Western thought, corresponds, in a certain sense, to the Western concept of a transcendental or absolute spirit self—important differences notwithstanding. The concept of *moksha* as the concept of the highest ideal has likewise been one of the concerns of Western thought, especially during the Christian Era, though it probably has never been as important as for the Hindu mind. Most Indian philosophies assume that *moksha* is possible, and the "impossibility of *moksha*" (*anirmoksha*) is regarded as a material fallacy likely to vitiate a philosophical theory.

In addition to *karma*, the lack of two other concerns further differentiates Indian philosophical thought from Western thought in general. Since the time of the Greeks, Western thought has been concerned with mathematics, and, in the Christian Era, with history. Neither mathematics nor history has ever raised philosophical problems for the Indian. In the lists of *pramanas*, or ways of knowing accepted by the different schools, there is none that includes mathematical knowledge or historical knowledge. Possibly connected with their indifference toward mathematics is the significant fact that Indian philosophers have not developed formal logic. The theory of the syllogism (a valid deductive argument having two premises and a conclusion) is, however, developed, and much sophistication has been achieved in logical theory. Indian logic offers an instructive example of a logic of cognitions (*jnanani*) rather than of abstract propositions—a logic not sundered and kept isolated from psychology and epistemology, because it is meant to be the logic of man's actual striving to know what is true of the world.

FORMS OF ARGUMENT AND PRESENTATION

There is, in relation to Western thought, a striking difference in the manner in which Indian philosophical thinking is presented as well as in the mode in which it historically develops. Out of the presystematic age of the Vedic hymns and the *Upanishads* and many diverse philosophical ideas current in the pre-Buddhistic era, there emerged with the rise of the age of the *sutras* (aphoristic summaries of the main points of a system) a neat classification of systems (*darshanas*), a classification that was never to be contradicted and to which no further systems are added. No new school was founded, no new *darshana* came into existence. But this conformism, like conformism to the Vedas, did not check the rise of independent thinking, new innovations, or original insights. There is, apparently, an underlying assumption in the Indian tradition that no individual can claim to have seen the truth for the first time and, therefore, that an individual can only explicate, state, and defend in a new form a truth that had been seen, stated, and defended by countless others before him: hence the tradition of expounding one's thoughts by affiliating oneself to one of the *darshanas*.

If one is to be counted as a great master (*acarya*), one has to write a commentary (*bhasya*) on the *sutras* of thesutra *darshana* concerned, or one must comment on one of the *bhasyas* and write a *tika* (subcommentary). The usual order is *sutra–bhasya–varttika* (collection of critical notes)–*tika*. At any stage, a person may introduce a new and original point of view, but at no stage can he claim originality for himself. Not even an author of the *sutras* could do that, for he was only systematizing the thoughts and insights of countless predecessors. The development of Indian philosophical thought has thus been able to combine, in an almost unique manner, conformity to tradition and adventure in thinking.

Roles of Sacred Texts, Mythology, and Theism

The role of the sacred texts in the growth of Indian philosophy is different in each of the different systems. In those systems that may be called *adhyatmavidya*, or sciences of spirituality, the sacred texts play a much greater role than they do in the logical systems (*anviksikividya*). In the case of the former, Shankara, a leading Advaita Vedanta philosopher (*c.* 788–820), perhaps best laid down the principles: reasoning should be allowed freedom only as long as it does not conflict with the scriptures. In matters regarding supersensible reality, reasoning left to itself cannot deliver certainty, for, according to Shankara, every thesis established by reasoning may be countered by an opposite thesis supported by equally strong, if not stronger, reasoning. The sacred scriptures, embodying as they do the results of intuitive experiences of seers, therefore, should be accepted as authoritative, and reasoning should be made subordinate to them.

Whereas the sacred texts thus continued to exercise some influence on philosophical thinking, the influence of mythology declined considerably with the rise of the systems. The myths of creation and dissolution of the universe persisted in the theistic systems but were transformed into metaphors and models. With the Nyaya (problem of knowledge)–Vaishesika (analysis of nature) systems, for example, the model of a potter making pots determined much philosophical thinking, as did that of a magician conjuring up tricks in the Advaita (nondualist) Vedanta. The *nirukta* (etymology) of Yaska, a 5th-century-BC Sanskrit scholar, tells of various attempts to interpret difficult Vedic mythologies: the *adhidaivata* (pertaining to the deities), the *aitihasika* (pertaining to the tradition), the *adhiyajna* (pertaining to the sacrifices), and the *adhyamika* (pertaining to the spirit). Such interpretations apparently prevailed in the *Upanishads*; the myths were turned into symbols, though some of them persisted as models and metaphors.

The issue of theism vis-à-vis atheism, in the ordinary senses of the English words, played an important role in Indian thought. The ancient Indian tradition, however, classified the classical systems (*darshanas*) into orthodox (*astika*) and unorthodox (*nastika*). *Astika* does not mean "theistic," nor does *nastika* mean "atheistic." Panini, a 5th-century-BC grammarian, stated that the former is one who believes in a transcendent world (*asti paralokah*) and the latter is one who does not believe in it (*nasti paralokah*). *Astika* may also mean one who accepts the authority of the Vedas; *nastika* then means one who does not accept that authority. Not all among the *astika* philosophers, however, were theists, and even if they were, they did not all accord the same importance to the concept of God in their systems. The Samkhya system did not involve belief in the existence of God, without ceasing to be *astika,* and Yoga (a mental–psychological–physical meditation system) made room for God not on theoretical grounds but only on practical considerations. The Purva-Mimamsa of Jaimini, the greatest philosopher of the Mimamsa school, posits various deities to account for the significance of Vedic rituals but ignores, without denying, the question of the existence of God. The Advaita Vedanta of Shankara rejects atheism in order to prove that the world had its origin in a conscious, spiritual being called Ishvara, or God, but in the long run regards the concept of Ishvara as a concept of lower order that becomes negated by a metaphysical knowledge of Brahman, the absolute, nondual reality. Only the non-Advaita schools of Vedanta and the Nyaya-Vaishesika remain zealous theists, and of these schools, the god of the Nyaya-Vaishesika school does not create the eternal atoms, universals, or individual souls. For a truly theistic conception of God, one has to look to the non-Advaita schools of Vedanta, the Vaishnava, and the Shaiva philosophical systems. Whereas Hindu religious life continues to be dominated by these last-mentioned theistic systems, the philosophies went their own ways, far removed from that religious demand.

A General History of Development and Cultural Background

S.N. Dasgupta, a 20th-century Indian philosopher, divided the history of Indian philosophy into three periods: the prelogical (up to the beginning of the Common Era), the logical (from the beginning of the Common Era up to the 11th century AD), and the ultralogical (from the 11th century to the 18th century). What Dasgupta calls the prelogical stage covers the pre-Mauryan and the Mauryan periods (*c.* 321–185 BC) in Indian history. The logical period begins roughly with the Kushanas (1st–2nd centuries AD) and finds its highest development during the Gupta era (3rd–5th centuries AD) and the age of imperial Kanauj (7th century AD).

THE PRELOGICAL PERIOD

In its early prelogical phase, Indian thought, freshly developing in the Indian subcontinent, actively confronted and assimilated the diverse currents of pre-Indo-European and non-Indo-European elements in the native culture that the Indo-Europeans sought to conquer and appropriate. The marks of this confrontation are to be noted in every facet of Indian religion and thought: in the Vedic hymns in the form of conflicts, with varying fortunes, between the Indo-Europeans and the non-Indo-Europeans; in the conflict between a positive attitude toward life that is interested in making life fuller and richer and a negative attitude emphasizing asceticism and renunciation; in the great variety of skeptics, naturalists, determinists, indeterminists, accidentalists, and no-soul theorists that filled the Ganges Plain; in the rise of the heretical, unorthodox schools of Jainism and Buddhism protesting against the Vedic religion and the Upanisadic theory of *atman*; and in the continuing confrontation, mutually enriching and nourishing, that occurred between the Brahmanic (Hindu priestly) and Buddhist logicians, epistemologists, and dialecticians. The Indo-Europeans, however, were soon followed by a host of foreign invaders, Greeks, Shakas and Hunas from Central Asia, Pashtuns, Mongols, and Mughals (Muslims). Both religious thought and philosophical discussion received continuous challenges and confrontations. The resulting responses have a dialectical character: sometimes new ideas have been absorbed and orthodoxy has been modified; sometimes orthodoxy has been strengthened and codified in order to be preserved in the face of the dangers of such confrontation; sometimes, as in the religious life of the Christian Middle Ages, bold attempts at synthesis of ideas have been made. Nevertheless, through all the vicissitudes of social and cultural life, Brahmanical thought has been able to maintain a fairly strong current of continuity.

In the chaotic intellectual climate of the pre-Mauryan era, there were skeptics (*ajnanikah*) who questioned the possibility of knowledge. There were also materialists, the chief of which were the Ajivikas (deterministic ascetics) and the Lokayatas (the name by which Carvaka doctrines—denying the authority of the Vedas and the soul—are generally known). Furthermore, there existed the two unorthodox schools of *yadrchhavada* (accidentalists) and *svabhavavaha* (naturalists), who rejected the supernatural. Kapila, the legendary founder of the Samkhya school, supposedly flourished during the 7th century BC. Pre-Mahavira Jaina ideas were already in existence when Mahavira (flourished 6th century BC), the founder of Jainism, initiated his reform. Gautama the Buddha (flourished 6th–5th centuries BC) apparently was familiar with all of these intellectual ideas and was as dissatisfied with them as with the Vedic orthodoxy. He sought to forge a new path—though not new in all respects—that was to assure blessedness to man. Orthodoxy, however, sought to preserve itself in a vast *Kalpa-* (ritual) *sutra* literature—with three parts: the *Shrauta-*, based on *shruti* (revelation); the *Grhya-*, based on *smrti* (tradition); and the *Dharma-*, or rules of religious law, *sutra*s—whereas the philosophers tried to codify their doctrines in systematic form, leading to the rise of the philosophical *sutra*s. Though the writing of the *sutra*s continued over a long period, the *sutra*s of most of the various *darshana*s probably were completed between the 6th and 3rd centuries BC. Two of the *sutra*s appear to have been composed in the pre-Maurya period, but after the rise of Buddhism; these works are the *Mimamsa-sutras* of Jaimini (*c.* 400 BC) and the *Vedanta-sutras* of Badarayana (*c.* 500–200 BC).

The Maurya period brought, for the first time, a strong centralized state. The Greeks had been ousted, and a new self-confidence characterized the beginning of the period. This seems to have been the period in which the epics *Mahabharata* and *Ramayana* were initiated, though their composition went on through several centuries before they took the forms they now have. Manu, a legendary lawgiver, codified the *Dharma-shastra*; Kautilya, a minister of King Chandragupta Maurya, systematized the science of political economy (*Artha-shastra*); and Patanjali, an ancient author or authors, composed the *Yoga-sutras*. Brahmanism tried to adjust itself to the new communities and cultures that were admitted into its fold: new gods—or rather, old Vedic gods that had been rejuvenated—were worshipped; the Hindu trinity of Brahma (the creator), Vishnu (the preserver), and Shiva (the destroyer) came into being; and the Pashupata (Shaivite), Bhagavata (Vaishnavite), and the Tantra (esoteric meditative) systems were initiated. The *Bhagavadgita*—the most famous work of this period—symbolized the spirit of the creative synthesis of the age. A new ideal of *karma* as opposed to the more ancient one of renunciation was emphasized. Orthodox notions were reinterpreted and given a new symbolic meaning, as, for example, the *Gita* does with the notion

of *yajna* ("sacrifice"). Already in the pre-Christian era, Buddhism had split up into several major sects, and the foundations for the rise of Mahayana ("Greater Vehicle") Buddhism had been laid.

THE LOGICAL PERIOD

The logical period of Indian thought began with the Kusanas (1st–2nd centuries). Gautama (author of the *Nyaya-sutras*; probably flourished at the beginning of the Christian Era) and his 5th-century commentator Vatsyayana established the foundations of the Nyaya as a school almost exclusively preoccupied with logical and epistemological issues. The Madhyamika ("Middle Way") school of Buddhism—also known as the Shunyavada ("Way of Emptiness") school—arose, and the analytical investigations of Nagarjuna (*c.* 200), the great propounder of Shunyavada (dialectical thinking), reached great heights. Though Buddhist logic in the strict sense of the term had not yet come into being, an increasingly rigorous logical style of philosophizing developed among the proponents of these schools of thought.

During the reign of the Guptas, there was a revival of Brahmanism of a gentler and more refined form. Vaishnavism of the Vasudeva cult, centring on the prince-god Krishna and advocating renunciation by action, and Shaivism prospered, along with Buddhism and Jainism. Both the Mahayana and the Hinayana ("Lesser Vehicle"), or Theravada ("Way of the

Elders"), schools flourished. The most notable feature, however, was the rise of the Buddhist Yogacara school, of which Asanga (4th century AD) and his brother Vasubandhu were the great pioneers. Toward the end of the 5th century, Dignaga, a Buddhist logician, wrote the *Pramanasamuccaya* ("Compendium of the Means of True Knowledge"), a work that laid the foundations of Buddhist logic.

The greatest names of Indian philosophy belong to the post-Gupta period from the 7th to the 10th century. At that time Buddhism was on the decline and the Tantric cults were rising, a situation that led to the development of the tantric forms of Buddhism. Shaivism was thriving in Kashmir, and Vaishnavism in the southern part of India. The great philosophers Mimamshakas Kumarila (7th century), Prabhakara (7th–8th centuries), Mandana Mishra (8th century), Shalikanatha (9th century), and Parthasarathi Mishra (10th century) belong to this age. The greatest Indian philosopher of the period, however, was Shankara. All of these men defended Brahmanism against the "unorthodox" schools, especially against the criticisms of Buddhism. The debate between Brahmanism and Buddhism was continued, on a logical level, by philosophers of the Nyaya school—Uddyotakara, Vacaspati Mishra, and Udayana (Udayanacarya).

THE ULTRALOGICAL PERIOD

Muslim rule in India had consolidated itself by the 11th century, by which time Buddhism, for all practical purposes, had disappeared from the country. Hinduism had absorbed Buddhist ideas and practices and reasserted itself, with the Buddha appearing in Hindu writings as an incarnation of Vishnu. The Muslim conquest created a need for orthodoxy to readjust itself to a new situation. In this period the great works on Hindu law were written. Jainism, of all the "unorthodox" schools, retained its purity, and great Jaina works, such as Devasuri's *Pramananayatattvalokalamkara* ("The Ornament of the Light of Truth of the Different Points of View Regarding the Means of True Knowledge," 12th century AD) and Prabhachandra's *Prameyakamalamartanda* ("The Sun of the Lotus of the Objects of True Knowledge," 11th century AD), were written during this period. Under the Chola kings (c. 850–1279) and later in the Vijayanagara kingdom (which, along with Mithilā in the north, remained strongholds of Hinduism until the middle of the 16th century), Vaiṣṇavism flourished. The philosopher Yamunacarya (flourished AD 1050) taught the path of *prapatti*, or complete surrender to God. The philosophers Ramanuja (11th century), Madhva, and Nimbarka (c. 12th century) developed theistic systems of Vedanta and severely criticized Shankara's Advaita Vedanta.

Toward the end of the 12th century, creative work of the highest order began to take place in the fields of logic and epistemology in Mithila and Bengal. The 12th–13th-century philosopher Gangesa's

Tattvacintamaṇi ("The Jewel of Thought on the Nature of Things") laid the foundations of the school of Navya-Nyaya ("New-Nyaya"). Four great members of this school were Pakshadhara Mishra of Mithila, Vasudeva Sarvabhauma (16th century), his disciple Raghunatha Shiromani (both of Bengal), and Gadadhara Bhattacaryya.

Religious life was marked by the rise of great mystic saints, chief of which are Ramananda, Kabir, Caitanya, and Guru Nanak, who emphasized the path of *bhakti*, or devotion, a wide sense of humanity, freedom of thought, and a sense of unity of all religions. Somewhat earlier than these were the great Muslim Sufi (mystic) saints, including Khwāja Mu'in-ud-Din Ḥasan, who emphasized asceticism and taught a philosophy that included both love of God and love of humanity.

The British period in Indian history was primarily a period of discovery of the ancient tradition (e.g., the two histories by Radhakrishnan, scholar and president of India from 1962 to 1967, and S.N. Dasgupta) and of comparison and synthesis of Indian philosophy with the philosophical ideas from the West. Among modern creative thinkers have been Mahatma Gandhi, who espoused new ideas in the fields of social, political, and educational philosophy; Sri Aurobindo, an exponent of a new school of Vedanta that he calls Integral Advaita; and K.C. Bhattacharyya, who developed a phenomenologically oriented philosophy of subjectivity that is conceived as freedom from object.

CHAPTER 5

INDIAN VISUAL ARTS

Despite a history of ethnic, linguistic, and political fragmentation, the people of the Indian subcontinent are unified by a common cultural and ethical outlook; a wealth of ancient textual literature in Sanskrit, Prakrit, and regional languages is a major unifying factor. Music and dance, ritual customs, modes of worship, and literary ideals are similar throughout the subcontinent, even though the region has been divided into kaleidoscopic political patterns through the centuries.

The close interrelationship of the various peoples of South Asia may be traced in their epics, as in the *Ramayana* and the *Mahabharata*. Kinship between the gods and heroes of regions far distant from each other is evident, and the place-names themselves often evoke common sources. Moreover, there have been continual attempts to impose a political unity over the region. In the 3rd century BC, for example, the emperor Ashoka had almost all of this region under his sway; in the 11th century AD, Rajendra I Chola conquered almost the whole of India and a good portion of Southeast Asia; and the great Mughal Akbar again achieved this in the 16th century. Though the expansion and attenuation of boundary lines, the bringing together or pulling apart politically of whole regions, have characterized all of South Asian history, the culture has remained essentially one.

The geography of the region encouraged a common adoration of mountains and rivers. The great Himalayas, which form the northern boundary, are the loftiest of mountains and are conceived to be the embodiment of nobility, the abode of immaculate snow, and the symbol of a cultural ideal. Similarly, the great rivers such as the Brahmaputra and the Indus are regarded as the mothers of their respective regions, assuring prosperity through their perennial supply of water.

The association of lakes and springs with water sprites and sylvan fairies, called *nagas* and *yakshas*, is common throughout the region. Karkota, the name of an early dynasty, itself signifies *naga* worship in Kashmir. Sculptures of *nagas* and *yakshas* found in widespread sites suggest a common spirit of adoration, as do sculptures, paintings, temples, and religious texts that for centuries were preserved within an oral tradition without losing their immaculate intonation. The same classical dance is seen in sculpture in Gandhara in Pakistan, in Bharhut in the north, and in Amaravati in the south.

The relation of the various arts to each other is very close in South Asia, where proficiency in several arts is necessary for specialization in any one. Thus, it is believed that without a good knowledge of dance there can be no proficiency in sculpture, for dance, like painting or sculpture, is a depiction of all the world. For its rhythmic movements and exposition of emotion, dance also requires musical accompaniments; hence, knowledge of musical rhythm is essential. For the stirring of emotion either in music or in dance, knowledge of literature and rhetoric is believed to be necessary; the flavour (*rasa*) to be expressed in music, dance, sculpture, or painting requires a literary background. Thus all the arts are closely linked together.

The arts were cultivated in South Asia not only as a noble pastime but also in a spirit of dedication, as an offering to a god. Passages in literature refer to princes studying works of art for possible defects. One inscription that mentions the name of the *sutra-dhara* ("architect") of the 8th-century Mallikārjuna temple at Pattadakal epitomizes the accomplishments and ideals, in both theory and practice, of the artist.

Artists traditionally have enjoyed a high position in South Asian societies. Poets, musicians, and dancers held honoured seats in the royal court. An inscription mentions the appreciation bestowed by Rajendra Chola on a talented dancer, and the architect of the temple at Tiruvorriyur, who was also patronized by Rajendra, was eulogized for his encyclopaedic knowledge of architecture and art. Nonetheless, the folk arts were closely linked with the elite arts. Tribal group dances, for example, shared common elements with classical art, dance, and music. Among the artistic traditions of the Indian subcontinent, sculpture in the round (*citra*) is considered the highest artistic expression of form, and sculpture in relief (*ardhacitra*) is next in importance. Painting (*citrabhasa*, literally "the semblance of sculpture") ranks third. Feeling for volume was so great that the effect of chiaroscuro (i.e., use of light and shade to indicate modelling) was considered very important in painting; a passage from a drama of the 5th-century poet Kalidasa describes how the eye tumbles over the heights and depths suggested in the modelling of a painting. A classical text on art, *Citrasutra* enumerates noteworthy factors in paintings: the line sketch, firmly and gracefully drawn, is considered the highest element by the masters; shading and depiction of modelling are valued by others; the decorative element appeals to feminine taste; and the splendour of colour appeals to common taste. The use of a minimum of drawing to produce the maximum effect in suggesting form is considered most admirable.

Portraits play an important role in the visual arts of South Asia, and there are many literary references to the effective depiction of portraits both in painting and in sculpture. A 6th-century text, the *Vishnudharmottara*, classifies portraiture into natural, lyrical, sophisticated, and mixed, and men and women are classified into types by varieties of hair—long and fine, curling to right, wavy, straight and flowing, curled and abundant; similarly, eyes may be bow-shaped, of the hue of the blue lotus, fishlike, lotus-petal-like, or globular. Artistic stances are enumerated, and principles of foreshortening are explained. Paintings or sculptures were believed to take after their creators, even as a poem reflects the poet.

Although South Asia has continually been subjected to strong outside influences, it has always incorporated them into native forms, resulting not in imitation but in a new synthesis. This may be seen even in the art of the Gandhara region of Pakistan, which in the 4th century BC was immersed in Greco-Roman tradition. In the sculpture of this period Indian themes and modes have softened the Western style. Foreign influence is evident after the invasion of the Kushans in the 1st century AD, but the native element predominated and overwhelmed the foreign influence. During the Mughal period, from the 16th century, when Muslims from Central Asia reigned in South Asia, the blend of Iranian and Indian elements produced a predominantly Indian school that spread throughout the region, making it a unified cultural area under imperial rule. The influence of Islamic art was enhanced by the second Mughal emperor, Humayun, who imported painters from the court of the shah of Persia and began a tradition that blended Indian and Persian elements to produce an efflorescence of painting and architecture.

Art in all these regions reflects a system of government, a set of moral and ethical attitudes, and social patterns. The desire of kings to serve the people and to take care of them almost as offspring is evident as early as the 3rd century BC. The ideal of the king as the unrivalled bowman, the unifier, the tall and stately noble spirit, the sacrificer for the welfare of the subjects, and the hero of his people (who conceive of him on a stately elephant) is comprehensively illustrated in a magnificent series of coins from the Gupta empire of North India of the 4th–6th centuries. The concepts of righteous conquest and righteous warfare are illustrated in sculpture. The long series of sculptures illustrating the history of the South Indian Pallava dynasty of the 4th–9th centuries gives an excellent picture of the various activities of government—such as war and conquests, symbolic horse sacrifices, the king's council, diplomatic receptions, peace negotiations, the building of temples, appreciation of the fine arts (including dance and music), and the coronation of kings—all clearly demonstrating what an orderly government meant to the people. Similarly, moral attitudes are illustrated in sculptures that lay stress on *dharma*—customs or laws governing duty. The doctrine of *ahimsa*, or noninjury to others, is often conceived symbolically as a deer, and the ideal of a holy place is represented as a place where the deer roams freely. The joy in giving and renunciation is clearly indicated in art. Sculptures illustrate simple and effective stories, as from the *Pancha-tantra*, one of the oldest books of fables in the world. The spirit of devotion, faith, and respect for moral standards that has throughout the centuries pervaded the subcontinent's social structure is continuously represented in South Asian painting and sculpture.

GENERAL CHARACTERISTICS OF INDIAN ART

Indian art is spread over a subcontinent and has a long, very productive history; but it nevertheless shows a remarkable unity and consistency. Works produced in the several geographical and cultural regions possess decidedly individual characteristics but at the same time have sufficient elements in common to justify their being considered manifestations of a general style. The existence of this style is evidence of the essential cultural unity of the subcontinent and to the uninterrupted contact between the various geographical units, at least from the historical period onward. Developments in one area have been quickly reflected in the others. The regional idioms have contributed to the richness of Indian art, and the mutual influences exercised by them have been responsible for the multi-faceted development of that art throughout the course of its long life.

THE UNITY OF INDIAN ART

The style of Indian art is largely determined not by a dynasty but by conditions of time and space. It has, essentially, a geographical rather than a dynastic basis, which is to say that the evolution of regional schools appears to have been largely independent of any particular dynasty that happened to rule over a specific region. The style does not change because of the conquest of one area by another dynasty; rather the influences exercised by one area on another are usually through the agency of factors other than conquest. Instances in which dynastic patronage changed the nature of a style are very few and confined mostly to the Islamic period. The political history of India is itself quite vague, and the areas in possession of a dynasty at various points in its history are even less susceptible to precise definition. For all these reasons, the classification of Indian art adopted here is not based on dynasties, for such a division has little meaning. Nevertheless, names of certain dynasties are used, for these have passed into common usage. When this is done, however, the name must be understood as little more than a convenient way of labelling a particular period.

The Materials of Indian Art

Indian art employs various materials, such as wood, brick, clay, stone, and metal. Most wooden monuments of the early period have perished but have been imitated in stone. Clay and brick were also abundantly used; but, particularly in later times, the favoured material seems to have been stone, in the dressing (facing and smoothing) and carving of which the Indian artist attained great excellence. The material may have influenced the form somewhat, but essentially Indian art tends to impose the form on the material. Thus, materials are generally regarded as interchangeable: wooden and clay forms are imitated in stone, and stone is imitated in bronze, and in turn stone sculpture assumes qualities appropriate to metal. It is as though the nature of the material presented a challenge that had to be met and overcome.

At the same time, Indian art stresses the plasticity of forms; sculpture is generally characterized by emphatic mass and volume; architecture is often sculpture on a colossal scale; and the elements of painting, particularly of the early period, are modelled by line and colour.

Indian and Foreign Art

Thanks to its geographical situation, the Indian subcontinent has been constantly fed by artistic traditions emanating from West and Central Asia. The Indian artist has shown a remarkable capacity for accepting these foreign influences naturally and assimilating and transforming them to accord with the nature of his own style. The process occurred frequently: in the Maurya period; in the first two centuries AD, when the Kushan dynasty attained imperial supremacy in the north; and at a much later period, in the 16th century, when the Mughals patronized a new school of architecture and painting.

Indian Art and Religion

Indian art is religious inasmuch as it is largely dedicated to the service of one of several great religions. It may be didactic or edificatory as is the relief sculpture of the last two centuries BC through the first two centuries AD; or, by representing the divinity in symbolic form (whether architectural or figural), its purpose may be to induce contemplation and thereby put the worshipper in communication with the divine. Not all Indian art, however, is purely religious, and some of it is only nominally so. There were periods when humanistic currents flowed strongly under the guise of edificatory or contemplative imagery, the art inspired by and delighting in the life of this world.

Although Indian art is religious, there is no such thing as a sectarian Hindu or Buddhist art, for style is a function of time and place and not of religion. Thus it is not strictly correct to speak of Hindu or Buddhist art, but, rather, of Indian art that happens to render Hindu or Buddhist themes. For example, an image of Vishnu and an image of Buddha of the same period are stylistically the same, religion having little to do with the mode of artistic expression. Nor should this be surprising in view of the fact that the artists belonged to nondenominational guilds, ready to lend their services to any patron, whether Hindu, Buddhist, or Jaina.

The religious nature of Indian art accounts to some extent for its essentially symbolic and abstract nature. It scrupulously avoids illusionistic effects, evoked by imitation of the physical and ephemeral world of the senses; instead, objects are made in imitation of ideal, divine prototypes, whose source is the inner world of the mind. This attitude may account for the relative absence of portraiture and for the fact that, even when it is attempted, the emphasis is on the ideal person behind the human lineaments rather than on the physical likeness.

THE ARTIST AND PATRON

Works of art in India were produced by artists at the behest of a patron, who might commission an object to worship for spiritual or material ends, in fulfillment of a vow, for the discharge of virtues enjoined by scripture, or even for personal glory. Once the artist received his commission, he fashioned the work of art according to his skill, gained by apprenticeship, and the written canons of his art, which possessed a holy character. There were prescribed rules for proportionate measurement, iconography, and the like, often with a symbolic significance. This is not to say that the individual artist was invariably aware of the symbolic meaning of the prescribed standards, based as these were on complex metaphysical and theological considerations; but the symbolism nevertheless formed part of the fabric of his work, ready to add an extra dimension of meaning to the initiated and knowledgeable spectator.

In these conditions it is not surprising that the artist as a person is for the most part anonymous, very few names of artists having survived. It was the skill with which the work of art was made to conform to established ideals, rather than the artist who possessed the skill, that held the place of first importance.

THE APPRECIATION OF INDIAN ART

According to Indian aesthetic theory, a work of art possesses distinct "flavours" (*rasa*), the "tasting" of which constitutes the aesthetic experience. Because the work of art operates at various levels, granting to the spectator what he is capable of receiving by virtue of his intellectual and emotional preparation, the appreciation of the beauty of form and line is considered an appropriate activity of the educated and cultured man. The supreme aesthetic experience, however, is believed to be much deeper and cognate to the experience of the Godhead. From this point of view, the work of art is in a sense irrelevant and unnecessary for a person at a high level of spiritual progress; and for the devout layman its excellence is measured by its efficacy in promoting spiritual development.

INDIAN SCULPTURE

On the Indian subcontinent, sculpture seems to have been the favoured medium of artistic expression. Even architecture and the little painting that has survived from the early periods partake of the nature of sculpture. Particularly is this true of rock-cut architecture, which is often little more than sculpture on a colossal scale. Structural buildings are also profusely adorned with sculpture that is often inseparable from it. The close relationship between architecture and sculpture has to be taken into account when considering individual works that, even if complete in themselves, are also fragments belonging to a larger context. Indian sculpture, particularly from the 10th century onward, thus cannot be studied in isolation but must be considered as part of a larger entity to the total effect of which it contributes and from which it in turn gains meaning.

The subject matter of Indian sculpture is almost invariably religious. This does not mean that it cannot be understood as a work of art apart from its religious significance; but, at the same time, an understanding of its motivation and intent enriches one's appreciation. Much of what is represented is the recounting of legend and myth, particularly in the two centuries BC, when narrative relief was much in vogue. The work at this time, didactic and edificatory in intent, generally expresses itself in forms that are surprisingly earthy and sensuous. The anthropomorphic representation of the Buddha is avoided, and the subsidiary gods and goddesses are very much creatures of this earth. The Buddha image formulated around the 1st century AD is not what one would expect of the meditative, compassionate, Master of the Law; he is presented rather as an energetic, earthy being radiating strength and power.

The foundations of traditional Hindu imagery were also laid about the same time that the Buddha image was first formulated: images with several arms, and sometimes heads, representing the Indian mind's attempt to define visually the infiniteness of divinity. In subsequent periods the image with many arms became a commonplace in Hindu, Buddhist, and Jaina iconography. Although the various pantheons expanded, they continued to share features of common derivation, expressing the belief that beyond the phenomenal multiplicity of forms lay the unity of the Godhead.

In addition to the major religions, there has always existed in India a substratum of folk beliefs and cults dedicated to the worship of powers that preside over the operation of the life processes of nature. These fertility cults, best expressed in the worship of the male and female divinities *yakshas* and *yakshis*, played an important part in the development of Indian art. Among the perennial motifs that spring from the cults, those expressing life and abundance—such as the lotus, the pot overflowing with vegetation, water, or the like, the tree, the amorous couple, and above all the *yakshas* and *yakshis* themselves—are most significant. The images of these divinities, in particular, are the source of a great deal of artistic imagery and played a leading part in the development of iconographic types such as the images of the Buddha, the goddess Shri, and other divinities. The maternal as the ideal of female beauty, which is manifested artistically in the emphasis on full breasts and wide hips, can be traced to the same beliefs. The very richness and exuberance of much Indian art is an expression of the view of life that equates beauty with abundance.

It is difficult to generalize about the style of a sculptural tradition that extended over a period of almost 5,000 years, but it is nevertheless clear that the distinguishing quality of Indian sculpture is its emphatic plasticity so obvious in Sanchi I and Mathura sculpture from the 1st–3rd century AD. Forms are seen as swelling from within in response to the power of an inner life, the sculptor's function being to make these more manifest. At the same time a vision of form that is carved from without rather than modelled from within is also present, as for example at Bharhut. The history of much of Indian sculpture, marked by periods of high achievement bursting with creativity followed by periods in which the potentialities so postulated are gradually worked out, is essentially the interaction of these two dominant tendencies.

INDUS VALLEY CIVILIZATION (*c.* 2500–1800 BC)

Sculpture found in excavated cities consists of small pieces, generally terra-cotta objects, soapstone, or steatite, seals carved for the most part with animals, and a few statuettes of stone and bronze. The terra-cotta figurines are summarily modelled and provided with elaborate jewelry, which was fashioned separately and applied to the surface of the piece. Most of the work is simple, but a small group of human heads with horns are very sensitively modelled. Animal figures are common, particularly bulls, which are often carved with a sure understanding of their bulky, massive form. This plastic quality is also found in the humped

bulls engraved on steatite seals, where the modelling is more refined and sensitive. A humpless beast, generally called a "unicorn," is another favourite animal, but it is frequently quite stylized. In addition to bisons, elephants, rhinoceroses, and tigers, seals are carved with images of apparent religious significance, often strongly pictographic.

The terra-cotta sculpture and the seals both show two clear and distinct stylistic trends, one plastic and sensuous, the other linear and abstract. These appear during the same period and are also seen in the small group of stone and bronze sculptures that date from this period (National Museum, New Delhi). Of extraordinarily full and refined modelling is a fragmentary torso from Harappa, barely four inches (10 centimetres) high but of imposing monumentality; the same feeling for massive form is present in a lesser known bronze buffalo. A jaunty bronze dancing girl with head tilted upward (about 4½ inches [11 centimetres] high), from Mohenjo-daro, and a headless figure of a male dancer from Harappa, shoulders twisted in a circular movement, clearly demonstrate, in the attenuated and wiry tension of their forms, the second component of Indus Valley art. Of great interest is a famous bearded figure from Mohenjo-daro wearing a robe decorated with a pattern composed of trefoil motifs. The tight, compressed shape of the body and the expansive modelling of the head demonstrate that the two aspects of form revealed in Indus Valley art were not compartmentalized but interacted with each other. This can also be seen in the interplay of modelled form and textured surface frequently found in works produced by this civilization.

MAURYA PERIOD (*c*. 3RD CENTURY BC)

Little is known of Indian art in the period between the Indus Valley civilization and the reign of the Maurya emperor Ashoka. When sculpture again began to be found, it was remarkable for its maturity, seemingly fully formed at birth. The most famous examples are great circular stone pillars, products of Ashoka's imperial workshop, found over an area stretching from the neighbourhood of Delhi to Bihar. Made of fine-grained sandstone quarried at Chunar near Varanasi (Benares), the monolithic shafts taper gently toward the top. They are without a base and, in the better preserved examples, are capped by campaniform lotus capitals supporting an animal emblem. The entire pillar was carefully burnished to a bright lustre commonly called the "Maurya polish." The most famous of these monuments

This terra-cotta figurine found at an Indus Valley excavation, shows jewelry that was made separately and attached to the sculpture, a typical feature of Indus Valley civilization art. Larry Burrows/Time & Life Pictures/Getty Images

Lion capital from Sarnath, Chunar sandstone, mid-3rd century BC; in the Sarnath Museum, Uttar Pradesh, India. P. Chandr

is the lion capital at Sarnath, consisting of the front half of four identical animals joined back to back. There is a naturalistic emphasis on build and musculature, and the modelling is hard, vigorous, and energetic, stressing physical strength and power.

Very similar, if not at the same level of achievement, is the quadruple lion capital at Sanchi. Single lions are found at Vaishali (Bakhra), Rampurva, and Lauriya Nandangarh. The Vaishali pillar is heavy and squat, and the animal lacks the verve of the other animals—features, according to some, designating it as an early work, executed before the Maurya style attained its maturity. By contrast, the Rampurva lion, finished with painstaking and concise artistry, represents the style at its best. His smooth, muscled contours, wiry sinews, rippling, flamboyant mane, and alert stance reveal the work of a superior artist. An example at Lauriya Nandangarh is interesting because the pillar and the lion are both complete and in their original place, giving a clear idea of the column as it appeared to its contemporaries.

The lion was the animal most often represented, but figures of elephants and bulls are also known. At Dhauli in Orissa, the fore part of an elephant is carved out of rock on a terrace above a boulder that carries several of Ashoka's edicts. The modelling here is soft and gentle, and the plump, fleshy qualities of the young animal's body, seen as emerging from the rock, are suffused with warmth and natural vitality. Since the contrast with the rather formal, heraldic lions could not be more complete, the sculpture clearly testifies to the simultaneous existence of a style different from that of the lion capitals. The style might very well represent the indigenous tradition of plastic form that appears consistently in later art and also in some of the animal capitals made in the imperial atelier, notably the damaged elephant that once crowned the pillar at Sankisa and, above all, the splendid bull from Rampurva. In this great work of art, the two opposing concepts of form merge in a work of harmonious power. The pronounced naturalism comes from the same source as do the lions, but the tense line and hard modelling yield to a form that wells from within and at the same time is given stability and strength by a vision imposed from without.

The sudden appearance of Maurya art with seemingly no tradition behind it has led to speculation that it was the creation of foreign artists, either Achaemenian or Hellenistic. Persian influence, particularly in the lotus capitals and the figures of lions can hardly be denied, but what is remarkable is the drastic reinterpretation of alien forms by Indian artists. This is a process that is repeatedly seen in the history of Indian art.

Besides the animal sculpture, some human figures, more or less life size, can also be assigned to the Maurya period, though scholarly opinion is by no means unanimous on the point. Among the most important are three images discovered at Patna (ancient Pataliputra, the Maurya capital), two of which are representations of *yakshas*, the popular male divinities associated with cults of fertility, and the third, found at Didarganj (a section of Patna), a representation of a *yakshi*, or female divinity. Stylistically the images are very similar. The standing *yakshas* (Indian Museum, Kolkata) are powerful creatures; the ponderous weight of their bodies, together with a certain refined appreciation of the soft flesh, is admirably rendered. The Didarganj *yakshi* (Patna Museum), a masterpiece, displays the Indian ideal of female beauty, the heavy hips and full breasts strongly emphasizing the maternal aspect. In a nude torso discovered at Lopanipur, the sophisticated and sensitive treatment of the surfaces and the gentle blending planes that avoid all harsh accents produce a work of much refinement.

Small stone discs (also called ring stones because several of them are perforated in the centre), found from Taxila to Patna, are clearly connected with the cult of a nude mother goddess. They represent Maurya sculpture on a smaller and more intimate scale but characterized by the same refined and exquisite workmanship. They are executed in bas-relief, which became the favourite form of sculpture in the subsequent period.

The terra-cotta art of the Maurya period is best represented by a substantial group of figurines, modelled for the most part, the clay sculptor performing work in his medium at the same level as the artist working in stone. Patna has yielded a large number of such works, but examples are found throughout the Gangetic Plain. The clothing and jewelry on the figurines are heavy and elaborate, the modelling, particularly of the head, is sensitive, and the expression is often one of great charm and refinement. There are also more archaic examples, distinguished by flat bodies, enormous hips, and modelled heads and breasts.

SECOND AND FIRST CENTURIES BC

The Maurya empire collapsed in the early years of the 2nd century BC, and with it passed the art with which it was intimately related. The sculpture that is found throughout India from the middle of the 2nd century BC is startlingly different, but the process by which this change took place in a relatively short period of time is not fully understood. Several schools, sharing common features but nevertheless possessing distinct individual characteristics, are known to have existed. The history of the schools of northern India is somewhat obscure, largely due to the great destruction wrought in the Gangetic heartland; but there appears to have flourished there and in adjacent areas a school of great importance represented by the remains discovered at Bharhut, Sanchi, Mathura, and Bodh Gaya. Western India had its own school, as revealed in the sculptures decorating the cave temples, notably those of Bhaja, Pitalkhora, and Karli. In the southeast, the important school of Andhradesha flourished in the Krishna River Valley at Amaravati, Jaggayyapeta, and associated sites; and in eastern India, what is now the modern state of Orissa, made its contribution in the rock-cut sculptures at Udayagiri-Khandagiri. The distinctive schools, though spread over a subcontinent, were not isolated from each other. The contacts fostered by a flourishing trade and by the constant movement of pilgrims were always very close, and it was never long before developments in one part of India were echoed in another.

Judging from extant remains, artists of the earlier period (c. 3rd century BC) preferred figures carved in the round, relief sculpture being quantitatively quite insignificant. By contrast, it was sculpture in low relief that was favoured in the first two centuries BC; the earlier tradition was not quite forgotten, but figures carved in the round are relatively few. Although there is no stylistic difference, relief sculpture is here considered first according to the various regional schools, and sculpture in the round is treated separately.

RELIEF SCULPTURE OF NORTHERN AND CENTRAL INDIA

Among the most important, and perhaps the earliest, remains in northern India are reliefs from the great *stupa* at Bharhut, dating approximately to the middle of the 2nd century BC. The work, suggesting a style imitating wooden sculpture, is characterized by essentially cubical forms, flat planes that meet at sharp angles, and very elaborate and precisely detailed ornamentation of surfaces. Most of the sculpture was confined to the railing of the *stupa*. Some of the supporting posts bear large image of *yakshas* and *yakshis* of popular religion, now clearly pressed into the service of Buddhism, while most of the others are decorated with medallions in the centre and crescent-shaped motifs, or lunates, at the top and bottom, all filled with lotus motifs. Some medallions contain amorous couples, the overflowing pot, the goddess Śrī standing on lotuses while being ceremonially bathed by elephants and other symbols of abundance; still others contain the earliest illustrations of events in the Buddha's life and of narratives of his former incarnations as related in the *Jataka* tales (a collection of tales about the Buddha). Although compositions are crowded, great economy of expression is evident because the artist confines himself to the representation of essentials. Figures are often carved in horizontal rows, sometimes asymmetrically, adapting themselves awkwardly to the circular space of the medallion. Continuous narrative, in which events succeeding in time are shown in the same space, is often resorted to—the first occurrence of what was to become a favourite narrative technique. There is no attempt at establishing any interrelationship, psychological or compositional, between the various figures, each of which is strictly

confined within its own space. The faces are masklike, without trace of emotion, lending a solemn and hieratic quality to their expression. Trapped between the background and a frontal plane beyond which they are not allowed to project, the figures are in a sense strictly two-dimensional, more so than in any other style of Indian sculpture. Often, however—particularly in the treatment of animals—the artist is more relaxed, giving glimpses of intimate observation and a natural rendering that anticipates the direction of future development. Like the posts, the top part, or coping, of the stone rail is also carved on both faces; on one of them is a continuous creeper bearing lotus flowers, leaves, and buds; on the other, again the winding stem of a creeper, but bearing other good things of life—such as clothes, jewelry, and fruits—and also scenes illustrating *Jataka* stories.

Bharhut is an extremely important monument inasmuch as it seems to mark a new beginning after the refined and naturalistic art of the Maurya empire. The sophistication, in spite of the archaic, hieratic manner, would indicate that a considerable body of sculptural tradition, particularly in wood, preceded it; but of this no traces have survived. Be that as it may, Bharhut states for the first time, and at some length, themes and motifs that would henceforth remain a part of Indian sculpture.

Stray finds of sculpture at Mathura and other sites in modern Uttar Pradesh indicate that the Bharhut style was spread over a large part of northern India, particularly the region roughly between that city and Varanasi and Bodh Gaya in the east. A closely related style is also found at Sanchi in eastern Malava, where a representative example is the sculpture of the railing of Stupa II. Although the themes and motifs found at Bharhut occur here, narrative representations are all but absent. The style is almost identical; the stiff and rigid contours are a little softer, but both the scale and richness of Bharhut are missing.

It is the sculpture of the four gateways (*toranas*) of the Great Stupa (Stupa I) at Sanchi, however, that is the principal glory of that site, carrying the promise of the Bharhut style to its fulfillment. The *toranas*, four in number, were attached to the plain railing around the middle of the 1st century BC. They consist of square posts with capitals supporting a triple architrave, or molded band, with voluted (turned in the shape of a spiral, scroll-shaped ornament) ends and a top crowned with Buddhist symbols. Bracket figures, in the form of *yakshis*, serve as additional supports. All parts of these gates, strongly reminiscent of wooden construction, are covered from top to bottom with the most exquisite sculpture. Subjects and motifs found at Bharhut are also found here, the same profusely flowering lotus stem and associated motifs, the same compositions with figures basically arranged in horizontal rows, the same love for clear detail; but to all of these are added a truly voluminous sense of form, a smoother and more energetic

movement, and a keen appreciation for the forms of nature, all of which endow the sculpture with a naïve and sensuous beauty unparalleled in Indian art.

Departures from the Bharhut style are particularly striking in the narrative reliefs. Their greater depth, taken together with their crowded composition, results in the background, visible at Bharhut, being submerged in shadow. The figures, in all their richness and abundance, flow out from the dark ground, secured in place by the frame of the panels. The Bharhut angular silhouette and the rigid, severe outline of the body yields at Sanchi to a gently swelling plasticity, animated by a soft, breathing quality that molds the contours without strain or tension. There is a pronounced concern with the organization of composition, and the narration is often leisurely and discursive; the artist does not just tell the basic story but also lingers over the details, amplifying them to give a vivid picture of everyday life. The emotional monotone of Bharhut survives in some Sanchi sculptures, but in others it is superseded by joyous faces and the emotional impact of vivid gesture and movement. Dejection is written large on the faces of the soldiers of Māra's army, who had tried to disturb the Buddha's meditation, as they stagger away from the scene of defeat, and the sensuousness of the amorous scenes is successfully evoked by the tender and intimate gestures of the couples. No longer transfixed in their own space, they turn to look at each other lovingly,

This detail shows a yakshi (a benevolent female spirit) on the East Gate to the Great Stupa in Sanchi, India. Eliot Elisofon/Time & Life Pictures/Getty Images

responding to each other with a deeply felt understanding.

Long and elaborate bas-reliefs carved on the architraves of the *toranas* are the summit of the Sanchi sculptor's art. Among the finest are representations of the wars for the relics, the defeat of Mara, the *Vishvantara Jataka*, and the *Shaddanta Jataka*. The compositions are rich and crowded with figures, and are arranged with great skill. Particularly striking is the masterly handling of animals, notably the elephant, whose fleshy body and graceful movement are captured unerringly. Deer, water buffaloes, bulls, monkeys—all of the beasts and birds of the forests—are rendered with a sense of intimacy indicating the artist's sense of the fellowship of man and animal in the world of nature. The lush Indian landscape is often carved with ornamental trees, waterfalls, pools, mountains, and rivers. The Sanchi sculptor also shows a marked preference for architectural settings, filling his compositions with numerous buildings that often provide the spatial context for the action. Entire cities, with surrounding walls, elaborate gate houses, and palatial mansions, are depicted. Depth is achieved by rendering side views, and multiple perspective continues to be the rule.

The several large images of *yakshis* serving as brackets supporting the lowermost architraves of the *toranas* are unique achievements. Like the same goddesses at Bharhut, they are shown in association with a tree to which they cling, but the style is remarkably different. The modelling shows a concern for the charms of the body, stressing the tactile nature of its flesh. The heavy jewelry and clothing that conceal the body are drastically reduced, revealing its nudity. The soft, melting sensuousness of the female form is so greatly emphasized that the belly and the folds of flesh at the waist are almost flabby, redeemed only by the smooth, firm breasts and the tender arms and limbs.

By comparison, reliefs adorning the railing around the Mahabodhi temple at Bodh Gaya (of about the same date or a little earlier) are in a somewhat impoverished idiom, lacking the rich proliferation both of Bharhut and Sanchi. The posts have the usual medallions, lunates filled with lotuses, and reliefs depicting the familiar scenes of Buddhist myth and legend. The artistry of Bodh Gaya, however, is of a lower level of achievement than that at either Bharhut or Sanchi: the relief is deeper than that at Bharhut but shallower than that at the Great Stupa of Sanchi; and crowded compositions are lacking, as are the clear and precise ornament and the rich floral motifs. The Bodh Gaya sculptor, however, though abbreviating even further the iconography of Bharhut, breaks up, as does the Sanchi sculptor, the spatial isolation that so uncompromisingly separated each individual figure at that site.

The great school of Mathura, also, seems to have come into existence about the 2nd century BC, though its period of greatest activity falls in the first two centuries AD. The city was repeatedly sacked in the course of the centuries, which may account for the paucity of materials, but enough has been discovered to reveal that the style, in its early stages, was very similar to that of Bharhut, characterized by flat two-dimensional sculpture decorated with abundant and precise ornament. Several fragments discovered at the site show the gradual stages by which this style evolved, leading to the sculpture of the Great Stupa at Sanchi on the one hand and to Bodh Gaya on the other.

RELIEF SCULPTURE OF ANDHRADESHA

Besides the schools of northern India, a very accomplished style also existed in southeast India; the most important sites are Jaggayyapeta and Amaravati, activity at the latter site extending well into the 2nd century AD. The early remains are strikingly similar to those at Bharhut, the relief generally even shallower and the modelling comparatively flat. In contrast to those found in northern India, the proportions of the human body are elongated; but in its flat, cubical modelling, angular, halting contours, and precise, detailed ornamentation, the style is essentially similar to contemporary work elsewhere, right down to the same conventional clothing and jewelry. The nervous, fluid treatment of surfaces, so characteristic of subsequent Andhra sculpture, is already present here. The preferred material is

marble rather than the sandstone invariably used in the north.

The style of the Andhradesha school developed in a manner consistent with other regions of India, becoming more voluminous and shedding the early rigidity fairly rapidly. A group of sculptures at Amaravati are characterized by the same qualities that distinguish the work at the Great Stupa of Sanchi: full and lissome forms, modelling that emphasizes mass and weight, and sensuously rendered surfaces.

RELIEF SCULPTURE OF WESTERN INDIA

The numerous rock-cut cave temples in the Western Ghats are, comparatively speaking, much less profusely adorned with sculpture than remains from other parts of India. The earliest works are undoubtedly the bas-reliefs on a side wall of the porch of a small monastery at Bhaja. They are commonly interpreted as depicting the god Indra on his elephant and the sun god Surya on his chariot but are more probably illustrations of the adventures of the mythical universal emperor Mandhata. What is immediately evident is that these sculptures are not imitations of wooden prototypes, like those at Bharhut, but, rather, reflect a tradition of terra-cotta sculpture, abundant examples of which are found in northern India and Bengal, where this medium was very popular because of the easy availability of fine clay. The terra-cotta tradition is reflected in the amorphous, spreading forms of Bhaja and in the fine striations used in depicting ornaments and pleated cloth, techniques natural and appropriate to the fashioning of wet clay. The fact that there are some similarities to the Bharhut style—the stilted postures of the figures and the flat contours of the body, for example—indicates that the beginnings of the western Indian school would also have to be placed about the middle of the 2nd century BC.

The next major group of sculptures in western India have been found at Pitalkhora. The colossal plinth of a monastery decorated with a row of elephants, the large figures of the door guardians, and several fragments recovered during the course of excavations are among the more important remains. A great proportion of the work represents an advance over the style of Bhaja, though features derived from terra-cotta sculpture continue to be found: the figures are carved in greater depth and volume, but the texture of the drapery, the soft contours of the body, and the high relief of the jewelry, which sometimes gives the impression of having been fashioned separately and then applied, testify to the continuing strength of the terra-cotta tradition. Although the hard line and sharp cutting of some sculpture is reminiscent of the earlier, wood-carving tradition as seen at Bharhut, the forms are more appropriate to the stone medium. Moreover, the expression is more explicit; and for the first time, both gently smiling and boldly laughing figures of *yakshas* appear, as

well as the figure of a lover blissfully drunk on wine offered to him by his beloved. These features are also found in the later sculpture of the Great Stupa at Sanchi and, to a more pronounced extent, in the sculpture of the Mathura school of the 1st centuries AD—for example, in the happily smiling *yakshis* from Bhutesar.

The cave temple at Kondane has, above the entrance hall, four beautiful panels depicting pairs of dancers. The forms retain the robust and full modelling of the more developed sculpture at Pitalkhora, but to this is added an ease of movement and considerable rhythmic grace. Traces of the terra-cotta tradition are now totally absent; nor do they occur in the next phase, best represented by a group of sculptures found in the rock-cut temples and monasteries at Bedsa and Nasik and in the *caitya*, or temple proper, at Karli. Sculpture at all these sites shows many affinities to the Great Stupa at Sanchi and should be approximately contemporary or a little earlier. Easily the most outstanding achievements of this region and period, and for that matter one of the greatest achievements of the Indian sculptor, are the large panels, depicting amorous couples, located in the entrance porch of the Karli *caitya*. Here the promise of early work achieves its fulfillment, the full weighty forms imbued with a warm, joyous life and a free, assured movement. The resemblance to work at the Great Stupa of Sanchi is obvious, though these figures at Karli are on a much larger scale and possess a massiveness and monumentality that is a characteristic of the distinct western Indian idiom.

RELIEF SCULPTURE OF ORISSA

Sculpture decorating the monasteries cut into the twin hills of Udayagiri and Khandagiri in Orissa represents yet another early Indian local idiom. The work is not of one period but extends over the first two centuries BC; the stages of development roughly parallel the styles observed at Sanchi Stupa No. II, Bodh Gaya, and the Great Stupa at Sanchi, but they possess, like other regional schools, fairly distinct and individual features. The earliest sculptures are the few simple reliefs found in the Alakapuri cave, humble works that recall the bas-reliefs of Sanchi Stupa II. The Mancapuri, Tatoka Gumpha, and Ananta cave sculptures—particularly the image of Surya riding a chariot—are more advanced and resemble work at Bodh Gaya. The forms are heavy and solid and lack the accomplished movement of the later cave sculpture adorning the Rani Gumpha monastery. These, like other sculptures here, are in a poor state of preservation, but they represent the finest achievements at the site. Most remarkable is a long frieze, stretching between the arched doorways of the top story, representing a series of incidents that have not yet been identified. The work parallels that of the Great Stupa at Sanchi, with the same supple modelling and crowded compositions. At the same time there is a nervous agitation, a fluid, agile movement together with a decided preference for tall, slender human figures. The reliefs on the guard rooms of Rani Gumpha are also quite remarkable, depicting forested landscapes filled with rocks from which waterfalls flow into lakes that are the sporting grounds of wild elephants. The fine work of this cave strikes a romantic and lyrical note seldom found in Indian art.

SCULPTURE IN THE ROUND AND TERRA-COTTA

The most important sculpture in the round are the life-size or colossal images of *yakshas* and *yakshis*, which reinterpret forms established by the two Patna *yakshas* and the Didarganj *yakshi* of the Maurya period—very much as a few animal capitals, particularly the *makaras* (a crocodile-like creature) from Kaushambi and Vidisha (Besnagar), echo the tradition of the superb Maurya animal capitals. It is the *yaksha* figures, however, that deserve special attention, for they played a significant part in the iconographic developments of the 1st century AD and later and contributed substantially to the imagery of the anthropomorphic Buddha icon.

The most famous of the *yaksha* images is a colossal figure recovered from the village of Parkham, near Mathura (Archaeological Museum). It is about 8 ⅔ feet (2.6 metres) in height, and, though

the two hands are broken and the head is considerably damaged, it is an image of great strength. Its squat neck, its head set close to the body, which tends toward corpulence, its swelling belly restrained by a flat band, and a broad chest adorned with necklaces—all of these features contribute to an image turgid with earthy power. The back is flat and cursively finished, so that the figure has the appearance more of a bifacial relief than of an image carved in the round. Although the forms retain some of the cubical modelling of Bharhut, the swelling limbs and torso have a massive weightiness that makes the image an appropriate representation of a divinity that presides over the productive processes of nature and endows plenty and abundance on his worshippers.

The Mathura region seems to have been an important centre of *yaksha* worship, for several images, most of them fragmentary, have been discovered there. Some images have also been found from the ancient city of Vidisha (Vidisha Museum), one of which is even larger than the Parkham example and is in a better state of preservation. The god holds a bag in one hand (the other was held below the chest), and the hair is tied in a large top knot over the forehead. The image is accompanied by a female consort (*yakshi*), wide-hipped and full-breasted, who also emphasizes and personifies the powers of fertility.

The widespread nature of the cult is evidenced by the occurrence of *yaksha* images throughout India. Fragments in the round (not to speak of the relief representations in a Buddhist context) of the 2nd to 1st centuries BC have been found from Madhyadesha, Orissa, Rajasthan, Andhradesha, and Maharashtra. At Pitalkhora there is an exceptionally fine image of a *yaksha* conceived as a pot-bellied dwarf carrying a shallow bowl on his head; the features, with a gently laughing mouth, are suffused with good humour. Similar *yakshas*, employed as atlantes (male figures used as supporting elements), are also found on the western gateway of the Great Stupa at Sanchi and at other sites, notably Sarnath.

The latest in the series of cult images is the image of the Yaksha Manibhadra, from Pawaya (Gwalior Museum). The sculpture is at present headless, but the rest of the body is well preserved. The right hand holds a fly whisk that flares over the shoulder; the modelling of the legs and torso is sensitive, and the folds of the garment wrapped around the body are full and voluminous, recalling the style of sculpture at Sanchi.

The terra-cotta sculpture of the period consists mainly of relief plaques made from molds found at numerous sites in northern India. These generally depict popular divinities; a richly dressed female figure loaded with profuse

Bust of a goddess, c. 9th century, from the fort at Gwalior, Madhya Pradesh, India. P. Chandra

jewelry, obviously a mother goddess, is the favoured subject. Scenes from daily life also abound—as well as what appear to be illustrations of current myths and stories. Superb examples have been found from Mathura, Ahichhatra, Kaushambi, Tamluk, and Chandraketugarh. The workmanship is often of the most exquisite clarity and delicacy, the style paralleling that of contemporary stone sculpture.

IN THE FIRST TO FOURTH CENTURIES AD

This period is characterized by the dominance in northern India of the ancient school of Mathura. Other schools, such as those that flourished at Sarnath and Sanchi in the first two centuries BC, for example, were markedly restricted in their artistic output. Much of their sculpture was imported from Mathura, and the few images they produced locally were strongly influenced by Mathura work. The narrative bas-relief tradition, consisting of elaborate compositions of edificatory character, was on the wane, and the emphasis was on carving individual figures, either in high relief or in the round. For the first time, images appear of the Buddha, bodhisattvas, and various other divinities including specifically Hindu images representing the gods Vishnu, Shiva, Varaha, and Devi slaying the buffalo demon; some of these figures begin to feature several arms, a characteristic of later iconography. There are also many images of yakshis, often in most alluring attitudes and gestures. Their enticing bodies are now presented as unified organic entities, lacking all traces of the stiff, puppet-like aspect that had not been entirely overcome even at the Great Stupa of Sanchi. During this period, also, a fresh incursion of foreign influence by way of western Asia was received, quickly assimilated, and transformed in the characteristic manner of Indian art.

The school of Gandhara, with Taxila in Pakistan as its centre and stretching into eastern Afghanistan, flourished alongside the Kushan school of Mathura. It is of a startlingly different aspect, stressing a relatively naturalistic rendering of form, ultimately of Greco-Roman origin. The school evolved a distinct type of Buddha image and was also rich in relief sculptures depicting Buddhist myth and legend. Drawing largely on Indian traditions of composition, it nevertheless reinterpreted them in its own manner. The schools of Mathura and Gandhara were in close proximity and undoubtedly influenced each other, but essentially each adheres to its own concept of style.

The ancient Indian relief style found its fullest expression and development at neither Mathura nor Gandhara but in Andhradesha, notably at the great sites of Amaravati and Nagarjunikonda. Railing pillars and other parts of stupas decorated with Jataka tales and scenes from the Buddha's life are found in great number and are of the most exquisite quality. Free-standing images of the Buddha, on the other hand, are relatively rare, being found only toward the close of the period.

MATHURA

One of the most important contributions of the school of Mathura was the development of the cult image of the Buddha, who had been previously represented by aniconic (not made as a likeness) symbols. There is a certain amount of controversy about whether Mathura or Gandhara originated the Buddha image, which appears to be insoluble in view of the circumstantial nature of the evidence. It is possible that the two schools independently developed their own separate types of images; but, at least as far as the Mathura image is concerned, it is clear that it is a natural development from the tradition of large *yaksha* sculptures found in this region. The development can easily be seen in a famous image (discovered at Sarnath and now in the Sarnath Museum) of Mathura manufactured and dedicated by the monk Bala. Carved in the round, the image is shown in a pose of strict frontality, the left hand held at the waist and the right arm, now damaged, originally raised to the shoulder—a posture immediately recalling that of the *yaksha* images. The jewelry, however, is appropriately omitted, and the body is clothed in simple monastic garments. The modelling throughout is strong and sensuous, and the radiant energy of the body, its affirmative, outgoing movement, is more appropriate to the personality of a *yaksha* than to that of the Buddha. This standing Buddha image, as seen in the Bala statue, is the standard Mathura type, several examples of which are known. Along with this one, a similar, seated type developed, of which the best example is the splendid image known as the Katra Buddha (Archaeological Museum). The modelling of the body is refined, the breasts characteristically heavy and prominent, and the flesh of the torso, with its subtle modulations, as convincingly rendered as the Bala image.

The new trends formulated early by the Mathura school do not indicate a sharp break from the traditions of the earlier schools. This is clear in a series of magnificent *ayagapatas*, or stone tablets originally set up outside *stupas* to receive worship and offerings. They are usually square or rectangular and richly decorated with auspicious and religious symbols as well as angelic and mythical beings. The extremely decorative, lavish surface treatment gives the immediate impression of a great profusion of multiple forms, akin in feeling to the sculpture of the Great Stupa of Sanchi. The organization of these forms, however, has none of the easy freedom of Sanchi. The figures, for example, are often cast in a regular, winding shape imitating the movement of the undulating lotus creeper. The same movement is seen in rows of animals depicted with haunches raised and chests touching the ground,

features seen in earlier art but now much more emphatically stylized. The bodies of the animals also begin to be overpowered by vegetal forms, the tails, for example, terminating in foliate tips; in a later age, this tendency results in the almost total disintegration of animal shapes under the pressure of the floral.

It is not to these bas-reliefs, however, that one turns for the most delightful creations of the Mathura school (for they are in fact the last vestiges of a style rapidly passing out of favour) but to the large number of railing pillars usually carved with representation of *yakshis* engaged in playful and enticing activities such as plucking blossoms from trees or leaning on its branches, dancing, bathing under a waterfall, and adorning themselves. Among the most beautiful of these is a group that was recovered from Kankali Tila and now in the State Museum at Lucknow. The modelling of the figures is generally heavy, the soft, plump bodies suffused with a slow, languorous movement. What is important, however, is the emotion, which is no longer expressed in the face alone but in the whole attitude of the body. The pensive mood of a woman holding a lamp, for instance, is evoked not only by the serene features of the face but by the gentle sway of the relaxed body. Present throughout is a fresh movement of life, a marked striving for diverse and varied effects of posture, movement, expression, and even dress and ornament that brings about vital changes in the nature of Indian sculpture. A remarkable group of railing posts decorated with *yakshi* images, which were recovered from Bhutesar near Mathura (Archaeological Museum), represent an even more refined achievement than the Kankali Tila figures. The heavy proportions, in spite of the full breasts and the wide hips, have been overcome; the happy faces express carefree joy, and the postures of the body are so alive with rhythm as to give the impression of a dancing figure.

Mathura, during this period, was ruled by the Kushan dynasty. A group of portrait sculptures of these rulers (Archaeological Museum), recovered from a village called Māt in the environs of Mathura, gives an interesting glimpse of the foreign influences entering India at the time. One of them (unfortunately lacking the head) represents the emperor Kaniska wearing heavy boots, a tunic, and a coat, and leaning on a mace. The image is quite different not only in dress but also in style from other contemporary works, being essentially linear, with the forms entirely set into the surface. The surfaces have little ornamentation and are marked by extreme simplicity; they are also uncompromisingly stiff and rigid.

Mathura is famed for its Buddhist-influenced art. This bas-relief detail comes from a temple in Mathura. Brand X Pictures/Dinodia Photos/Getty Images

It is possible that these images represent attempts by a Mathura artist to imitate a style preferred by his imperial masters; but it was not long before the foreign elements were assimilated into the Mathura style proper, for later images of Kushan chiefs have the same expanding and voluminous form that characterizes other sculptures of this school. A large number of ornamental motifs that now appear in India for the first time undergo a similar process of transformation.

The extent of Mathura influence on Indian art of this period can be gauged by the sculpture of the school found at several sites in different parts of northern India, notably Ahichhatra, Kaushambi, Sarnath, and Sanchi. Most of these sites had been flourishing centres earlier, but only a very limited amount of sculpture was produced during the ascendancy of the Mathura school; and whatever local sculpture was produced at this time was heavily influenced by the Mathura style. At Sarnath, for example, both the Bala Buddha imported from Mathura and its local imitations have been found.

Ivory plaques discovered at Bagram in Afghanistan are closely related to the school of Mathura. These are of great importance; for, though ivory must have been a favourite medium of sculpture, little has been preserved of the early work. Most of it is in very low engraved relief, with fluent, sweeping outlines. The figures are depicted in easy and elegant postures, and the workmanship often attains considerable virtuosity.

GANDHARA

Contemporary with the school of Mathura, and extending almost into the 6th century, is the Gandhara school, whose style is unlike anything else in Indian art. It flourished in a region known in ancient times as Gandhara, with its capital at Taxila in the Punjab, and in adjacent areas including the Swat Valley and eastern Afghanistan. The output of the school was very large; numerous images, mostly of Buddhas and *bodhisattvas*, and narrative reliefs illustrating scenes from the Buddha's life and legends have been found. The favoured material is gray slate or blue schist and, particularly during the later phases, stucco. Except for objects excavated at a few well-known sites (such as Taxila, Peshawar, and the Swat Valley, in Pakistan, and Jalalabad, Hadda, and Bamiyan, in Afghanistan), most of the finds have been the result of casual discovery or clandestine treasure hunts and plunder, so their correct provenance is not known. If to this are added the large variety of idioms that appear to have existed simultaneously and the total absence of securely dated images, the wide divergence of scholarly opinion with regard to the schools' evolution can be understood. In the present day, there is general agreement, however, that its most flourishing period probably coincided with Kushan rule, particularly the reigns of the emperor Kaniska and his successors, and that the school did not long outlast the growth of the Gupta school in the 5th century.

The origins of the Gandhara style are ultimately Greco-Roman, though, recently, emphasis has been placed on Roman art as the more immediate source. It has also been suggested that the school was created by foreign craftsmen imported into India and by their Indian pupils.

The Gandhara school is also credited by some scholars with the invention of the anthropomorphic Buddha image. Whether this is correct or not, the Gandhara image is quite different from that of Mathura and illustrates the difference between the two schools. Instead of the powerful images directly descended from *yaksha* prototypes, the Gandhara version is an adaptation of an Apollo figure, with rather sweet and sentimental features. The definite volume and substance given to the pleated folds of the monastic robes make this image more naturalistic than anything found in Indian art. At the same time, the iconographical features are of Indian origin. Large numbers of *bodhisattva* images conceived in the image of royalty, some with strongly individualized facial features, have also been found.

In contrast to Mathura, narrative relief sculpture was very popular in Gandhara art. Again, in composition and iconography these reliefs are largely dependent on the earlier Indian schools, but the style is quite distinct. Instead of continuous narrative, incidents separated in time are separately represented, though often arranged in sequence. Violent emotions are realistically rendered. The compositions range from simple horizontal placement of figures to rich and complex arrangements, which often attempt to render space illusionistically.

In the course of time, Indian influence was increasingly felt in the art of Gandhara, and an abstract vision began to obscure the Greco-Roman naturalism of the earlier forms. In spite of the new influence (and the many graceful but cloying stucco sculptures that are representative of this late phase) the style shows no signs of vital change. This conservatism, together with the large artistic production, gives an overall impression of considerable monotony. Without any real roots in India and with marked foreign features, the avenues of natural development seem to have been closed to the school, which thus finally disappeared. Nevertheless it made vital contributions to the art of Central and eastern Asia, and several features, drastically transformed, were incorporated in Gupta art.

ANDHRADESHA

Besides the schools of Mathura and Gandhara, a most accomplished school of sculpture flourished in Andhradesha during the three centuries AD, the most important centres being Amaravati and Nagarjunakonda. The remains consist mainly of carved railings and rectangular slabs that decorated the great Buddhist *stupas*, which have largely disappeared. The finds are thus fragmentary and belong to several phases of construction or to separate monuments spanning the 1st, 2nd, and 3rd centuries AD.

Unlike the school of Mathura, which concentrates on the carving of single figures, the Amaravati school carried to the fullest limit of its development the ancient tradition of relief sculpture, which flourished in the two centuries BC at sites such as Bharhut, Sanchi, and Amaravati itself. The marble railing posts are decorated with central medallions and lunates at the top and bottom, all filled with lotus flowers of a very rich design. Often the medallions also contain reliefs illustrating scenes from the Buddha's life and from the *Jataka* stories, and these are the principal glory of the site.

Two broad phases in the development of narrative relief can be distinguished. In the first, the artist builds on the achievements of early relief sculpture as seen on the Great Stupa of Sanchi. The forms are still comparatively heavy, the figures increasingly soft and fleshy, the movement freer but still pervaded by a sense of calm repose. This type of work, represented by relatively few examples, is followed by a phase in which the compositions achieve an extraordinary elaboration and complexity. Most striking is the restless, energetic movement, often nervous and flurried, that possesses the participants in any given scene. Complex relationships and patterns are established between the figures; and space is so articulated that the eye participates in the swirling inner movement of the composition that effectually dissolves the ground on which the figures are carved, while the figures themselves flow out in an endless movement from the ground. The setting is dramatic in the extreme. The loving workmanship, reminiscent of ivory carving, and the superb technical proficiency mark the Amaravati reliefs as the culminating point of the entire relief style.

The figures, of both men and women, are of unprecedented suppleness and plasticity, the forms rendered in every variety of torsion and flexion. A fluent, gliding line, often more appropriate to painting than to sculpture, encloses the figures, and pervading the whole is a subtle voluptuousness. The reliefs are often only nominally religious, a pretext for the sculptor's pleasure in representing the leisured and sophisticated life of the time.

Nagarjunakonda sculpture marks the last phase of the relief style. The figures become stiffer and puppet-like, the patterns of movement frozen and mechanical but still possessing the energy and richness that always characterize this style.

The Buddha is represented in Andhradesha by both symbolic and anthropomorphic forms. The iconographic formula developed shows him clad in a rather thick garment with stylized folds, and the postures are not as formal and hieratic as the Mathura. This type of Buddha exercised considerable influence in the development of the Buddha image in Sri Lanka. In several other features as well, the Andhra style also contributed to the development of early sculpture in Southeast Asia.

TERRA-COTTA

The quality of terra-cotta figurines of this period is generally inferior to work produced in the first two centuries BC. Many heads of crude workmanship, with protruding eyes, apparently representing foreigners, were found at sites such as Mathura, Ahichhatra, and Kaushambi. At the same time, there are some well-modelled heads that imitate the style of stone sculpture and are equally expressive.

GUPTA PERIOD (*C.* 4TH–6TH CENTURIES AD)

During the 4th and the 5th centuries, when much of northern India was ruled by the Gupta dynasty, Indian sculpture entered what has been called its classic phase. The promise of the earlier schools was now fully realized, and at the same time new forms and artistic ideals were formulated that served as the source for development in succeeding centuries. The more or less sensuous and earthy rendering of form was drastically transformed, so that artistic expression closely conformed to the religious vision. The forms are refined and treated with sure and unsurpassed elegance. The volumes, impelled by an inner life, still swell from within but are restrained and controlled, made to flow in smooth and abstract rhythms in an organic and unified concept in which the sensual and the spiritual are inextricably blended. The edificatory, didactic intent of early relief sculpture is abandoned; instead, the works produced are pronouncedly meditative; and the repose and calm that settles on the images of the Buddha, the master of the inner contemplative life, is also seen on images of other divinities. Decorative ornament is in perfect harmony with the volumes it adorns, each emphasizing the other, so that in every respect this classic style of the Gupta period is one of great composure and perfect balance.

MATHURA

The impetus for the new schools seems to have come from Mathura, which is hardly surprising in view of the preponderant role played by the city in the preceding period. The transformation into the new idiom is best illustrated by a splendid image of the Buddha which is dated AD 384 (Indian Museum, Kolkata [Calcutta]). Memories of the rather massive and ponderous weight of the earlier style are present, but the calm face no longer looks out at the world; rather, the vision is turned within, the mood being one of serene contemplation. The style, which consistently uses the local red sandstone, undergoes further refinement, seen in a series of magnificent life-size Buddha images of the 5th century (now scattered in museums throughout the world). The more delicate face radiates a feeling of calm inner bliss, and the body is most subtly modelled by smoothly flowing planes that both suggest the swelling force of life and subordinate it to the spiritual vision of the whole. Mathura images generally show the Buddha wearing a diaphanous robe, the folds of which are rendered by stringlike ridges in a reinterpretation of a Gandhara convention. The gestures of the hand are delicate and varied. The hair is usually rendered by rows of small curls that conceal the conical protuberance. These Mathura images established an iconographical type that became the norm for the Buddha image.

In addition to the Buddha figure, Mathura has yielded large numbers of images of the various Hindu divinities, particularly Vishnu-Krishna. This is in keeping with the increasing strength of the various Hindu cults and the intimate association of Mathura with the god Krishna. The famous image of Vishnu from Katra Keshavadeva in Mathura is one of the finest (National Museum, New Delhi). The god is conceived as a royal figure, wearing a crown and appropriate jewelry, his features imbued with a dignified calm that is suitable to his function as the preserver and is also characteristic of most Gupta art.

SARNATH

This famous centre of Indian art developed a sweeter and more elegant version of the Buddha image than Mathura's. Instead of the rather strict frontal posture, the weight of the body is thrown more on one leg, resulting in a very subtle contrapposto position, in which the hips, shoulders, and head are turned in different directions. This lends a certain movement to the figure, so that it does not quite possess the static, steadfast quality of Mathura. The robes are no longer ridged with folds but are plain, and the surface of the stone is even more abstractly handled than is the Mathura. The faces are heart-shaped, the transitions from one part of the body to another smoother, so that the images have great refinement even if they do not possess the strength of Mathura. The characteristic Sarnath style, the preferred material of which is the local buff Chunar sandstone, seems to have developed in the late 5th century, the few earlier works being closer to the Mathura school. The most famous image from the site and one of the masterpieces of Indian art is that of the seated Buddha preaching (Sarnath Museum). It is exceptionally well preserved and delicately carved. The face, with serene features and a gentle smile playing on the lips, suggests the joy of supreme spiritual achievement. The halo behind the Buddha is also very beautifully carved, with exquisite floral patterns. Large numbers of Buddha and *bodhisattva* images have been excavated at Sarnath and are to be found in the museum at the site and in major collections throughout the world.

CENTRAL INDIA

In addition to the major schools of Sarnath and Mathura, important sculpture of the 5th and 6th centuries is found at several sites in central India. The sculptures here are often in their original locations, surviving not as isolated images torn from their architectural context but in association with the temples of which they formed a part. At Udayagiri, near Vidisha, are a series of simple rock-cut caves of the opening years of the 5th century. The sculpture, made of soft stone, has suffered greatly, but whatever has survived reveals a style that stresses strength and power. Perhaps the most magnificent work is a great relief panel depicting the boar incarnation of Vishnu lifting the earth goddess from the watery deeps into which she had been dragged by a demon. The massive figure of the god, with the body of a man and the head of a boar, is carved in a surging movement across the face of the rock, the goddess resting easily on his shoulder, while a host of beings, human and divine, celebrate this great triumph.

The Shiva temple at Bhumara has also yielded some sculpture of fine quality. The stone is carved with great precision and skill, nowhere more evident than in the handling of exuberant floral ornament. Little in Indian decorative sculpture can match the brilliance of the large panels filled with lotus stems and floriated scrolls discovered at this site and at Nachna Kuthara.

Some of the finest Gupta sculpture adorns the walls of the Vishnu temple at Deogarh. Particularly striking are three large relief panels depicting Vishnu lying on the serpent Shsa, the elephant's rescue, and the penance of Nara-Narayana. The compositions tend to be dramatic; the carving and decoration, sumptuous, the sturdy forms recalling Mathura rather than the attenuated grace of Sarnath. The door frame of the sanctum of this temple is an especially fine example of architectural decoration popular in this period. Bands of floral scrolls, amorous couples, and flying angels of great elegance are carved around the entrance. Particularly impressive are groups of worshippers at the base, their swaying bodies related to each other with an easy rhythm.

MAHARASHTRA

A great revival of artistic activity seems to have taken place in this region during the reign of the Vakataka dynasty and its successors, best expressed in the splendid sculpture decorating the cave temples of Ajanta and Elephanta. The idioms established in the North were adapted here to the needs of a style that conceived figures on a massive scale, as determined by the demands of the great expanses of rock out of which they were carved. Although the sculpture at Ajanta (mostly of the late 5th century) combines the old weightiness with the new restraint and elegance, the style finds its supreme expression in the magnificent cave temple at Elephanta. The central image of this great temple is of immense size and in deep relief. It represents Shiva in his cosmic aspect, the central head clam, introspective, self-sufficient, and transcending time, the heads to the sides, in their sensuous beauty and awesome terror, reflecting the creative and the destructive aspects of the supreme divinity.

Other Regions

The impact of the Gupta style of the 5th and 6th centuries was felt in many parts of India, though actual remains thus far discovered are more abundant in some parts than in others. There appears to have been, in Bihar, a distinct school characterized by rather heavy, compact forms; and Gujarat and southern Rajasthan developed an individual style of considerable voluptuousness and plasticity. Among the notable sculpture of the Idar region are groups of mother goddesses whose massive forms are rendered with an easy grace and intimacy. In the Karnataka country, to the south, the cave temples of Badami reveal yet another distinct idiom, somewhat direct and elemental but nevertheless belonging to the same general style, with local variations, that prevailed over the greater part of India.

Terra-Cotta

Terra-cotta sculpture, like art in other mediums, was greatly developed. Fairly large and elaborate plaques were used to adorn brick *stupas* and Hindu temples from Sind to Bengal. The polychrome relief images of the Buddha from Mirpur Khas are delicate and slender, with traces of Gandhara feeling. Representations of divinities and mythological scenes from temples in Bikaner, Ahichhatra,

Bhitargaon, and Shravasti are works on a more popular level, possessing an earthy ponderousness. A large number of figurines, particularly fragments of heads with elaborate coiffures and delicate, smiling features, have been found at Rajghat in Varanasi (Benares) and at other sites.

Medieval Indian Sculpture

Indian sculpture from the 7th century onward developed, broadly speaking, into two styles that flourished in northern and southern India, respectively. In each of these regions there also developed additional local idioms, so that there was a wide variety of schools. All, however, evolved in a consistent manner, the earlier phase marked by relatively plastic forms, the later phase by a style that emphasizes a more linear rendering. The sculpture was used mainly as a part of the architectural decor, and the quantity required was vast. This often entailed a mechanical production, with the result that works of quality are few in proportion to the numbers.

Besides the two main idioms, the local schools of Maharashtra and Karnataka are of particular interest because they possess considerable individuality and often show both northern and southern features.

Sculpture in bronze was also produced in fairly large quantities in this period. Again, several local schools can be distinguished, the most important of which are those of eastern and southern India.

NORTH INDIA

The history of North Indian sculpture from the 7th to the 9th centuries is one of the more obscure periods in Indian art. Two trends, however, are clear: one exhibits the decline and disintegration of classical forms established during the 5th and 6th centuries; and the other, the evolution of new styles that began to possess overall unity and stability only in the 10th century.

A breakdown of the Gupta formula is observable from at least the 7th century onward, if not a little earlier: harmonious proportion, graceful movement, and supple modelling begin to yield to squat proportions, a halting movement, and a more congealed form. Toward the 8th century, signs of a new movement become evident in a group of sculptures that departs from the progressively lifeless working out of the Gupta idiom. The modelling emphasizes breadth but with a pronounced feeling for rhythm, and the delineation of decorative detail is fairly restrained. In the 9th century, particularly during the second half, a distinct change came over the styles of all of northern India. A new elegance, a richer decorativeness, and a staccato rhythm so characteristic of the medieval styles of the 10th and 11th centuries begin to be clearly seen and felt. Sculpture of this period reaches a standard of elegance never surpassed in the medieval period: the grace and voluminousness of earlier work are modified but not lost; the harsh angularity of later work, avoided. An idea of the style can be formed from an important group of sculptures at Abaneri, the Shiva temple at Indore, and the Teli-ka-Mandir temple at Gwalior, as well as from individual works in various North Indian museums.

With the 10th century, the conventions of North Indian sculpture became fairly well established. The style is represented by examples from such monuments as the Lakshmana temple at Khajuraho (dated 941), the Harasnath temple at Mt. Harsha (c. mid-10th century), in Rajasthan, and numerous other sites scattered all over northern India. These works are executed in a style that has become harder and more angular, the figures covered with a profusion of jewelry that tends to obscure the forms it decorates. These features are further accentuated in the 11th century, when many temples of great size, adorned with prodigious amounts of sculpture, were erected all over northern India. There is a decline in the general level of workmanship: the carving is often entirely conventional and lifeless, the features rigid and masklike, and the contours stiff and unyielding. The ornamentation, consisting of a profusion of beaded jewelry, is for the most part as dull, repetitive, and lifeless as the rest of the sculpture. This phase of artistic activity is represented at important centres from Gujarat to Orissa; one of them is Khajuraho, with a vast amount of sculpture, all in a good state of preservation but conceived and executed as perfunctory architectural ornamentation. Not all sculpture, however, is

Atrium of the Great Sas-Bahu Temple at Gwalior, Madhya Pradesh, India. Milt and Joan Mann/CameraMann International

of inferior quality; the hard, metallic carving and angular, stylized line sometimes result in works possessing a cold brilliance.

The 12th century marks the end of traditional sculpture all over northern India, except for a few pockets not yet penetrated by the Islamic invasions. A rigid line imposed itself on the forms, which in turn became desiccated and hard, so that whatever unity of surface may have existed was entirely shattered.

A brief revival took place in parts of Gujarat and Rajasthan in the 15th century, but the sculpture merely imitated the work of the late medieval phase. The pure geometry of their forms, however, sometimes results in works possessing a curious archaistic power.

Sculpture in eastern India (consisting of Bangladesh and the modern Indian states of Bihar, West Bengal, and Orissa), though sharing in the broad pattern of development of the rest of northern India, nevertheless represents a distinct idiom. The flatness of planes and angularity of contours are less pronounced, the figures retaining a sense of mass and weight for a greater period of time and to a greater degree. This can be clearly seen in sculpture from Konarak, in Orissa. Dating to the 13th century, the style retains a considerable semblance of plasticity at a period when sculpture in other parts of northern India had assumed a very wooden appearance. In Bihar and Bengal a flourishing school of bronze sculpture also developed, as evidenced by the large number of finds, notably from the sites of Nalanda and Kurkihar. The style generally parallels works in stone, emphasizing plastic values to a great degree. The most flourishing period was the 9th century, when a series of magnificent images representing the gods and goddesses of the Buddhist pantheon were made at Kurkihar and Nalanda. The work of the 10th and 11th centuries is more decorative and often very skillfully and elaborately cast. Of relatively small size and therefore easily transportable, bronze sculpture from this area played an important part in the diffusion of Indian influence in Southeast Asia.

Kashmir sculpture tends to be weightier and more massive than works in other parts of India. Some Gandhara memories survive, particularly in the fleshy rendering of the body and the drapery, but the sculpture is very much a part of the stylistic developments in northern India. Representative examples of the style, dating to around the mid-9th century, have been found from Avantipura. A flourishing school of bronze sculpture also existed, numerous examples having come to light in recent years. One of the finest, discovered at Devsar (Sir Pratap Singh Museum, Srinagar), is a large 9th-century ornamental frame, 6 ½ feet (two metres) high, decorated with various incarnations of Vishnu, all filled with great energy and movement. A good number of ivory images of Kashmir workmanship have also been preserved. These are generally of miniature size, polychromed, and of extremely fine and delicate workmanship. Influences of the Kashmir style of sculpture were strongly felt in the neighbouring Himalayan region, including both Tibet and Nepal.

SOUTHERN INDIA

The medieval phase in southern India opened with elegant 7th-century sculptures at Mahabalipuram, by far the most impressive of which is a large relief depicting the penance of Arjuna (previously identified as an illustration of the mythical descent of the Ganges). It is carved on the face of a granite boulder with a deep cleft in the centre, representing a river, down which water actually flowed from a reservoir situated above. On both sides are carved numerous figures of divinities, human beings, and animals that crowd the hermitage where Arjuna, practicing penance, is visited by Shiva. The tall, slender figures, with supple tubular limbs, remotely recall the proportions of Amaravati, now greatly transformed; and the numerous animals, including the elephant herd with its young, show the same intimate feeling for animal life that characterizes all Indian sculpture, but in a manner that has seldom been surpassed.

The light, aerial forms gained stability and strength in subsequent centuries, culminating in superb sculptures adorning small, elegant shrines built during the late 9th century when the Chola dynasty was consolidating its power. The temples at Tiruvalishvaram, Kodumbalur, Kilaiyur, Shrinivasanalur, Kumbakonam, and a host of other sites of this period are only sparingly adorned with sculpture, but it is of superb quality. With the 10th and 11th centuries, South Indian sculpture, like its counterpart in the north though to a lesser degree, was carved in flatter planes and more angular forms, and the fresh, blooming life of earlier work is gradually lost. This can be seen, for example, in the sculpture of the numerous temples of Thanjavur and Gangaikondacholapuram. The subsequent phase, extending up to the 13th century, is represented by work at Darasuram and Tribhuvanam; although the forms become increasingly congealed, brittle works of fine quality—often capturing outer movement with great skill—continue to be produced. Sculpture in southern India continued when artistic activity was interrupted in the north by the Islamic invasions but, in spite of technical virtuosity, became progressively lifeless. Artistic activity continued in the south into the 17th century, the elaborately sculptured halls at Madura and the masses of stucco sculpture adorning the immense entrances, or *gopuras*, testifying to the prodigious output and the undistinguished quality of the work produced.

South Indian bronze sculpture has a special place in the history of Indian art. A large number of images were made (some of them still in worship in the mid-20th century and others unearthed from the ground by chance), but examples before the 8th century are quite rare. In bronze, as in stone, the 9th and 10th centuries were periods of high achievement, and many images of excellent quality have survived. They are all cast by the lost-wax, or cire perdue, process (in which a wax model is used) and technically are very accomplished. In the early stages the forms were smooth and flowing, with a fine balance maintained between the body and the complex jewelry, the lines of which follow and reinforce every movement of the plastic surface. The bronzes of the later period lose this cohesiveness, the ornament, by virtue of its hardness, tending to divide and fragment the body it covers. The modelling also became flatter and sharper, though not quite as rapidly in bronze sculpture as in stone. Ancient traditions of workmanship survive to the present day, and a few guilds of craftsmen continue to make competent if somewhat lifeless images.

Most South Indian bronze images are representations of Hindu divinities, notably Vishnu and Shiva. One particular form deserves special notice as a striking

This 11th-century statue of Shiva as Nataraja (Lord of the Dance) is an elegant example of one of the bronze sculptures of the Chola dynasty of southern India. Shaun Curry/AFP/ Getty Images

southern contribution to Indian iconography. It is that of a four-armed Shiva as Lord of the Dance (Nataraja), shown within a flaming halo, or aureole, one hand holding the doubleheaded drum symbolizing sound, or creation, and the other holding the fire that puts an end to all that is created. The palm of the third hand faces the devotee, assuring him of freedom from fear, while the fourth hand points to the raised foot, the place of refuge from ignorance and delusion, which

are symbolized by the dwarf demon crushed beneath the other foot. Several splendid images are known, the finest being, perhaps, the great image still worshipped in the Brhadishvara temple at Thanjavur.

MAHARASHTRA AND KARNATAKA

The Karnataka country possessed a flourishing school of sculpture in the 7th and 8th centuries, as seen in examples from

Aihole, Pattadkal, and Alampur. As in architecture, influences from the north are discernible, but the style is basically southern, emphasizing rugged strength and power compared to the more elegant and delicate forms of the Tamil country. In Maharashtra, cave temples at Ellora carry the most important examples of this phase of sculpture. Here the tradition is continued of images of great size that, in their primitive strength, partake of the nature of the rock out of which they are carved. A series of large, splendid panels (6th century AD) depicting incidents from Hindu mythology in high relief are to be found in the Ramesvara cave; notable among them is a fearsome representation of the dancing Kali, goddess of death. The Kailasa temple (c. 757–783) has a remarkable group of elephants struggling with lions all around the plinth. Of the several large reliefs, also at Kailasa, the depiction of Ravana shaking Kailasa is a composition of considerable grace and charm.

Toward the 13th and 14th centuries, a very distinctive style developed in the Karnataka country, which was then largely ruled by kings of the Hoysala dynasty. The materials employed are varieties of stone that are soft when freshly quarried but harden on exposure, which may account partially for the extreme richness of the work. The sculpture is in very high relief, often undercut and literally covered with the most elaborate ornaments and jewelry from top to toe. This unrestrained extravaganza is unique even for Indian art, which shows a preference for intricate and elaborate ornament at all stages of its history.

INDIAN PAINTING

Literary works testify to the eminence of painting as an art form in India, particularly in the decoration of walls, but climate has taken a devastating toll, leaving behind only a few tantalizing examples. By far the bulk of the preserved material consists of miniature painting, initially done on palm leaf but later on paper. The subject matter is generally religious (illustrating divinities, myths, and legends) and literary (illustrating poetry and romances, for example), though the Mughal school was also concerned with historical and secular themes. The styles were rich and varied, often closely connected with one another and sometimes developing and changing rapidly, particularly from the 16th century onward. The work also shows a surprising vitality under strained circumstances, surviving up to the very eve of the modern period when the other arts had deteriorated greatly.

PREHISTORIC AND PROTOHISTORIC PERIODS

Painting in India should have a history stretching as far back as any of the other arts but, because of its perishable nature, little has survived. None of the examples found in rock shelters over almost all of India, and chiefly representing scenes of hunting and war, appears to be earlier than the 8th century BC, and all may be as late as the 10th century AD. A faint idea of the painter's art in the Indus Valley civilization can be had from the pottery, elaborately decorated with leaf designs and geometrical patterns.

ANCIENT WALL PAINTING

The earliest substantial remains are those found in rock-cut cave temples at Ajanta, in western India. They belong to the 2nd or 1st century BC and are in a style reminiscent of the relief sculpture at Sanchi. Also found at Ajanta are the most substantial remains of Indian painting of about the 5th century AD and a little later, when ancient Indian civilization was in full flower. The paintings, the work of several ateliers, decorate the walls and ceilings of the numerous cave temples and monasteries at the site. They are executed in the tempera technique on smooth surfaces, prepared by application of plaster. The themes, nominally Buddhist, illustrate the major events of the Buddha's life, the *Jataka* tales, and the various divinities of the expanding Buddhist pantheon. The ceilings are covered with rich motifs, based generally upon the lotus stem and the world of animals and birds. The style is unlike anything seen in later Indian art, expansive, free, and dynamic. The graceful figures are painted by a sweeping and accomplished brush; and they are given body and substance by modelling in colour and by a schematic distribution of light and shade that has little to do with scientific chiaroscuro. The narrative compositions, handled with utmost dexterity, are a natural outgrowth of the long traditions of relief sculpture and reflect the splendour and maturity of contemporary sculpture. The large images of the *bodhisattvas* in Cave 1, combining rich elegance with spiritual serenity, reflect a vision that sees the shifting world of matter and the transcendental calm of Nirvana as essentially one.

Except for a large and magnificent painting of a dance scene found at the rock-cut cave at Bagh—a painting executed in a style closely resembling Ajanta—hardly any other work of this great period survives. Cave temples at Badami, in the Karnataka country, and Sittanavasal, in Tamil Nadu, probably of the late 6th and 7th centuries AD are already but echoes of the style of the 5th century, which appears to have died out around this time.

EASTERN INDIAN STYLE

Small illustrations on palm leaf, chiefly painted at the great Buddhist establishments of eastern India, appear to have conserved some elements of this ancient style; but they have lost its dramatic impact, which is replaced by a studied preciosity and an inhibited meticulousness. The surviving paintings date from the 11th and 12th centuries and are conventional icons of the numerous Buddhist gods and goddesses, narrative representations having largely disappeared. With the destruction of these Buddhist centres by the Islamic invader, the east Indian style seems to have come to an end.

WESTERN INDIAN STYLE

The style of Ajanta is succeeded in western India by what has been appropriately named the western Indian style. Among the earliest examples are a few surviving wall paintings of the Kailasa temple (mid-8th century) at Ellora and the Jaina temples, built at the same site a hundred years later. The plastic sense of form, so evident at Ajanta, is emphatically replaced by a style that even at this early stage is heavily dependent on line. The contours of the figures are sharp and angular, the forms dry and abstract; and the fluent, stately rhythms of Ajanta have become laboured and halting.

The most copious examples of this style, however, have survived not on the walls of temples but in the large number of illustrated manuscripts commissioned by members of the Jaina community. The earliest of these are contemporary with eastern Indian manuscripts and are also painted on palm leaf; but the style, instead of attempting to cling to ancient traditions, moves steadily in the direction already established at Ellora. It is a perfect counterpart of contemporary sculpture in western India, relying for its effect on line, which progressively becomes more angular and wiry until all naturalism has been deliberately erased. The figures are almost always shown in profile, the full-face view generally reserved for representations of the *tirthankaras*, or the Jaina saviours. A convention that appears unfailingly for the duration of the western Indian style is the eye projecting beyond the face shown in profile, meant to represent the second eye, which would not be visible in this posture. The colours are few and pure: yellow, green, blue, black, and red, which was preferred for the background. In the beginning, the illustrations are simple icons in small panels; but gradually they become more elaborate, with scenes from the lives of the various Jaina saviours as told in the *Kalpa-sutra* and from the adventures of the monk Kalaka as related in the *Kalakaharyakatha* the most favoured.

Even greater elaboration was possible with the increasing availability of paper from the late 14th century; with larger surfaces to paint on, by the middle of the 15th century artists were producing opulent manuscripts, such as the *Kalpa-sutra* in the Devasanopada library, Ahmadabad. The text is written in gold on coloured ground, the margins gorgeously illuminated with richest decorative and figural patterns, and the main paintings often occupying the entire page. Blue and gold, in addition to red, are used with increasing lavishness, testifying to the prosperity of the patron. The use of such costly materials, however, did not necessarily produce works of quality, and one is often left with the impression of cursive and hasty workmanship. With some variations—but hardly any substantial departures from the bounds that it had set for itself—the style endured throughout the 16th century and even extended into the 17th. The political subjugation of the country by the forces of Islam may have contributed to the conservatism of the style but did not result in its total elimination, as seems to have been the case in eastern India. Indeed, in the course of its long life, the western Indian school became a national style, painting at other centres in India interpreting and elaborating its forms in their own individual manner. In the province of Orissa, painting on palm leaf and in a manner entirely dependent on the western Indian style has continued up to the present day.

TRANSITION TO THE MUGHAL AND RAJASTHANI STYLES

The belief held earlier by scholars that the new Islamic rulers of India did not patronize any painting until the rise of the Mughal dynasty in the 16th century is being abandoned in the face of the literary testimony and the discovery or recognition of illustrated manuscripts that were painted at Indian courts. Nor should this be surprising, as the Muslim kings of India had before them the example of other rulers of the Islamic world who were great patrons of painting in spite of the injunctions of orthodox Islam against the portrayal of living beings. The taste of these Indian rulers, however, did not turn to the western Indian style but to the flourishing traditions of Islamic painting abroad, notably neighbouring Iran. As many painters as architects had in all probability been invited from foreign countries; and illustrated manuscripts,

handily transported, must have been easily available. As a result there appears to have developed what can only be called an Indo-Persian style, based essentially on the schools of Iran but affected to a greater or lesser extent by the individual tastes of the Indian rulers and by the local styles. The earliest known examples are paintings dating from the 15th century onward. The most important are the *Khamseh* ("Quintet") of Amīr Khosrow of Delhi (Freer Gallery of Art, Washington, D.C.), a *Bostān* painted in Mandu (National Museum, New Delhi), and, most interesting of all, a manuscript of the *Ne'mat-nāmeh* (India Office Library, London) painted for a sultan of Malwa in the opening years of the 16th century. Its illustrations are derived from the Turkmen style of Shīrāz but show clear Indian features adapted from the local version of the western Indian style.

Though the western Indian style was essentially conservative, it was not unfailingly so. It began to show signs of an inner change most notably in two manuscripts from Mandu, a *Kalpa-sutra* and a *Kalakaharyakatha* of about 1439, and a *Kalpa-sutra* painted at Jaunpur in 1465. These works were done in the opulent manner of the 15th century, but for the first time the quality of the line is different, and the uncompromisingly abstract expression begins to make way for a more human and emotional mood. By the opening years of the 16th century, a new and vigorous style had come into being. Although derived from the western

Indian style, it is clearly independent, full of the most vital energy, deeply felt, and profoundly moving. The earliest dated example is an *Aranyaka Parva* of the *Mahabharata* (1516; The Asiatic Society of Mumbai), and among the finest are series illustrating the *Bhagavata-Purana* and the *Caurapancashika* of Bilhana, scattered in collections all over the world. A technically more refined variant of this style, preferring the pale, cool colours of Persian derivation, a fine line, and meticulous ornamentation, exists contemporaneously and is best illustrated by a manuscript of the ballad *Candamyana* by Mullā Dāūd (c. first half of the 16th century; Prince of Wales Museum of Western India, Mumbai). The early 16th century thus appears to have been a period of inventiveness and set the stage for the development of the Mughal and Rajput schools, which thrived from the 16th to the 19th century.

AKBAR PERIOD (1556–1605)

Although the Mughal dynasty came to power in India with the great victory won by Babar at the Battle of Panipat in 1526, the Mughal style was almost exclusively the creation of Akbar. Trained in painting at an early age by a Persian master, Khwāja ‘Abd-ul-Ṣamad, who was employed by his father, Humāyūn, Akbar created a large atelier, which he staffed with artists recruited from all parts of India. The atelier, at least in the initial stages, was under the superintendence of Akbar's teacher and another great Persian master, Mīr Sayyid ‘Alī; but the distinctive style that evolved here owed not a little to the highly individual tastes of Akbar himself, who took an interest in the work, inspecting the atelier frequently and rewarding painters whose work was pleasing.

The work of the Mughal atelier in this early formative stage was largely confined to the illustration of books on a wide variety of subjects: histories, romances, poetic works, myths, legends, and fables, of both Indian and Persian origin. The manuscripts were first written by calligraphers, with blank spaces left for the illustrations. These were executed largely by groups of painters, including a colourist, who did most of the actual painting, and specialists in portraiture and in the mixing of colours. Chief of the group was the designer, generally an artist of top quality, who formulated the composition and sketched in the rough outline. A thin wash of white, through which the initial drawing was visible, was then applied and the colours filled in. The colourist's work proceeded slowly, the colour being applied in several thin layers and frequently rubbed down with an agate burnisher, a process that resulted in the glowing, enamel-like finish. The colours used were mostly mineral but sometimes consisted of vegetable dyes; and the brushes, many of them exceedingly fine, were made from squirrel's tail or camel hair.

The earliest paintings (c. 1560–70) of the school of Akbar are illustrations of *Ṭūṭī-nāmeh* ("Parrot Book"; Cleveland

Museum of Art) and the stupendous illustrations of the *Dāstān-e Amīr Ḥamzeh* ("Stories of Amīr Ḥamzeh"; Museum of Applied Arts, Vienna), which originally consisted of 1,400 paintings of an unusually large size (approximately 25 inches by 16 inches [65 by 40 centimetres]), of which only about 200 have survived. The *Ṭūṭī-nāmeh* shows the Mughal style in the process of formation: the hand of artists belonging to the various non-Mughal traditions is clearly recognizable, but the style also reveals an intense effort to cope with the demands of a new patron. The transition is achieved in the *Dāstān-e Amīr Ḥamzeh*, in which the uncertainties are overcome in a homogeneous style, quite unlike Persian work in its leaning toward naturalism and filled with swift, vigorous movement and bold colour. The forms are individually modelled, except for the geometrical ornament used as architectural decor; the figures are superbly interrelated in closely unified compositions, in which depth is indicated by a preference for diagonals; and much attention is paid to the expression of emotion. One of the last manifestations of this bold and vigorous early manner is the *Dārāb-nameh* (c. 1580) in the British Museum.

Immediately following were some very important historical manuscripts, including the *Tārīkh-e Khāndān-e Tīmūrīyeh* ("History of the House of Timur," c. 1580–85; Khuda Baksh Library, Patna) and other works concerned with the affairs of the Timurid dynasty, to which the Mughals belonged. Each of these manuscripts contains several

hundred illustrations, the prolific output of the atelier made possible by the division of labour that was in effect. Historical events are recreated with remarkable inventiveness, though the explosive and almost frantic energy of the *Dāstān-e Amīr-Ḥamzeh* has begun to subside. The scale was smaller and the work began to acquire a studied richness. The narrative method employed by these Mughal paintings, like that of traditional literature, is infinitely discursive; and the painter did not hesitate to provide a fairly detailed picture of contemporary life—both of the people and of the court—and of the rich fauna and flora of India. Like Indian artists of all periods, the Mughal painter showed a remarkable empathy for animals, for through them flows the same life that flows through human beings. This sense of kinship allowed him to achieve unqualified success in the illustration of animal fables such as the *Anwār-e Suhaylī* ("Lights of Caropus"), of which several copies were painted, the earliest dated 1570 (School of Oriental and African Studies, London). It was in the illustrations to Persian translations of the Hindu epics, the *Mahabharata* and the *Ramayana*, that the Mughal painter revealed to the full the richness of his imagination and his unending resourcefulness. With little precedent to rely on, he was nevertheless seldom dismayed by the subject and created a whole series of convincing compositions. Because most of the painters of the atelier were Hindus, the subjects must have been close to their hearts; and, given the opportunity by a tolerant and sympathetic patron, they rose to great heights. It is no wonder, therefore, that the *Razm-nāmeh* (City Palace Museum, Jaipur), as the *Mahabharata* is known in Persian, is one of the outstanding masterpieces of the age.

In addition to large books containing numerous illustrations, which were the products of the combined efforts of many artists, the imperial atelier also cultivated a more intimate manner that specialized in the illustration of books, generally poetic works, with a smaller number of illustrations. The paintings were done by a single master artist who, working alone, had ample scope to display his virtuosity. In style the works tend to be finely detailed and exquisitely coloured. A *Dīvān* ("Anthology") of Anwarī (Fogg Art Museum, Cambridge, Massachusetts), dated 1589, is a relatively early example of this manner. The paintings are very small, none larger than five inches by 2½ inches (12 by 6 centimetres) and most delicately executed. Very similar in size and quality are the miniatures illustrating the *Dīvān* of Ḥāfeẓ (Reza Library, Rāmpur). On a larger scale but in the same mood are the manuscripts that represent the most delicate and refined works of the reign of Akbar: the *Bahāristān* of Jāmī (1595; Bodleian Library, Oxford), a *Khamseh* of Neẓāmī (1593; British Museum, London), a *Khamseh* of Amīr Khosrow (1598; Walters Art Gallery, Baltimore and Metropolitan Museum of Art, New York), and an *Anwār-e Suhaylī* (1595–96; Bharat Kala Bhavan, Vārānasī).

Also prepared in the late 1590s were magnificent copies of the *Akbar-nāmeh* ("History of Akbar"; Victoria and Albert Museum, London) and the *Kitāb-e Changīz-nāmeh* ("History of Genghis Khan"; Gulistan Library, Tehran). These copiously illustrated volumes were produced by artists working jointly, but the quality of refinement is similar to that of the poetic manuscripts.

Of the large number of painters who worked in the imperial atelier, the most outstanding were Dasvant and Basavan. The former played the leading part in the illustration of the *Razm-nāmeh*. Basavan, who is preferred by some to Dasvant, painted in a very distinctive style, which delighted in the tactile and the plastic, and with an unerring grasp of psychological relationships.

JAHĀNGĪR PERIOD (1605–27)

The emperor Jahāngīr, even as a prince, showed a keen interest in painting and maintained an atelier of his own. His tastes, however, were not the same as those of his father, and this is reflected in the painting, which underwent a significant change. The tradition of illustrating books began to die out, though a few manuscripts, in continuation of the old style, were produced. For Jahāngīr much preferred portraiture; and this tradition, also initiated in the reign of his father, was greatly developed. Among the most elaborate works of his reign are the great court scenes, several of which have survived, showing Jahāngīr surrounded by his numerous courtiers. These are essentially large-scale exercises in portraiture, the artist taking great pains to reproduce the likeness of every figure.

The compositions of these paintings have lost entirely the bustle and movement so evident in the works of Akbar's reign. The figures are more formally ordered, their comportment in keeping with the strict rules of etiquette enforced in the Mughal court. The colours are subdued and harmonious, the bright glowing palette of the Akbarī artist having been quickly abandoned. The brushwork is exceedingly fine. Technical virtuosity, however, is not all that was attained, for beneath the surface of the great portraits of the reign there is a deep and often spiritual understanding of the character of the person and the drama of human life.

Many of the paintings produced at the imperial atelier are preserved in the albums assembled for Jahāngīr and his son Shāh Jahān. The Muraqqah-e Gulshan is the most spectacular. (Most surviving folios from this album are in the Gulistan Library in Tehran and the National Museums of Berlin.) There are assembled masterpieces from Iran, curiosities from Europe, works produced in the reign of Akbar, and many of the finest paintings of Jahāngīr's master painters, all surrounded by the most magnificent borders decorated with a wide variety of floral and geometrical designs. The album gives a fairly complete idea of Jahāngīr as a patron, collector, and connoisseur of the arts, revealing a person with a wide range of taste and a curious, enquiring mind.

Jahāngīr esteemed the art of painting and honoured his painters. His favourite was Abū al-Hasan, who was designated Nādir-ul-Zamān ("Wonder of the Age"). Several pictures by the master are known, among them a perceptive study of Jahāngīr looking at a portrait of his father. Also much admired was Ustād Mansūr, designated Nādir-ul-'Asr ("Wonder of the Time"), whose studies of birds and animals are unparalleled. Bishandās was singled out by the emperor as unique in the art of portraiture. Manohar, the son of Basavan, Govardhan, and Daulat are other important painters of this reign.

SHĀH JAHĀN PERIOD (1628–58)

Under Shāh Jahān, attention seems to have shifted to architecture, but painting in the tradition of Jahāngīr continued. The style, however, becomes noticeably rigid. The portraits resemble hieratic effigies, lacking the breath of life so evident in the work of Jahāngīr's time. The colouring is jewel-like in its brilliance, and the outward splendour quite dazzling. The best work is found in the *Shāhjahānnāmeh* ("History of Shāh Jahān") of the Windsor Castle Library and in several albums assembled for the emperor. Govardhan and Bichitra, who had begun their careers in the reign of Jahāngīr, were among the outstanding painters; several works by them are quite above the general level produced in this reign.

AURANGZEB AND THE LATER MUGHALS (1659–1806)

From the reign of Aurangzeb (1659–1707), a few pictures have survived that essentially continue the cold style of Shāh Jahān; but the rest of the work is nondescript, consisting chiefly of an array of lifeless portraits, most of them the output of workshops other than the imperial atelier. Genre scenes, showing gatherings of ascetics and holy men, lovers in a garden or on a terrace, musical parties, carousals, and the like, which had grown in number from the reign of Shāh Jahān, became quite abundant. They sometimes show touches of genuine quality, particularly in the reign of Muḥammad Shāh (1719–48), who was passionately devoted to the arts. This brief revival, however, was momentary, and Mughal painting essentially came to an end during the reign of Shāh ʿĀlam II (1759–1806). The artists of this disintegrated court were chiefly occupied in reveries of the past, the best work, for whatever it is worth, being confined to copies of old masterpieces still in the imperial library. This great library was dispersed and destroyed during the uprising of 1857 against the British.

DECCANI STYLE

In mood and manner, Deccani painting, which flourished over much of the Deccan Plateau from at least the last quarter of the 16th century, is reminiscent of the contemporary Mughal school. Again, a homogeneous style evolved from a combination of foreign (Persian and Turkish) and Indian elements, but with a distinct local flavour. Of the early schools, the style patronized by the sultans of Bijapur—notably the tolerant and art-loving Ibrāhīm ʿĀdil Shāh II of Bijapur, famous for his love of music—is particularly distinguished. Some splendid portraits of him, more lyrical and poetic in concept than contemporary Mughal portraits, are to be found. A wonderful series depicting symbolically the musical modes (*ragamala*) also survives. Of illustrated manuscripts,

COMPANY SCHOOL

The style of miniature painting that developed in India in the second half of the 18th century was known as Company school or Patna painting. It was so called because it developed in response to the tastes of the British serving with the East India Company. The style first emerged in Murshidabad, West Bengal, and then spread to other centres of British trade: Benares (now Varanasi), Delhi, Lucknow, and Patna.

The paintings were executed in watercolours on paper and on mica. Favourite subjects were scenes of Indian daily life, local rulers, and sets of festivals and ceremonies, in line with the "cult of the picturesque" then current in British artistic circles. Most successful were the studies of natural life, but the style was generally of a hybrid and undistinguished quality.

the most important are the *Nujūm-ul-ʻulūm* ("The Stars of the Sciences," 1590; Chester Beatty Library, Dublin) and the *Tārīf-e H·useyn-Shāhī* (Bharata Itihasa Samshodhaka Mandala, Pune), painted about 1565 in the neighbouring state of Ahmadnagar. The sultanate of Golconda also produced work of high quality—for example, a manuscript of the *Dīvān* of Muh·ammad Qulī Qut·b Shāh in the Salar Jang Library, Hyderabad, and a series of distinguished portraits up to the end of the 17th century (dispersed in various collections). The state of Hyderabad, founded in the early 18th century and headed by a grandee of the Mughal empire, was a great centre of painting. The work that was produced there reflects both Golconda traditions and increasing Mughal and Rajasthani influences.

RAJASTHANI STYLE

This style appears to have come into being in the 16th century, about the same time the Mughal school was evolving under the patronage of Akbar; but, rather than a sharp break from the indigenous traditions, it represented a direct and natural evolution. Throughout the early phase, almost up to the end of the 17th century, it retained its essentially hieratic and abstract character, as opposed to the naturalistic tendencies cultivated by the Mughal atelier. The subject matter of this style is essentially Hindu, devoted mainly to the illustration of myths and legends, the epics, and above all the life of Krishna;

particularly favoured were depictions of his early life as the cowherd of Vraja, and the mystical love of Vraja's maidens for him, as celebrated in the *Bhagavata-Purana*, the *Gitagovinda* of Jayadeva, and the Braj Bhasha verses written by Surdas and other poets. The style of the painting, no less than the literature, is a product of the new religious movements, all of which stressed personal devotion to Krishna as the way to salvation. Related popular themes were pictorial representations of the musical modes (*ragamala*) and illustrations of poetical works such as the *Rasikapriya* of Keshavadasa, which dealt with the sentiment of love, analyzing its varieties and endlessly classifying the types of lovers and beloveds and their emotions. Portraits, seldom found in the early phase, became increasingly common in the 18th century—as did court scenes, scenes of sporting and hunting events, and other scenes concerned with the courtly life of the great chiefs and feudal lords of Rajasthan.

The Rajasthani style developed various distinct schools, most of them centring in the several states of Rajasthan, namely Mewar, Bundi, Kotah, Markar, Bikaner, Kishangarh, and Jaipur (Amber). It also had centres outside the geographical limits of present-day Rajasthan, notably Gujarat, Malwa, and Bundelkhand. The study of Rajasthani painting is still in its infancy, for most of the material has been available for study only since the mid-1940s.

The Mughal and Rajasthani styles were always in contact with each other, but in general the Rajasthani schools were not essentially affected by the work produced at the Mughal court during the greater part of the 17th century. This became less true in the 18th century, when the sharp distinction between the two became progressively obscured, though each retained its distinctive features right up to the end.

Mewar

The Mewar school is among the most important. The earliest dated examples are represented by a *ragamala* series painted at Chawand in 1605 (Gopi Krishna Kanoria Collection, Patna). These simple paintings, filled with bright colour, are only a step removed from the pre-Rajasthani phase. The style became more elaborate in the first quarter of the 17th century when another *ragamala*, painted at Udaipur in 1628 (formerly in the Khajanchi Collection, Bikaner; now dispersed in various collections), showed some superficial acquaintance with the Mughal manner. This phase, lasting until about 1660, was one of the most important for the development of painting all over Rajasthan. Ambitious and extensive illustrations of the *Bhagavata*, the *Ramayana*, the poems of Surdas, and the *Gitagovinda* were completed, all full of strength and vitality. The name of Sāhabadī is intimately connected with this phase; another well-known painter is Manohar. The intensity and richness associated with their atelier began to fade toward the close of the 17th century,

and a wave of Mughal influence began to affect the school in the opening years of the 18th century. Portraits, court scenes, and events in the everyday world of the ruling classes are increasingly found. Although the emotional fervour of the 17th century was never again attained, this work is often of considerable charm. The 19th century continued to create work in the tradition of the 18th, one of the most important centres being Nathdwara (Rajasthan), the seat of the Vallabha sect. Large numbers of pictures, produced here for the pilgrim trade, were spread over all parts of Rajasthan, northern India, Gujarat, and the Deccan.

Bundi and Kotah

A school as important as that of Mewar developed at Bundi and later at Kotah, which was formed by a partition of the parent state and ruled by a junior branch of the Bundi family. The earliest examples are represented by a *ragamala* series of extraordinarily rich quality, probably dating from the end of the 16th century. From the very beginning the Bundi style seemed to have found Mughal painting an inspiring source, but its workmanship was as distinctively Rajasthani as the work of Mewar. The artists of this school always displayed a pronounced preference for vivid movement, which is unique in all of Rajasthan. Toward the second half of the 17th century, work at Bundi came unmistakably under the influence of Mewar; many miniatures, including several series illustrating the *Rasikapriya*,

Krishna lifting Mount Govardhana, Mewar miniature painting, early 18th century; in a private collection. P. Chandra

indicate that this was a period of prolific activity. The sister state of Kotah also appears to have become an important centre of painting at this time, developing a great fondness for hunting and sport scenes, all filled with great vigour and surging strength. This kind of work continued well into the 19th century, and if the workmanship is not always of the highest quality, the style maintained its integrity against the rapidly increasing Western influence right up to the end.

Malwa

It has been suggested but not definitely determined that the school itself does not belong to Malwa but to some other area, probably Bundelkhand. In contrast to the Bundi school, miniatures generally thought to have been painted in Malwa are quite archaic, with mannerisms inherited from the 16th century retained until the end of the 17th. The earliest work is an illustrated version of the *Rasikapriya* (1634), followed by a series illustrating a Sanskrit poem called the *Amaru Shataka* (1652). There are also illustrations of the musical modes (*ragamala*), the *Bhagavata-Purana*, and other Hindu devotional and literary works. The compositions of all of these pictures is uncompromisingly flat, the space divided into registers and panels, each filled with a patch of colour and occupied by figures that convey the action. This conservative style disappeared after the close of the 17th century. The course of Malwa painting in the 18th century and later is not known.

Marwar

A *ragamala* series dated 1623 reveals that painting in this state shared features common to other schools of Rajasthan. Miniatures of the second half of the 17th century are distinguished by some splendid portraits that owe much to the Mughal school. A very large amount of work was done in the 19th century, all of which is highly stylized but strong in colour and often of great charm.

Bikaner

Of all Rajasthani schools, the Bikaner style, from its very inception in the mid-17th century, shows the greatest indebtedness to the Mughal style. This is due to the presence in the Bikaneratelier of artists who had previously worked in the Mughal manner at Delhi. They and their descendants continued to paint in a style that could only be classed as a provincial Mughal manner had it not been for the quick absorption of influences from the Rajasthani environment and a sympathy for the religious and literary themes favoured by the royal Hindu patrons. Delicacy of line and colour are consistent characteristics of Bikaner painting even when, toward the end of the 18th century, it assumed stylistic features associated with the more orthodox Rajasthani schools.

Kishangarh

The Kishangarh school, which came into being toward the mid-18th century, was also indebted to the contemporary Mughal style but combined a rich and refined technique with deeply moving religious fervour. Its inspiring patron in the formative phase was Savant Singh, more of a devotee and a poet than a king. The style established by him, characterized by pronounced mystical leanings and a distinctive facial type, continued to the middle of the 19th century, though at a clearly lower level of achievement.

Jaipur (Amber)

The rulers of the state were closely allied to the Mughal dynasty, but paintings of the late 16th and early 17th centuries possessed all of the elements of the Rajasthani style. Little is known about the school until the opening years of the 18th century, when stiff, formal examples appear in the reign of Savai Jai Singh. The finest works, dating from the reign of Pratap Singh, are sumptuous in effect and include some splendid portraits and some large paintings of the sports of Krishna. Although the entire 19th century was extremely productive, the work was rather undistinguished and increasingly affected by Western influences. Of the Rajasthani styles of this period, the Jaipur school was the most popular, examples having been found all over northern India.

PAHARI STYLE

Closely allied to the Rajasthani schools both in subject matter and technique is the Pahari style, so-named because of its prevalence in the erstwhile hill states of the Himalayas, stretching roughly from Jammu to Garhwal. It can be divided into two main schools, the Basohli and the Kangra, but it must be understood that these schools were not confined to the centres after which they are named but extended all over the area. Unlike Rajasthan, the area covered by the Pahari style is small, and the probability of artists travelling from one area to another in search of livelihood was much greater. Thus, attempts to distinguish regional schools are fraught with controversy, and it has been suggested that a classification based upon ateliers and families is likely to be more tenable than those presently current among scholars. Because the Basohli and the Kangra schools show considerable divergences, scholars have postulated the existence of a transitional phase, named the pre-Kangra style.

Basohli School

The origins of this remarkable style are not yet understood, but it is clear that the style was flourishing toward the close of the 17th century. The earliest dated paintings are illustrations to the *Rasamanjari* of Bhanudatta (a Sanskrit work on poetics), executed for a ruler of Basohli (1690; Boston Museum of Fine Arts). Bold colour, vigorous drawing, and primitive intensity of feeling are outstanding qualities in these paintings, quite surpassing the work of the plains. In addition to other Hindu works such as the *Gitagovinda* and the *Bhagavata-Purana*, a fairly large number of idealized portraits have also been discovered.

Kangra School

The Basohli style began to fade by the mid-18th century, being gradually replaced by the Kangra style, named after the state of Kangra but, like the Basohli style, of much wider prevalence. A curvilinear line, easy flowing rhythms, calmer colours, and a mood of sweet lyricism easily distinguish the work from that of the Basohli style. The reasons for this change are to be sought in strong influences from the plains, notably the Mughal styles of Delhi and Lucknow. These influences account for the more refined technique; but whatever was borrowed was transmuted and given a fresh and tender aspect. Among the greatest works are large series illustrating the *Bhagavata-Purana* (National Museum, New Delhi), the *Gitagovinda*, and the *Satsai* of Bihari (both in the collection of the maharaja of Tehri-Garhwal), all painted in 1775–80. The corpus of work produced is very large and, although it seldom fails to please, works of high achievement are rare. The school flourished from about 1770 to almost the end of the 19th century, but the finest work was produced largely from 1775 to 1820.

MODERN PERIOD

Toward the late 19th century traditional Indian painting was rapidly dying out, being replaced by feeble works in a variety of idioms, all strongly influenced by the West. A reaction set in during the early 20th century, symbolized by what is called the Bengal school. The glories of Indian art were rediscovered, and the school consciously tried to produce what it considered a truly Indian art inspired by the creations of the past. Its leading artist was Abanindranath Tagore and its theoretician was E.B. Havell, the principal of the Calcutta School of Art. Nostalgic in mood, the work was mainly sentimental though often of considerable charm. The Bengal school did a great deal to reshape contemporary taste and to make Indian artists aware of their own heritage. Amrita Sher-Gil, who was inspired by the Postimpressionists, made Indian painters aware of new directions. Mid-20th-century Indian painting is very much a part of the international scene, the artists painting in a variety of idioms, often attempting to come to terms with their heritage and with the emergence of India as a modern culture.

INDIAN DECORATIVE ARTS

Fragmentary ivory furniture (c. 1st century AD) excavated at Begram is one of the few indications of the existence in ancient India of a secular art concerned with the production of luxurious and richly decorated objects meant for daily use. Objects that can be clearly designated as works of decorative art become much more extensive for the later periods, during which Islamic traditions were having a profound effect on Indian artistic traditions. The reign of the Mughal emperors, in particular, produced works of the most elaborate and exquisite craftsmanship; the decorative tradition is clearly preserved in architectural ornament, though surviving decorative objects themselves, particularly before the 17th century, are far fewer than might be expected. Economic conditions, including competition with machine-made goods imported from English factories, and a change in taste from increasing European influence had disastrous consequences for traditional craftsmanship, especially in the late 19th and 20th centuries.

PRE-ISLAMIC PERIOD

Of the very few objects surviving from the pre-Islamic period, the most important are fragments of ivory caskets, chairs, and footstools found at Begram, in eastern Afghanistan, but obviously of Indian origin and strongly reminiscent of the school of Mathura in the 1st century AD. The work is profusely decorated with carved panels and confirms the wide reputation for superb ivories that India had in ancient times. Nothing as spectacular has come down from the succeeding periods, but stray examples such as the so-called Charlemagne chessman (c. 8th century; Cabinet des Medailles, Paris) and two magnificent throne legs, of Orissan workmanship, carved in the shape of griffins with elephant heads (13th century; Freer Gallery of Art, Washington D.C., and Philadelphia Museum of Art), indicate

that ivory craftsmanship was always vital. Ancient traditions, relatively unaffected by Islamic influence, continued in southern India up to modern times. An exquisitely carved box from Vijayanagar (16th century; Prince of Wales Museum of Western India, Mumbai) is representative; many other exquisite objects of this period and later are among the treasures of South Indian temples.

There is even less evidence of what the decorative work in metal was like. The practice of re-using the metal by melting unserviceable items may account for the paucity of objects, for there is little doubt that the craft was always flourishing. A hoard found at Kolhapur, consisting of plates, various kinds of vessels, lamps and objets d'art, including a superb bronze elephant with riders, constitutes the most important surviving group of metal objects and is datable to about the 2nd century AD. Some fine examples of ritual utensils, notably elaborate incense burners, of the 8th–9th century have been excavated at Nālandā; and a large number of 14th-century ceremonial vessels of complex design and excellent workmanship, and apparently belonging to the local temple, were discovered at Kollur, in Mysore state.

Gold played an extremely important role in the manufacture of jewelry, but once again the finds are hardly commensurate with tradition. Small amounts of gold jewelry have been excavated at Mohenjo-daro and Harappa (3rd millennium BC); and, in the historical period, a very important group, of delicate workmanship, has been excavated at Taxila (*c.* 2nd century AD).

From earliest times, India has been famous for the variety and magnificence of its textiles. In this case, however, the Indian climate has been particularly destructive; virtually nothing has survived the heat and moisture. Besides the testimony of literature and the evidence of figural sculpture, only a few fragments of printed textiles are preserved—at Fusṭāṭ in Egypt, where they had been exported. These date approximately to the 14th century.

ISLAMIC PERIOD

Traditions of craftsmanship established during the Islamic period came to full flower during the reign of the Mughal dynasty. Surviving works of decorative art are more abundant, though once again there are hardly as many examples as might be expected, particularly from the 16th and 17th centuries. According to literary testimony and the few available examples, the finest objects were undoubtedly made in the imperial workshops set up in large number at the capital and in the great cities of the empire, where they were nourished by local traditions. Well-organized, these shops specialized in particular items, such as textiles, carpets, jewelry, ornamental arms and armour, metalware, and jade. Textile manufacture must have been enormous, considering the demands of court and social etiquette and ritual. Contributing to the popularity of

tapestries, curtains, draperies, canopies, and carpets in contemporary architecture were the nomadic tenting traditions of the Mughal rulers.

The variety of techniques employed in the manufacture of textiles was infinite, ranging from printed and painted patterns to the exquisite embroidery decoration of woolen shawls and the costly figured brocading of silk. An important contribution to carpet weaving was the landscape carpet that reproduced pictorial themes inspired by miniature painting. Much of the surviving textile work dates from the 18th century or later, though the 16th and 17th centuries produced works of the most outstanding quality.

In response to growing European trade, a considerable amount of furniture (chairs, cabinets, chests of drawers, and the like) was produced, mostly wood inlaid with ivory. Many of these pieces have been preserved in the kinder European climate. Although the furniture made for export gives some idea of the craft in India, it must be emphasized that only the ornamental and figural work was Indian, while the form was European. Also in a hybrid Indo-European style were the Christian objects produced by a local school of ivory carvers at Goa.

Metal objects of sumptuous quality were also made, a unique example of which is a splendid, elaborately chiselled 16th-century cup in the Prince of Wales Museum of Western India in Mumbai. This tradition was continued in the 17th and particularly the 18th century, when vessels made of a variety of metals and adorned with engraved, chiselled, inlaid, and enamelled designs were very popular. Arms and armour, in particular, were decorated with the skill of a jeweler. Particularly striking are the carved hilts, often done in animal shapes.

Jade or jadeite was much fancied by the rich and was used together with crystal to make precious vessels as well as sword and dagger hilts. A rather large number of 18th- and 19th-century objects have survived, but they are often of nondescript quality. The greatest period for jade carving seems to have been the 17th century; a few outstanding examples associated with the emperors Jahāngīr and Shāh Jahān are of singular delicacy and perfection. The practice of inlaying jade, and also stone, with precious or semiprecious stones became more popular with the reign of Shāh Jahān and increasingly characteristic of Indian jade craftsmanship from that time on.

Architectural decoration provides a clear idea of the range of ornamental patterns used by the Mughal artist. They consisted mainly of arabesques (intricate interlaced patterns made up of flower, foliage, fruit, and sometimes animal and figural outlines) and infinitely varied geometric patterns—motifs shared with the rest of the Muslim world—together with floral scrolls and other designs adapted from Indian traditions. As a whole, the Mughal decorative style tends to endow ornamental patterns with a distinctive plasticity not seen in the more truly two-dimensional Iranian and Arab work. From the 17th century, a type of floral spray became the most favoured motif and was found on almost every decorated object. The motif, symmetrical but relatively naturalistic at the beginning, became progressively stiff and stylized, but never lost its importance in the ornamental vocabulary.

CHAPTER 6

INDIAN MUSIC

Traditional Indian music is divided between the Hindustani (northern) and Karnatak (Carnatic; southern) schools. (The Hindustani style is influenced by musical traditions of the Persian-speaking world.) Instrumental and vocal music is also varied and frequently played or sung in concert (usually by small ensembles). It is a popular mode of religious expression, as well as an essential accompaniment to many social festivities, including dances and the narration of bardic and other folk narratives. Some virtuosos, most notably Ravi Shankar (composer and sitar player) and Ali Akbar Khan (composer and sarod player), have gained world renown. The most popular dramatic classical performances, sometimes choreographed, relate to the great Hindu epics the *Ramayana* and the *Mahabharata*. Regional variations of classical and folk music abound. All of these genres have remained popular—as has devotional Hindu music—but interest in Indian popular music has grown rapidly since the late 20th century, buoyed by the great success of motion picture musicals. Western classical music is represented by such institutions as the Symphony Orchestra of India, based in Mumbai, and some individuals (notably conductor Zubin Mehta) have achieved international renown.

FOLK, CLASSICAL, AND POPULAR MUSIC

The wide field of musical phenomena in South Asia ranges from the relatively straightforward two- or three-tone melodies of some of the hill tribes in central India to the highly cultivated art music heard in concert halls in the large cities. This variety reflects the heterogeneous population of the subcontinent in terms of ethnic heritage, religion, language, and social status.

RURAL AREAS

In the villages, music is not just a form of entertainment but is an essential element in many of the activities of daily life and plays a prominent part in most rituals. These include life-cycle events, such as birth, initiation, marriage, and death; events of the agricultural cycle, such as planting, transplanting, harvesting, and threshing; and a variety of work songs. Much of this music could be described as functional, for it serves a utilitarian purpose; for instance, a harvest song might well give thanks to God for a bountiful harvest, but underlying this is the idea that singing this song in its traditional manner will help to ensure that the next harvest will be equally fruitful. These songs are usually sung by all the members participating in the activity and are sung not for a human audience but for a spiritual one. They are often sung in the form of leader and chorus, and the musical accompaniment, if any, is generally provided by drone instruments (those sustaining or reiterating a given note or notes), usually of the lute family, or percussion instruments, such as drums, clappers, and pairs of cymbals. Occasionally, a fiddle or flute might also accompany the singers, who often dance while they sing.

In each area and even within a single area, different social groups have their own individual songs whose origins are lost in antiquity. The songs are passed on from one generation to another, and in most cases the composers are unknown. Apart from folk songs, one also hears outdoor instrumental music in villages. The music is provided by an ensemble of varying size, which consists basically of an oboe type of instrument (usually a *shehnai* in North India and *nagaswaram* in the south) and a variety of drums. Sometimes straight, curved, or S-shaped horns may be added. These groups play at weddings, funerals, and religious processions. The musicians are professional or semiprofessional and usually belong to a very low caste. Such ensembles are found in tribal and other predominantly rural societies as well as in villages and cities.

Other professional music is also found in the rural regions. Most areas are visited by religious mendicants, many of whom travel around the countryside singing devotional songs, accompanying themselves either with a one-, two-, or three-stringed lute that generally provides only a drone or with a frame (tambourine-like) drum. They carry with them a small begging bowl and maintain themselves entirely on what they receive in alms. There are also itinerant magicians, snake charmers, acrobats, and storytellers who travel in the rural areas. Music is often involved in their acts, and the storyteller generally sings his tales, which may be taken from the two epics, the *Mahabharata* and the *Ramayana*, or from the Puranas, the legends that describe the adventures of the incarnations of God as they rid the world of evil. Sometimes the narrative songs are concerned with historical characters and describe the wars and the heroic deeds of the regional rulers. Some storytellers specialize in generally tragic stories of romance and of lovers.

During certain religious festivals, the villages might be visited by a travelling band of players who enact some of the mythological episodes connected with the festival. Such performances are accompanied by music and may also include dances. During the festivals villagers may visit neighbourhood shrines or temples, there encountering religious mendicants singing devotional songs and perhaps watching elaborate enactments of the episodes connected with the festival. Thus, the villagers become familiar with the mythological and philosophical aspects of their religion, in spite of low levels of literacy in many rural areas and the difficulties of communication via the overland infrastructure, which may be limited to a narrow dirt road traversed by bullock carts.

Especially since the mid-20th century, there has been considerable interaction between rural and urban cultures. Travelling cinemas, set up quickly and easily in tents, have visited the rural areas for many years, not only bringing Western-influenced film music—the source of most Indian popular songs—but also contributing to changing musical tastes and aesthetics across the countryside. Conversely, film music and other popular genres, such as the now ubiquitous *bhangra* music, have clearly been inspired by rural traditions. Although many distinct rural and urban musics continue to be practiced in the 21st century, the traditions are increasingly intertwined.

CLASSICAL MUSIC

Many different forms of music can be heard in the cities. Of these, best known in the West are the classical music of North India (including Pakistan), also called Hindustani music, and that of South India, also called Karnatak music. Both classical systems are supported by an extensive body of literature and elaborate musical theory. Until modern times, classical music was patronized by the princely courts and to some extent also by wealthy noblemen. Since India gained independence in 1947, and with the abolition of the princely kingdoms, the emphasis has shifted to the milieu of large concert halls. The concertgoer, radio, and the cinema are now the main patrons of the classical musicians. Meanwhile, the growth of university music programs, particularly involving classical music, has placed greater emphasis on music history and theory and has provided a further source of income for musicologists and musicians. The traditional system of private instruction, however, still continues to this day.

India's music, both classical and popular, has drawn more fans in recent years. Here, musicians perform during the Indian musical Bharati *at the ICC Center on January 2, 2007, in Berlin, Germany.* Christian Jakubaszek/Getty Images

Classical music is based on two main elements, raga and tala. The word *raga* is derived from a Sanskrit root meaning "to colour," the underlying idea being that certain melodic shapes, involving specific intervals of the scale, produce a continuity of emotional experience and "colour" the mind. Since neither the melodic shapes nor their sequence are fixed precisely, a raga serves as a basis for composition and improvisation. Indian music has neither modulation (change of key) nor changing harmonies; instead, the music is invariably accompanied by a drone that establishes the tonic, or ground note, of the raga and usually its fifth (i.e., five notes above). These are chosen to suit the convenience of the main performer, as there is no concept of fixed pitch. While a raga is primarily a musical concept, specific ragas, particularly in North Indian music, possess a number of nonsonic elements in their association with particular periods of the day, seasons of the year, colours, deities, and specific moods.

The second element of Indian music, tala, is best described as time measure and has two main constituents; the duration of the time measure in terms of time units that vary according to the tempo chosen; and the distribution of stress within the time measure. Tala, like raga, serves as a basis for composition and improvisation.

Indian classical music is generally performed by small ensembles of not more than five or six musicians. Improvisation plays a major part in a performance, and great emphasis is placed on the creativity and sensitivity of the soloist. A performance of a raga usually goes through well-defined stages, beginning with an improvised melodic prelude that is followed by a composed piece set in a particular time measure. The composition is generally quite short and serves as a frame of reference to which the soloist returns at the conclusion of his improvisation. There is no set duration for the performance of a raga. A characteristic feature of North Indian classical music is the gradual acceleration of tempo, which leads to a final climax.

NONCLASSICAL MUSIC OF THE CITIES

Classical music interests only a small proportion of the peoples of South Asia, even in the cities. Since about the 1930s a new genre, associated with the cinema, has achieved extraordinary popularity. Most Indian films are very much like Western musicals and generally include six or more songs. Film music derives its inspiration from a number of sources, both Indian and Western; classical, folk, and devotional music are the main Indian sources, while Western influence is seen most obviously in the use of large orchestras that employ both Western and Indian instruments. The influence of Western popular music, too, is very evident. In spite of the eclectic nature of Indian film music, most of the songs maintain an Indian feeling that arises largely from the vocal technique of the singers and the ornamentation of the melody line. This music is a continuously developing form, and much of it has incorporated harmony, counterpoint, and other features of Western music. But the film music differs from typical Western music in that the melody line is generally not dictated by harmonic progressions and in that the harmonies used are incidental additions.

Aside from classical and film music, there are several other forms of urban music, some of which closely resemble the music of the rural areas. In city streets one is likely to encounter an outdoor band of oboes and drums announcing a wedding or a funeral. Street musicians, religious mendicants, snake charmers, storytellers, and magicians perform at every available opportunity, and work songs are sung by construction workers and other labourers. In private homes, still other forms of music are performed, ranging from religious chanting to traditional folk and devotional songs. In public places of entertainment, the listener may encounter, apart from classical and film music, theatrical music from one of the many

Popular Indian film star Shilpa Shetty performs on stage during a preview of a musical called Miss Bollywood. Andreas Rentz/Getty Images

forms of regional theatre. In the lowbrow places of entertainment, courtesans still sing and dance in traditional fashion. In the larger cities there are performances of Western chamber music and occasionally symphony concerts, as well as popular dance music, rock, and jazz in the night clubs.

ANTIQUITY

In a musical tradition in which improvisation predominates, and written notation, when used, is skeletal and more a tool of the theorist than of the practicing musician, the music of past generations is irrevocably lost. References to music in ancient texts, aesthetic formulations, and depictions and written discussions of musical instruments can offer clues. In rare instances an ancient musical style may be preserved in unbroken oral tradition. For most historical eras and styles, surviving treatises explaining musical scales and modes—the framework of melody—provide a particularly important means of recapturing at least a suggestion of the music of former times, and tracing the musical theory of the past makes clear the position of the present musical system.

Little is known of the musical culture of the Indus valley civilization of the 3rd and 2nd millennia BC. Some musical instruments, such as the arched, or bow-shaped, harp and more than one variety of drum, have been identified from the small terra-cotta figures and among the pictographs on the seals that were probably used by merchants. Further, it has been suggested that a bronze statuette of a dancing girl represents a class of temple dancers similar to those found much later in Hindu culture. It is known that the Indus civilization had established trade connections with the Mesopotamian civilizations, so that it is possible that the bow harp found in Sumeria would also have been known in the Indus valley.

Vedic Chant

It is generally thought among scholars that the Indus valley civilization was terminated by the arrival of bands of sem-inomadic tribesmen, the Indo-Europeans, who descended into India from the north-west, probably in the first half of the 2nd millennium BC. An important aspect of Vedic religious life was the bard-priest who composed hymns in praise of gods, to be sung or chanted at sacrifices. This tradition was continued in the invaders'

new home in northern India until a siz-able body of oral religious poetry had been composed.

Compilation of Hymns

By about 1000 BC this body of chanted poetry had apparently grown to unman-ageable proportions, and the best of the poems were formed into an anthology called Rigveda, which was then canon-ized. It was not committed to writing, but text and chanting formula were care-fully handed down by word of mouth from one generation to the next, up to the present period.

The poems in the Rigveda are arranged according to the priestly fami-lies who used and, presumably, had composed the hymns. Shortly after this a new Veda, called the Yajurveda, basi-cally a methodical rearrangement of the verses of the Rigveda with certain addi-tions in prose, was created to serve as a kind of manual for the priest officiating at the sacrifices. At approximately the same time, a third Veda, the Samaveda, was created for liturgical purposes. The Samaveda was also derived from the hymns of the Rigveda, but the words were distorted by the repetition of sylla-bles, pauses, prolongations, and phonetic changes, as well as the insertion of cer-tain meaningless syllables believed to have magical significance. A fourth Veda, the Atharvaveda, was accepted as a Veda considerably later and is quite unrelated to the other three. It represents the more popular aspects of the Vedic religion and consists mostly of magic spells and incantations.

Each of these Vedas has several ancillary texts, called the Brahmanas, Aranyakas, and Upanishads, which are also regarded as part of the Vedas. These ancillary texts are concerned primarily with mystical speculations, symbolism, and the cosmological significance of the sacrifice. The Vedic literature was oral and not written down until very much later, the first reference to a written Vedic text being in the 10th century AD. In order to ensure the purity of the Vedas, the slightest change was forbidden, and the priests devised systems of checks and counterchecks so that there has been virtually no change in these texts for about 3,000 years. Underlying this was the belief that the correct recitation of the Vedas was "the pivot of the universe" and that the slightest mistake would have disastrous cosmic consequence unless expiated by sacrifice and prayer. The Vedas are still chanted by the Brahmin priests at weddings, initiations, funerals, and the like, in the daily devotions of the priests, and at the now rarely held so-called public sacrifices.

From the Vedic literature it is apparent that music played an important part in the lives of the Indo-European peoples, and there are references to stringed instruments, wind instruments, and several types of drums and cymbals. Songs, instrumental music, and dance are mentioned as being an integral part of some of the sacrificial ceremonies. The bow harp (*vina*), a stringed instrument (probably a board zither) with 100 strings, and the bamboo flute were the most prominent melody instruments. Little is known of the music, however, apart from the Vedic chanting, which can still be heard today.

CHANT INTONATION

The chanting of the Rigveda and Yajurveda shows, with some exceptions, a direct correlation with the grammar of the Vedic language. As in ancient Greek, the original Vedic language was accented, with the location of the accent often having a bearing on the meaning of the word. In the development of the Vedic language to Classical Sanskrit, the original accent was replaced by an automatic stress accent, whose location was determined by the length of the word and had no bearing on its meaning. It was thus imperative that the location of the original accent be inviolate if the Vedic texts were to be preserved accurately. The original Vedic accent occurs as a three-syllable pattern: the central syllable, called *udatta*, receives the main accent; the preceding syllable, *anudatta*, is a kind of preparation for the accent; and the following syllable, *svarita*, is a kind of return from accentuation to accentlessness. There is some difference of opinion among scholars as to the nature of the original Vedic accent; some have suggested that it was based on pitch, others on stress; and one theory proposes that it referred to the relative height of the tongue.

In the most common style of Rigvedic and Yajurvedic chanting found today, that of the Tamil Aiyar Brahmins, it is clear that the accent is differentiated in terms of pitch. This chanting is based on three tones; the *udatta* and the non-accented syllables (called *prachaya*) are recited at a middle tone, the preceding *anudatta* syllable at a low tone, and the following *svarita* syllable either at the high tone (when the syllable is short) or as a combination of middle tone and high tone. The intonation of these tones is not precise, but the lower interval is very often about a whole tone, while the upper interval tends to be slightly smaller than a whole tone but slightly larger than a semitone. In this style of chanting the duration of the tones is also relative to the length of the syllables, the short syllables generally being half the duration of the long.

The more musical chanting of the Samaveda employs five, six, or seven tones and is said to be the source of the later secular and classical music. From some of the phonetic texts that follow the Vedic literature, it is apparent that certain elements of musical theory were known in Vedic circles, and there are references to three octave registers (*sthana*), each containing seven notes (*yama*). An auxiliary text of the Samaveda, the Naradishiksha, correlates the Vedic tones with the accents described above,

suggesting that the Samavedic tones possibly derived from the accents. The Samavedic hymns as chanted by the Tamil Aiyar Brahmins are based on a mode similar to the D mode (D-d on the white notes of the piano; i.e., the ecclesiastical Dorian mode). But the hymns seem to use three different-sized intervals, in contrast to the two sizes found in the Western church modes. They are approximately a whole tone, a semitone, and an intermediate tone. Once again, the intervals are not consistent and vary both from one chanter to another and within the framework of a single chant. The chants are entirely unaccompanied by instruments, and this may account for some of the extreme variation of intonation.

The changes brought by the 20th century weakened the traditional prominent position of the Vedic chant. The Atharvaveda is seldom heard in India now. Samavedic chant, associated primarily with the large public sacrifices, also appears to be dying out. Even the Rigveda and Yajurveda are virtually extinct in some places, and South India is now the main stronghold of Vedic chant.

THE CLASSICAL PERIOD

The ritual of the Vedas involves only the three upper classes, or castes, of Indo-European society: the Brahman, or priestly class; the Kshatriya, or prince-warriors; and the Vaishya, or merchants. The fourth caste, the Sudra, or labourers, were excluded from Vedic rites. The primary sources of religious education and inspiration for the Sudra were derived from what is sometimes called the fifth Veda: the epic poems *Ramayana* and *Mahabharata*, as well as the collections of legends, called the Puranas, depicting the lives of the various incarnations of the Hindu deities. The *Ramayana* and the *Mahabharata* were originally secular in character, describing the heroic deeds of kings and noblemen, many of whom are not recorded in history. Subsequently, religious matter was added, including the very famous sermon *Bhagavadgita* ("Song of the Lord"), which has been referred to as the most important document of Hinduism; and many of the heroes of the epics were identified as incarnations of the Hindu deities. The legends were probably sung and recited by wandering minstrels and bards even before the advent of the Christian Era, in much the same way as they still are. The stories were also enacted on the stage, particularly at the time of the religious festivals. The earliest extant account of drama is to be found in the *Natya-shastra* ("Treatise on the Dramatic Arts"), a text that has been dated variously from the 2nd century BC to the 5th century AD and even later. It is virtually a handbook for the producer of stage plays and deals with all aspects of drama, including dance and music.

Theatrical music of the period apparently included songs sung on stage by the actors, as well as background music provided by an orchestra (which included singers) located offstage, in what was very like an orchestra pit. Melodies were composed on a system of modes, or *jatis*, each of which was thought to evoke one or more particular sentiments (*rasa*) by its emphasis on specific notes. The modes were derived in turn from the 14 *murchanas*—seven pairs of ascending seven-note series beginning on each of the notes of two closely related heptatonic (seven-note) parent scales, called *sadjagrama* and *madhyamagrama*. The *murchana*s were thus more or less analogous to the European modal scales that begin progressively on D, E, F, G, etc. A third parent scale, *gandharagrama*, was mentioned in several texts of the period and some even earlier but is not included in the system laid out in the *Natya-shastra*.

QUALITIES OF THE SCALES

The two parent scales differed in the positioning of just one note, which was microtonally flatter in one of the scales. The microtonal difference, referred to as *pramana* ("measuring") *shruti*, presumably served as a standard of measurement. In terms of this standard, it was determined that the intervals of the *murchana*s were of three different sizes, consisting of two, three, or four *shruti*s, and that the octave comprised 22 *shruti*s. An interval of one *shruti* was not used. Several modern scholars have suggested that the *shruti*s were of unequal size; from the evidence in the *Natya-shastra*, it would appear, however, that they were thought to be equal. There has been no attempt to determine the exact size of the *shrutis* in any of the traditional Indian musical treatises until relatively modern times (18th century).

The term *shruti* was also used to define consonance and dissonance, as these terms were understood in the period. In this connection, four terms are mentioned: *vadi*, comparable to the Western term *sonant*, meaning "having sound"; *samvadi*, comparable to the Western *consonant* (concordant; reposeful); *vivadi*, comparable to *dissonant* (discordant; lacking repose); and *anuvadi*, comparable to *assonant* (neither consonant nor dissonant). As in the ancient Greek Pythagorean system, which influenced Western music, only fourths and fifths (intervals of four or five tones in a Western scale) were considered consonant. In the Indian system of measurement, tones separated by either nine or 13 *shrutis* correspond in size to Western fourths and fifths and are described as being consonant to each other. "Dissonant" in this system referred only to the minor second, an interval of two *shrutis*, and to its inversion (complementary interval), the major seventh (20 *shrutis*). All other tones, including the major third, were thought to be assonant.

The musical difference between the two parent scales is best seen not in terms of the microtonal deviation mentioned earlier but rather in terms of a musically influential consonance found in one but lacking in the other and vice versa. In each of the parent scales there are two nonconsonances, one of which is the tritone (interval of three Western whole tones, such as F-B) of 11 *shrutis* inevitable in all diatonic scales (seven-note scales of the major scale and *murchana* type) and which in medieval Europe was described as *diabolus in musica* ("the devil in music").

The second is a microtonal nonconsonance unique to this ancient Indian system.

The nonconsonance arises from variances of one *shruti* from the fundamental consonances of the fourth and the fifth—a variance of about a quarter tone. In the *sadjagrama* scale the interval *ri-pa* (E to A) contains 10 *shrutis*; i.e., one more than the nine of the consonant fourth. Comparably, in the *madhyamagrama* scale the interval *sa-pa* (D to A) contains 12 *shrutis*, or one fewer than the consonant fifth. These variances involve the consonant relationships of two melodically prominent notes, the first and the fifth. In the *madhyamagrama* the first note, *sa*, has no consonant fifth, and perhaps for this reason this scale is said to begin not on the *sa* (D) but on its fourth, the note *ma* (G); hence, it resembles the G mode—i.e., the ecclesiastical Mixolydian mode—whereas the *sadjagrama* resembles the D mode, the ecclesiastical Dorian.

There is a striking resemblance of the *sadjagrama* scale to the intervals used by the Tamil Aiyar Brahmins in their chanting of the Samaveda. Not only are their hymns set in a mode similar to the D mode, but they seem to use three different-sized intervals, the intermediate one corresponding to the three-*shruti* interval. The *Natya-shastra* claims to have derived song (*gita*) from the chanting of the Samaveda, and the resemblances between the two may not be entirely fortuitous.

The two parent scales are complementary and between them supply all the consonances found in the ancient Greek Pythagorean scale. Thus, if in a mode the consonance *ri-pa* (E–A) were needed, one would tune to the *madhyamagrama* scale. But, if the consonance *sa-pa* (D–A) were important, it could be obtained with the *sadjagrama* tuning. There was a further development in this system caused by the introduction of two additional notes, called *antara ga* (F♯) and *kakali ni* (C♯), which could be substituted for the usual *ga* (F) and *ni* (C). The *antara ga* eliminates the 11-*shruti* tritone between *ga* and *dha* (F–B), but its use creates a further tritone between F♯ and C. The second additional note, *kakali ni* (C♯), eliminates this tritone but once again creates a new one, this time between C♯ and G. This process of adding notes, if carried further, would eventually lead to the circle, or, rather, the spiral, of fourths or fifths found in Western music (whereby a sequence of fifths, such as C–G, G–D, D–A, etc., leads eventually back to a microtonally out-of-tune C); there is no evidence that such a circle or spiral was known in ancient India.

MODE, OR *JATI*

From each of the two parent scales were derived seven modal sequences (the *murchana*s described above), based on each of the seven notes. The two *murchana*s of a corresponding pair differed from each other only in the tuning of the note *pa* (A), the crucial distinction in the tunings of the two parent scales. One of each pair was selected as the basis for a "pure" mode, or *shuddha-jati*; in the groups of seven pure modes, four used the tuning of the *sadjagrama* and three that of the *madhyamagrama*. In addition to these seven pure modes, a further 11 "mixed" modes, or *vikrita-jatis*, are also mentioned in the *Natya-shastra*. These were derived by a combination of two or more pure modes, but the text does not explain just in what way these derivations were accomplished.

The *jatis* were similar to the modern concept of raga in that they provided the melodic basis for composition and, presumably, improvisation. They were not merely scales, but were also assigned 10 melodic characteristics: *graha*, the initial note; *amsha*, the predominant note; *tara*, the note that forms the upper limit; *mandra*, the note that forms the lower limit; *nyasa*, the final note; *apanyasa*, the secondary final note; *alpatva*, the notes to be used infrequently; *bahutva*, the notes to be used frequently; *shadavita*, the note that must be omitted in order to create the hexatonic (six-note) version of the mode; and *audavita*, the two notes that must be omitted to create the pentatonic (five-note) version of the mode.

No written music survives from this early period. It is not clear from the description whether or not the music was like that of the present period. There is no mention of a drone, nor do the instruments of the orchestra—consisting of the *vipanchi* and *vina*, bamboo flute, a variety of drums, and singers—appear to include any specifically drone instrument, such as the modern tamboura. The evidence tends rather to suggest, from the emphasis on consonance and some of the playing techniques, that some form of organum (two or more parts paralleling the same melody at distinct pitch levels) and even some type of rudimentary harmony may have been characteristic.

MEDIEVAL PERIOD

It is not clear just when the *jati* system fell into disuse. Later writers refer to *jatis* merely out of reverence for Bharata, the author of the *Natya-shastra*.

PRECURSORS OF THE MEDIEVAL SYSTEM

Later developments are based on musical entities called *grama-ragas*, of which seven are mentioned in the 7th-century Kutimiyamalai rock inscription in Tamil Nadu state. Although the word *grama-raga* does not occur in the *Natya-shastra*, the names applied to the individual *grama-ragas* are all mentioned. Two of

them, *sadjagrama-raga* and *madhyama-grama-raga*, are obviously related to the parent scales of the *jati* system. The other five seem to be variants of these two *grama-ragas* in which either or both the altered forms of the notes *ga* and *ni* (F♯ and C♯) are used. In the *Natya-shastra* the reference to the various *grama-ragas* is far removed from the main section in which the *jati* system is discussed, and there is no obvious connection between the two. Each of the *grama-ragas* is said to be used in one of the seven formal stages of Sanskrit drama.

FURTHER DEVELOPMENT OF THE *GRAMA-RAGAS*

In the next significant text on Indian music, the *Brihaddeshi*, written by the theorist Matanga about the 10th century AD, the *grama-ragas* are said to derive from the *jatis*. In some respects at least, the *grama-ragas* resemble not the *jatis* but their parent scales. The author of the *Brihaddeshi* claims to be the first to discuss the term *raga* in any detail. It is clear that raga was only one of several kinds of musical entities in this period and is described as having "varied and graceful ornaments, with emphasis on clear, even, and deep tones and having a charming elegance." The ragas of this period seem to have been named after the different peoples living in the various parts of the country, suggesting that their origin might lie in folk music. Matanga appears to contrast the two terms *marga* and *deshi*. The term *marga* (literally "the path") apparently refers to the ancient traditional musical material, whereas *deshi* (literally "the vulgar dialect spoken in the provinces") designates the musical practice that was evolving in the provinces, which may have had a more secular basis. Although the title *Brihaddeshi* ("The Great Deshi") suggests that the latter music might have been the focus of the treatise and that the *grama-ragas* were possibly out of date by the time it was written, the surviving portion of the text does not support such a theory.

The mammoth 13th-century text *Sangitaratnakara* ("Ocean of Music and Dance"), composed by the theorist Sharngadeva, is often said to be one of the most important landmarks in Indian music history. It was composed in the Deccan (south-central India) shortly before the conquest of this region by the Muslim invaders and thus gives an account of Indian music before the full impact of Muslim influence. A large part of this work is devoted to *marga*—that is, the ancient music that includes the system of *jatis* and *grama-ragas*—but Sharngadeva mentions a total of 264 ragas. Despite the use in both the *Brihaddeshi* and the *Sangitaratnakara* of a notation equivalent to the Western tonic sol–fa (i.e., with syllables, as do-re-mi...) to illustrate the ragas, modern scholars have not yet been able to reconstruct them with assurance.

The basic difficulty scholars face lies in determining the intervals used in each of the ragas. In the ancient system, the *jatis* were something like the ancient Greek and medieval church modes in that each was derived from a parent scale by altering the ground note and the tessitura (range). In modern Indian music, however, the ragas are all transposed to a common ground note. This change may well be connected with the introduction of the drone and the evolution of the long-necked-lute family on which the drone is usually played. In the old system, with the changing ground note, it would have been necessary to retune drone instruments from one raga to another, which would have been a cumbersome and impractical operation to carry out during a recital. It may have been this factor that provided the impetus for the change to the standard ground-note system. There is no conclusive evidence to show just when this change might have taken place, and it is not clear whether the *Brihaddeshi* and the *Sangitaratnakara* are using the old ground-note system or one similar to that used in modern times.

THE ISLAMIC PERIOD

The Muslim conquest of India can be said to have begun in the 12th century, although Sindh (now in Pakistan) had been conquered by the Arabs as early as the 8th century. Muslim writers such as al-Jāḥiẓ and al-Mas'ūdī had already commented favourably on Indian music in the 9th and 10th centuries, and the

Muslims in India seem to have been very much attracted by it.

IMPACT ON MUSICAL GENRES AND AESTHETICS

In the beginning of the 14th century, the great poet Amīr Khosrow, who was considered to be extremely proficient in both Persian and Indian music, wrote that Indian music was superior to the music of any other country. Further, it is stated that, after the Muslim conquest of the Deccan under Malik Kāfūr (c. 1310), a large number of Hindu musicians were taken with the royal armies and settled in the north. Although orthodox Islam considered music illegal, the acceptance of the Sufi doctrines, in which music was an accepted means to the realization of God, enabled Muslim rulers and noblemen to extend their patronage to this art. At the courts of the Mughal emperors Akbar, Jahāngīr, and Shah Jahān, music flourished on a grand scale. Apart from Indian musicians, there were also musicians from Persia, Afghanistan, and Kashmir in the employ of these rulers; nevertheless, it appears that it was Indian music that was most favoured. Famous Indian musicians, such as Svami Haridas and Tansen, are legendary performers and innovators of this period. After the example set by Amīr Khosrow, Muslim musicians took an active interest in the performance of Indian music and added to the repertoire by inventing new ragas, talas, and musical forms, as well as new instruments.

The Muslim patronage of music was largely effective in the north of India and has had a profound influence on North Indian music. Perhaps the main result of this influence was to de-emphasize the importance of the words of the songs, which were mostly based on Hindu devotional themes. In addition, the songs had been generally composed in Sanskrit, a language that had ceased to be a medium of communication except among scholars and priests. Sanskrit songs were gradually replaced by compositions in the various dialects of Hindi, Braj Bhasha, Bhojpuri, and Dakhani, as well as in Urdu and Persian. Nevertheless, the problems of communication, in terms of both language and subject matter, were not easily reconciled.

A new approach to religion was, in any case, sweeping through India at about this time. This emphasized devotion (*bhakti*) as a primary means to achieving union with God, bypassing the traditional Hindu beliefs of the transmigration of the soul from body to body in the lengthy process of purification before it could achieve the Godhead. The Islamic Sufi movement was based on an approach similar to that of the *bhakti* movements and also gained many converts in India. A manifestation of these devotional cults was the growth of a new form of mystic-devotional poetry composed by wandering mendicants who had dedicated their lives to the realization of God. Many of these mendicants have been sanctified and are referred to as poet-saints or singer-saints, since their poems were invariably set to music. A number of devotional sects sprang up all over the country—some Muslim, some Hindu, and others merging elements from both. These sects emphasized the individual's personal relationship with God. In their poetry, human love for God was often represented as a woman's love for a man and, specifically, the love of the milkmaid Radha for Krishna, a popular incarnation of the Hindu god Vishnu. In the environment of the royal courts, there was a less idealistic interpretation of the word "love," and much of the poetry, as well as the miniature painting, of the period depicts the states of experience of the lover and the beloved.

This attitude is also reflected in the musical literature of the period. From early times, both *jatis* and ragas in their connection with dramatic performance were described as evoking specific sentiments (*rasa*) and being suitable for accompanying particular dramatic events. It was this connotational aspect, rather than the technical one, that gained precedence in this period. The most popular method of classification was in terms of ragas (masculine) and their wives, called *raginis*, which was extended to include *putras*, their sons, and *bharyas*, the wives of the sons. The ragas were personified and associated with particular scenes, some of which were taken from Hindu mythology, while others represented aspects of the relationship between two lovers. The climax of this personification is found in the *ragamala* paintings, usually in a series of 36, which depict the ragas and *raginis* in their emotive settings.

THEORETICAL DEVELOPMENTS

From the middle of the 16th century, a new method of describing ragas is found in musical literature. It was also at about this time that the distinction between North and South Indian music became clearly evident. In the literature, ragas are described in terms of scales having a common ground note. These scales were called *mela* in the South and *mela* or *thata* in the North.

It was in the South that a complete theoretical system of *melas* was introduced, in the *Caturdandiprakashika* ("The Illuminator of the Four Pillars of Music"), a text written in the middle of the 17th century. This system was based on the permutations of the tones and semitones, which had by this time been reduced to a basic 12 in the octave. The octave was divided into two tetrachords, or four-note sequences, C–F and G–c, and six possible tetrachord species were arranged in an order showing their relationship with each other. It will be noted in the sequence of tetrachords shown below that each lower tetrachord has an analogous upper tetrachord and that the outer notes of each are constant, whereas the inner notes change their pitch.

1. C D♭ E♭♭ F   and   G A♭ B♭♭ c
2. C D♭ E♭ F   G A♭ B♭ c
3. C D♭ E F   G A♭ B c
4. C D E♭ F   G A B c
5. C D E F   G A B c
6. C D♯ E F   G A♯ B c

The list could have extended further, except that apparently no pitch distinction was made between the enharmonic pairs D–E♭♭, D♯–E♭, A–B♭♭, and A♯–B♭. (Enharmonic notes have different pitch names but sound either the same pitch or, in some tuning systems, have very slight differences in pitch.)

By utilizing all possible combinations of a lower with an upper tetrachord, 36 melas, or raga scales, were derived; a further 36 were formed by using F♯ in place of the F in the lower tetrachord. The melas were named in such a way that the first two syllables of the name, when applied in a code, gave the number of that mela in the sequence. The musician, given the number, could easily reconstruct the scale of the mela. The names of the melas were often derived from prominent ragas in those melas, with a two-syllable prefix that supplied the code numbers; for instance, the name of the mela Dhira-shankarabharana is derived from the raga Shankarabharana, the two syllables dhira giving the code number 29, which indicates a scale similar to the Western major scale, or C mode. The Caturdandiprakashika acknowledges the theoretical nature of its analytical system and mentions clearly that only 19 of the possible 72 melas were in use at the time that the text was written.

Although North Indian texts also describe ragas in terms of melas or thatas, there is no attempt to arrange them systematically. In the Ragatarangini ("The River of Raga"), probably of the 16th century, 12 melas are mentioned:

bhairavī	C	D	E♭	F	G	A	B♭	c	
toṛī	C	D♭	E♭	F	G	A♭	B♭	c	
gaurī	C	D♭	E	F	G	A♭	B	c	
karnāta	C	D	E	F	G	A	B♭	c	
kedāra	C	D	E	F	G	A	B	c	
imana	C	D	E	F♯	G	A	B	c	
sāraṅga	C	D	E♯	F♯	G	A♯	B	c	
megha	C	D	E	F	G	A♯	B	c	
dhanāśrī	C	D♭	E	F♯	G	A♭	B	c	
pūravā	C	D	E	F♯	G	A⁺	B	c	
mukhārī	C	D	E♭	F	G	A♭	B♭	c	
dīpaka	no description								

Although it appears from the description of saranga and megha melas that enharmonic intervals were used, there is good reason to believe that the E♯ and A♯ in the two melas really represent their chromatic counterparts, F and B♭, and that F and F♯ (and B and B♭) do not appear in sequence. The A⁺ in the mela purava is said to be raised by one shruti. The description of the ragas in these melas shows that the North Indian system was by this time also based on 12 semitones.

THE MODERN PERIOD

With the collapse of the Mughal empire in the 18th century and the emergence of the British as a dominant power in India, the subcontinent was divided into many princely states. Music continued to be patronized by the rulers, although the courts were never again to achieve their former opulence.

Musically, there has been a continuous evolution from the Islamic period to the present, and both North and South Indian classical music have continued to expand. South Indian music has clearly been influenced more by theory than has that of the North. The 72-*mela* system continues to be the basis of classifying the ragas in South India, but it has had more than a classificatory significance. Many new ragas have been composed in the past few centuries, some of them inspired by the theoretical scales of the *mela* system. As a result, there are now ragas in all of the 72 *melas*.

In North Indian music, theory has had little influence on performance practice. This can be ascribed to the language problem, an especially significant influence on the many Muslim musicians in North India, who were not able to cope with the Sanskrit musical literature. Thus, there had been no attempt to systematize the music, and there was a considerable gap between performance and theory until the present century. Vishnu Narayana Bhatkande, one of the leading Indian musicologists of this century, contributed a great deal toward diminishing the gap. Being both a scholar and a performer, he devoted much effort to collecting and notating representative versions of a number of ragas from musicians belonging to different family traditions, or *gharanas*. Based on this collection, he concluded that most of the ragas of North Indian music can be grouped into the following scales, called *thatas* (compare the South Indian *melas* shown above in Theoretical developments):

kalyāṇa	C	D	E	F♯	G	A	B	c
bilāvala	C	D	E	F	G	A	B	c
khamāja	C	D	E	F	G	A	B♭	c
bhairava	C	D♭	E	F	G	A♭	B	c
pūrvī	C	D♭	E	F♯	G	A♭	B	c
mārvā	C	D♭	E	F♯	G	A	B	c
kāfī	C	D	E♭	F	G	A	B♭	c
āsāvarī	C	D	E♭	F	G	A♭	B♭	c
bhairavī	C	D♭	E♭	F	G	A♭	B♭	c
toṛī	C	D♭	E♭	F♯	G	A♭	B	c

The *thatas* do not cover all the ragas used in North Indian music, but there is reason to believe that most of the ragas having scales other than the above are relatively modern innovations. New ragas are constantly being created, and some North Indian musicians are using the vast potential of the South Indian *mela* system as their source of inspiration.

Mela and *thata* are theoretical devices for the classification of ragas. Ragas have scalar elements, such as specified ascending and descending movements, that might or might not employ adjacent steps. They may also employ oblique or zigzag movements. Ragas can be heptatonic, hexatonic, or pentatonic and may also have accidentals (sharpened or flattened notes) that occur only in specific melodic contexts. A further distinction between scale and raga is found in the varying emphasis placed on different notes in a raga. Ragas, furthermore, also have melodic elements, such as certain recurrent nuclear motives (brief melodic fragments) that enable the raga to be identified more easily. One scale type can be the basis for perhaps 20 or 30 ragas, in which case it is the nonscalar elements that provide the distinguishing features of each raga in the group.

RHYTHMIC ORGANIZATION

Just as the system of classifying raga is better organized in South Indian music, so too is the system of classifying tala, or time measure. In North Indian music the talas are fewer and not organized in any systematic manner.

SOUTH INDIA

The main group is composed of 35 talas, called the *suladi-talas*. Each tala is composed of one, two, or three different units: short, medium, and long. The medium unit is twice the duration of the short; the long unit is, however, a variable and may be three, four, five, seven, or nine times the duration of the short. There are seven basic tala patterns, and, because the long unit of these talas can be of five different durations, the total number of talas in this system is 35. The basic tala patterns are:

dhruva-tāla—long, medium, long, long
mathya-tāla—long, medium, long
rūpaka-tāla—medium, long
jhampā-tāla—long, short, medium
triputa-tāla—long, medium, medium
āta-tāla—long, long, medium, medium
eka-tāla—only a single long.

The total duration of each pattern is controlled by the duration of the variable long; thus, if the long unit is five times the short, a tala pattern such as *dhruva-tala* will be 5 + 2 + 5 + 5, or 17 units. Several of these talas have the same total duration but are distinguished from each other by their internal subdivisions. In the course of a performance, the vocalist as well as the audience may mark the time by clapping, hand waving, and finger counting.

In addition to the *suladi-talas*, there are four *chapu-talas* that are used in South Indian classical music. Said to derive from folk music, they consist of two sections of unequal length, 1 + 2, 2 + 3, 3 + 4, and 4 + 5. Of these, the 3 + 4 combination is the most prominent. On rare occasions a performer may use one of the "classical" talas referred to in Sanskrit texts. These generally involve long time cycles composed of as many as 100 short units. The most frequently heard time measures, however, are *adi-tala*, a modified eight-beat version of *triputa-tala* (4 + 2 + 2); *mishra-chapu-tala* (3 + 4); and *rupaka-tala* (4 + 2). The difficult and long talas are used primarily as a tour de force. Each tala may be performed in either slow, medium, or quick tempo. There is no gradual acceleration as in North Indian music.

NORTH INDIA

As in South Indian music, the two main factors are the duration of the time cycle and the subdivisions within the cycle. Each of these subdivisions is marked by a clap or a wave, with the greatest emphasis falling on beat 1 of the cycle, which is called *sam*. North Indian talas have a further feature, the *khali* ("empty"), a conscious negation of stress occurring at one or more points in each tala where one would expect a beat. It often falls at the halfway point in the time cycle and is marked by a wave of the hand. There is nothing comparable to the *khali* in the South Indian system. A further distinguishing feature found only in North Indian talas is the emphasis placed on the characteristic drum pattern of each tala, called *theka*. Two talas might have the same duration and subdivisions but might, nevertheless, be differentiated from each other by different characteristic drum patterns. In addition, the talas are also associated with different forms of song and even particular tempi. The usual North Indian talas range from six to 16 time units in duration. The most popular are *tin-tala* (4 + 4 + 4 + 4), *eka-tala* (2 + 2 + 2 + 2 + 2 + 2), *jhap-tala* (2 + 3 + 2 + 3), *kaharava* (4 + 4), *rupaka-tala* (3 + 2 + 2), and *dadra* (3 + 3). *Tin-tala* should not be confused with Western 4/4, or common time, for the time cycle repeats only after 16 units and is more like four bars of common time.

MUSICAL FORMS AND INSTRUMENTS

Both raga and tala provide bases for composition and improvisation in Indian classical music. A performance usually begins with an improvised section, called *alapa*, played in free time without accompaniment of drums. It may have various sections and might on occasion last half an hour or longer. It is followed by a composed piece in the same raga, set in a particular tala.

SOUTH INDIA

In South Indian music all composed pieces are primarily for the voice and have lyrics. In North India, however, there are also some purely instrumental compositions, called *gat* and *dhun*. The emphasis on the composition varies in the different forms of song and, to some extent, in the interpretation of the performer. In South Indian music the composed piece is generally emphasized more than in the North. Much of the South Indian repertoire of compositions stems from three composers, Tyagaraja, Muthuswami Dikshitar, and Syama Sastri, contemporaries who lived in the second half of the 18th and the beginning of the 19th centuries. The devotional songs that they composed, called *kriti*, are a delicate blend of text, melody, and rhythm and are the most popular items of a South Indian concert. The composed elements in these songs sometimes include sections such as *niraval*, melodic variations with the same text, and *svara-kalpana*, passages using the Indian equivalent of the sol–fa syllables, which are otherwise improvised.

The longest item in the South Indian concert, called *ragam-tanam-pallavi*, is, on the other hand, mostly improvised. It begins with a long *alapa*, called *ragam* in this context, presumably because this elaborate, gradually developing *alapa* is intended to display the raga being performed in as complete a manner as possible, without the limitations imposed by a fixed time measure. This is followed by another improvised section, *tanam*, in which the singer uses meaningless words to produce more or less regular rhythms, but still without reference to time measure. This section, too, is without drum accompaniment. The final section, *pallavi*, is a composition of words and melody set in a particular tala, usually a long or complex one. The *pallavi* may have been composed by the performer himself and be unfamiliar to his accompanists, usually a violinist who echoes the singer's phrases and a drummer who plays the *mridangam*, a double-ended drum. The statement of the composition is followed by elaborate rhythmic and melodic variations that the accompanists are expected to follow. It is customary to have a drum solo at the end of the *pallavi*, and the performance concludes with a brief restatement of the *pallavi*.

Other forms used in South Indian classical music derive largely from the musical repertoire of *bharata natyam*, the classical South Indian dance. The *varnam*, a completely composed piece, serves mainly as a warming up and is performed at the beginning of a concert.

Pada and *javali* are two kinds of love songs using the poetic imagery characteristic of the romantic-devotional movement mentioned earlier. *Tillana* has a text composed mostly of meaningless syllables, which may include the onomatopoeic syllables used to represent the different drum sounds. This is a very rhythmic piece and is usually sung in fast tempo.

The ensemble used in present-day South Indian classical music consists of a singer or a main melody instrument, a secondary melody instrument, one or more rhythmic percussion instruments, and one or more drone instruments. The most commonly heard main melody instruments are the *vina*, a long-necked, fretted, plucked lute with seven strings; the *venu*, a side-blown bamboo flute; the *nagaswaram*, a long, oboe-like, double-reed instrument with finger holes; the violin, imported from the West in the 18th century, played while seated on the floor with the scroll resting on the player's left foot; and the *gottuvadyam*, a long-necked lute without frets, played like the Hawaiian guitar, with a sliding stop in the left hand.

The violin is by far the most common secondary melody instrument in South India. It plays in unison where the passage is composed but imitates the voice or main melody instrument in the improvised passages. Of the rhythm instruments, the *mridangam*, a double-conical, two-headed drum, is the most common. Others include the *kanjira*, a tambourine; the *ghatam*, an earthenware pot without skin covering; the *morsing*, a metallic jew's harp; and the *tavil*, a slightly barrel-shaped, double-ended drum, which accompanies the *nagaswaram*. The most prominent drone instrument is the four-stringed *tamboura*, a long-necked lute without frets. It accompanies the voice and all melody instruments, except the *nagaswaram*, which is usually accompanied by the *ottu*, a longer version of the *nagaswaram* but without finger holes. A hand-pumped harmonium drone, called *shruti* or *shruti* box, sometimes replaces the *ottu* or the tamboura.

NORTH INDIA

The most common vocal form in North Indian classical music at the present time is the *khayal*, a Muslim word meaning "imagination." The *khayal* is contrasted to the *dhruvapada* (now known as *dhrupad*), which means "fixed words." The two forms existed side by side in the Islamic period, and it is only since the 19th century that the *khayal* has been predominant. There are two types of *khayal*. The first is sung in extremely slow tempo, with each syllable of the text having extensive melisma (prolongation of a syllable over many notes), so that the words are virtually unrecognizable. It is not usually preceded by a lengthy *alapa*; instead, *alapa*-like phrases are generally sung against the very slow time measure to the accompaniment of the drums. Also characteristic of the *khayal* are the

sargam tanas, passages using the Indian equivalent of the sol–fa syllables, and the *a-kar tanas*, which are rapid runs sung to the syllable *aah*. The second type of *khayal*, which may be as much as eight times faster than the slow and is generally set in a different tala, follows the slow. Its composed portion is usually quite short, and the main features of the improvisation are the *a-kar tanas*. Occasionally, a composition called *tarana*, made up of meaningless syllables, may replace the fast-tempo *khayal*.

The *thumri* is another North Indian vocal form and is based on the romantic-devotional literature inspired by the *bhakti* movement. The text is usually derived from the Radha-Krishna theme and is of primary importance. The words are strictly adhered to, and the singer attempts to interpret them with his melodic improvisations. It is quite usual for a singer to deviate momentarily from the raga in which the composition is set, by using accidentals and evoking other ragas that might be suggested by the words, but he always returns to the original raga.

Some of the North Indian musical forms are very like the South Indian. The vocal forms *dhrupad* and *dhamar* resemble the *ragam-tanam-pallavi*. They begin with an elaborate *alapa* followed by the more rhythmic but unmeasured *non-tom* using meaningless syllables such as *te, re, na, nom,* and *tom*. Then follow the four composed sections of the *dhrupad* or *dhamar*, the latter being named after *dhamar-tala* of 14 units (5 + 5 + 4) in which it is composed, the former name derived from *dhruvapada*. The song, usually in slow or medium tempo, is first sung as composed. Then the performer introduces variations, the words often being distorted and serving merely as a vehicle for the melodic and rhythmic improvisations.

Instrumental music has gained considerable prominence in North India in recent times. The most common instrumental form is the *gat*, which seems to have derived its elements from both *dhrupad* and *khayal*. It is usually preceded by *alapa* and *jor*, which resemble the *alapa* and *non-tom* sections of the *dhrupad*. On plucked stringed instruments these two movements are often followed by *jhala*, a fast section in which the rhythmic plucking of the drone strings is used to achieve a climax. The performer usually pauses before the composed *gat* is introduced. Like the *khayal*, the *gat* can be in slow or fast tempo. The composition is generally short, and the emphasis is on the improvisations of the melody instrumentalist and the drummer, who for the most part alternate in their extemporizing. The final climax may once again be achieved by a *jhala* section, in which the tempo is accelerated quite considerably. Other forms played on instruments are the *thumri*, basically an instrumental rendering of a vocal *thumri*, and *dhun*, which is derived from a folk tune and does not usually follow a conventional raga. One may also hear a piece called *raga-mala*

(literally, "a garland of ragas"), in which the musician modulates from one raga to another, finally concluding with a return to the original raga.

The most prominent melody instruments used in North Indian classical music are the sitar, a long-necked fretted lute; *surbahar*, a larger version of the sitar; the sarod, a plucked lute without frets and with a shorter neck than that of the sitar; the *sarangi*, a short-necked bowed lute; the *bansuri*, a side-blown bamboo flute with six or seven finger holes; the *shehnai*, a double-reed wind instrument similar to the oboe, but without keys; and the violin, played in the same manner as in South India. Secondary melody instruments are used only in vocal music, the two most common being the *sarangi* and the keyboard harmonium, an import from the West. The violin and the *surmandal*, a plucked board zither, are also used in this context. Since the mid-20th century, instrumental duets, in which the musicians improvise alternately, have grown in popularity. In these duets the musicians may imitate each other's phrases, temporarily creating something of the effect of a secondary melody instrument.

As with South Indian music, the drone is usually provided by a tamboura (Bangla *tanpura*) or a hand-pumped reed drone similar to the harmonium but without a keyboard, called *sur-peti* in North India. The *shehnai* is usually accompanied by one or more drone *shehnais*, called *sur*.

A group of Indian musicians, the two in the foreground playing the tabla (left) and sitar. Bert Hardy/Hulton Archive/Getty Images

The rhythmic accompaniment is usually provided on the tabla, a pair of small drums played with the fingers. As accompaniment to the somewhat archaic *dhrupad*, however, the *pakhavaj*, a double-conical drum, similar to the South Indian *mridangam*, is generally used. The *shehnai* in classical music is usually accompanied by a small pair of kettledrums, called *dukar-tikar*.

TABLA

The pair of small unmatched drums that is fundamental (since the 18th century) to Hindustani music of northern India, Pakistan, and Bangladesh is the tabla. The higher-pitched of the two drums, which is played with the right hand, is also referred to individually as the tabla or as the daya (dahina or dayan, meaning "right"). It is a single-headed drum usually of wood and having the profile of two truncated cones bulging at the centre, the lower portion shorter. It is about 25 cm (10 inches) in height and 15 cm (6 inches) across. Skin tension is maintained by thong lacings and wooden dowels that are tapped with a hammer in retuning. It is usually tuned to the tonic, or ground note, of the raga (melodic pattern).

The baya (bahina or bayan, meaning "left"), played with the left hand, is a deep kettledrum measuring about 25 cm (10 inches) in height, and the drum face is about 20 cm (8 inches) in diameter. It is usually made of copper but may also be made of clay or wood, with a hoop and thong lacings to maintain skin tension. Pressure from the heel of the player's hand changes the tone colour and pitch. The tuning of the baya

An Indian worker repairs a tabla, a traditional Indian two-headed drum. *Noah Seelam/AFP/Getty Images*

varies, but it may be a fifth or an octave below the daya. A disk of black tuning paste placed on the skin of each drum affects pitch and also generates overtones characteristic of the drums' sound. The musician plays the tabla while seated, with the baya to the left of the daya. Sound is produced on the drums through a variety of different finger and hand strokes. Each drum stroke can be expressed by a corresponding vocable, used for both teaching and performance purposes. The intricate music of the drums reflects the rhythmic pattern (tala) of the piece.

Tabla can be documented in India from the late 18th century. Originally associated with courtesan dance traditions, tabla now are used in a variety of genres and styles of Hindustani music. Distinguished players of the tabla include Alla Rakha and his son Zakir Hussain.

INTERACTION WITH WESTERN MUSIC

It is in the sphere of musical instruments that the influence of Western music is most obvious. In addition to the violin and the harmonium, many other Western instruments are used in Indian classical and popular music. Of the melodic instruments, these include, most notably, the clarinet, saxophone, trumpet, guitar, mandolin, and organ. Scholars have criticized the use of some of these instruments on the ground that their tuning, being based on the Western tempered scale (having 12 equal semitones), is not suitable for the performance of Indian music, and All-India Radio forbade the use of the harmonium in its programs for a number of years in the late 20th century. Most of the leading North Indian singers, however, have been using the harmonium as a secondary melody instrument for many years and have continued to do so in concerts and on recordings.

Apart from the area of musical instruments, Indian classical music appears to have absorbed very little of Western music. It is possible, however, that some developments in the tradition might have been inspired by Western music. These include the slightly increased use of chromaticism (using a succession of semitones) and some of the new drone tunings in which the major third is added (making for example, the drone on the first, third, and fifth notes of the scale, rather than on the first and fifth only).

But the evidence is not conclusive, and it could equally be argued that these are natural developments within the system.

Advancements in technology have, of course, had a profound influence on Indian music. Sound-amplification devices have made concerts available to large audiences, and the intimate atmosphere in which the music was traditionally performed is now seldom encountered. The Indian musician has been obliged to adapt his music, once played before a select and musically educated group of listeners, to new circumstances involving a mass of people, many of whom are unfamiliar with the finer points of the music. The use of microphones during concerts has had a marked effect on voice production, and, since the voice no longer needs to project over distances, many singers now perform with a relaxed throat and produce a more mellow tone.

Since the mid-1950s, Indian classical music has been performed fairly regularly in the West. Initially, the audiences were composed mainly of South Asians, but now a large and increasing number of Westerners attend the concerts. Perhaps the music would not have reached beyond a very limited audience were it not for the interest shown by the American violinist Yehudi Menuhin, who sponsored a number of collaborative programs in the West in the 1960s, and the British popular-music group the Beatles, who pioneered the incorporation of the sitar and other elements of Indian culture into the world of Western popular music. At the same time, several North Indian instrumentalists, such as Ravi Shankar, Ali Akbar Khan, Vilayat Khan, Imrat Khan, and Nikhil Banerjee, were received with overwhelming enthusiasm by Western audiences. By about 1970 the sitar and tabla were heard frequently in Western pop music, jazz, cinema, and television programs, as well as in radio and television advertisements.

Since the late 20th century the interaction between the musics of India, the West, and the world at large has become both more intense and more diverse. In the realm of popular music, jazz-rock (fusion) artists such as British guitarist John McLaughlin have gained international recognition with their energetic and eclectic assimilation of Indian music elements. Meanwhile, British-Indian world-music artist Sheila Chandra has blended the aesthetics of Western popular music with the ragas and drones of Indian music and the vocal techniques of Indian, Arab, Irish, and Scottish traditions to create a unique Asian fusion sound. Within the purview of classical music, Ravi Shankar composed and recorded a number of successful works for sitar and orchestra. Both he and his daughter, sitarist Anoushka Shankar, performed these compositions to wide international acclaim in the early 21st century. Anoushka, moreover, worked to strengthen the bridge between the classical and popular traditions of India and the West through touring and performing with such bands as the art rock group Jethro Tull.

CHAPTER 7

INDIAN PERFORMING ARTS

The royal courts and temples of India traditionally have been the chief centres of the performing arts. In ancient times, Sanskrit dramas were staged at seasonal festivals or to celebrate special events. Some kings were themselves playwrights; the most notable of the playwright-kings was Shudraka, the supposed 4th-century author of *Mrichchakatika* ("The Little Clay Cart"). Other well-known royal dramatists include Harsha, who wrote *Ratnavali* in the 7th century; Mahendravikramavarman, author of the 7th-century play *Bhagavad-Ajjukiya*; and Vishakhadatta, creator of the 9th-century drama *Mudrarakshasa*.

In the 4th century BC, Kautilya, the chief minister of Emperor Chandragupta, referred in his book on the art of government, the *Artha-shastra*, to the low morals of players and advised the municipal authorities not to build houses in the midst of their villages for actors, acrobats, and mummers. But, in the glorious era of the Hindu kings during the first eight centuries AD, actors and dancers were given special places of distinction. This tradition continued in the princely courts of India even under British rule. *Kathakali* dance-drama, for instance, was created by the raja of Kottarakkara, ruler of one of the states of South India in the 17th century. The powerful *peshwas* (chief ministers) of the Maratha kingdom in the 18th century patronized the *tamasha* folk theatre. Nawab Wajid Ali Shah (flourished mid-19th century) was an expert *kathak* dancer and producer of Krishnalore plays in which his palace maids danced as the *gopis* (milkmaids who were devotees of Krishna). Maharajas of Travancore and Mysore competed with each other for the excellence of their dance troupes. In the 20th century the maharaja of Varanasi carried on this tradition by being patron and producer of the spectacular *ramlila*, a 31-day cycle play on Rama's life that he witnessed every night while sitting on his royal elephant. On special nights the spectators numbered more than 30,000.

Dance is a part of all Hindu rituals. Farmers dance for a plentiful harvest, hunters for a rich bag, fishermen for a good catch. Seasonal festivals, religious fairs, marriages, and births are celebrated by community dancing. A warrior dances before the image of his goddess and receives her blessings before he leaves for battle. A temple girl dances to please her god. The gods dance in joy, in anger, in triumph. The world itself was created by the Cosmic Dance of Lord Shiva, who is called Nataraja, the king of dancers, and worshipped by actors and dancers as their patron.

Religious festivals are still the most important occasions for dance and theatrical activity. The *ramlila krishnalala* and *raslila* in North India (Uttar Pradesh, Delhi, Rajasthan, Haryana, and Punjab), the *chhau* masked dance-drama in Saraikela region in Jharkhand, and the *bhagavatha mela* in Melatur village in Tamil Nadu are performed annually to celebrate the glory of their particular deities. During the Dashahara festival every village in North India enacts for a fortnight the story of Rama's life, with songs, dances, and pageants. The *jatra* in West Bengal is a year-round dramatic activity, but the number of troupes swells to many thousands in Kolkata during the Puja festival. The hill and tribal people dance all night to celebrate their community festivals and weddings rich in masks, pageants, and carnivals. In more-remote areas of South Asia, people may not have seen a drama, but there will be hardly a person who has not witnessed or taken part in a community dance.

In folk theatre, traditional dance, classical music, and poetical symposia, performances are held in the open air or in a well-lit canopied courtyard so that the players can see the spectators and be motivated by their reactions.

For the usually all-night folk dramas, people come with their children, straw mats, and snacks, making themselves at home. At these performances there is a constant inflow and outflow of spectators. Some go to sleep, asking their neighbours to awaken them for favourite scenes. Stalls selling betel leaves, peanuts, and spicy fried things, adorned with flowers and incense and lighted by oil lamps, surround the open-air arena.

The clown, an essential character in every folk play, comments on the audience and contemporary events. Zealous spectators offer donations and gifts in appreciation of their favourite actor or

Cluster of betel nuts, seeds of the betel palm (Areca catechu). *Betel nuts are traditionally sold at folk plays.* Wayne Lukas–Group IV—The National Audubon Society Collection/Photo Researchers

dancer, who receives them in the middle of the performance and thanks the donor by singing or dancing a particular piece of his choice. The audience thus constantly throws sparks to the performer, who throws them back. People laugh, weep, sigh, or suddenly fall silent during a moving scene.

In both folk and classical forms of drama, the performer may lengthen or shorten his piece according to audience response. During a *kathak* dance, the drummer, in order to test the perfection of the dancer, disguises the main beat of his drum by slurs and offbeats, a secret he shares with the audience and announces by a loud thump that is synchronized with the dancer's stamping of the foot. At this point in the dance, the spectators shout, swaying their heads in admiration. They show their approval and disapproval through delighted groans or sullen headshakes as the performance goes on. In the raslila, the audience joins in singing the refrain and marks the beat by hand clapping. At a climactic point the people rock and sway, rhythmically clapping and singing. These practices bind the performers, chanters, and spectators together in a sense of aesthetic pleasure.

Instrumental music and singing are integral parts of Indian dance and theatre. Musicians, chanters, and drummers sit on the stage in view, a tradition observed throughout almost all of Asia. They watch the dancer and play on their instruments following his movements, whereas in the West the movements of a ballerina are timed and controlled by the already written music. An Indian dancer is constantly reacting to the accompanying musician, and vice versa. He may signal the chanters and drummers and even instruct them during the performance without spoiling its aesthetic effect.

In some classical dance forms, such as *kuchipudi*, the dancer sings in voiceless whispers as she dances. In *bharata natyam* the dance movements are like sculpted music in space, and the accompanying musician is invariably a dance guru (teacher). In *kathak* the rhythmic syllables beaten out by the dancer with her feet are vocalized by the singer and then chirped out by the drummer. No folk dancing is complete without the use of drum and vocal singing. Women's folk singing such as the *giddha* in the Punjab and the men's *kirtan* in West Bengal

takes the form of dance when the rhythm becomes fast.

In folk theatre this relationship is even more apparent. *Raslila* dance sequences are interspersed with the singing as a decorative frill, to accentuate emotional appeal, or to mark the climax of a song. The *yakshagana* hero gives a brisk dance number to announce his entry. In many folk forms of opera (*bhavai, terukkuttu,* and *nautanki*), the characters sing and dance at the same time or alternate. Ballad singers from the states of Orissa and Andhra Pradesh dramatize their singing by strong facial gestures and rhythmic ankle bells and execute dance phrases between the narrative singing. On the other hand, no one can imagine a dancer who is not at the same time a musician. This double aesthetic discipline enriches both of these arts, and the Indian audience is conditioned to this tradition.

INDIAN DANCE

Dance in India can be organized into three categories: classical, folk, and modern. Classical dance forms are among the best-preserved and oldest practiced in the 21st century. The royal courts, the temples, and the guru to pupil teaching tradition have kept this art alive and stable. Folk dancing has remained in rural areas as an expression of the daily work and rituals of village communities. Modern Indian dance, a product of the 20th century, is a creative mixture of the first two forms, with freely improvised movements and rhythms to express the new themes and impulses of contemporary India.

The popularity of dance in contemporary India can be judged from the fact that there is hardly any Indian motion picture that does not have half a dozen dances in it. In the typical "boy meets girl" film the heroine dances everywhere and anywhere. A film company may not have a script writer (in some cases the financier writes the story himself), but it must have a dance director. To provide ample dance opportunities, motion pictures have been made on the lives of poets, courtesans, and temple dancers and on mythological themes. For these the services of expert dancers are sought.

In the 20th century, classical dance left the temples and royal courts and came to be presented regularly on the stage in large cities. Rich industrialists, international hotels, and the wealthy families of the upper class are the chief patrons. It is not uncommon to have a classical dance recital by a major performer at a business dinner or for the annual function of a club. Some universities have dance as a regular subject in their curricula. Women learn it as a social grace, and young girls learn a few classical dances for greater eligibility in marriage. Folk dancing has also become more common as a contemporary cultural event in the cities. Most colleges have their folk-dance troupes, and even the police of the Punjab have their folk-dance groups to perform the *bhangra*.

CLASSICAL DANCE

Through its classical and folk traditions, India has developed a type of dance drama that is a form of total theatre. The actor dances out the story through a complex gesture language, a form that, in its universal appeal, cuts across the multi-language barrier of the subcontinent.

THE DANCE-DRAMA

Some of the classical dance-drama forms (e.g., *kathakali, kuchipudi, bhagavatha mela*) enact well-known stories derived from Hindu mythology. In the 20th century, dancers Uday Shankar and Shanti Bardhan created ballets that were inspired by such traditional dance-dramas. Contemporary Indian directors and writers are re-examining traditional dance forms and are using these in their current works for greater psychological appeal and deeper artistic impact. Millions in villages are still entertained by dance-dramas. In spite of the popularity of straight prose plays in the cities, the appeal of dance-drama is unquestionably deeper and more satisfying to the rural Indian, whose aesthetics are still rooted in tradition.

The chief source of classical dance is Bharata Muni's *Natya-shastra* (1st century BC to 3rd century AD), a comprehensive treatise on the origin and function of *natya* (dramatic art that is also dance), on types of plays, gesture language, acting, miming, theatre architecture, production, makeup, costumes, masks, and various *bhavas* ("emotions") and *rasas* ("sentiments"). No other book of ancient times contains such an exhaustive study of dramaturgy.

Techniques and Types of Classical Dance

According to the *Natya-shastra,* the dancer-actor communicates the meaning of a play through four kinds of *abhinaya* (histrionic representations): *angika,* transmitting emotion through the stylized movements of parts of the body; *vachika,* speech, song, pitch of vowels, and intonation; *aharya,* costumes and makeup; and *sattvika,* the entire psychological resources of the dancer-actor.

The actor is equipped with a complicated repertoire of stylized gestures. Conventionalized movements are prescribed for every part of the body, the eyes and hands being the most important. There are 13 movements of the head, seven of the eyebrows, six for the nose, six for the cheek, seven for the chin, nine for the neck, five for the breasts, and 36 for the eyes. There are 32 movements of feet, 16 on the ground and 16 in the air. Various positions of the feet (strutting, mincing, tromping, splaying, beating, etc.) are carefully worked out. There are 24 single-hand gestures (*asamyuta-hasta*) and 13 for combined hands (*samyuta-hasta*). One gesture (*hasta*) may mean more than 30 different things quite unrelated to each other. The *pataka* gesture of the hand, for example, in which all the fingers are extended and held close together with the thumb bent, can represent heat, rain, a crowd of men, the night, a forest, a horse, or a flight of birds. The *pataka* hand with the third finger bent (*tripataka*) can mean a crown, a tree, marriage, fire, a door, or a king. In *karkata* ("crab"), one of the combined hand gestures, the fingers of the hands are interlocked, and this may indicate a honeycomb, yawning after sleep, or a conch shell. Of course, for each of these different meanings, a *hasta* is given a different body posture or action.

The male or female classical dancer portraying a story in a solo performance simultaneously plays two or three principal characters by alternating facial expressions, gestures, and moods. Krishna, his jealous wife Satyabhama, and his gentle wife Rukmini, for example, may be played by one person.

The aesthetic pleasure of Hindu dance and theatre is determined by how successful the artist is in expressing a particular emotion (*bhava*) and evoking the *rasa.* Literally, *rasa* means "taste" or "flavour." The *rasa* is that exalted sentiment or mood that the spectator experiences after witnessing a performance. The critics do not generally concern themselves so much about plot construction or technical perfection of a poem or play as about the *rasa* of a particular work. There are nine *rasas*: erotic, comic, pathetic, furious, heroic, terrible, odious, marvelous, and spiritually peaceful. There are nine corresponding *bhavas*: love, laughter, pathos, anger, energy, fear, disgust, wonder, and quietude.

Four distinct schools of classical Indian dance—*bharata natyam, kathakali, kathak,* and *manipuri*—exist in the 21st century, along with two types of temperament—*tandava*, representing the fearful male energy of Shiva, and *lasya*, representing the lyrical grace of Shiva's wife Parvati. *Bharata natyam*, which takes its name from Bharata's *Natya-shastra*, has the *lasya* character, and its home is Tamil Nadu, in South India. *Kathakali*, a pantomimic dance-drama in the *tandava* mood with towering headgear and elaborate facial makeup, originated in Kerala. *Kathak* is a mixture of *lasya* and *tandava* characterized by intricate footwork and mathematical precision of rhythmic patterns; it flourishes in the north. *Manipuri*, with its swaying and gliding movements, is *lasya*, and it has been preserved in Manipur state in the Assam Hills. In 1958 the Sangeet Natak Akademi (National Academy of Music, Dance, and Drama) in New Delhi bestowed classical status on two other schools of dance—*kuchipudi*, from Andhra Pradesh, and *orissi*, from Orissa. These two styles overlap the *bharata natyam* school and therefore are not as distinctly different in temperament and style as other forms.

THE *BHARATA NATYAM* SCHOOL

Bharata natyam (also called *dasi attam*) has survived to the present through the *devadasi*s, temple dancing girls who devoted their lives to their gods through this medium. Muslim invasions from the north destroyed the powerful Hindu kingdoms in the south but could not disrupt their arts, which took shelter in the temples. After the 16th century the Muslims overpowered the south completely until the British came, thus giving a setback to Hindu dance. Slowly the institution of *devadasi* fell into disrepute, and temple dancing girls became synonymous with prostitutes. In the latter half of the 19th century in Tanjore (Thanjavur), four talented dancers who were brothers—Chinniyah, Punniah, Vadivelu, and Shivanandam—revived the original purity of *dasi attam* by studying and following the ancient texts and temple friezes, with missing links supplied by the socially spurned *devadasis*. Their popularized form of *dasi attam* was called *bharata natyam*.

A performance of *bharata natyam* lasts for about two hours and consists of six parts, beginning with *allarippu* (Telegu language, "to decorate with flowers"), a devotional prologue that shows off the elegance and grace of the dancer. The second part is *jatisvaram*, a brilliant blaze of *jatis* ("dance phrases") with *svaras* ("musical sounds"). This is followed by *shabdam*, the singing words that prepare the dancer to interpret through *abhinaya* (gesture language) interspersed with pure dance. The fourth part is *varnam*, a combination of expressive and pure dance. Then follow the *padams*, songs in

Telegu, Tamil, or Kannada that the dancer dramatizes by facial expressions and hand gestures. The accompanying singer chants the line again and again, and the dancer enacts the clashing and contrasting meanings. Her virtuosity consists of exhausting all possible shades of suggestion. The performance ends with *tillana*, a pure dance accompanied by meaningless musical syllables chanted to punctuate the rhythm. The dancer explodes into leaps and jumps forward and backward, from right and left, in a state of ecstasy. *Tillana* ends with three clangs of the cymbals while the dancer executes a triple blaze of *jati*s, thumping her feet with a jingling flourish of ankle bells.

Bharata natyam has attained world recognition as one of the most exquisite forms of classical dance. Its aspirants go to Tamil Nadu to learn from gurus who still live in villages. Because of its *lasya* character, performing artists have always been women. But their teachers have invariably been old men who chant the lines to tiny cymbals, controlling the complex rhythm without dancing themselves.

The major performers associated with the *bharata natyam* school of dance in the 20th century were T. Balasaraswathi, especially known for her *abhinaya* (expressive interpretation) of *padam*s; Rukmini Devi, who popularized *bharata natyam* among the upper classes in the 1930s; Yamini Krishnamurthi; and Shanta Rao. Two of the most important gurus were Minakshisundaram Pillai,

who injected vigour into *bharata natyam* by his choreography, and his son-in-law, Chokkalingam Pillai.

THE *KATHAKALI* SCHOOL

Kathakali (*katha*, "story"; *kali*, "performance") originated in the 17th century in Kerala, the lush tropical coastal strip of South India washed by the Arabian Sea. It was devised by the raja of Kottarakkara, who, angry over the refusal of a neighbouring prince to allow his dancers to perform a Sanskrit dance-drama in his court, decided to create his own dance troupe using Malayalam, the spoken language of the people. This school has its own *hastas*, based on a regional text influenced by the *Natya-shastra* and later treatises. It also has marked elements of energetic ritualistic dances. The makeup has its roots in the grotesque pre-Hindu demon masks. Themes are taken mainly from the *Ramayana*, the *Shiva-purana*, the *Bhagavata-purana*, the *Mahabharata*, and other religious texts. The superhuman characters represent primal forces of good and evil at war. Because of its terrifying vigour, men play all the roles.

Most *kathakali* characters (except those of women, Brahmans, and sages) wear towering headgear and billowing skirts and have their fingers fitted with long silver nails to accentuate hand gestures. The principal characters are classified into seven types. (1) *Pachcha* ("green") is the noble hero whose face is painted bright green and framed in a white bow-shaped sweep from ears to chin. Heroes such as Rama, Lakshmana, Krishna, Arjuna, and Yudhishthira fall into this category. (2) *Katti* ("knife"), haughty and arrogant but learned and of exalted character, has a fiery upcurled moustache with silver piping and a white mushroom knob at the tip of his nose. Two walrus tusks protrude from the corners of his mouth, his headgear is opulent, and his skirt is full. Duryodhana, Ravana, and Kichaka belong to this type. (3) *Chokannatadi* ("red beard"), power-drunk and vicious, is painted jet black from the nostrils upward. On both cheeks semicircular strips of white paper run from the upper lip to the eyes. He has black lips, white warts on nose and forehead, two long curved teeth, spiky silver claws, and a blood-red beard. (4) *Velupputadi* ("white beard") represents Hanuman, son of the wind god. The upper half of his face is black and the lower red, marked by a tracery of curling white lines. The lips are black, the nose is green, black squares frame the eyes, and two red spots decorate the forehead. A feathery gray beard, a large furry coat, and bell-shaped headgear give the illusion of a monkey. (5) *Karupputadi* ("black beard") is a hunter or forest dweller. His face is coal black with crisscross lines drawn around the eyes. A white flower sits on his nose, and peacock feathers closely woven into a cylinder rise above his head. He carries a bow, quiver, and sword. (6) *Kari* ("black") is intended to be disgusting and gruesome. Witches and ogresses, who fall into this category, have black faces marked with queer patterns in white and huge, bulging breasts. (7) *Minnukku* ("softly shaded") represents sages, Brahmans, and women. The men wear white or orange dhotis (loincloths). Women have their faces painted light yellow and sprinkled with mica, and their heads are covered by saris.

Under a flower-decked canopy on a square ground-level stage, a tall brass worship lamp brimming with coconut oil burns brightly. The musicians and dancers bow before it before they start performing. Drummers standing in one corner pound the *cenda*, a barrel-shaped drum with a piercing, clattering sound suited for battle scenes, and continue throughout the performance, almost without respite. Two men hold a 12-by-6-foot (4-by-2-metre) embroidered hand curtain from behind which the principal characters make their entrances. They dance, grab the trembling curtain, and give vivid facial expressions with fearful glances and grunts. This "peering over the curtain," called *tiranokku*, is a close-up that offers an actor full scope to display his art. At a climactic moment the curtain is whisked away, and the character enters in full splendour. The performance lasts all night, the singers singing the text that the dancers act out in an elaborate gesture language.

Well-known performers of *kathakali* include Guru Chandu Panikkar, Guru Kunju Kurup, Ramunni Nair, and

Kalamandalam Krishna Nair. The dancers Guru Gopi Nath and Krishnan Kutty have both emphasized simplification of the use of towering headgear and thick-crusted, elaborate makeup, so that the art may be more commonly understood.

THE *KATHAK* SCHOOL

Kathak, born of the marriage of Hindu and Muslim cultures, flourished in North India under Mughal influence. *Kathak* dancers retain their 17th-century costumes but are steeped in Radha and Krishna love lore. Krishna, playing his flute in the Vrindavana woods on the bank of the Yamuna River, is surrounded by the *gopi*s ("milkmaids"). Their play is the eternal game of the god and his devotees, the hide-and-seek of man and woman. This spiritual relationship is deeply passionate, with erotic love-play. Slowly the dance degenerated and found shelter in bawdy houses, where professional dancing girls practiced the art to make themselves more tantalizing. In the beginning of the 20th century it was reclaimed and revived, however, mainly through the efforts of Kalkaprasad Maharaj, whose three sons—Achchan, Lachchu, and Shambhu—perfected the art.

Because of its mixed *lasya* and *tandava* temperament, *kathak* is popular with both females and males. In *bharata natyam*, footwork is synchronized with hand gestures and eye movements, but *kathak* has no such rigid technique. It takes its movements from life, stylizes them, and adds complex rhythmic patterns. The mathematical precision in doubling and quadrupling the beat with quick transfers and shifts makes the onlookers dizzy.

A female *kathak* dancer generally wears a brocade blouse, a long, wide, shimmering silk skirt, a transparent tissue scarf of gold threads, and a heavy cluster of ankle bells. A musician, generally the guru, sits beside the drummer on the floor and vocalizes the complicated syllables of the drum that the dancer beats out with her feet. *Kathak's* basic dance posture and some of the steps can be traced to the *rasilla* of Braj Bhoomi. The musical refrain, which is called *lehra*, provides the base on which the drummer and the dancer execute a rich tapestry of rhythmic patterns. Beats are called *matra*s and the footwork *tatkar*. Important elements of the dance are *chakkar*s, *torah*s, and *tihai*s. *Chakkar* denotes whirling with great speed and stopping for a fraction of time after each whirl within the prescribed beat while at the same time maintaining the beauty of the form. *Torah* is a composition consisting of rhythmic syllables. *Tihai* is the repetition of a phrase of rhythmic syllables used to adorn the concluding part of a *torah*. There are two styles of *kathak*: Jaipur *gharana* and Lucknow *gharana*. While the Lucknow *gharana* excels in *bhava*, the Jaipur *gharana* specializes in brilliance of footwork.

In the 20th century the major performers of *kathak* included Shambhu

Maharaj, who specialized in *bhavapradarshan* ("display of emotion"), and Sunder Prasad, who concentrated on the tala and *layakari* aspects of the dance. Birju Maharaj, Gopi Krishan, Sitara Devi, and Damayanti Joshi all have important reputations in India as well as abroad.

THE *MANIPURI* SCHOOL

Manipuri has survived in the sheltered valley of Manipur in the Assam Hills. It remained aloof not only from foreign influences but also from the main Indian trends. Its isolation was broken only in the 1920s, when Rabindranath Tagore visited the valley and invited a leading guru of the area, Atomba Singh, to teach at his school in Santiniketan. The supple movements of *manipuri* dance were suitable for Tagore's lyrical dramas, and he therefore employed them in his plays and introduced the dance as a part of the curriculum at his institution.

The *manipuri* dancer wears a large, stiff skirt that is glittering with round mirror pieces and a shimmering gauze veil. Her hair is done up in a high rolled crown that is adorned with chains of white blossoms, and her luminous cheeks and forehead are decorated with dots of sandalwood paste.

Known for its femininity, *manipuri* is marked by a slow, swooning rhythm. The dancer, with her hips thrust back and head tilted on one side, turns and sways and glides as if in a dream. The immobility of her face, like that of a mask, is in sharp contrast with the other three schools of dance, in which the face and eyes are a major source of expression.

The *manipuri* drummer, his bare torso in a white dhoti with a red border tucked up above his knees, dances while he plays on the drum. He slaps and thumps; the drum rumbles and howls and chuckles. Drunk with its rhythm, the drummer dances in wild, frenzied leaps. His energetic and electric movements are a masculine counterpart to the slow, undulating patterns woven by the female dancer.

Chief 20th-century exponents of *manipuri* included Atomba Singh, who preserved the tradition of *ras* dancing, and Amubi Singh.

THE *KUCHIPUDI* SCHOOL

Kuchipudi dance-dramas owe their origin to the small village of Kuchipudi (Kuchelapuram) in Andhra Pradesh. Their form was originated in the 17th century by Sidhyendra Yogi, creator of the superb dance-drama *Bhama Kalapam*, which is the story of charming Satyabhama, jealous wife of Lord Krishna. Sidhyendra Yogi taught the art to Brahman boys of Kuchipudi and gave a performance with them in 1675 for the nawab of Golconda, who was so pleased that he granted Kuchipudi to the Brahman Bhavathas for the preservation of this art. Even into the 20th century, every Brahman of Kuchipudi was expected to perform at least once in his life the role of Satyabhama as an offering to Lord Krishna.

The *kuchipudi* dance begins with worship rituals. A male dancer moves about sprinkling holy water, and then incense is burned. *Indra-dhvaja* (the flagstaff of the god Indra) is planted on the stage to guard the performance against outside interference. Women sing and dance with worship lamps, followed by the worship of Ganesha, the elephant god, who is traditionally petitioned for success before all enterprises. The *bhagavatha* (stage manager-singer) sings invocations to the goddesses Sarasvati (Learning), Lakshmi (Wealth), and Parashakti (Parent Energy), in between chanting drum syllables.

Two men hold up the traditional coloured curtain. A long gold-embroidered braid is hung on the curtain as a challenge to anyone among the spectators who dares to act and dance. If anyone should take up this braid, the hero playing the female character Satyabhama will cut off "her" hair. The principal characters are introduced from behind the curtain after each one has done a brisk dance, and at that time the *bhagavatha* sings out the background and function of each. All roles are traditionally played by men (but since the mid-20th century by women also), and all the four elements of *abhinaya* are used—dance, song, costume, and psychological resources. Thus, *kuchipudi* differs from other classical dances in which the performers do not sing.

Among the major *kuchipudi* dancers of the 20th century were Guru Chinta Krishnamurthi, Vedantam Satyanarayana, and Yamini Krishnamurthi.

THE *ODISSI* TRADITION

Odissi, practiced in Orissa, claims to be over 2,000 years old and the true inheritor of the *Natya-shastra* tradition. It originated and was initially developed in the temples and later flourished in the courts as well. Many of the 108 basic dance units (*karanas*) mentioned in the *Natya-shastra* can be found only in *odissi*, and many of its dance poses are sculpted on the exterior of the temples of Bhubaneswar, Konarak, and Puri. Kelu Charan Mahapatra and Indrani Rehman were the principal 20th-century figures associated with *odissi*.

OTHER CLASSICAL DANCE FORMS

Among other classical or semiclassical dance forms are *bhagavatha mela*, *mohini attam*, and *kuravanchi*. Performed at the annual Narasimha Jayanti festival in Melatur village in Tamil Nadu, the *bhagavatha mela* uses classical gesture language with densely textured Karnatak (South Indian classical) music. Its repertoire was enriched by the musician-poet Venkatarama Sastri (1759–1847), who composed important dance-dramas in the Telugu language. *Mohini attam* is based on the legend of the Hindu mythological seductress Mohini, who tempted Shiva. It is patterned on *bharata natyam* with elements of *kathakali*. It uses Malayalam songs with Karnatak music. *Kuravanchi* is a dance-drama of lyrical beauty prevalent in Tamil Nadu. It is performed by four to eight women, with a gypsy fortune-teller as initiator of the story of a lady pining for her lover. Formally, it is a mixture of the folk and classical types of Indian dance.

FOLK DANCE

Indian folk dances have an inexhaustible variety of forms and rhythms. They differ according to region, occupation, and caste. The Adivasis (aboriginal tribes) of central and eastern India (Murias, Bhils, Gonds, Juangs, and Santals) are the most uninhibited in their dancing. There is hardly a national fair or festival where these dances are not performed. The most impressive occasion occurs every January 26 on Republic Day, when dancers from all parts of India come to New Delhi to dance in the vast arena of the National Stadium and along a five-mile parade route.

It is difficult to categorize Indian folk dances, but generally they fall into four groups: social (concerned with such labours as tilling, sowing, fishing, and hunting); religious (in praise of deities or in celebration of spiritual fulfillment); ritualistic (to propitiate a deity with magical rites); and masked (a type that appears in all the above categories).

The *kolyacha* is among the better-known examples of social folk dance. A fisherman's dance indigenous to the Konkan coast of west-central India, the *kolyacha* is an enactment of the rowing of a boat. Women wave handkerchiefs to their male partners, who move with sliding steps. For wedding parties, young Kolis dance in the streets carrying household utensils for the newlywed couple, who join the dance at its climax.

The national social folk dance of Rajasthan is the *ghoomar*, danced by women in long full skirts and colourful *chuneris* (squares of cloth draping head and shoulders and tucked in front at the waist). Especially spectacular are the *kachchi ghori* dancers of this region. Equipped with shields and long swords, the upper part of their bodies each arrayed in the traditional attire of a bridegroom and the lower part concealed by a brilliant-coloured papier-mâché horse built up on a bamboo frame, they enact jousting contests at marriages and festivals. Bawaris generally are expert in this form of folk dance.

In the Punjab region, which spans parts of India and Pakistan, the most dynamic social folk dance is the male harvest dance, *bhangra*. This dance is always punctuated by a song. At the end of every line the drum thunders. The last line is taken up by all the dancers in a chorus. In ecstasy they spring, bellow, shout, and gallop in a circle, madly wiggling their shoulders and hips. Any man of any age can join.

The Lambadi women of Andhra Pradesh wear mirror-speckled headdresses and skirts and cover their arms

This young dancer from Rajasthan performs a traditional ghoomar dance during celebrations for the 14th National Youth Festival in Amritsar in 2009. Narinder Nanu/AFP/Getty Images

with broad, white bone bracelets. They dance in slow, swaying movements, with men acting as singers and drummers. Their social dance is imbued with impassioned grace and lyricism.

The bison-horn dance of the Muria tribe in Madhya Pradesh is performed by both men and women, who traditionally have lived on equal terms. The men wear a horned headdress with a tall tuft of feathers and a fringe of cowry shells dangling over their faces. A drum shaped like a log is slung around their necks.

The women, their heads surmounted by broad, solid-brass chaplets and their breasts covered with heavy metal necklaces, carry sticks in their right hands like drum majorettes. Fifty to 100 men and women dance at a time. The male "bison" attack and fight each other, spearing up leaves with their horns and chasing the female dancers, while imitating various movements of a bison.

The Juang tribe in Orissa performs bird and animal dances with vivid miming and powerful muscular agility.

Some major examples of religious folk dances are the *dindi* and *kala* dances of Maharashtra, which are expressions of religious ecstasy. The dancers revolve in a circle, beating short sticks (*dindis*) to keep time with the chorus leader and a drummer in the middle. As the rhythm accelerates, the dancers form into two rows, stamp their right feet, bow, and advance with their left feet, making geometric formations. The *kala* dance features a pot symbolizing fecundity. A group of dancers forms a double-tiered circle with other dancers on their shoulders. On top of this tier a man breaks the pot and splashes curds over the torsos of the dancers. After this ceremonial opening, the dancers twirl sticks and swords in a feverish battle dance.

Garaba, meaning a votive pot, is the best-known religious dance of Gujarat. It is danced by a group of 50 to 100 women every year for nine nights in honour of the goddess Amba Mata, known in other parts of India as Durga or Kali. The women move in a circle, bending, turning, clapping their hands, and sometimes snapping their fingers. Songs in praise of the goddess accompany this dance.

Of the endless variety of ritualistic folk dances, many have magical significance and are connected with ancient cults. The *karakam* dance of Tamil Nadu state, mainly performed on the annual festival in front of the image of Mariyammai (goddess of pestilence), is to deter her from unleashing an epidemic. Tumbling and leaping, the dancer retains on his head without touching it a pot of uncooked rice surmounted by a tall bamboo frame. People ascribe this feat to the spirit of the deity, which, it is believed, enters his body. The Therayattam festival in Kerala is held to propitiate the gods and demons recognized by the pantheon of the Malayalis. The dancers, arrayed in awe-inspiring costumes and frightening masks, enact colourful rituals before the village shrine. A devotee makes an offering of a cock. The dancer grabs it, chops off its head in one stroke, gives a blessing, and hands it back to the devotee. This ceremony is punctuated by a prolonged and ponderous dance.

The greatest number of masked folk dances are found in Arunachal Pradesh, where the influence of Tibetan dance may be seen. The yak dance is performed in the Ladakh section of Kashmir and in the southern fringes of the Himalayas near Assam. The dancer impersonating a yak dances with a man mounted on his back. In *sada topo tsen* men wear gorgeous silks, brocades, and long tunics with wide flapping sleeves. Skulls arranged as a diadem are a prominent feature of their grotesquely grinning wooden masks representing spirits of the other world. The dancers rely on powerful, rather slow, twirling movements with hops.

The *chhau*, a unique form of masked dance, is preserved by the royal family of the former state of Saraikela in Jharkhand. The dancer impersonates a god, animal, bird, hunter, rainbow, night, or flower. He acts out a short theme and performs a series of vignettes at the annual Chaitra Parva festival in April. *Chhau* masks have

BHANGRA

Bhangra is a folk dance and a music of the Punjab (northwestern India and northeastern Pakistan) and the popular music genre that emerged from it in the mid-to-late 20th century. Cultivated in two separate but interactive styles—one centred in South Asia, the other within the South Asian community of the United Kingdom—the newer bhangra blends various Western popular musics with the original Punjabi tradition. It enjoys an immense following in South Asia and within the South Asian diaspora.

The term bhangra originally designated a particular dance performed by Sikh and Muslim men in the farming districts of the Punjab region of South Asia. The dance was associated primarily with the spring harvest festival Baisakhi, and it is from one of the major products of the harvest—bhang (hemp)—that bhangra drew its name. In a typical

These Indian young people perform bhangra, a traditional Punjabi folk dance, during Republic Day in Amritsar, India, on January 26, 2010. *Narinder Nanu/AFP/Getty Images*

performance, several dancers executed vigorous kicks, leaps, and bends of the body to the accompaniment of short songs called boliyan and, most significantly, to the beat of a dhol (double-headed drum). Struck with a heavy beater on one end and with a lighter stick on the other, the dhol imbued the music with a syncopated (accents on the weak beats), swinging rhythmic character that has generally remained the hallmark of any music that has come to bear the bhangra name.

In the mid-20th century the bhangra dance began to gain popularity beyond the Punjab, and, as it did so, it became divorced from the agricultural cycle, emerging as a regular feature of wedding festivities, birthday parties, local fairs, and other celebrations. With the change in context came changes in other aspects of tradition. The term bhangra expanded to encompass not only the dance but also the instrumental and vocal music that was associated with it; the large dhol was replaced by the similar yet smaller dholak, played with the hands; various local instruments—such as the flute, zither, fiddle, harmonium (a portable, hand-pumped organ), and tabla—were added to the accompaniment; and the topics of the song texts broadened from agricultural themes to include literary, romantic, and subtly comic material. In the later 20th century, guitar, mandolin, saxophone, synthesizer, drum set, and other Western instruments were added to the ensemble.

Bit by bit, bhangra began to amass an audience that extended beyond the boundaries of South Asia to Britain. There the music gained momentum as a positive emblem of South Asian identity, particularly in Southall, the predominantly South Asian suburb of London's West End.

Aside from matters of musical style, British bhangra differed from South Asian bhangra in other significant ways. These events provided a venue for men and women to dance together as couples to the sound of South Asian music. The new bhangra eventually seeped into the night-club scene.

In the mid-1990s, however, British musicians, began to use their music as a vehicle for poignant social commentary. Not only did these and other artists address such issues as racial conflict and the HIV/AIDS epidemic, but they tapped stylistic features of reggae, rap, and other African American and Afro-Caribbean popular music genres. Alongside these topical changes, the song texts shifted increasingly from Punjabi to English or to a mixture of the two. Meanwhile, bhangra in South Asia experienced similar changes, although its style generally retained a clearer link to its rural folk roots. Gurdas Maan is largely credited for elevating Punjabi music from a regional tradition to one that draws audiences throughout South Asia. Expanding the music's listenership was indeed one of Maan's priorities; to that end, he sang in a simplified Punjabi for Hindi-speaking audiences and also composed songs in Urdu, a language closely related to Hindi and spoken in northern India and Pakistan.

Both bhangras have continued to develop—albeit along somewhat different trajectories—in the 21st century. The South Asian style enjoys a tremendous following, particularly within South Asia. The British style, by contrast, has a strong listenership not only in the United Kingdom but also within South Asian communities of Canada and the United States.

predominantly human features slightly modified to suggest what they are portraying. With serene expressions painted in simple, flat colours, they differ radically from the elaborate facial makeup of *kathakali* or the exaggerated ghoulishness of the Kandyan masks. His face being expressionless, the *chhau* dancer's body communicates the total emotional and psychological tensions of a character. His feet have a gesture language; his toes are agile, functional, and expressive. The dancer is mute; no song is sung. Only instrumental music accompanies him. In another form of *chhau*, practiced in the Mayurbhanj district of Orissa, the actors do not wear masks, but through deliberately stiff and immobile faces they give the illusion of a mask. The style of their dance is vigorous and acrobatic.

MODERN INDIAN DANCE

While in the West the theatrical elements of spoken words, music, and dance developed independently and evolved in the forms of drama, opera, and ballet, Indian theatrical tradition continued to combine the three in its dramas. Indian films still follow this rule (the heroine suddenly bursts into a song or dances for the hero). Since the mid-20th century, dance in the form of ballet with choreography in the Western sense has emerged as a distinct form.

Modern Indian ballet started with Uday Shankar, who went to England to study the plastic arts and was chosen by the Russian ballerina Anna Pavlova to be her partner in the ballet *Radha and Krishna*. Young Shankar returned to India fired with enthusiasm. After studying the essentials of the four major styles of classical dance, he created new ballets with complex choreography and music, mixing the sounds from wooden clappers and metal cymbals with those of traditional instruments. He used classical and folk rhythms. Employing Western stage techniques, he presented his ballets with a skill and style previously unknown to Indian audiences. These ballets included *Shiva-Parvati* and *Lanka Dahan* ("The Burning of Lanka"), in which he used wooden masks from Sri Lanka. In *Rhythm of Life* (1938) and in *Labour and Machinery* (1939), he employed contemporary political and social themes. He established a culture centre at Almora in 1939 and during its four years' existence created a whole generation of modern dancers.

Shanti Bardhan, a junior colleague of Uday Shankar, produced some of the most imaginative dance-dramas of the 20th century. After founding the Little Ballet Troupe in Andheri, now in Mumbai, in 1952 he produced *Ramayana*, in which the actors moved and danced like puppets. His posthumous production *Panchatantra (The Winning of Friends)* is based on an ancient fable of four friends (Mouse, Turtle, Deer, and Crow), in which he used masks and the mimed movements of animals and birds.

Narendra Sharma and Sachin Shankar, both pupils of Uday Shankar, continued his tradition. Other important figures who have shaped modern

Indian dance include Menaka, Ram Gopal, and Mrinalini Sarabhai, who has experimented with conveying modern themes through the *bharata natyam* and *kathakali* styles.

DANCE-TRAINING CENTRES

Dance training in small academies and local *kala kendras* ("art centres") is available all over contemporary India. Most universities have introduced dance as a subject in their curricula. The gurus still impart specialized training to pupils who go to live with them in villages and learn the art over a number of years. But there are many state-run or public-financed training centres, most organized in the 20th century, that attract students from all over the world. Among the most important of these are Kerala Kalamandalam (Kerala Institute of Arts), near Shoranur; Kalakshetra at Adyar, Tamil Nadu; Kathak Kendra, a dance branch of the Shriram Bharatiya Kala Kendra in New Delhi; Triveni Kala Sangam (Centre of Music, Dance, and Painting), at New Delhi; Darpana Academy in Ahmadabad, Gujarat; Visva-Bharati (founded by Rabindranath Tagore), at Santiniketan, West Bengal; and the Jawaharlal Nehru Manipuri Dance Academy, at Imphal.

INDIAN THEATRE

Aphorisms on acting appear in the writings of Panini, the Sanskrit grammarian of the 5th century BC, and references to actors, dancers, mummers, theatrical companies, and academies are found in Kautilya's book on statesmanship, the *Artha-shastra* (4th century BC).

CLASSICAL THEATRE

The structure, form, and style of acting and production with aesthetic rules, however, were not consolidated until Bharata Muni wrote his treatise on dramaturgy, *Natya-shastra*. Bharata defines drama as a

> *mimicry of the actions and conduct of people, rich in various emotions, depicting different situations. This relates to actions of men good, bad and indifferent and gives courage, amusement, happiness, and advice to all of them.*

Bharata classified drama into 10 types. The two most important are *nataka* ("heroic"), which deals with the exalted themes of gods and kings and draws from history or mythology (Kalidasa's *Shakuntala* and Bhavabhuti's *Uttararamacharita* fall into this category), and *prakarana* ("social"), in which the dramatist invents a plot dealing with ordinary human beings, such as a courtesan or a woman of low morals (Shudraka's *Mrichchakatika*, "The Little Clay Cart," belongs to this type). Plays range from 1 to 10 acts. There are many types of one-act plays, including *bhana* ("monologue"), in which a single character carries on a dialogue with an invisible one, and *prahasana* ("farce"), which is classified into two categories—superior and inferior, both dealing with courtesans and crooks. King Mahendravikramavarman's 7th-century-AD *Bhagavad-Ajjukiya* ("The Harlot and the Monk") and *Mattavilasa* ("Drunken Revelry") are examples of *prahasana.*

There are three structural types of classical theatre: oblong, square, and triangular, each further divided into large, medium, and small sizes. According to the *Natya-shastra,* the playhouse was "like a mountain cave" with two floors at different levels, small windows so that outside noise and wind would not interfere with the acoustics, and a backstage for actors to do makeup, costumes, and offstage noise effects. Bharata disapproved of a large playhouse and recommended the medium-size structure meant for court productions.

The ancient Hindus insisted on a small playhouse, because dramas were acted in a highly stylized gesture language with subtle movements of eyes and hands. Hindu theatre differed from its Greek counterpart in temperament and method of production. The three unities rigidly followed by the Greeks were totally unknown to Sanskrit dramatists. Less time was consumed by a Greek program of three tragedies and a farce than by a single Sanskrit drama, with its subsidiary plots and wide variety of characters and moods. The Greeks laid emphasis on plot and speech, the Hindus on the four types of acting and visual demonstration. People were audiences to the Greeks and spectators to the Hindus. The aesthetic rules also differed.

Aristotle's theory of catharsis bears no resemblance to Bharata's theory of *rasa.* The Greek conception of tragedy is totally absent in Sanskrit dramas, as is the aesthetic principle that prohibits any death or defeat of the hero on stage.

There were two types of Hindu productions: the *lokadharmi,* or realistic theatre, with natural presentation of human behaviour and properties catering to the popular taste, and the *natyadharmi,* or stylized drama, which, using gesture language and symbols, was considered more artistic. In *Shakuntala* the king enters riding an imaginary chariot, and Shakuntala plucks flowers that are not there; in "The Little Clay Cart" the thief breaks through a nonexistent wall, and Maitreya passes through Vasantasena's seven courtyards by miming.

A classical play traditionally opened with the *nandi,* a benediction of eight to 12 lines of verse in praise of the gods, after which the *sutra-dhara* (stage manager) entered with his wife and described the place and occasion of the action. The last sentence of his prologue served as a bridge leading to the action of the play. In *Shakuntala* he refers to the bewitching song of his wife, which has made him forget his surroundings as the pursuit of a deer has made the king forget his state affairs. At this point the king enters, riding his hunting chariot, and the spectators are plunged into action of the play.

The *vidushaka* (clown) is a noble, good-hearted, blundering fool, the trusted friend of the hero. A bald-headed glutton, comic in speech and manners, he is the darling of the spectators. With the decline of Sanskrit drama the folk theatre in various regional languages inherited the conventions of the opening prayer song, the *sutra-dhara*, and the *vidushaka*.

The only surviving Sanskrit drama is *kudiyattam*, still performed by the Chakkayars of Kerala. Some principles of the *Natya-shastra* are evident in their presentations.

The earliest available classical dramas are 13 plays edited in 1912 by Pandit Ganapati Sastri, who dug out their manuscripts in Trivandrum, the capital of Kerala state. These, ascribed to Bhasa (1st century BC–1st century AD), include the one-act *Urubhanga* ("The Broken Thigh"), a tragedy that is a departure from Sanskrit convention, and the six-act *Svapnavasavadatta* ("The Dream of Vasavadatta").

The most acclaimed dramatist is Kalidasa. Other important playwrights succeeding him include Harsha, Mahendravikramavarman, Bhavabhuti, and Vishakhadatta. An exception is King Shudraka, whose work is perhaps the most theatrical in the entire Sanskrit range.

The title of "The Little Clay Cart" represents a departure from Sanskrit tradition, in which a *prakarana* was generally named after its hero and heroine. *Malavikagnimitra*, for example, is the love story of Princess Malavika and King Agnimitra, *Vikramorvashi* is the tale of King Pururavas and the heavenly nymph Urvashi, and *Malati-Madhava* is the love drama of Malati and Madhava. Shudraka, as if to mock tradition, chose an insignificant homely incident—the hero's son playing with a toy cart—and elevated this to the title.

"The Little Clay Cart" has a wide range of characters. The plot does not progress in a straight line but zigzags along a winding path. During its 10 acts the hero does not appear in four of them, the heroine is absent from three, and the lustful villain disappears after the first act until the eighth. Each act is an almost independent play. The device used to link the acts is that of ending them with subtitles that sum up their particular themes or plots.

"The Little Clay Cart" has been successful in the West, whereas Indian audiences, still fed on poetic-flavoured characters and romances of an ethereal type, have favoured *Shakuntala*. Western audiences find "The Little Clay Cart" more in their own tradition of realism and individualized characterization. Its "lisping villain," gamblers, and rogues have something in common with Shakespeare's comic characters and Molière's crooks. "The Little Clay Cart" is better theatre, whereas *Shakuntala* is better poetry.

FOLK THEATRE

After the decline of Sanskrit drama, folk theatre developed in various regional languages from the 14th through the 19th century. Some conventions and stock characters of classical drama (stage preliminaries, the opening prayer song, the *sutra-dhara*, and the *vidushaka*) were adopted into folk theatre, which lavishly employs music, dance, drumming, exaggerated makeup, masks, and a singing chorus. Thematically, it deals with mythological heroes, medieval romances, and social and political events, and it is a rich store of customs, beliefs, legends, and rituals. It is a "total theatre," invading all the senses of the spectators.

The most crystalized forms are the *jatra* of Bengal, the *nautanki, ramlila,* and *raslila* of North India, the *bhavai* of Gujarat, the *tamasha* of Maharashtra, the *terukkuttu* of Tamil Nadu, and the *yakshagana* of Karnataka.

Folk theatre is performed in the open on a variety of arena stages; round, square, rectangular, multiple-set. The *bhavai*, enacted on a ground-level circle, and the *jatra*, on a 16-foot (5-metre) square platform, have gangways that run through the surrounding audience and connect the stage to the dressing room. Actors enter and exit through these gangways, which serve a function similar to the *hanamichi* of the Japanese Kabuki theatre. In the *ramlila* the action sometimes occurs simultaneously at various levels on a multiple set. Actors in *nautanki* and *bhavai* sit on the stage in full view instead of exiting and sing or play an instrument as a part of the chorus. In the *ramlila* the actor playing Ravana removes his 10-headed mask when he is not acting and continues sitting on his throne, but for the spectators he is theatrically absent. Asides, soliloquies, and monologues abound. Scenes melt into one another, and the action continues in spite of change of locale.

In most folk forms the art of the actor is hereditary. He learns by watching his elders throughout childhood. He starts with drumming, then dancing, plays female roles, and then major roles.

All roles are played by men except that of the *tamasha* woman, who is always a dancer-singer-actress. Since the mid-20th century, women have increasingly played female roles in the *jatra*, but they have yet to achieve the artistic stature of their professional male counterparts.

In the *ramlila* and *raslila* the principal characters—Rama and Krishna—are always played by boys under age 14, because tradition decreed they must be pure and innocent. They are considered representatives of the gods and are worshipped on these occasions. In the *ramlila* the *vyas* ("director"), present on the stage throughout the performance, prompts and directs the characters loudly enough for the audience to hear. This is not regarded as disturbing, because it is an accepted part of the tradition. Adult roles such as Ravana and Hanuman are sometimes played by the same individual throughout his life.

Of the nonreligious forms, the *jatra* and the *tamasha* are most important. The *jatra*, also popular in Orissa and eastern Bihar, originated in Bengal in the 15th century as a result of the *bhakti* movement, in which devotees of Krishna went singing and dancing in processions and in their frenzied singing sometimes went into acting trances. This singing with dramatic elements gradually came to be known as *jatra*, which means "to go in a

This young actor is dressed in jewels and makeup to perform in the Ramlila, *the stage play of the great Hindu epic the* Ramayana, *in Varanasi (Benares), Uttar Pradesh, India.* John Henry Claude Wilson/Robert Harding World Imagery/Getty Images

procession." In the 19th century the *jatra* became secularized when the repertoire swelled with love stories and social and political themes. Until the beginning of the 20th century, the dialogue was primarily sung. The length has been cut from all night to four hours. The *jatra* performance consists of action-packed dialogue with only about six songs. The singing chorus is represented by a single character, the *vivek* ("conscience"), who can appear at any moment in the play. He comments on the action, philosophizes, warns of impending dangers, and plays the double of everybody. Through his songs he externalizes the inner feelings of the characters and reveals the inner meaning of their outer actions.

The *tamasha* (a Persian word meaning "fun," "play," or "spectacle") originated at the beginning of the 18th century in Maharashtra as an entertainment for the camping Mughal armies. This theatrical form was created by singing girls and dancers imported from North India and the local acrobats and tumblers of the lower-caste Dombari and Kolhati communities with their traditional manner of singing. It flourished in the courts of Maratha rulers of the 18th and 19th centuries and attained its artistic apogee during the reign of Baji Rao II (1796–1818). Its uninhibited *lavani*-style singing and powerful drumming and dancing give it an erotic flavor. The most famous *tamasha* poet and performer was Ram Joshi (1762–1812) of Sholapur, an upper-class Brahman who married the courtesan Bayabai. Another famous singer-poet was Patthe Bapu Rao (1868–1941), a Brahman who married a beautiful low-caste dancer, Pawala. They were the biggest *tamasha* stars during the first quarter of the 20th century. The *tamasha* actress, commonly called the *nautchi* (meaning "nautch girl," or "prostitute") is the life and soul of the performance. Because of their bawdy elements, women never see *tamasha* plays, nor do respectable men.

In the 20th century, *jatra* and *tamasha* both became highly organized and commercially run. Troupes are now in heavy demand and work for nine months. Hundreds of *tamasha* troupes with many dancer-actresses tour the rural areas, ultimately providing a living for thousands of people. The *jatra* is the most successful commercially. Its star actors draw more than any other professional actor in the theatrical centre of Kolkata.

Popular in North India are the *putliwalas* ("puppeteers") of Rajasthan, who operate marionettes made of wood and bright-coloured cloth. The puppet plays deal with kings, lovers, bandits,

and princesses of the Mughal period. Generally, the puppeteer and his nephew or son operate the strings from behind, while the puppeteer's wife sits on her haunches in front of the miniature stage playing the drums and commenting on the action. The puppeteer chirps, whimpers, and squeals in animal–bird voices and creates battles and tragic moments, expresses pathos, anger, and laughter.

In Andhra Pradesh the puppets, called *tholu bommalata* ("the dance of leather dolls"), are fashioned of translucent, coloured leather. These are projected on a small screen, like colour photographic transparencies. Animals, birds, gods, and demons dominate the screen. The puppeteer manipulates them from behind with two sticks. Strong lamps are arranged so that the size, position, and angle of the puppets change with the distance of the light. They are similar to the *wayang kulit* puppets of Indonesia but are much smaller and quicker-moving.

In the absence of a powerful Indian city theatre (with the exception of a few in Kolkata, Mumbai, and Tamil Nadu), folk theatre has kept the rural audiences entertained for centuries and has played an important part in the growth of modern theatres in different languages. The 19th-century dramatist Bharatendu Harishchandra, who was responsible for the birth of Hindi drama, used folk conventions—the opening prayer song, tableaux, comic interludes, duets, stylized speech—and combined these with Western theatrical forms in vogue at that time. Parsi companies adapted the

In Rajasthan, performances with ornately decorated and clothed traditional string puppets such as these are a popular form of entertainment. Christopher and Sally Gable/Dorling Kindersley/Getty Images

popular folk techniques for their extravaganzas and were a major influence until the 1930s. Rabindranath Tagore, rejecting the heavy sets and realistic decor of the commercial companies, created a lyrical theatre of the imagination. Much influenced by the *baul* singers and folk actors of Bengal, he introduced the Singing Bairagi and the Wandering Poet (similar to the *vivek* of the *jatra*) in his dramas. In the late 20th century, folk theatre came to be viewed as a form that can add colour and vitality to contemporary theatre.

MODERN THEATRE

Modern Indian theatre first developed in Bengal at the end of the 18th century as a result of Western influence. The other regional theatres more or less followed Bengal's pattern, and within the next 100 years they took the same meandering path, though they never achieved the same robust growth.

The British conquered Bengal in 1757 and influenced local arts by their educational and political systems. Their clubs performed Shakespeare, Molière, and Restoration comedies, introducing Western dramatic structure and the proscenium stage to the Indian intelligentsia. With the help of Golak Nath Dass, a local linguist, Gerasim Lebedev, a Russian bandmaster in a British military unit, produced the first Bangla play, *Chhadmabes* ("The Disguise"), in 1795 on a Western-style stage with Bengali players of both sexes. Subsequently, Bengali playwrights began synthesizing Western styles with their own folk and Sanskrit heritage. With growing national consciousness, theatre became a platform for social reform and propaganda against British rule. Among the most important playwrights were Michael Madhu Sudan (1824–73), Dina Bandhu Mitra (1843–87), Girish Chandra Ghosh (1844–1912), and D.L. Roy (1863–1913).

The success of Dina Bandhu Mitra's *Nildarpan* ("Mirror of the Indigo"), dealing with the tyranny of the British indigo planters over the rural Bengali farm labourers, paved the way for professional theatre. The actor-director-writer Girish Chandra Ghosh founded in 1872 the National Theatre, the first Bangla professional company, and took *Nildarpan* on tour, giving performances in the North Indian cities of Delhi and Lucknow. The instigatory speeches and lurid scenes of British brutality resulted in the banning of this production. To overcome censorship difficulties, playwrights turned to historical and mythological themes with veiled symbolism that was clearly understood by Indian audiences. The heroes

and villains of these plays came to represent the Indian freedom fighter against the British oppressor. Girish's historical tragedies *Mir Qasim* (1906), *Chhatrapati* (1907), and *Sirajuddaulah* (1909) bring out the tragic grandeur of heroes who fail because of some inner weakness or betrayal of their colleagues. D.L. Roy emphasized the same aspect of nationalism in his historical dramas *Mebarapatan* (The Fall of Mebar), *Shahjahan* (1910), and *Chandragupta* (1911).

Girish introduced professional efficiency and showmanship. His style of acting was flamboyant, with fiery grace. Actors such as Amar Datta and Dani Babu carried his style into the early 1920s. The acting and production methods of the Star, the Minerva, and the Manmohan Theatres (all professional) were modelled on Girish's pioneer work.

The first elements of realism were introduced in the 1920s by Sisir Kumar Bhaduri, Naresh Mitra, Ahindra Chowdhuri, and Durga Das Banerji, together with the actresses Probha Devi and Kanka Vati. In his Srirangam Theatre (closed in 1954), Sisir performed two most memorable roles: the again Mughal emperor Aurangzeb and the shrewd Hindu philosopher-politician Chanakya. Sisir's style was refined by actor-director Sombhu Mitra and his actress wife Tripti, who worked in the Left-wing People's Theatre movement in the 1940s. With other actors they founded the Bahurupee group in 1949 and produced many Tagore plays including *Rakta Karabi* ("Red Oleanders") and *Bisarjan* ("Sacrifice").

Rabindranath Tagore (1861–1941), steeped in Hindu classics and indigenous folk forms but responsive to European techniques of production, evolved a dramatic form quite different from those of his contemporaries. He directed and acted in his plays along with his cousins, nephews, and students. These productions were staged mostly at his school, Santiniketan, in Bengal as a nonprofessional and experimental theatre. The elite of Calcutta and foreign visitors were attracted to these performances.

A painter, musician, actor, and poet, Tagore combined these talents in his productions. He used music and dance as essential elements in his latter years and created the novel opera-dance form in which a chorus sat on the stage and sang while the players acted out their roles in dance and stylized movements. Sometimes Tagore himself sat on a stool acting as the *sutra-dhara* and chanted to the accompaniment of music and drum as the dancing players became visual moving pictures.

In northern and western India, theatre developed in the latter half of the 19th century. The Mumbai Parsi companies, using Hindi and Urdu, toured all over India. Their spectacular showmanship, based on a dramatic structure of five acts with songs, dances, comic scenes, and declamatory acting, was copied by regional theatres. The Maharashtrian theatre, founded in 1843 by Visnudas Bhave, a singer-composer-wood-carver in the court of the Raja of Sangli, was developed by powerful dramatists such as Khadilkar and Gadkari, who emphasized Maratha nationalism. The acting style in Maharashtrian theatre remained melodramatic, passionately arousing audiences to laughter or tears.

In the south the popularity of dance-dramas has limited the growth of theatrical realism. Tamil commercial companies with their song and dance extravaganzas have dominated Andhra Pradesh, Kerala, and Mysore. One of the most outstanding Tamil companies in the second half of the 20th century was the T.K.S. Brothers of Madras (Chennai), famous for trick scenes and gorgeous settings. Also a pioneer of realistic Tamil theatre was the actor-producer-proprietor Nawab Rajamanickam Pillai, who specialized in mythological plays with an all-male cast, using horses, chariots, processions, replicas of temples, and even elephants.

Urdu and Hindi drama began with the production of *Indrasabha* by Nawab Wajid Ali Shah in 1855 and was developed by the Parsi theatrical companies until the 1930s.

Parsi theatre was an amalgam of European techniques and local classical forms, folk dramas, farces, and pageants. Mythical titans thundered on the stage. Devils soared in the air, daggers flew, thrones moved, and heroes jumped from high palace walls. Vampire pits, the painted back cloth of a generalized scene, and mechanical devices to operate flying figures were direct copies of the 19th-century Lyceum melodramas and Drury Lane spectacles in London.

The star film actor Prithvi Raj Kapoor founded Prithvi Theatres in Mumbai in

DANCE AND THEATRE IN KASHMIR

The Vale of Kashmir, predominantly populated by Muslims, has remained aloof from the main cultural currents of India. The ancient caves and temples of Kashmir, however, reveal a strong link with Indian culture at the beginning of the Common Era. At one time the classical dances of the south are believed to have been practiced. When Islam was introduced, in the 14th century, dancing and theatrical arts were suppressed, being contrary to a strict interpretation of the Qur'ān. These arts survived only in folk forms and were performed principally at marriage ceremonies. The popular hafiza *dance performed by Kashmiri women at weddings and festivals to the accompaniment of* sufiana kalam *(devotional music of the Muslim mystics known as Sufis) was banned in the 1920s by the ruling maharaja, who felt this dance was becoming too sensual. It was replaced by the* bacha nagma, *performed by young boys dressed like women. A popular entertainment at parties and festivals, it is also customarily included in modern stage plays.*

Theatrical productions in Kashmir are generally offered irregularly by amateur troupes. There is, however, the bhand jashna *("festival of clowns"), a centuries-old genre of folk theatre. Performed in village squares, it satirizes social situations through dance, music, and clowning.*

The Kashmiri-language theatre was founded in 1947, when a new national consciousness, the aftermath of the independence of the Indian subcontinent from Britain, inspired playwrights and folk actors to dramatize topical events and create a "visual newspaper" for the people. Some theatrical presentations carried a political agenda, such as the left-wing propaganda plays Zamin Sanz *("Who Owns the Land?") and* Jangbaaz *("The Warmonger"). Especially notable among those who have written for the stage has been the poet Nadim, author of two operas,* Bambur-yambarzal *(The Bumblebee) and* Himal Nagraj *(The Beautiful Woman and the Snake Prince).*

Since the 1960s the Jammu and Kashmir Academy of Art, Culture, and Languages has promoted theatre in the Kashmiri and Dogri languages, with an emphasis on literary dramas and folk-dance festivals of regional appeal.

1944 and brought robust realism to Hindi drama, then closed down in 1960 with a sense of completion after many tours throughout India. Prithvi's sons, nephews, and old associates worked in his large company, which became a training centre for many actors who later joined the films. Among these was the outstanding stage actress Zohra Sehgal, a former dance partner of Uday Shankar in the 1930s who had tremendous emotional depth and range, rare in actresses on the Hindi stage. Out of Prithvi's eight productions, in which he always played the lead, the most successful was *Pathan* (1946), which ran for 558 nights. It deals with the friendship between a tribal Muslim leader and a Hindu administrator and is set in the rugged frontier from which Prithvi came. This tragedy of two archetypes in which the tribal leader sacrifices his son to save the life of his friend's son had intensity of action, smoldering passion, and unity of mood and achieved the highest quality of realism on the Hindi stage to this day.

Among the actors who molded regional-language theatres are Shri Narayan Rao Rajhans (popularly known as the Bala Gandharva of the Maharashtra stage), Jayashankar Bhojak Sundari of Gujarat, and Sthanam Narasimhrao of Andhra. All three specialized in female roles and were star attractions during the first quarter of the 20th century.

In the second half of the 20th century, two outstanding actor-directors were Ebrahim Alkazi, director of the National School of Drama in New Delhi, and Utpal Dutt, who founded the Calcutta Little Theatre Group in 1947, which originally performed plays in English and in 1954 changed to productions in Bangla. Dutt was an actor fully committed to the revolutionary ideology of the Chinese communist leader Mao Zedong. He acted on open-air stages in rural areas of Bengal, where he exerted a strong artistic and political influence.

Since Lebedev in 1795 there has been a continuous stream of Western-trained actors and producers who have been revitalizing regional-language theatrical groups. Nawab Wajid Ali Shah had visiting French opera composers in his mid-19th-century court. Tagore did his first opera, *Valmiki Pratibha* ("The Genius of Valmiki"), in 1881, after returning from England, where he became familiar with Western harmonies. Prithvi Raj Kapoor,

E. Alkazi, and Utpal Dutt all had their earlier training in English productions. Norah Richards, an Irish-born actress who came to the Punjab in 1911, produced in 1914 the first Punjabi play, *Dulhan* ("The Bride"), written by her pupil I.C. Nanda. For 50 years she promoted rural drama and inspired actors and producers, including Prithvi Raj Kapoor.

India's genius still lies in its dance-dramas, which have a unique form based on centuries of unbroken tradition. There are very few professional theatre companies in the whole of India, but thousands of amateur productions are staged every year by organized groups. Out of this intense experimental activity, the Indians have aimed to create a national theatre that incorporates contemporary, internationally recognized techniques but retains a distinctly Indian flavour.

Many centres for theatrical training that were established in the mid-20th century have continued to operate in the 21st century, despite some name changes and mergers with other institutions. Among the most important of these are the National School of Drama in New Delhi, Sangeet Natak Akademi (National Academy of Music, Dance, and Drama) in New Delhi, and the National Institute for the Performing Arts in Mumbai. Bharatiya Natya Sangh, the union of all Indian theatre groups, was founded in 1949 and is centered in New Delhi. Affiliated with UNESCO's branch of the International Theatre Institute, it organizes drama festivals and seminars, as well as serving as a centre for information.

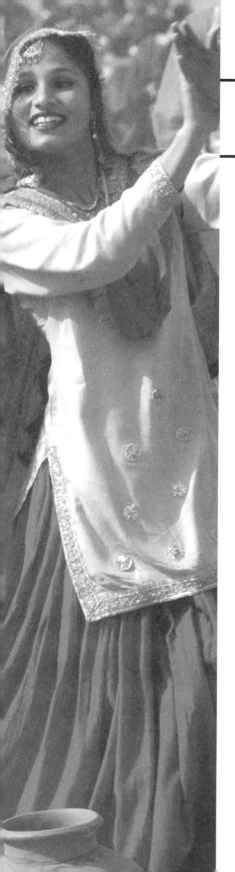

CHAPTER 8

INDIAN ARCHITECTURE

The favoured material of early Indian architecture appears to have been wood, but little has survived the rigours of the climate. Wooden forms, however, affected work in other mediums and were sometimes quite literally copied, as, for example, in early cave temples of western India. The principles of wooden construction also played an important part in determining the shape of Indian architecture and its various elements and components.

Baked or sun-dried brick has a history as ancient as that of wood; among the earliest remains are buildings excavated at sites of the Indus Valley civilization. The use of brick is once again evident from about the 6th century BC, and its popularity was undiminished in subsequent centuries. Many brick monuments have been discovered, particularly in areas in which good clay was easily available, such as the Gangetic Basin. Although more durable than wood, few brick buildings from before the 5th century AD have survived in a good state of preservation.

Traditions of stone architecture appear to be more recent than wood or brick, the earliest examples of the use of dressed stone for building purposes not predating the 6th century BC. The Indian architect, however, soon gained great proficiency in its use, and, by the 7th century AD, the use of stone for monumental buildings of considerable size had become quite popular. The preference for stone can also be seen in Islamic monuments of India, which contrast markedly with the brick and tile structures popular in neighbouring West Asia.

Most surviving examples of Indian architecture before the Islamic period are of a religious nature, consisting mainly of Buddhist shrines, or stupas, and temples. Monastic residences give some idea of civil architecture, but, surprisingly, very few examples of palaces and secular dwellings have been found.

INDUS VALLEY CIVILIZATION
(C. 2500–1800 BC)

From excavated remains, it is clear that the Indus Valley civilization possessed a flourishing urban architecture. The major cities associated with the civilization, notably Mohenjo-daro, Harappa, and Kalibangan, were laid out on a grid pattern and had provisions for an advanced drainage system. The residential buildings, which were serviceable enough, were mainly brick and consisted of an open patio flanked by rooms. For monumental architecture, the evidence is slight, the most important being a "sacred" tank (thought to be for ritual ablution) and associated structures. Corbel vaulting (arches supported by brackets projecting from the wall) was known, and, to a limited extent, timber was used together with brick; whatever architectural ornamentation existed must have been of brick or plaster.

THE MAURYA PERIOD
(C. 321–185 BC)

The state of Indian architecture in the period between the Indus Valley civilization and the rise of the Maurya empire is largely unknown since most work was done in such perishable material as wood or brick. Excavations at Rajgir, Kaushambi, and other sites, however, testify to the existence of fortified cities with stupas, monasteries, and temples of the type found at the later Maurya sites of Nagari and Vidisha; and there is evidence of the use of dressed stone in a palace excavated at Kaushambi. Considering the power of the Maurya empire and the extensive territory it controlled, the architectural remains are remarkably few. The most important are stupas (later enlarged) such as a famous example of Sanchi; the ruins of a hall excavated at the site of Kumrahar in Patna (ancient Pataliputra), the capital city; and a series of rock-cut caves in the Barabar and Nagarjuni Hills near Gaya, which are interesting because they preserve in the more permanent rock some types of wooden buildings popular at that time.

The stupa, the most typical monument of the Buddhist faith, consists essentially of a domical mound in which sacred relics are enshrined. Its origins are traced to mounds, or tumuli, raised over the buried remains of the dead that were found in India even before the rise of Buddhism: Stupas appear to have had a regular architectural form in the Maurya period: the mound was sometimes provided with a parasol surrounded by a miniature railing on the top, raised on a terrace, and the whole surrounded by a large railing consisting of posts, crossbars, and a coping (the capping on the top course), all secured by tenons and mortices in a technique appropriate to craftsmanship in wood. The essential feature of the stupa, however, always remained the domical mound, the other elements being optional.

Along with stupas were erected roofless, or hypaethral, shrines enclosing a sacred object such as a tree or an altar. Temples of brick and timber with vaulted or domical roofs were also constructed, on plans that were generally elliptical, circular, quadrilateral, or apsidal (i.e., having an apse, or semicircular plan, at the sanctum end). These structures have not survived, but some idea of their shape has been obtained from the excavated foundations and the few examples imitating wooden originals that were cut into the rock, notably the Sudama and the Lomas Rsi caves in the Nagarjuni and Barabar hills near Gaya. The latter has an intersesting entrance showing an edged barrel-vault roof (an arch shaped like a half cylinder) in profile supported on raked pillars, the ogee arch (an arch with curving sides, concave above and convex toward the top) so formed filled with a trellis to let in light and air. The interiors of most caves are highly polished and consist of two chambers: a shrine, elliptical or circular in plan with a domed roof (Sudama cave); and an adjacent

antechamber, roughly rectangular and provided with a barrel vault. Remains of structural buildings have been excavated at Bairat and Vidisha, where wood and brick shrines with timber domes and vaults once existed. A temple (No. 40) at Sanchi was apsidal in plan and perhaps had a barrel-vault roof of timber.

A hall excavated at Kumrahar in Patna had a high wooden platform of most excellent workmanship, on which stood eight rows of 10 columns each, which once supported a second story. Only one stone pillar has been recovered, and it is circular in shape and made of sandstone that has been polished to a high lustre. The capitals that topped them must have been similar to others found in neighbouring Lohanipur and almost certainly consisted of one or two pairs of addorsed (set back to back) animals, recalling Persepolitan examples. Indeed, there is much about Maurya architecture and sculpture to suggest Iranian influence, however substantially transformed in the Indian environment.

EARLY INDIAN ARCHITECTURE (2ND CENTURY BC–3RD CENTURY AD)

Except for stupas, architectural remains from the 2nd century BC (downfall of the Maurya dynasty) to the 4th century AD (rise of the Gupta dynasty) continue to be rare, indicating that most of the work was done in brick and timber. Once again, examples cut into the rock and closely imitating wooden forms give a fairly accurate idea of at least some types of buildings in this period.

The stupas become progressively larger and more elaborate. The railings continue to imitate wooden construction and are often profusely carved, as at Bharhut, Sanchi II, and Amaravati. These were also provided with elaborate gateways, consisting of posts supporting from one to three architraves, again imitating wooden forms and covered with sculpture (Bharahut, Sanchi I, III). In the course of time an attempt was made to give height to the stupas by multiplying the terraces that supported the dome and by increasing the number of parasols on top. In Gandhara and southeastern India, particularly, sculptured decoration was extended to the stupa proper, so that terraces, drums, and domes—as well as railing—were decorated with figural and ornamental sculpture in bas-relief. Stupas in Gandhara were not provided with railings but, instead, had rows of small temples arranged on a rectangular plan.

Cave temples of western India, cut into the scarp of the Western Ghats and stretching from Gujarat to southern Maharashtra, constitute the most extensive architectural remains of the period. Two main types of buildings can be distinguished, the temple proper (*caitya*) and the monastery (*vihara, sangharama*). The former is generally an apsidal hall with a central nave flanked by aisles. The apse is covered by a half dome; and two rows of pillars, which demarcate the nave, support a barrel-vault roof that covers the rest of the building. In the apsidal end is placed the object to be worshipped, generally a stupa, the hall being meant for the gathered congregation. In front of the hall is a porch, separated from it by a screen wall provided with a door of considerable size, together with an arched opening on top clearly derived from wooden buildings of the Lomas Rsi type and permitting air and dim light to filter into the interior. Other influences of wooden construction are equally striking, particularly in the vaulting ribs that cover the entire ceiling and that are sometimes actually of wood, as at Bhaja, where the pillars are also raked in imitation of the exigencies of wooden construction. The pillars are generally octagonal with a pot-shaped base and a capital of addorsed animals placed on a bell-shaped, or campaniform, lotus in the Maurya tradition. The most significant example is at Karli, dating approximately to the closing years of the 1st century BC. The Bhaja *caitya* is certainly the earliest, and important examples are to be found at Bedsa, Kondane, Pitalkhora, Ajanta, and Nasik. Toward the end of the period, a quadrilateral plan appears more and more frequently, as, for example, at Kuda and Sailarwadi.

In addition to the *caitya*, or temple proper, numerous monasteries (*viharas*) are also cut into the rock. These are generally provided with a pillared porch and a screen wall pierced with doorways leading into the interior, which consists of a "courtyard" or congregation hall in the three walls of which are the monks' cells.

The surviving rock-cut examples are all of one story, though the facade of the great monastery at Pitalkhora simulates a building of several stories.

Monasteries carved into the rock are also known from Orissa (Udayagiri-Khandagiri), in eastern India. These are much humbler than their counterparts in western India, and consist of a row of cells that open out into a porch, the hall being absent. At Uparkot in Junagadh, Gujarat, is a remarkable series of rock-cut structures dating from the 3rd–4th century AD, which appear to be secular in character and in all probability served as royal pleasure houses.

The large number of representations of buildings found on relief sculpture from sites such as Bharhut, Sanchi, Mathura, and Amaravati are a rich source of information about early Indian architecture. They depict walled and moated cities with massive gates, elaborate multi-storied residences, pavilions with a variety of domes, together with the simple, thatched-roofed huts that remained the basis of most Indian architectural forms. A striking feature of this early Indian architecture is the consistent and profuse use of arched windows and doors, which are extremely important elements of the architectural decor.

THE GUPTA PERIOD (4TH–6TH CENTURIES AD)

Dating toward the close of the 4th and the beginning of the 5th century AD is a series of temples that marks the opening phase of an architecture that is no longer content with merely imitating wooden building but initiates a new movement, ultimately leading to the great and elaborate temples of the 8th century onward.

Two main temple types have been distinguished in the Gupta period. The first consists of a square, dark sanctum with a small, pillared porch in front, both covered with flat roofs. This type of temple answers the simplest needs of worship, a chamber to house the deity and a roof to shelter the devotee. Temple No. 17 at Sanchi is a classic example of this flat-roofed type. The plain walls are of ashlar masonry (made up of squared stone blocks), composed of sizable blocks, which are spanned by large slabs that constitute the ceiling. The pillars of the porch have a campaniform lotus capital, one of the last times this form appears in Indian architecture. Another temple of this type is the Kankali Devi shrine at Tigowa, which has more elaborate pillars, provided with the overflowing vase, or the vase-and-foliage (*ghata-pallava*), capital that became the basic north Indian order.

It is the second type of temple that points the way to future developments. It also has a square sanctum, or cella, but instead of a flat roof there is a pyramidal superstructure (*shikhara*). Among the most interesting examples are a brick temple at Bhitargaon and the Vishnu temple at Deogarh, built entirely of stone. The pyramidal superstructure of each consists essentially of piled-up cornice moldings of diminishing size, which are decorated primarily with *chandrashala* (ogee arch) ornament derived from the arched windows and doors so frequently found in the last centuries BC and the earliest centuries AD. The sanctums of both temples are square in plan, with three sides provided with central offsets (vertical buttress-like projections) that extend from the base of the walls right up to the top of the *shikhara* (spire); the section of the central offset that extends across the wall is conceived in the form of a niche, in which is placed an image. The Deogarh temple is also noteworthy for the large terrace with four corner shrines (now ruined) on which it is placed, pre-figuring the quincunx, or *panchayatana*, grouping (one structure in each corner and one in the middle) popular in the later period. The doorway surround, too, is very elaborate, carved with several bands carrying floral and figural motifs. At the base of the surround are rows of worshippers, and in the crossette (projection at the corner) on top are images of graceful river goddesses.

The Parvati Devi temple at Nacna Kutthara, also of this period, is interesting for the covered circumambulatory provided around the sanctum and the large hall in front. When first discovered, the temple had an entire chamber above the sanctum (which subsequently collapsed). Though provided with a door, there seems to have been no access to it; thus, for all practical purposes it constituted a false story and, aside from a

symbolic meaning, served no other purpose than to emphasize the importance of the sanctum. The principle of gaining height not by the superimposition of ornamental cornice moldings with *chandrashala* decoration but by the multiplication of stories, each imitating the story below, also distinguished the later architectural style of southern India.

The great Mahabodhi temple at Bodh Gaya, commemorating the spot where the Buddha attained enlightenment, though burdened with later restorations, is essentially a temple of this period. It has a particularly majestic *shikhara*, decorated with ornamental niches and *chandrashalas*, rising over a square sanctum to a great height.

Along with temples, stupas continued to be built. These also aspired to height, which was achieved by multiplication and heightening of the supporting terraces and elongating the drum and dome. A good example of this new form is the Dhamekh at Sarnath. Along more conventional lines, but quite elaborate, are the brick stupas in Sind, notably a fine example at Mirpur Khas.

The rock-cut temple and monastery tradition also continued in this period, notably in western India, where the excavations—especially at Ajanta acquire extreme richness and magnificence. The monasteries are characterized by the introduction of images into some of the cells, so that they partake of the nature of temples instead of being simple residences. Temples with an apsidal plan and

barrel-vault roofs, however, soon went out of fashion, and are found very rarely in the subsequent period. The early 5th-century cave temples at Udayagiri, Madhya Pradesh, are similar to the simple flat-roofed temples with a hall and are not descended from ancient traditions as preserved in western India.

MEDIEVAL TEMPLE ARCHITECTURE

Architectural styles initiated during the 5th and 6th centuries found their fullest expression in the medieval period (particularly from the 9th to the 11th centuries), when great stone temples were built. Two main types can be broadly distinguished, one found generally in northern India, the other in southern India. To these can be added a third type, sharing features of both and found in Karnataka and the Deccan. These three types have been identified by some scholars with the *nagara, dravida,* and *vesara* classes referred to in some Sanskrit texts, though the actual meaning of these terms is far from clear. In spite of the havoc wrought by the destructive Islamic invasions, particularly in the Indo-Gangetic Plains, an extremely large number of monuments have survived in almost every other part of India, particularly in the south, and these continue to be discovered and recorded to the present day.

NORTH INDIAN STYLE

North Indian temples generally consist of a sanctum enshrining the main image, usually square in plan and shaped like a hollow cube, and one or more halls (called *mandapas*), aligned along a horizontal axis. The sanctum may or may not have an ambulatory, but it is invariably dark, the only opening being the entrance door. The doorway surrounds are richly decorated with bands of figural, floral, and geometrical ornament and with river-goddess groups at the base. A vestibule (*antarala*) connects the sanctum to the halls, which are of two broad types: the *gudhamandapas*, which are enclosed by walls, light and air let in through windows or doors; and open halls, which are provided with balustrades rather than walls and are consequently lighter and airier. The sanctum almost invariably, and the *mandapas* generally, have *shikharas*; those on the sanctum, appropriately, are the most dominant in any grouping. Internally, the sanctum has a flat ceiling; the *shikhara* is solid theoretically, though hollow chambers to which there is no access must be left within its body to lessen the weight. The ceilings of the halls, supported by carved pillars, are coffered (decorated with sunken panels) and of extremely rich design.

The sanctum is often set on a raised base, or a plinth (*pitha*), above which is a

Mahabodhi temple, Bodh Gaya, Bihar, India. Frederick M. Asher foundation block, or socle (*vedibandha*), decorated with a distinct series of moldings; above the *vedibandha* rise the walls proper (*jangha*), which are capped by a cornice or a series of cornice moldings (*varandika*), above which rises the *shikhara*. One, three, and sometimes more projections extend all the way from the base of the temple up the walls to the top of the *shikhara*. The central offset (*bhadra*) is the largest and generally carries an image in a niche; the other projections (*rathas*), too, are often decorated with statuary.

The entire temple complex, including sanctum, halls, and attendant shrines, may be raised on a terrace (*jagati*), which is sometimes of considerable height and size. The attendant shrines—generally four—are placed at the corners of the terrace, forming a *panchayatana*, or quincunx, arrangement that is fairly widespread. The temple complex may be surrounded by a wall with an arched doorway (*torana*).

The *shikhara* is the most distinctive part of the North Indian temple and provides the basis for the most useful and instructive classification. The two basic types are called *latina* and *phamsana*. Curvilinear in outline, the *latina* is composed of a series of superimposed horizontal roof slabs and has offsets called *latas*. The edges of the *shikhara* are interrupted at intervals with grooved discs, each one demarcating a "story." The surface of the entire *shikhara* is covered with a creeper-like tracery, or interlaced work, composed of diminutive ornamental *chandrashalas*.

The *shikhara* is truncated at the top and capped by a shoulder course (*skandha*), above which is a circular necking (*griva*), carrying a large grooved disc called the *amalasaraka*. On it rests a pot and a crowning finial (*kalasha*).

Unlike the *latina*, the *phamsana shikhara* is rectilinear rather than curvilinear in outine, and it is lower in height. It is composed of horizontal slabs, like the *latina*, but is capped by a bell-shaped member called the *ghanta*. The surface of this type of *shikhara* may have projections, like the *latina shikhara*, and be adorned with a variety of architectural ornament.

From the 10th century onward, the *shekhari* type of spire, an elaboration of the *latina* type, became increasingly popular. In its developed form it consisted of a central *latina* spire (*mulashrnga*) with one or more rows of half spires added on the sides (*urah-shrnga*) and the base strung with miniature spires (*shrngas*). The corners, too, are sometimes filled with quarter spires, the whole mass of carved masonry recalling a mountain with a cluster of subsidiary peaks.

The *latina* and *shekhari* spires are generally found on the sanctum, while the *phamsana* and its variants are usually confined to the *mandapas*, or halls. The sanctum spires also have a large and prominent projection in front (*shukanasa*), generally rising above the vestibule (*antarala*). These projections are essentially large ogee arches of complex form, which often contain the image of the presiding deity.

Tomb of Itimad al-Dawlah, Agra, Uttar Pradesh, India. Frederick M. Asher

A particularly rich and pleasing variety of North Indian *shikhara*, popular in Malwa, western India, and northern Deccan, is the *bhumija* type. It has a central projection on each of the four faces, the quadrants so formed filled with miniature spires in vertical and horizontal rows right up to the top.

Although basically reflecting a homogeneous architectural style, temple architecture in northern India developed a number of distinct regional schools. A detailed elucidation of all has yet to be made, but among the most important are the styles of Orissa, central India, Rajasthan, and Gujarat. The style of Kashmir is distinct from the rest of northern India in several respects, and hardly any examples of the great schools that flourished in modern Uttar Pradesh, Bihar, and Bengal are left standing. The North Indian style also extended for some time into the Karnataka territory, situated in the southern Deccan, though the architecture of Tamil Nadu was relatively unaffected by it.

ORISSA

The greatest centre of this school is the ancient city of Bhuvaneshvara, in which are concentrated almost 100 examples of the style, both great and small, ranging in date from the 7th to the 13th century. Among the earliest is the Parashurameshvara temple (7th–8th century), with a heavy, stately *latina shikhara*, to which is attached a rectangular *gudhamandapa* with double sloping roofs. The walls are richly carved, but the interiors, as in almost all examples of the style, are left plain. The Mukteshvara temple (10th century), which has a hall with a *phamsana* roof, is the product of the most exquisite workmanship. The enclosing wall and the arched entrance, or *torana*, are still present, giving a clear idea of a temple with all its parts fully preserved. The Brahmeshvara temple, which is dated on the basis of an inscription to the mid-10th century, is a *panchayatana*, with subsidiary shrines at all of the corners. The most magnificent building, however, is the great Lingaraja temple (11th century), an achievement of Orissan architecture in full flower. The *latina* spire soars to

Surya Deula (Sun Temple), Konarak, Orissa state, India. Frederick M. Asher

a considerable height (over 125 feet [40 metres]); the wall is divided into two horizontal rows, or registers, replete with statuary; and the attached hall is exquisitely and minutely carved.

The most famous of all Orissan temples, however, is the colossal building at Konarak, dedicated to Surya, the sun god. The temple and its accompanying hall are conceived in the form of a great chariot drawn by horses. The *shikhara* over the sanctum has entirely collapsed; and all that survives are the ruins of the sanctum and the *gudhamandapa*, or enclosed hall, and also a separate dancing hall. Of these, the *gudhamandapa* is now the most conspicuous, its gigantic *phamsana shikhara* rising in three stages and adorned with colossal figures of musicians and dancers.

Because the Orissan style usually favours a *latina shikhara* over the sanctum, the *shekhari* spire of the Railani temple (11th century) at Bhuvaneshvara (Bhubaneswar) is quite exceptional. Of particular interest as a late survival of early building traditions is the Vaital Deul (8th century), the sanctum of which is rectangular in plan, its *shikhara* imitating a pointed barrel vault. Besides Bhuvaneshvara, important groups of temples are to be found at Khiching and Mukhalingam.

CENTRAL INDIA

The area roughly covered by the modern state of Madhya Pradesh was the centre of several vigorous schools of architecture, of which at least four have been identified. The first flourished at Gwalior and adjacent areas (ancient Gopadri); the second in modern Bundelkhand, known in ancient times as Jejakabhukti; the third in the eastern and southeastern parts in the ancient country of Dahala, of which Tripuri, near modern Jabalpur, was the capital; and the fourth in the west, in an area bordering Gujarat and Rajasthan in the fertile land of Malava (Malwa).

The earliest examples in the Gwalior area are a group of small shrines at Naresar, a few miles from Gwalior proper; dating to the 8th century, the shrines have *latina* spires and sparsely ornamented walls. In the 9th century a series of magnificent temples was built, including the Mala-de at Dyaraspur, the Shiva temples at Mahka and Indore, and a temple dedicated to an unidentified mother goddess at Barwa-Sagar. The period appears to have been one of experimentation, a variety of plans and spires having been tried. The Mala-de temple is an early example of the *shekhari* type in its formative stages; the Indore temple has a star-shaped plan; and the Barwa-Sagar example has a twin *latina* spire over a rectangular sanctum. The masonry work is of the finest quality and the architectural ornament is crisply carved. (The figural sculptures are few.) The temple at Umri, with a *latina* spire, is small and exquisitely finished; but the largest and perhaps the finest temple is the Teli-ka-Mandir on Gwalior Fort, rectangular in plan and capped by a pointed barrel vault, recalling once again the survival of ancient roof forms. The walls are decorated with niches (empty at present) topped by tall pediments (triangular gable ornament).

The style of this region became increasingly elaborate from the 10th century, during the supremacy of the Kacchapaghata dynasty. The many examples from this period are distinguished by a low plinth and rich sculptural decoration on the walls. Outstanding among them are the Kakan-madh at Suhania (1015–35) and the Sas-Bahu temple (completed 1093) in Gwalior Fort. The several temples at Surwaya and Kadwaha, though smaller in size, are distinguished for their extremely rich and elegant workmanship.

The style is best represented by a large group of temples at Khajuraho, the capital of the Chandela dynasty, though examples are also to be found in Mahoba and at several other sites in the Jhansi district of Uttar Pradesh, notably Chandpur and Dudhai.

All of the distinctive characteristics of the fully developed style can be seen in the Lakshmana temple at Khajuraho (dated 941), which is a *panchayatana* placed on a tall terrace enclosed by walls. The sanctum has an ambulatory and, facing it, a series of halls, including the *gudhamandapa*, a porch, and a small

Lakshmana temple, Khajuraho, Madhya Pradesh, India. Frederick M. Asher

intermediate hall. Both the ambulatory and the *gudhamandapa* are provided with lateral, balconied arms, or transepts, which let in light and air. Each hall has its own pyramidal *shikhara*, all skillfully correlated to ascend gradually to the main *shekhari* spire over the sanctum. Extraordinary richness of carving, both in the interior and on the exterior, where the walls carry as many as three rows of sculpture, and a skillful handling of the main spire to suggest ascent are distinguishing features of the style. The largest temple of the group, very similar to the Lakshmana, is the Kandariya Mahaheo;

and among the most distinguished are the Vishvanatha and the Parshvanatha temples. The Duladeo temple, which does not have an ambulatory, represents the closing phase of the group and probably belongs to the 12th century.

The earliest temples of the Dahala area, dating from the 8th–9th century, are the simple shrines at Bandhogarh, which consist of a sanctum with *latina* spire and porch. To the 10th century, when the local Kalacuri dynasty was rapidly gaining power, belong the remarkable Shiva temples at Chandrehe and Masaun, the former being circular in plan, with a *latina*

Tomb at Allahabad, Uttar Pradesh, India. Frederick M. Asher

spire covered with rich *chandrashala* tracery. The Gola Math at Maihar has the more conventional square sanctum, with a very elegant *latina shikhara*, the walls of which are adorned with two rows of figural sculpture. There must have existed at Gurgi a large number of temples, though all of them now are in total ruin. Judging from a colossal image of Shiva-Parvati and a huge entrance, which have somehow survived, the main temple must have been of very great size. Another important site is Amarkantak, where there are a large group of temples, the most important of which is the Karna. Although generally of the 11th century, they are quite simple, lacking the rich sculptural decoration so characteristic of the period. By contrast, the Virateshvara temple at Sohagpur, with an unusually tall and narrow *shekhari* spire, is covered with sculptural ornamentation as rich as that of Khajuraho.

The Malava region, ruled largely by the Paramara dynasty, appears to have been the first to develop the *bhumija* type of *shikhara* (10th century). The finest and most representative group of these structures is at Un. Though, unfortunately, they are considerably damaged, judging from the remains, they must have been very elegant structures. The best preserved and easily the finest *bhumija* temple is the Udayeshvara (1059–82), situated at Udaipur in Madhya Pradesh. The *shikhara*, based on a stellate plan, is divided into quadrants by four *lata*s, or offsets, each one of which

has five rows of aediculae. The large hall has three entrance porches, one to the front and two to the sides, and walls that are richly carved. The whole complex, including seven subsidiary shrines, is placed on a broad, tall platform. The Siddheshvara temple at Nemawar (early 12th century) is even larger than the Udayeshvara, though the proportions are not as well balanced and the quality of the carving is inferior. Structures in the *bhumija* manner continued to be made in Malava up to the 15th century; the Malvai temple at Alirajpur is a good example of the late phase.

From Malava, the *bhumija* style spread to the neighbouring regions. To the north in Rajasthan, the Mahanaleshvara temple at Menal (c. 11th century), the Sun temple at Jhalrapatan (11th century), the Shiva temple at Ramgarh (12th century), and the Endeshvara temple (12th century) at Bijolian are important examples. To the west, in Gujarat, are temples at Limkheda and Sarnal of the 11th and 12th centuries. The style was particularly favoured in Maharashtra, to the south. Among surviving examples, the most impressive is the Ambarnath temple near Mumbai (11th century); Balsane and Sinnar also have pleasing temples. The style continued up to the 16th century, many examples having been found in north Deccan and Berar. The *bhumija* style also spread to the east of Malava; the Bhand Dewal at Arang (11th century), for example, is a Dahala adaptation.

ELLORA CAVES

Near the village of Ellora (Elura) in northwest-central Maharashtra state, western India, are a series of 34 magnificent rock-cut temples. They are located 19 miles (30 km) northwest of Aurangabad and 50 miles (80 km) southwest of the Ajanta Caves. Spread over a distance of 1.2 miles (2 km), the temples were cut from basaltic cliffs and have elaborate facades and interior walls. The Ellora complex was designated a UNESCO World Heritage site in 1983.

The 12 Buddhist caves (in the south) date from about 200 BC to AD 600, the 17 Hindu temples (in the centre) date from about AD 500 to 900, and the 5 Jaina temples (in the north) date from about 800 to 1000. The Hindu caves are the most dramatic in design, and the Buddhist caves contain the simplest ornamentation. Ellora served as a group of monasteries (viharas) and temples (caityas); some of the caves include sleeping cells that were carved for itinerant monks.

The most remarkable of the cave temples is Kailasa (Kailasanatha; cave 16), named for the mountain in the Kailas Range of the Himalayas where the Hindu god Shiva resides. Unlike other temples at the site, which were first delved horizontally into the rock face, the Kailasa complex was excavated downward from a basaltic slope and is therefore largely exposed to sunlight. Construction of the temple in the 8th century, beginning in the reign of Krishna I (c. 756–773), involved the removal of 150,000 to 200,000 tons of solid rock. The complex measures some 164 feet (50 metres) long, 108 feet (33 metres) wide, and 100 feet (30 metres) high and has four levels, or stories. It contains elaborately carved monoliths and halls with stairs, doorways, windows, and numerous fixed sculptures. One of its better-known decorations is a scene of Vishnu transformed into a man-lion and battling a demon. Just beyond the entrance, in the main courtyard, is a monument to Shiva's bull Nandi. Along the walls of the temple, at the second-story level, are life-size sculptures of elephants and other animals. Among the depictions within the halls is that of the 10-headed demon king Ravana shaking Kailasa mountain in a show of strength. Erotic and voluptuous representations of Hindu divinities and mythological figures also grace the temple. Some features have been damaged or destroyed over the centuries, such as a rock-hewn footbridge that once joined two upper-story thresholds.

The Vishvakarma cave (cave 10) has carvings of Hindu and Buddhist figures as well as a lively scene of dancing dwarfs. Notable among the Jaina temples is cave 32, which includes fine carvings of lotus flowers and other elaborate ornaments. Each year the caves attract large crowds of religious pilgrims and tourists. The annual Ellora Festival of Classical Dance and Music is held there in the third week of March.

RAJASTHAN

A group of temples at Osian, dating to about the 8th century, represents adequately the opening phases of medieval temple architecture in Rajasthan. They stand on high terraces and consist of a sanctum, a hall, and a porch. The sanctum is generally square and has a *latina* spire. The walls, with one central and two subsidiary projections, are decorated with sculpture, often placed in niches with tall pediments. The halls are Badoligenerally of the open variety, provided with balustrades rather than walls, so that the interiors are well lit. The surrounds of the doorway sanctum are quite elaborate, with four or five bands of decoration and the usual river-goddess groups at the base. The pillars, with *ghata-pallava* (vase-and-foliage) capitals, are also decorated, richness of sculpture and architectural elaboration being a characteristic of this group of monuments. The Mahavira temple, which is the largest, belongs to the 8th century, though renovated in later times, when the *torana* (gateway) and the *shikhara* were added. Other important temples are Harihara Nos. 1, 2, and 3 and two temples dedicated to Vishnu. The ruined Harshat Mata temple at Abaneri, of a slightly later date (c. 800), was erected on three stepped terraces of great size and is remarkable for the exquisite quality of the carving. Some of the finest temples of the style date from the 10th century, the most important of which are the Ghateshvara temple at Badoli and the Ambika-Mata temple at Jagat. The simple but beautiful Badoli temple consists of a sanctum with a *latina* superstructure and an open hall with six pillars and two pilasters (columns that project a third of their width or less from the wall) supporting a *phamsana* spire. Only the central projections of the sanctum walls are decorated with niches containing sculpture. A large open hall was built in front of the temple at a later date. The Ambika-Mata temple at Jagat, of the mid-10th century, is exceptionally fine. It consists of a sanctum, a *gudhamandapa*, or enclosed hall, and a parapeted porch with projecting eaves. The walls of the sanctum and the hall are covered with fine sculpture, the superstructures being of the *shekhari* and the *phamsana* types.

Temples, too numerous to mention, dating from the 10th and—to an even greater extent—the 11th century onward, are found throughout Rajasthan. The styles of Rajasthan and neighbouring Gujarat during these centuries grew closer and closer together until the differences between them were gradually obliterated. This coalescence resulted in the emergence of a composite style found throughout Gujarat and Rajasthan. Temples situated in the two areas are discussed separately here, but this is for the sake of convenience and does not signify any real stylistic difference.

The temples at Kiradu in Rajasthan, dating from the late 10th and 11th centuries, are early examples of the style shared by Rajasthan and Gujarat. The

Someshvara temple (*c.* 1020) is the most important and clearly shows the movement toward increasing elaboration and ornamentation. Each of the constituent parts became more complex; the moldings of the plinth, for example, are multiplied to include bands of elephants, horses, and soldiers. The walls are covered with sculpture, and the spire is of the rich *shekhari* type. Situated in Rajasthan, but again in the composite style, are the extraordinarily sumptuous temples known as the Vimala Vasahi (1031) and the Luna Vasahi (1230) at Mt. Abu. The Vimala Vasahi consists of a sanctum, a *gudhamandapa*, and a magnificent assembly hall added in mid-12th century. The plain, uncarved exterior walls of the rectangular enclosure of the temple have on the inside rows of cells containing images of divinities. The interiors are very richly carved, the coffered ceilings loaded with a wealth of detail. The Luna Vasahi is even more elaborate, though the quality of the work had begun to decline perceptibly.

Traditional architecture continued even after the Islamic invasions, particularly during the reign of Rana Kumbha of Mewar (*c.* 1430–69). During this period, the tall nine-storied Kirttistambha and other temples at Chittaurgarh and also the great Chaumukha temple at Ranakpur (1438) were built.

GUJARAT

Gujarat was the home of one of the richest regional styles of northern India. A temple at Gop (*c.* 600), with a tall terrace and a cylindrical sanctum with high walls capped by a *phamsana* roof, and other temples in Saurashtra show the formative phases of the style. Its distinctive features are clear in an interesting group of temples from Roda (*c.* 8th century). The sanctum is square in plan and has *latina* spires that are weighty and majestic. The walls are relatively plain, with niches, housing images, provided only on the central projection. The masonry work is exceptionally good, a characteristic of Gujarat architecture throughout its history. The Ranakdevi temple at Wadhwan, of the early 10th century, is also characterized by plain walls and a *latina* spire, while the Shiva temple at Kerakot has a *shekhari* spire and also a *gudhamandapa*. The great Sun Temple at Modhera, datable to the early years of the 11th century, represents a fully developed Gujarat style of great magnificence. The temple consists of a sanctum (now in ruins), a *gudhamandapa*, an open hall of extraordinary richness, and an arched entrance in front of which was the great tank. The Navalakha temple at Sejakpur continued this tradition. The Rudramala at Siddhapur, the most magnificent temple of the 12th century, is now in a much ruined condition, with only the *torana* (gateway) and some subsidiary structures remaining. Successively damaged and rebuilt, the Somanatha at Prabhasa Patan was the most famous temple of Gujarat, its best known structure dating from the time of Kumarapala (mid-12th century). It has been now dismantled, but a great temple built at the site in recent years testifies to the survival of ancient traditions in modern Gujarat.

The hills of Satrunjaya and Girnar house veritable temple cities. Most of the shrines, which are of late date, are picturesque but otherwise of little significance. With the Islamic conquest, the Gujarat architect adapted his considerable skills to meet the needs of a patron of different religion and quickly produced a totally successful Indian version of Islamic architecture.

KARNATAKA

The North Indian style was largely confined to India above the Vindhyas, though for a short period it also flourished in a region of southern India known as Karnataka from ancient times and now largely part of Karnataka state. Here, temples of the northern and the southern styles are found next to each other, notably at Aihole and Pattadkal. The earliest appears to be the Ladh Khan at Aihole, closely related to the 5th-century temple at Nachna Kuthara in northern India. The northern style was also cultivated at Pattadkal, where the most important examples are the Kashivishvanatha, the Galaganatha, and the Papanatha. Alampur, now in Andhra Pradesh, has eight temples of the northern style with *latina* spires. These belong to the late 7th and early 8th centuries and are the finest and among the last examples of the northern style in southern India.

KASHMIR

The architectural style of the Kashmir region is quite distinct: unlike other regions, in which the sanctum usually has a *latina* or *shekhari* spire, the roof of the Kashmir sanctum is of the *phamsana* type, with eaves raised in two stages. The greatest example to survive is the ruined Sun Temple at Martand (mid-8th century), which, though its *shikhara* is missing, gives a good idea of the characteristic features of the style. The temple is placed in a rectangular court enclosed by a series of columns. Access to the court is through an imposing entrance hall, the walls of which have doorways with gabled pediments and a trefoil (shaped like a trifoliate leaf) recess. The Avantisvami temple of the mid-9th century, now quite ruined, must have been similar, though much more richly ornamented. The style continued up to the 12th century; the Rilhaneshvara temple at Pandrenthan is a comparatively well-preserved example of this period.

SOUTH INDIAN STYLE

The home of the South Indian style, sometimes called the *dravida* style, appears to be the modern state of Tamil Nadu; examples, however, are found all over southern India, particularly in the adjoining regions of Karnataka and Andhradesha, now largely covered by the states of Karnataka and Andhra Pradesh. Both Andhradesha and Karnataka developed variants, particularly Karnataka, which evolved a distinct manner, basically South Indian but with features of North Indian origin. The Karnatic style extended northward into Maharashtra, where the Kailasa temple at Ellora is the most famous example.

A typical South Indian temple consists of a hall and a square sanctum that has a superstructure of the *kutina* type. Pyramidal in form, the *kutina* spire consists of stepped stories, each of which simulates the main story and is conceived as having its own "wall" enclosed by a parapet. The parapet itself is composed of miniature shrines strung together: square ones (called *kutas*) at the corners and rectangular ones with barrel-vault roofs (called *shalas*) in the centre, the space between them connected by miniature wall elements called *harantaras*. (Conspicuous in the early temples, these stepped stories of the superstructure with their parapets became more and more ornamental, so that in the course of time they evolved into more or less decorative bands around the pyramidal superstructure.) On top of the stepped structure is a necking that supports a solid dome, or cupola (instead of the North Indian grooved disc), which in turn is crowned by a pot and finial. The walls of the sanctum rise above a series of moldings, constituting the foundation block, or socle (*adhisthana*), that differ from North Indian temples; and the surface of the walls does not have the prominent offsets seen in North Indian temples but is instead divided by pilasters. In the Karnatic version, particularly from the

late 10th century onward (sometimes called the *vesara* style), this arrangement of the superstructure is loaded with decoration, thus considerably obscuring the component elements. At the same time, these elements—particularly the central offset with its subsidiaries that carry *chandrashala* motifs—are so manipulated that they tend to form distinct vertical bands, in this respect closely recalling the *shikharas* of northern India.

The design of the hall-temple roofed by a barrel vault, popular in the last centuries BC and the earliest centuries AD, was adopted in southern India for the great entrance buildings, or *gopuras*, that give access to the sacred enclosures in which the temples stand. Relatively small and inconspicuous in the early examples, they had, by the mid-12th century, outstripped the main temple in size.

TAMIL NADU (7TH–18TH CENTURY)

The early phase, which, broadly speaking, coincided with the political supremacy of the Pallava dynasty (*c.* 650–893), is best represented by the important monuments at Mahabalipuram. Besides a fine group of small cave temples (early 7th century), among the earliest examples of their type in southern India, there are here several monolithic temples carved out of the rock, the largest of which is the massive three-storied Dharmaraja-ratha (*c.* 650). The finest temple at this site and of this period is an elegant complex of three shrines called the Shore Temple (*c.* 700), not cut out of rock but built of stone.

The Talapurishvara temple at Panamalai is another excellent example. The capital city of Kanchipuram also possesses some fine temples—for example, the Kailasanatha (dating a little later than the Shore Temple), with its stately superstructure and subsidiary shrines attached to the walls. The enclosure wall has a series of small shrines on all sides and a small *gopura*. Another splendid temple at Kanchipuram is the Vaikuntha Perumal (mid-8th century), which has an interesting arrangement of three sanctums, one above the other, encased within the body of the superstructure.

The 9th century marked a fresh movement in the South Indian style, revealed in several small, simple, but most elegant temples set up during the ascendancy of the Chola and other contemporary dynasties. Most important of a large number of unpretentious and beautiful shrines that dot the Tamil countryside are the Vijayalaya Cholishvara temple at Narttamalai (mid-9th century), with its circular sanctum, spherical cupola, and massive, plain walls; the twin shrines called Agastyishvara and Cholishvara, at Kilaiyur (late 9th century); and the splendid group of two temples (originally three) known as the Muvarkovil, at Kodumbalur (c. 875).

These simple beginnings led rapidly (in about a century) to the mightiest of all temples in the South Indian style, the Brhadishvara, or Rajarajeshvara, temple, built at the Chola capital of Thanjavur. A royal dedication of Rajaraja I, the temple was begun about 1003 and completed about seven years later. The main walls are raised in two stories, above which the superstructure rises to a height of 190 feet (60 metres). It has 16 stories, each of which consists of a wall with a parapet of shrines carved in relatively low relief. The great temple at Gangaikondacholapuram, built (1030–40) by the Chola king Rajendra I, is somewhat smaller than the Brhadishvara; but the constituent elements of its superstructure, whose outline is concave, are carved in bolder relief, giving the whole a rather emphatic plasticity. The Airavateshvara (1146–73) and Kampahareshvara (1178–1223) temples at Darasuram and Tribhuvanam follow the tradition of the 11th century but are smaller and considerably more ornate. They bring to a close a great phase of South Indian architecture extending from the 11th to the 13th century.

From the middle of the 12th century onward, the *gopuras*, or entrance buildings, to temple enclosures began to be greatly emphasized. They are extremely large and elaborately decorated with sculpture, quite dominating the architectural ensemble. Their construction is similar to that of the main temple except that they are rectangular in plan and capped by a barrel vault rather than a cupola, and only the base is of stone, the superstructure being made of brick and plaster. Among the finest examples are the Sundara Pandya *gopura* (13th century) of the Jambukeshvara temple at Tiruchchirappalli and the *gopuras* of a great Shiva temple at Chidambaram, built largely in the 12th–13th century. Even larger *gopuras*, if not of such fine quality, continued to be built up to the 17th century. Such great emphasis was placed on the construction of *gopuras* that enclosure walls, which were not really necessary, were especially built to justify their erection. In the course of time several walls and *gopuras* were successively built, each enclosing the other so that at the present day one often has to pass through a succession of walls with their *gopuras* before reaching the main shrine. A particularly interesting example is the Ranganatha temple at Srirangam, which has seven enclosure walls and numerous *gopuras*, halls, and temples constructed in the course of several centuries. The *gopuras* of the Minakshi temple at Madurai are also good representative examples of this period.

In addition to the *gopuras*, temples also continued to be built. Although they never achieved colossal size, they are often of very fine workmanship. The Subrahmanya temple of the 17th century, built in the compound of the Brhadishvara temple at Thanjavur, indicates the vitality of architectural traditions even at this late date.

KARNATAKA

The early phase, as in Tamil Nadu, opens with the rock-cut cave temples. Of the elaborate and richly sculptured group at Badami, one cave temple is dated 578, and two cave temples at Aihole are early 8th century. Among structural temples built during the rule of the Chalukyas of Bahami are examples in the North Indian style; but, because the Karnataka region was more receptive to southern influences, there are a large number of examples that are basically South Indian with only a few North Indian elements. The Durga temple (*c.* 7th century) at Aihole is apsidal in plan, echoing early architectural traditions; the northern *latina shikhara* is in all probability a later addition. The Malegitti Shivalaya temple at Bahami (early 8th century), consisting of a sanctum, a hall with a parapet of *shalas* and *kutas* (rectangular and square miniature shrines), and an open porch, is similar to examples in Tamil Nadu. The Virupaksha at Pattadkal (*c.* 733–746) is the most imposing and elaborate temple in the South Indian manner. It is placed within an enclosure, to which access is through a *gopura*; and the superstructure, consisting of four stories, has a projection in the front, a feature inspired by the prominent projections, or *shukanasa*, of North Indian temples. Belonging to the 9th century is the triple shrine (the three sanctums sharing the same *mandapa*, or hall) at Kambadahalli and the extremely refined and elaborately carved Bhoganandishvara temple at Nandi. The Chavundarayabasti (*c.* 982–995) at Shravana-Belgola is also an impressive building, with an elegant superstructure of three stories.

With the 10th century, the Karnatic idiom begins to show an increasing individuality that culminates in the distinctive style of the 12th century and later. The Kalleshvara temple at Kukkanur (late 10th century) and a large Jaina temple at Lakkundi (c. 1050–1100) clearly demonstrate the transition. The superstructures, though basically of the South Indian type, have offsets and recesses that tend to emphasize a vertical, upward movement. The Lakkundi temple is also the first to be built of chloritic schist, which is the favoured material of the later period and which lends itself easily to elaborate sculptural ornamentation. With the Mahadeva temple at Ittagi (c. 1112) the transition is complete, the extremely rich and profuse decoration characteristic of this shrine being found in all work that follows. Dating from the reign of the Hoysala dynasty (c. 1141) is a twin Hoysaleshvara temple at Halebid, the capital city. The sanctums are stellate in form but lack their original superstructures. The pillars of the interior are lathe-turned in a variety of fanciful shapes. The exterior is almost totally covered with sculpture, the walls carrying the usual complement of images; the base, or socle, is decorated with several bands of ornamental motifs and a narrative relief. Among other temples that were constructed in this style, the most important are the Chenna Keshava temple at Belur (1117), the Amrteshvara temple at Amritpur (1196), and the Keshava temple at Somnathpur (1268).

MAHARASHTRA, ANDHRADESHA, AND KERALA

The traditions of cave architecture are stronger in Maharashtra than in any other part of India; there, great shrines were cut out of rock right up to the 9th century AD and even later. Of those belonging to the early phase, the most remarkable is a temple at Elephanta (early 6th century); equally impressive are numerous temples at Ellora (6th–9th centuries). The Karnatic version of the South Indian style extended northward into Maharashtra, where the Kailasa temple at Ellora, erected in the reign of the Rashtrakuta Krishna I (8th century), is its most stupendous achievement. The entire temple is carved out of rock and is over 100 feet (30 metres) high. It is placed in a courtyard, the three sides of which are carved with cells filled with images; the front wall has an entrance *gopura*. The tall base, or plinth, is decorated with groups of large elephants and griffins, and the superstructure rises in four stories. Groups of important temples in the southern style are also found in the Andhra country, notably at Biccavolu, ranging in date from the 9th to the 11th centuries. The 13th-century temples at Palampet are the counterparts of the elaborate Karnatic style of the same period, but without its overpowering elaboration. The temples of Kerala represent an adaptation of the South Indian style to the great main fall of this region and are provided with heavy sloping roofs of stone that imitate timber originals required for draining away the water.

ISLAMIC ARCHITECTURE OF THE DELHI AND PROVINCIAL SULTANATES

Although the province of Sind was captured by the Arabs as early as 712, the earliest examples of Islamic architecture to survive in the subcontinent date from the closing years of the 12th century; they are located at Delhi, the main seat of Muslim power throughout the centuries. The Qūwat-ul-Islām mosque (completed 1196), consisting of cloisters around a courtyard with the sanctuary to the west, was built from the remains of demolished temples. In 1198 an arched facade (*maqṣūrah*) was built in front to give the building an Islamic aspect, but its rich floral decoration and corbelled (supported by brackets projecting from the wall) arches are Indian in character. The Qutb Mīnār, a tall (288 feet [87.7 m] high), fluted tower provided with balconies, stood outside this mosque. The Arhāi-dīn-kā-jhompṛā mosque (*c.* 1119), built at Ajmer, was similar to the Delhi mosque, the *maqṣūrah* consisting of engrailed (sides ornamented with several arcs) corbel arches decorated with greater restraint than the Qutb example. The earliest Islamic tomb to survive is the Sultān Gharī, built in 1231, but the finest is the tomb of Iltutmish, who ruled from 1211 to 1236. The interior, covered with Arabic inscriptions, in its richness displays a strong Indian quality. The first use of the true arch in India is found in the ruined tomb of Balban (died 1287). From 1296 to 1316 ‘Alā’-ud-Dīn Khaljī attempted to expand the Qūwat-ul-Islām mosque, which already had been enlarged in 1230, to three times its size; but he was unable to complete the work. All that has survived of it is the Alai Darkāzah, a beautiful entrance.

In contrast to this early phase, the style of the 14th century at Delhi, ushered in by the Tughluq dynasty, is impoverished and austere. The buildings, with a few exceptions, are made of coarse rubble masonry and overlaid with plaster. The tomb of Ghiyās-ud-Dīn Tughluq (*c.* 1320–25), placed in a little fortress, has sloping walls faced with panels of stone and marble. Also to be ascribed to his reign is the magnificent tomb of Shāh Rukn-e ‘Ālam at Multān in Pakistan, which is built of brick and faced with exquisite tile work. The Kotla Fīrūz Shāh (1354–70), with its mosques, palaces, and tombs, is now in ruins but represents the major building activity of Fīrūz Shāh, who took a great interest in architecture.

Many mosques and tombs of this period and of the 15th century are found in Delhi and its environs; the most notable of them are the Begampur and Khirkī mosques and an octagonal tomb of Khān-e Jahān Tilangānī. In the early 16th century, Shēr Shāh Sūr refined upon this style, the Qal‘ah-e Kuhnah Masjid and his tomb at Sasaram (*c.* 1540) being

Tomb and palace of Fīrūz Shah, Delhi, India, c. 1380 AD. P. Chandra

the finest of a series of distinguished works that were created during his reign.

The provinces, which gradually became independent sultanates, did not lag behind in architectural activity. In West Bengal, at Pandua, is the immense Ādīna Masjid (1364–69), which utilized remains of Indian temples. In Jaunpur, Uttar Pradesh, are a group of elegant mosques, notably the Aṭalā Masjid (1377–1408) and the Jāmiʿ Masjid (c. 1458–79), characterized by *maqṣūrahs* that have the aspect of imposing gateways. The

sultans of Malwa built elegant structures at Māndu and at Chanderi in the middle of the 15th century. The sultanate of Gujarat is notable for its great contribution to Islamic architecture in India. The style, which is basically indigenous, reinterprets foreign influences with great resourcefulness and confidence, producing works notable for their integrity and unity. The city of Ahmadabad (Ahmedabad) is full of elegant buildings; the Jāmiʿ Masjid (c. 1424), for example, is a masterly exposition of the style.

Jāmi' Masjid (Great Mosque), Ahmadabad, Gujarat, India. Frederick M. Asher

Fine examples dating from the second half of the 15th century are the small but exquisite mosques of Muḥāfiz Khān (1492) and Rānī Sabra'i (1514) at Ahmadabad and the handsome Jāmi' Masjid at the city of Champaner.

The Deccan was another great centre, but in contrast to Gujarat it took little from the indigenous building traditions. Among the earliest works is the Jāmi' Masjid at Gulbarga (1367), with its extraordinary cloisters consisting of wide arches on low piers, producing a most solemn effect. The city of Bidar possesses many remains, including a remarkable series of 12 tombs, the most elaborate of which is that of 'Alā-ud-Dīn Aḥmad Bahmanī (died 1457), which has extremely fine decorations in coloured tile. Some of the finest examples of Islamic architecture in the Deccan, however, are in Bijapur. The most important buildings of this city are the great Jāmi' Masjid (begun in 1558) with its superb arched cloisters; the ornate Ibrāhīm Rawẕa; and the Dol Gunbad (built by Muḥammad 'Ādil

Mausoleum of Rani Sabra'i, Ahmadabad, Gujarat state, India. Frederick M. Asher

Shāh), a tomb of exceptional size and grandeur, with one of the largest domes in existence.

The Hindu kingdoms that managed to retain varying degrees of independence during the period of Islamic supremacy also produced important works. These structures naturally bore the imprint of what survived of traditional Indian architecture to a greater extent than did those monuments patronized by Muslims. Among the Hindu structures of this period are the extensive series of palaces, all in ruin, built by Rana Kumbha (c. 1430–69) at Chittaurgarh, and the superb Man Mandir palace at Gwalior (1486–1516), a rich and magnificent work that exerted considerable influence on the development of Mughal architecture at Fatehpur Sikri.

ISLAMIC ARCHITECTURE OF THE MUGHAL STYLE

The advent of the Mughal dynasty marks a striking revival of Islamic architecture

Buland Darwaza (Victory Gate) of the Jāmiʻ Masjid (Great Mosque) at Fatehpur Sikri, Uttar Pradesh, India. Shostal Associates

in northern India: Persian, Indian, and the various provincial styles were successfully fused to produce works of unusual refinement and quality. The tomb of Humāyūn, begun in 1564, inaugurates the new style. Built entirely of red sandstone and marble, it shows considerable Persian influence. The great fort at Agra (1565–74) and the city of Fatehpur Sikri (1569–74) represent the building activities of the emperor Akbar. The former has the massive so-called Delhi gate (1566) and lengthy and immense walls carefully designed and faced with dressed stone throughout. The most important achievements, however, are to be found at Fatehpur Sikri; the Jāmiʻ Masjid (1571), with the colossal gateway known as the Buland Darwāza, for example, is one of the finest mosques of the Mughal period.

Other notable buildings include the palace of Jodha Bal, which has a strongly indigenous aspect; the exquisitely carved Turkish Sultana's house; the Panch-Mahal; the Dīvān-e ʻĀmm; and

Interior of Jodha Bai's palace, Fatehpur Sikri, Uttar Pradesh, India. Frederick M. Asher

the so-called hall of private audience. Most of the buildings are of post and lintel construction, arches being used very sparingly. The tomb of the emperor, at Sikandara, near Agra, is of unique design, in the shape of a truncated square pyramid 340 feet (103 metres) on each side. It consists of five terraces, four of red sandstone and the uppermost of white marble. Begun about 1602, it was completed in 1613, during the reign of Akbar's son Jahāngīr. Architectural undertakings in this emperor's reign were not very ambitious, but there are fine buildings, chiefly at Lahore. The tomb of his father-in-law I'timāh-ul-Dawla, at Agra, is small but of exquisite workmanship, built entirely of delicately inlaid marble. The reign of Shāh Jahān (1628–58) is as remarkable for its architectural achievements as was that of Akbar. He built the great Red Fort at Delhi (1639–48), with its dazzling hall of public audience, the flat roof of which rests on rows of columns and pointed, or cusped, arches, and the Jāmi' Masjid (1650–56), which is among the finest mosques in India.

Red Fort, Agra, Uttar Pradesh, India. Frederick M. Asher

But it is the Taj Mahal (*c.* 1632–*c.* 1649), built as a tomb for Queen Mumtāz Mahal, that is the greatest masterpiece of his reign. All the resources of the empire were put into its construction. In addition to the mausoleum proper, the complex included a wide variety of accessory buildings of great beauty. The marble mausoleum rises up from a tall terrace (at the four corners of which are elegant towers, or minars) and is crowned by a graceful dome. Other notable buildings of the reign of Shāh Jahān include the Motī Masjid (*c.* 1648–55) and the Jāmi' Masjid at Agra (1548–55).

Architectural monuments of the reign of Aurangzeb represent a distinct decline; the tomb of Rābī'ah Begam at Aurangabad, for example (1679), is a poor copy of the Taj Mahal.

The Pearl Mosque (Moti Masjid) and the fort at Agra, Uttar Pradesh, India. Picturepoint

The royal mosque at Lahore (1673–74) is of much better quality, retaining the grandeur and dignity of earlier work; and the Motī Masjid at Delhi (1659–60) possesses much of the early refinement and delicacy. The tomb of Safdar Jang at Delhi (c. 1754) was among the last important works to be produced under the Mughal dynasty and had already lost the coherence and balance characteristic of mature Mughal architecture.

EUROPEAN TRADITIONS AND THE MODERN PERIOD

Buildings imitating contemporary styles of European architecture, often mixed with a strong provincial flavour, were known in India from at least the 16th century. Some of this work was of considerable merit, particularly the baroque architecture of the Portuguese colony of Goa, where splendid buildings were erected in the second half of the 16th

Bibika Makbara tomb, near Aurangabad, Maharashtra, India, the mausoleum of Rābī'ah Begam, Aurangzeb's wife. Frederick M. Asher

century. Among the most famous of these structures to survive is the church of Bom Jesus, which was begun in 1594 and completed in 1605.

The 18th and 19th centuries witnessed the erection of several buildings deeply indebted to Neoclassic styles; these buildings were imitated by Indian patrons, particularly in areas under European rule or influence. Subsequently, attempts were made by the British, with varying degrees of success, to engraft the neo-Gothic and also the neo-Saracenic styles onto Indian architectural tradition. At the same time, buildings in the great Indian metropolises came under increasing European influence; the resulting hybrid styles gradually found their way into cities in the interior. In recent years an attempt has been made to grapple with the problems of climate and function, particularly in connection with urban development. The influence of the Swiss architect Le Corbusier, who worked on the great Chandigarh project, involving the construction of a new capital for Punjab, in the early 1950s, and that of other American and European masters has brought about a modern architectural movement of great vitality, which is in the process of adapting itself to local requirements and traditions.

Conclusion

As we have seen, India has functioned as a virtually self-contained political and cultural arena since the time of the Indus Valley civilization. The region gave rise to a distinctive tradition that was associated primarily with Hinduism, the roots of which can largely be traced to the Indus civilization. Other religions, notably Buddhism and Jainism, originated in India—though their presence there is now quite small—and throughout the centuries residents of the subcontinent developed a rich intellectual life in such fields as mathematics, astronomy, and architecture.

Throughout its history, India was intermittently disturbed by incursions from beyond its northern mountain wall. Especially important was the coming of Islam, brought from the northwest by Arab, Turkish, Persian, and other raiders beginning early in the 8th century AD. Eventually, some of these raiders stayed; by the 13th century much of the subcontinent was under Muslim rule, and the number of Muslims steadily increased. Only after the arrival of the Portuguese navigator Vasco da Gama in 1498 and the subsequent establishment of European maritime supremacy in the region did India become exposed to major external influences arriving by sea, a process that culminated in the decline of the ruling Muslim elite and absorption of the subcontinent within the British Empire.

Direct administration by the British, which began in 1858, effected a political and economic unification of the subcontinent. When British rule came to an end in 1947, the subcontinent was partitioned along religious lines into two separate countries—India, with a majority of Hindus, and Pakistan, with a majority of Muslims; the eastern portion of Pakistan later split off to form Bangladesh. Many British institutions stayed in place (such as the parliamentary system of

The Rumi Darwaza, or Turkish Gate, in Lucknow, Uttar Pradesh, India. The Rumi Darwaza was modeled (1784) after the Sublime Porte (Bab-i Hūmayun) in Istanbul. © Ann & Bury Peerless Slide Resources & Picture Library

government); English continued to be a widely used lingua franca; and India remained within the Commonwealth. Hindi became the official language (and a number of other local languages achieved official status), while a vibrant English-language intelligentsia thrived.

Apart from its many religions and sects, India is home to innumerable castes and tribes, as well as to more than a dozen major and hundreds of minor linguistic groups from several language families unrelated to one another. Religious minorities, including Muslims, Christians, Sikhs, Buddhists, and Jains, still account for a significant proportion of the population; collectively, their numbers exceed the populations of all countries except China. In its sheer numbers the country remains a force to be reckoned with. In its ancient monuments, its human variety, its vibrant spirit, and its celebrations, India is nothing short of a cultural treasure.

Glossary

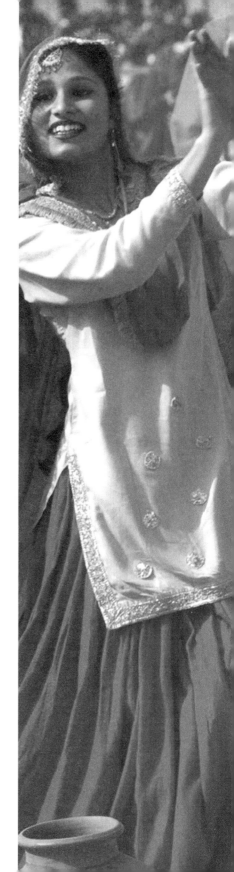

ascetic Denying oneself pleasure, goods, and personal affectations as a sign of spiritual devoutness.

ahimsa The principle of nonviolence to all people, especially important to Jains.

ashram A religious retreat (Sanskrit: ashrama, "retreat," or "hermitage").

atman Self.

beau ideal An ideal type, an idea of perfect beauty.

bhakti ("sharing or "devotion") a tradition of a loving God that is associated with Indian poet-saints.

cella An enclosed chamber inside a temple.

determinist Follower of a philosophical doctrine in which all events are inevitable consequences of previous conditions and not the result of free will.

diglossia When a language has two distinctive varieties, such as formal and informal dialects.

dharma World maintenance; the principle by which the universe is organized; the religious obligation of an individual.

ghat A set of stairs that rises up from a river, especially a river used for bathing.

gotras Lineages.

hagiographic Referring to writing about saints, or an overly uncritical treatment of a subject by a biographer.

hegemony A preponderant influence or authority over others.

karma The influence of one's actions on one's present and future lives.

jatis Social or caste group.

miri/piri Spiritual leader/earthly leader.

moksha Liberation from the imperfection of the world.

monism The philosophical belief that reality is made up of a single element.

mudras Symbolic hand gestures used in religious ceremonies and dances of India.

prasad Blessing or grace, or food that has already been offered to a god. Blessed leftovers, returned portion of a worshiper's ritual offering, such as fruit, coconut, or candy.

pratima "Likeness," an expression of a god's nature.

Puranas A class of Hindu sacred literature.

raga A series of five or more notes upon which a melody is based.

rasa Taste or flavour.

samsara The Hindu concept of a never-ending cycle of death and rebirth.

Scheduled Castes Formerly "untouchables"; official designation of groups that historically occupied a low position within the traditional caste system.

Shaivite The cult of the Hindu god Shiva.

shakti Creative power.

shruti Revelation.

smrti Tradition.

sitar A stringed instrument similar to a lute.

sutras Summaries given in aphorisms of the main points of Vedic teaching.

syncretism The combination of different forms of belief.

tabla A musical instrument made up of two small drums.

Vaishnavism The worship of the god Vishnu.

FOR FURTHER READING

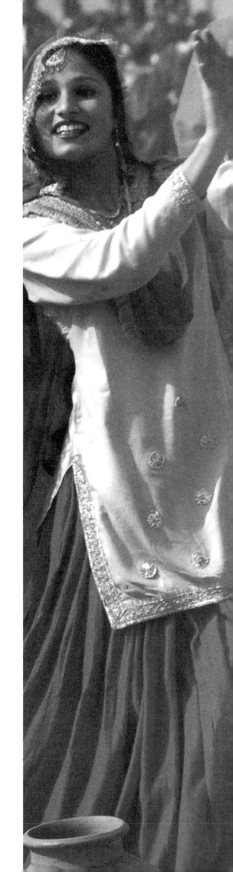

Behl, Boy K., (author) and Milo Beach (forward). *The Ajanta Caves, Ancient Paintings of Buddhist India*. New York, NY: Thames & Hudson, 2005.

Bindloss, Joe. *India (Lonely Planet Country Guide)*. Oakland, CA: Lonely Planet, 2009.

Danielou, Alain, (author) and Kenneth F. Hurry (translator). *A Brief History of India*. Rochester, VT: Inner Traditions, 2003.

Eck, Diana L. *Darsan: Seeing the Divine Image in India*. New York, NY: Columbia University Press, 1998.

Eraly, Abraham. *India*. New York, NY: DK Pub, 2008.

Eraly, Abraham. *The Mughal Throne: The Saga of India's Great Emperors*. London: Phoenix, 2004.

Fisher, Robert E. *Buddhist Art and Architecture*. New York, NY: Thames and Hudson, 2002.

Fitzgerald, Michael Oren. *Introduction to Hindu Dharma: Illustrated*. Bloomington, IN: World Wisdom, Inc., 2008.

Grihault, Nicki. *India—Culture Smart! The Essential Guide to Customs and Culture*. New York, NY: Random House, 2008.

Grover, Nirad. *100 Wonders of India*. Mumbai, India: Roli Books, 2008.

Gupta, Roxanne Kamayani. *A Yoga of Indian Classical Dance: The Yogini's Mirror*. Rochester, VT: Inner Traditions, 2000.

Koch, Ebba. *The Complete Taj Mahal*. New York, NY: Thames & Hudson, 2006.

Matane, Paulias, and M.L. Ahuja. *India: A Splendour in Cultural Diversity*. New Delhi, India: Anmol Publications Pvt. Ltd., 2004.

Michell, George. *Hindu Art and Architecture* (World of Art). New York, NY: Thames & Hudson, 2000.

Mitter, Partha. *Indian Art* (Oxford History of Art). New York, NY: Oxford University Press, 2001.

Narayan, Shoba. *Monsoon Diary: A Memoir with Recipes*. New York, NY: Random House, 2004.

Shah, Jagan. *Contemporary Indian Architecture*. New Delhi, India: Lustre Press, 2008.

Thapar, Bindia, Surat Kumar Manto, and Suparna Bhalla. *Introduction to Indian Architecture*. Singapore: Periplus Editions, 2004

Thapar, Romila. *Early India: From the Origins to AD 1300*. Berkeley, CA: University of California Press, 2004.

Venkataraman, Leela, and Avinash Pasricha. *Indian Classical Dance: Tradition in Transition*. New Delhi, India: Roli Books, 2004.

Wolpert, Stanley. *A New History of India*. New York, NY: Oxford University Press, 2004.

Wood, Michael. *India*. New York, NY: Basic Books, 2007.

INDEX